GA

"Gayle Wilson will go far in romantic
books have that special 'edge' that lifts them out of the ordinary. They're always tautly written, a treasure trove of action, suspense and richly drawn characters."
—*New York Times* bestselling author Linda Howard

"...an exhilarating continual action thriller that never slows down."
—*TheBestReviews.com* on *Double Blind*

"Wilson gives her readers just what they want: more thrilling adventure and heart-wrenching suspense.... Inspiring. Wilson is destined to become one of the suspense genre's brightest stars."
—*Romantic Times BOOKreviews,* 4 1/2 stars, on *Wednesday's Child*

"Gayle Wilson pulls out all the stops to give her readers a thrilling chilling read that will give you goose bumps in the night."
—*ReadertoReader.com* on *In Plain Sight*

"Writing like this is a rare treat."
—*Gothic Journal*

"Rich historical detail, intriguing mystery, romance that touches the heart and lingers in the mind. These are elements that keep me waiting impatiently for Gayle Wilson's next book."
—*USA TODAY* bestselling author BJ James

Also by GAYLE WILSON

THE INQUISITOR
DOUBLE BLIND
WEDNESDAY'S CHILD
IN PLAIN SIGHT

And watch for the newest novel from
Gayle Wilson

VICTIM

Coming soon

GAYLE WILSON

BOGEYMAN

ISBN-13: 978-0-7783-2361-7
ISBN-10: 0-7783-2361-7

BOGEYMAN

www.MIRABooks.com

Printed in U.S.A.

This book is dedicated to the strongest, most wonderful group of women I know, with my love, my gratitude and my deepest admiration...

Jill, Kelley, Connie, Lisa, Michelle, Dorien, Peg, Linda, LJ, Karen, Sherry, Geralyn, Stef, Teresa, Diane, Nic, Donna, Julie and Allison.

Thank you for everything!

And a very special dedication to Angelon. She knows all the reasons why.

Dear Reader,

While doing research for this book, I learned that no one is totally sure of the origins of the word *bogeyman.* What we do know is that in the mythology of childhood, a bogeyman is something to be feared. A dreaded creature of the night. Something—or someone—intent on doing harm. The bogeyman of my title is certainly all of those—and more.

At the center of this novel is a brutal, twenty-five-year-old murder of a little girl. A crime that, if ever one did, cries out for justice. And in this case, it's entirely possible that plea may come from beyond the grave.

When Blythe Wyndham brings her four-year-old back to the small Alabama town where she was born, she never dreams Maddie will be the one called upon to respond to that cry. Nor could she have imagined when she made her decision to come home that, with the help of Sheriff Cade Jackson, she will be forced to try to solve the savage killing of another child in order to prevent her own daughter's death.

Although I cannot deny there are elements of this novel that may be difficult for you to read, its themes are universal. A mother's love and determination to protect her child, no matter the cost. A modern lawman's reluctance to admit that not all evidence can be examined under a microscope or proven in a court of law. And an evil that is as old as time and as current as today's headlines.

I invite you to enter their world. And to follow—if you dare—the terrifying hunt for...the BOGEYMAN.

Gayle

BOGEYMAN

Prologue

Twenty-five Years Earlier…

She had known he would come tonight. In spite of the rain and the cold. In spite of her praying "Please, Jesus" over and over again since Rachel had turned out the light.

She listened, but there was no sound now except her sister's breathing, slightly whistling on each slow intake of air. And the rain, of course, pelting down on the tin roof overhead.

It made enough noise to drown out anything else, she reassured herself. Whatever she thought she'd heard—

The sound came again, and this time there was no doubt what it was. She had anticipated this, dreaded it too many nights not to recognize that soft tapping on the glass.

She opened her eyes to the darkness, staring up at the ceiling as if she could see through it to the storm above. Maybe if she waited—if she pretended to be asleep—maybe this time Rachel would hear him and wake up. Or maybe Mama would get up to check and see if they were warm enough.

The tapping came again. Louder. Demanding.

Her sister's breathing hesitated, a long pause during which she repeated her talisman phrase again. Then the sounds Rachel made settled back into that same pattern of wheezing inhalation followed by sibilant release.

Mama always said Rachel slept like the dead.

Mama...

If she got out of bed and tiptoed across the floor to the door, surely with the noise of the rain, she could open it without him hearing. And if he didn't hear, then he would never know that she'd told.

If you ever tell anyone...

She quickly destroyed the image his words created. Denied them because she couldn't bear to think about what would happen if she didn't go to the window....

She took a breath, squeezing her eyes shut to stop the burn of tears. *Please, dear Jesus.*

Except Jesus hadn't answered her prayers any of the other times. Somewhere inside her heart she knew he wasn't going to answer tonight.

Which meant that nobody would. There was nobody she could turn to. Nobody who could do anything about what he'd told her he would do if she didn't mind him. Nobody but her.

She opened her eyes, raising her arm to scrub at them with the sleeve of her nightgown. He didn't like it when she cried. He said it spoiled everything. And that if she wasn't real careful—

She drew another breath, fighting to keep it from turning into a sob. Then, moving as carefully as she could, she pushed back the sheet and the piled quilts and sat up, putting her bare feet on the stone-cold floor.

By the time he tapped again, she was at the window. As she put her fingers around the metal handles of the sash to lift it, she couldn't find even enough hope left inside her heart to repeat the words she'd prayed all night. The ones they had told her at Sunday school would protect her from evil.

Now she knew that they, too, had lied.

1

Present Day…

The storm had increased in intensity, rain pounding against the windows as if demanding admittance. Not for the first time Blythe Wyndham regretted the isolation of the small rental house she and her daughter had moved into two months ago.

She'd never been easily spooked—not by thunderstorms or by being alone—but right now she was wondering why she hadn't taken her grandmother up on her offer to move back into the family home. The hundred-year-old farmhouse, which the Mitchells had occupied since its construction, was almost as isolated as the one in which she and Maddie were currently living. Still, it had been home for most of Blythe's childhood, and she had always felt completely safe there.

Safe?

Blythe shook her head, wondering at her use of the word. There was no reason to think the house they were in *wasn't* safe. She couldn't ever remember consciously worrying about that before. Why the thought would cross her mind tonight—

"We haven't said my prayers."

Her daughter's reminder destroyed Blythe's momentary uneasiness. Smiling, she brushed strands of pale blond hair away from the forehead of the little girl she'd just tucked into bed.

No matter what else might have gone wrong in her life, Maddie was the one thing that had *always* been right. And the reason Blythe had chosen to return to the small Alabama community where she'd been raised.

"Then say them now," she prompted.

Maddie closed her eyes, putting her joined hands in front of her face, small thumbs touching her lips. "Now I lay me down to sleep. I pray the Lord my soul to keep. If I should die before I wake, I pray the Lord my soul to take."

Blythe wondered who had decided that was an appropriate prayer for a child. Of course Maddie, who said the words by rote, was probably not even cognizant of their meaning.

Thank God.

"God bless Mommy and Miz Ruth and Delores." Maddie's listing of personal blessings that had grown by two since their move to Crenshaw. "And God keep Daddy safe in heaven. Amen."

"Amen," Blythe repeated softly.

Her daughter's blue eyes flew open to catch her mother studying her face. "You didn't close your eyes."

"If I did, I couldn't look at you."

"But you aren't *supposed* to look at me. You're supposed to bow your head and close your eyes. Everybody knows that."

As Blythe herself had always been, Maddie was an obeyer of rules. The trait made her an easy child to handle, but Blythe often wondered if it shouldn't be her role to introduce the occasional urge to rebel into her daughter's well-ordered existence.

"Sorry. I guess I forgot," Blythe said, her smile widening at the note of concern in Maddie's voice.

"You better ask forgiveness. *Before* you go to sleep. You hear me?"

The culture of the area was obviously making inroads, not only on the little girl's speech, but on her thinking as well. Blythe could hardly complain, since that was one of the reasons she'd brought Maddie back. That and the fact that the only family she had left in the world was here.

"I will, I promise. And you promise to sleep tight, okay?"

"Okay." Maddie turned slightly to one side, one hand sliding under the feather pillow, another item on loan from her great-grandmother's house.

The necessity of that kind of borrowing had also, like it or not, played a part in their homecoming. The little insurance money that had been left after the bills had all been paid, including those incurred by the move, wouldn't have extended to luxuries like feather pillows. With her grandmother's generosity, it would go a little further and hopefully keep them solvent until Blythe could find some kind of permanent employment.

"Just don't say that thing Miz Ruth always says," Maddie ordered without opening her eyes.

"What thing?"

"About the bugs biting me."

Blythe could almost hear her grandmother's voice, its distinctive Southern accent repeating the same good-night wish she'd whispered to Blythe when she was a child. *Sleep tight. Don't let the bedbugs bite.*

"That's just a silly old saying." She bent over to press a kiss on the little girl's temple. "There are no bedbugs here *or* at Miz Ruth's."

Maddie had quickly picked up on the name by which most of the inhabitants of Crenshaw referred to Ruth Mitchell. Or maybe because that was how her grandmother's housekeeper always addressed her, and the little girl spent her mornings with the two old women.

In any case, given the growing closeness between them, Blythe had decided that it didn't matter what Maddie called her great-grandmother. Ruth Mitchell would be for Maddie exactly what she had been for Blythe—friend, confidante and role model. The child couldn't have a better one.

Blythe pushed up from her perch on the edge of the bed, reaching over to turn off the bedside lamp as she did. The flash of lightning that illuminated the darkened room was followed closely by a clap of thunder.

Blythe glanced down at the little girl in the bed, but

her eyes were still closed. Apparently the storm didn't bother her.

Normally, they didn't bother Blythe either. There was something about this one, however, that had kept her slightly on edge since the rain had started. If the power went out—

That's what she had intended to do, she remembered. Locate the flashlight and gather up any candles she could find. Despite having been here for a couple of months, she hadn't managed to get everything unpacked.

Of course, working at Raymond Lucky's law office half a day made it hard to get much done at the house. And she couldn't have managed either the job or the unpacking had her grandmother and Delores not been so eager to look after Maddie for her.

When she'd started with Ray, Blythe had intended to prove herself so invaluable that he'd be forced to hire her full-time. Now she knew he didn't have enough clients to warrant that expenditure. Although her greatest fear was that Ray would decide he couldn't afford her any longer, she had already started putting out feelers for more permanent—and more lucrative—positions.

Despite the obvious advantages of her move back home, that was the major drawback to living in this small, rural community. A lack of jobs that related to any of her skills.

Without the required education courses that would allow her to teach, her English degree seemed worthless in this setting. As did the five years before Maddie's birth that she'd spent as editor of one of Boston's small entertainment magazines.

Such as they are, she acknowledged.

Denying the rush of bitterness over the turn her life had taken, Blythe flipped the switch for the overhead light as she entered the kitchen, welcoming its glow. Despite her earlier uneasiness, the room seemed warm and familiar.

Safe.

She rummaged through the drawers, searching for the utility candles she knew she'd brought with her. This was where she'd always kept them in the old house. She couldn't imagine where else she might have put them when she'd unpacked the container they'd been in.

Which probably indicated she hadn't. And that meant they were in one of the boxes lined up along the wall in what had been the house's front parlor.

She debated letting the candles go and simply going back upstairs to bed. That way if the power did go out, she'd never know.

Not unless Maddie has another nightmare.

The thought was enough to send her out of the kitchen and into the hall. She stopped a moment at the foot of the stairs, listening for any sounds coming from the little girl's bedroom. She could hear nothing but the steady beat of the rain against the roof.

She crossed the hall to open the door of the parlor. She kept this room shut off in an attempt to keep the utility bill down. Besides, other than using it as storage, she couldn't imagine that she would ever need the space.

By force of habit she flipped the switch, remembering only when nothing happened that she'd not yet replaced the bulbs in the overhead fixture. So far, she had only worked in here in the daytime, so that until tonight, there had been no need. And too many other things that demanded her time.

Blowing out an exasperated breath, she walked over to the boxes. She squatted before the first, trying to read the words she'd carefully printed in indelible marker as she'd packed them. Despite the occasional flare of lightning, that proved impossible. Why the hell hadn't she brought the flashlight?

Because you're operating on too little sleep and too much stress.

Putting her hand on the top of the box, she pushed herself up. Screw the candles. The flashlight would be enough.

As long as it had working batteries. Given the way the night was going...

She started across the parlor, heading back to the hall. With the lack of furniture in the room, her footsteps seemed unnaturally loud as she crossed the wooden floor. Halfway to the door she realized that wasn't all she was hearing.

She stopped, tilting her head toward the hallway. For a few seconds there was nothing, and then the noise came again.

Even over the omnipresent rain she could hear it. A low, muffled tapping.

She had heard the same sound a couple of times before, always at night, and always as she lay in that state between waking and sleeping. It had seemed too much trouble to get up and locate the source then, but she'd better figure it out tonight or, combined with her feeling of anxiety about the storm, the noise would keep her awake. If there was anything she didn't need, it was another night of interrupted sleep.

A shutter? she wondered. Or a branch brushing against the house? Except there didn't seem to be enough wind to cause either.

She hurried into the front hall, once more stopping at the foot of the staircase. Again she cocked her head to listen.

Other than the rain, the house was now silent. She took a breath of relief. In the middle of it, the tapping came again. Whatever its cause, it was definitely coming from upstairs.

The faint light spilling out into the hall to the den reminded her that she had been headed to the kitchen to retrieve the flashlight. Once she had it, she'd go upstairs and locate whatever was making the racket. When that had been taken care of, she'd check on Maddie and then get into her own bed. Maybe they could manage to make it through one night without any further disturbances.

The flashlight was lying on the counter where she'd put it when she'd started rummaging through the drawers. She picked it up and then walked over to check the dead bolt and chain lock on the back door. Both were secure.

She pushed aside the sheer curtain that covered the glass top half of the door, intending to peer out into the darkness. For an instant her reflection made it seem as if someone was out there looking in at her. Although her realization of what she was really seeing was almost instantaneous, the jolt of adrenaline that initial sensation created caused her to jerk the fabric back over the pane.

Still fighting that ridiculous surge of panic, she turned, taking a last look around the kitchen before she retraced her steps. She hesitated in the doorway, her fingers finding the switch several seconds before they pulled it down. She waited, giving her eyes a chance to adjust to the sudden lack of light.

This was her normal routine. Cutting off the lights down here and making her way up the stairs in the dark. Since she no longer closed Maddie's door at night, she didn't want to turn on the light at the top of the stairs and chance waking her.

She hadn't taken two steps into the hall before the tapping sounded again, seeming louder than before. Maybe the rain had slackened, allowing her to hear whatever was brushing against the house more clearly.

As she started toward the stairs, she pushed the button on the flashlight forward with her thumb. A narrow cone of light appeared before her, but before she could focus it on the bottom step, it blinked out.

"*Damn* it." Angry at herself for not making better preparations in case of an emergency, she shook the flashlight. The batteries rattled inside their metal case, and almost miraculously, the light reappeared, this time without wavering.

At least she knew what to do if she really needed the thing. Which she didn't right now.

She slid the button back into the off position, conserving what life was left in the batteries. Putting her left hand on the banister, she began to climb the narrow stairs. Halfway up, the tapping began again.

This time she didn't stop to listen. She took the last few risers in a rush, trying to get to the top of the staircase so that she could determine the direction from which the sound was coming. By the time she'd reached the upstairs hall, however, there was only the noise of the rain.

Check on Maddie. Maybe by the time she'd done that, whatever she was hearing would sound again.

She walked down the hall, guided by the night-light she'd put in Maddie's room after the first of the terrors. A flare of lightning, turning the night sky as bright as day, illuminated the window at the end of the hallway. It was immediately followed by a boom of thunder that literally shook the house.

Certain that some object nearby had been struck, Blythe waited, her heart in her throat, for the sound of a falling tree or for Maddie's screams. When neither occurred, she continued down the hall, her eyes fastened on the dark panes of the window at its end.

In the faint light provided by the night-light, she could see her reflection again, distorted by the mullions and the waviness of the old glass. Given the multiple images portrayed in the window, she had to fight the urge to look over her shoulder to make sure she was alone.

She turned into Maddie's room, expecting the little girl to be as distraught by the storm as she was. Instead, Maddie was lying on her side, just as she had been when Blythe had gone downstairs. Her eyes were closed.

Instead of the relief she should have felt, Blythe's first reaction was a renewed sense of uneasiness. How could the child sleep through the noise of the storm?

She tiptoed closer to the bed, spending a few seconds watching the regular rise and fall of Maddie's breathing. The little girl's lashes rested unmoving against her cheek.

Although her inclination was to pull the piled quilts over her daughter's small, exposed shoulder, Blythe stepped back from the bed. It would be stupid to take a chance on waking Maddie, who was obviously fine.

And obviously dealing with the storm much better than you are.

Blythe turned, intending to make her way to her own bedroom. If she couldn't sleep, there was a sack of paperbacks that her grandmother had pressed on her when she'd picked Maddie up after work yesterday. Most of them would be romances, but maybe that was exactly what she needed. Something positive. Life affirming. With a happily-ever-after guarantee.

She had already reached the doorway to Maddie's room when the tapping came from behind her. She whirled, looking immediately toward the window to her right.

There was no doubt in her mind that something had struck its glass. She walked across the room, leaning over the small secretary she'd placed in front of the window.

Below was the roof of a narrow screened porch that had been added to the original structure. There were no trees. No branches to brush against the house, even if there had been enough wind to move them. And, she remembered, there were no shutters on the windows at the back.

Realizing that she still held the flashlight in her hand, she pushed the switch forward, pointing the beam outside the window. Rain streaked the glass, but there was nothing out there. She leaned forward as much as she could, directing the flashlight in a circle—above, to the right, below the window and then to the left. Nothing.

She straightened, trying to understand how she could have been wrong about the direction of the sound. It *had* come from here.

Obviously, it didn't. You were wrong. So what else is new?

Her thumb had already begun to apply pressure to the off switch when the tapping came again. This time there was no mistake. The sound was right in front of her. She could even see the glass tremble slightly in its frame.

The cone of light from the flashlight was focused directly on the window. With a growing sense of horror she realized that there was nothing out there. Nothing touching the window. Nothing moving against it. Nothing that *could* move against it. Nothing.

Even as she came to that realization, the beam blinked out, leaving her looking at an empty blackness beyond the glass. Despite her success downstairs, she didn't even try to shake the thing back on.

She backed away from the window instead. Then, without being conscious of having made a decision, she ran across to the bed and pulled back the covers. She scooped Maddie up and had already started to carry her across the room when the little girl's eyes opened.

"What's wrong?"

"Nothing," she lied. "I thought you might like to sleep in my bed. Because of the storm."

Her voice trembled, but she prayed that, roused from a deep sleep, her daughter wouldn't notice. The wide blue eyes looked over her shoulder, seeming to fasten for a moment on the window above the secretary.

Then Maddie turned her head, looking up at her. "Don't be frightened, Mama. There's nothing to be afraid of. It's only the rain."

Unable to speak, Blythe nodded.

No doubt there was a perfectly logical explanation for what had just happened. Whatever that might be, right now she wasn't interested.

All she was interested in at this moment was getting Maddie out of this room. And maybe even out of this house.

2

As he entered his utility room, Cade Jackson struck his rain-soaked uniform hat against his leg before he hung it on one of the row of hooks by the back door. Then, sitting down on the bench, he removed his low-topped boots and socks, both of which were even wetter than the rest of his attire.

The Sheriff's Department had been asked to help the state troopers work a tanker-trailer wreck out on the interstate. Cade and his deputies had done little more than direct traffic around the area of the possibly toxic spill. The thunderstorm, which had grown in intensity while the highway crews had worked to clean up the mess, had complicated things, dragging out the final all-clear for several hours.

As a result, Cade was cold and tired and hungry. And right now he wasn't sure which of those pressing needs should take precedence.

Shower first, he decided, standing again to slip out of his yellow slicker. The hotter the better. To be followed by a couple of packets of aspirin powder to put a dent in the headache that had developed as he'd squinted through the driving rain at the oncoming headlights. Once those two things were accomplished, then he could think about taking something from freezer to microwave and out again in a matter of minutes.

He walked into the kitchen, fingers working over the buttons on his shirt. The light on the answering machine that sat on the counter was blinking.

Whatever this was, given the night he'd had, it couldn't be good. Still, delaying wouldn't make the news any better. Blowing out a breath, he stabbed Play.

While he waited for the message to begin, he pulled his shirt out of his pants to undo the last of its buttons. He was in the act of shrugging out of the damp garment when Teresa Payne's voice, with its distinctive nasal drawl, came through the speaker.

"Hey, Cade. Just touching base. When you get in, give me a call about tomorrow night."

Returning this particular call was way down on his list of priorities. He had run out of excuses to avoid Teresa's invitations. And he wasn't up to coming up with anything creative tonight.

So tell her the truth. Tell her you aren't interested. And that you aren't ever going to be.

There was enough of his good-ol'-boy upbringing left that he knew he was incapable of being that blunt. At least at this point. If Teresa didn't figure it out pretty soon, he wouldn't have much choice. As for tonight…

Carrying the balled-up shirt in his hand, he

walked down the hall, not bothering to turn on a light. He'd grown up in this house. He knew every crack and crevice of it. Every squeak of the cross-sawn oak floorboards.

He flipped on the overhead in the bathroom. Dropping the shirt onto the floor, he unbuckled his belt and unzipped his uniform pants. He stepped out of those, leaving them on the tile beside the discarded shirt.

With one hand, he reached back and gripped the fabric between his shoulders to pull his T-shirt over his head. He pitched it to lie on top of the pants and shirt. Seconds later, his boxers had joined the growing pile.

He shivered a little in the cold. He should have turned up the thermostat, he realized. If he had, by the time he'd finished his shower, the house would be habitable.

Nude, he stepped out into the hall and pushed the lever up with his thumb. The furnace in the basement came to life with a whoosh, sending heated air through the vents.

He went back into the bathroom, reaching into the shower to turn on the hot water. Given the location of the heater, it would take longer for that to get warm.

Since Maria had come today, the racks had all been stripped bare for the washing machine. As he reached for a clean towel from the stack above the john, he caught a glimpse of himself in the mirror.

Dampness from the rain had spiked his hair. It glistened like jet in the light of the fluorescent. Even the twin swatches of gray at his temples were darkened by the moisture.

He had shaved around five this morning, but the ever-present afternoon stubble now made him look slightly sinister. And the shadows under his eyes made him look old.

Hell, you are old. Thirty-seven going on a hundred. Especially on nights like this.

As he turned away from the image in the mirror, exhaustion in every aching muscle, he wondered if he could be coming down with something. Probably not that lucky, he decided. The luxury of a couple of days off, spent inside a warm house, would work wonders. Both the cold and the rain were supposed to continue well into next week, and he would have no choice but to be out in them.

He slid back the glass door and stepped in, turning his back to the water. For several seconds he didn't move, letting the force of the spray pound the bunched muscles between his shoulders. After a couple of minutes, he leaned his head back, eyes closed, to let the shower slough the cold moisture of the rain from his hair.

As his body began to lose the bone-deep chill, his tiredness, too, seemed to ease. He scrubbed every inch of his skin, literally trying to wash away the day's tensions.

It seemed to work. When he stepped out of the shower, the bathroom was at least ten degrees warmer than it had been when he'd entered. He grabbed the towel he'd taken from the shelf, using it first to dry his hair and then his body.

When he was finished, he wrapped the towel

around his waist and opened the bathroom door. Steam wafted out into the cooler hall as he headed toward his bedroom.

Left hand on the top of the chest, he fished a pair of clean pajama bottoms out of the second drawer. He sat down on the end of the bed, which was made—the last time it would be until Maria showed up again next week—and put them on.

He stood, pulling the pajamas up to his waist. He went back to the chest of drawers for a clean T-shirt. Now all he needed were the aspirin and something to eat.

Two packets of powdered aspirin, a product everyone in the department swore by, had begun to make inroads on his headache by the time the microwave sounded. Ignoring the baleful light of the answering machine, he carried his dinner, still in its black plastic tray, along with a fork into the den.

He sat down on the couch, putting his food on the coffee table in front of him. Despite the tempting aromas of meat loaf, potatoes and gravy, he used the remote to turn on the TV.

He wolfed down the contents of the plastic tray, almost without looking at them, while he watched a rain-fogged video of the wreck his men had worked. When the local news cut to commercials, he glanced back into the kitchen.

The unanswered phone call would nag at him until he'd returned it. When he had, and had made a final check-in with the department's dispatcher, he could crawl into bed and forget about the needs of the citizens of Davis County until the phone—or better yet, the alarm—woke him.

He pushed up from the deep cushions of the couch and made his way back to the kitchen counter. He listened to the message again, before he glanced down at his watch.

Decision made, he called up the number on caller ID and then pushed Talk. He listened to the electronic beeps, trying to decide what he was going to say this time.

"Hey, Cade," Teresa said. "I was afraid you were still out working that mess on 65."

"Got in about half an hour ago. The state finally decided that whatever the guy was hauling, it wasn't a public threat."

"That's good to know. Hope you all don't catch pneumonia from standing out in this rain."

"Yeah, me, too." He leaned against the cabinet, allowing the silence to lengthen.

Nothing was going to change. He was only delaying the inevitable. He might as well get this over with so he could go to bed.

"About tomorrow night..." he began and then hesitated.

This whole thing was his fault, and he knew it. He should never have opened the door even the crack he'd allowed. When it had started, he hadn't seen the harm in their friendship. By the time he did, it was too late.

Teresa laughed. The sound was soft, but its bitterness apparent. "I can hear it coming."

"Hear what coming?"

"Whatever you've got on. You're either working. Or you've promised somebody you'll do something for them. Or help them do something."

"Teresa—"

"And that isn't ever going to change, is it? Why don't you just tell me to quit bothering you?"

"You aren't bothering me."

"Oh, hell, Cade. Don't lie. That just makes it worse."

"Look, why don't we—"

"No. No pity arrangements. You and I are a little old for those kinds of games."

There was nothing he could say to that. She was right. They were both too old for games. He had been for five years. Ever since Jean had walked out on him.

"I don't blame you," she said, speaking quickly now. "I just thought that maybe… I don't know. There aren't that many singles our age in Crenshaw. I just thought we had a lot in common. At least I hoped we did."

They did. More than Cade and his ex-wife had ever had.

And look how well that worked out.

At least he and Teresa had had the same upbringing, right here in Davis County. And like him, she wasn't interested in living anywhere else.

Despite knowing that, there was nothing there. No

spark of interest. Not on his part. Knowing himself as he did, he knew there would never be.

He resisted the urge to offer more platitudes. The quicker they got through this, the less painful it would be. For both of them.

"I guess I was wrong," she added.

"I'm sorry." Despite his intentions, the apology slipped had out.

He hadn't meant to hurt her. The fact that he wasn't interested in a relationship didn't have anything to do with Teresa. Maybe if he told her that…

"It isn't you."

"Oh, Lord, Cade. At least spare me the crap."

"I'm sorry."

"And for God's sake, stop *saying* that."

He obeyed, willing himself not to prolong this. Again the silence grew.

"You're a good man, Cade Jackson," Teresa said finally. "Even if you aren't, and won't ever be, *my* man. You don't owe me any explanations, so don't bother trying to think them up. Just… If you ever change your mind…"

He waited, lips pressed together. She never finished the sentence. Instead, there was a low click and then the dial tone in his ear.

After a moment he put the receiver back on the stand, stopping the sound. Despite his exhaustion, despite the promise he'd made to himself, he didn't move. Not to cut off the light or to head to bed.

You and I are a little old for those kinds of games. That

went along with what he'd been thinking when he'd looked into the mirror tonight. Thirty-seven going on a hundred.

In every way that mattered, Teresa Payne was far too young for him. And he no longer believed he was ever going to find someone who wasn't.

She had been right last night, Blythe realized. There was no overhanging branch up there. No shutter. And absolutely nothing to bang against that window.

"What are you looking at?"

Blythe turned to find Maddie standing at her elbow, blue eyes shifting from her face up to the bedroom window. The little girl was wearing only her nightgown. Although it was made of thick flannel, with long sleeves and a deep flounce, long enough to brush the winter-browned grass, it offered too little protection against the early morning cold.

"There was something bumping against your window last night. I could hear it. I thought maybe I could see whatever it was from down here."

She had come downstairs and out through the screened porch as soon as she'd woken up, leaving Maddie asleep in her bed. Or so she had thought.

"I didn't hear anything."

"You don't remember?"

"I didn't hear it."

This was the same kind of stonewalling with which Maddie replied to questions about her nightmares.

Stonewalling? She's four. *If she says she doesn't re-*

member, then she doesn't. She isn't capable of that kind of deception.

And how does a little girl not remember something tapping against her window? Or dreams that make her scream hysterically?

"Well, whatever it was, it doesn't seem to be there now," Blythe said, turning to look down at her daughter with a smile. "How about some breakfast?"

"Egg McMuffin?"

"Not exactly what I had in mind. How about bacon and eggs and toast?" That was the kind of food she never had time to prepare in the mornings as she was rushing to get Maddie ready for Ruth's and herself ready for work.

"That's what Delores always fixes."

Of course. Delores and Miz Ruth couldn't imagine starting the day without a cooked breakfast.

"So what would you like? Other than McDonald's."

"Cereal. Coco Charlies."

The Egg McMuffin would probably have been a more nutritious choice, Blythe thought. Death by sugar.

Despite the unfortunate choice of words, Blythe managed to hold on to her smile as, hand between the small shoulders, she turned the little girl back toward the house. "Coco Charlies it is."

"It makes its own chocolate milk," Maddie said cheerfully, skipping along in front of her.

With its concrete floor and open walls, the screened porch was almost as cold as the outside. The small kitchen, however, had already warmed in the few minutes since Blythe had turned up the heat. This house might have its problems, but at least the plumbing and the furnace were reliable.

Fingers crossed.

While Maddie took her place at the table, Blythe retrieved the box of cereal from the old-fashioned pantry. On her way across the room, she opened the fridge and took out a quart of milk. She set both on the table and reached into the cabinet above the sink for a bowl.

Easier than eggs and bacon. And if the sugar made Maddie hyper, then there was no one to be bothered by it but her.

If Ruth and Delores at their age could put up with her daughter's energy day after day, then she certainly had nothing to complain about.

Except maybe too many nights of lost sleep.

"So you really didn't hear anything last night?" She dumped a cup or so of the brown pebbles into the bowl and covered them with milk.

"Rain. And the thunder."

"You didn't mind that?"

Maddie shook her head, digging her spoon into the mess in the bowl. She was right, Blythe realized. The milk had already taken on a decidedly brown tinge.

"Do you?" Maddie asked, looking up from under her bangs.

"Do I what?"

"Mind the rain?"

"Not most of the time."

"Maybe that's what you heard."

"I don't think so." She didn't want to make Maddie fearful. "Maybe it was a bird," she suggested, sticking the milk back in the refrigerator. "Or a squirrel." She turned back to see Maddie's eyes come up again, widened with interest.

"Trying to get out of the rain?"

"Maybe. Maybe they were just cold," she added with a smile.

"Then...would it be all right to open it for them the next time?"

"Open the window?" For some reason, despite the winter sunlight flooding the kitchen, last night's chill was back.

"So that whatever is knocking can come in."

In Maddie's world, the one Blythe herself had created, you took care of those who couldn't take care of themselves. You fed strays and rescued chipmunks from the neighbor's cat. And if something was cold and hungry, you let it in.

Except not this time. Even though Blythe couldn't explain the certainty she felt about that, she knew that whatever had caused the tapping she'd heard last night wasn't something she wanted to let into her home.

And especially not into Maddie's bedroom.

3

"Mama! Help me! Somebody help me!"

The screams pulled Blythe out of a sleep so deep that, despite her exhaustion, she couldn't believe she'd achieved it. After all, she had tossed and turned in Maddie's narrow bed for what seemed like hours. Listening for the tapping. Straining to identify every creak of the old house. She had finally drifted off, only to be awakened as suddenly as if someone had poured ice water over her.

She scrambled from under the covers, not stopping to pull on the woolen robe that lay across the foot of the bed. She ran across the heart-pine floors, bare feet skidding across their smooth surfaces as she made the turn through the doorway of Maddie's bedroom and headed down the hall toward her own.

In the cold light of day—when her heart wasn't frozen with fear or her mind imagining ridiculous scenarios—she hadn't been able to justify letting the child sleep with her again. But she also couldn't bring herself to put her back in that bedroom.

She had wondered if whatever she'd heard tapping at the window last night in Maddie's room could precipitate the night terrors. Obviously, she'd been wrong.

"Mama, wake up. Please, Jesus. Please, somebody help me. Daddy. No. Daddy."

By the time Blythe reached the doorway of her bedroom, the panicked screams had increased in volume. Following the now-familiar pattern, the little girl's shrieks were growing so frenzied, words were no longer distinguishable. Piercing and hysterical, the screams echoed and reechoed through the room, even when Blythe turned on the bedside lamp.

As always when the child was in the grip of a terror, Maddie's eyes were open, their dilated pupils eating up the blue iris. Blythe knew from experience that the little girl was totally unaware of her surroundings, still trapped in the horror of whatever she was dreaming about.

Blythe threw back the covers and then lifted her daughter to hold her against her heart. She rocked her back and forth in a rhythm familiar to them both since Maddie had been a baby.

"Shh. I'm here. I've got you. Everything's all right."

After what seemed an eternity, the little girl responded, turning her head to bury her face between her mother's breasts. Through the thickness of her flannel gown, Blythe could feel the sweat-soaked hair. At least the shrieks had faded to whimpers.

Over the top of Maddie's head, Blythe released a sigh of relief. Her own nightmare was that one night her daughter wouldn't return from whatever terrifying place the dream took her. Tonight she had, and Blythe sent a silent prayer of thanks heavenward.

She had done that far more often since she'd come back to Crenshaw. Prayed. It was something she couldn't remember doing much of during the last few years. Not even during those terrible months of John's illness.

Maybe she'd sought divine intervention more often because she had returned to her roots, the town where she'd spent her childhood, which had certainly not lacked for religious instruction. Or maybe, she admitted, it was that she was at the end of her own very human resources in knowing how to deal with what was going on.

Why wouldn't she be? How could she be expected to know what to do with night terrors so severe she literally feared for her daughter's life—or her sanity. Or with inexplicable noises that chilled her to the bone.

She leaned back, attempting to put some space between them so that she could look down into those normally lucent and guileless eyes. Maddie refused to look up, clutching her more tightly instead, small fingers locked into the fabric of Blythe's gown.

"It's all right," she whispered again. "It was just a dream. I'm right here, and I have you."

There was no response. At least Maddie was no longer trembling.

Gradually Blythe's own panic began to ease. With the light of day, she might again be able to convince herself that this scene, which had been repeated no less than a dozen times in the last few weeks, had not been nearly as frightening as she remembered.

With one hand, she brushed damp tendrils of fine blond hair away from her daughter's face. In response to the gesture, Maddie finally leaned back, looking up at her.

In the glow from the lamp, the little girl's features seemed illuminated, as if lit from within. The blue eyes had now lost the look of horror they'd held only moments before.

"What's wrong?" Maddie's pale brows were drawn together in puzzlement.

Unsure how to answer the question, Blythe forced a smile. "You had a bad dream. Don't you remember?"

The child shook her head. She raised a fist, rubbing her eyes in that timeless gesture of sleepiness.

"Don't you remember *anything,* Maddie? Not even what made you call me?"

Another negative motion of the sweat-drenched head, and then her daughter leaned tiredly against her chest again. As she did, she put the thumb of the hand she'd used to rub her eyes into her mouth. In the stillness, Blythe listened to the sound of her sucking it.

The psychologist she'd taken Maddie to had advised she not make an issue of this, although the habit was something the little girl had outgrown years ago. Ignore it and everything else, the woman had said.

She had reassured Blythe that night terrors weren't uncommon in children Maddie's age. Although there was definitely a genetic component to them, they were usually triggered by stress.

Probably the result of her father's death, combined with the move, the psychologist had suggested. She just needed lots of love and reassurance that she was safe and that you'll always be there for her. Other than that, it was better to completely ignore the nightmares.

Blythe had had to fight against her instinct, which was to ignore the advice rather than the nightmares. She wanted to question Maddie about her dreams. To talk to her about them. To find out if there really were, as it seemed, no lingering traces of whatever horror paralyzed her in the darkness.

Instead, she had listened to the expert. About that, as well as about not sleeping with her daughter, which was one bit of advice she no longer intended to follow. At least not right now.

"I think I'll sleep in here with you the rest of the night," she said, pulling the covers back.

Obediently the little girl scooted over in the bed, making room. Blythe slipped between the warm sheets, settling the quilts around them again.

Before she reached over to turn off the lamp, she took one last look at her daughter. The little girl had already cuddled down on her side, her thumb back in her mouth. Her lashes lay motionless against the apple of her cheek, her breathing again relaxed and even.

Asleep? Was it possible that she'd already dropped off, despite the state in which Blythe had found her only minutes before? Something she obviously had no memory of.

Thank God, Blythe thought, completing the motion she'd begun. *And while you're at it, dear Heavenly Father, would you please give me that same blessed forgetfulness?*

There was no answer to her prayer. At least not an affirmative one. Just as there had been no answer to any of the others she had prayed since she'd returned.

"Land sakes, child. You look like death warmed over. You sickening for something?"

"Too little sleep," Blythe said, taking the cup of coffee her grandmother held out to her.

As soon as she had it in her hands, she turned her gaze back to the scene revealed through the kitchen window. Maddie was playing in her great grandmother's sunlit back garden, the one where Blythe had spent so many happy hours during her own childhood.

The tire swing she'd played on still hung from the lowest branch of a massive oak. Maddie's body was draped through it now, her jean-clad bottom and legs and the soles of her scuffed sneakers all that were visible from this angle.

"She having more of those nightmares?"

Blythe turned to find her grandmother still standing at her elbow, her gaze also fastened on the little girl. In an attempt to hide the sudden thickness in her throat at the genuine concern in the old woman's voice, Blythe lifted the steaming cup and took a sip. Despite the strong flavor of chicory, a remnant of her grandmother's childhood in St. Francisville, the coffee warmed her almost as much as entering this house always did.

"Night terrors," she corrected softly, finding it difficult to believe that the child they were watching was the same one who had trembled in her arms only hours before. "An appropriate name. She's certainly terrified by whatever she sees."

"But if she doesn't remember—"

"*I* remember. I thought last night—" Blythe stopped, hesitant to put her fear into words, lest doing so should give it some actual power.

"You thought what?" her grandmother asked when the silence stretched between them.

"I'm afraid she won't come back from wherever she is."

"Oh, child. You don't believe that. You can't." With one weathered hand, its fingers knotted with arthritis and the blue veins across the back distended beneath the thin skin, her grandmother touched her fingers as they gripped the cup, seeking warmth for the coldness that seemed to have settled permanently in her chest.

"You haven't seen her. And anyone seeing her now..." Blythe didn't finish the thought, knowing that she could never explain the gap between the picture below and the events of last night.

"Why don't you tell me exactly what happens?" her grandmother suggested. "Sit down at the table, and we'll drink our coffee while you tell me all about it."

"I should watch her—"

"In Crenshaw? Who you gonna watch her from here?"

The old woman was right. The backyard was as safe as church, to use one of her grandfather's favorite expressions. There was no reason to fear for Maddie's safety. That was one of the reasons Blythe had decided to come home.

She'd been reluctant to talk to anyone about the terrors. More reluctant to mention the tapping. The kindness in her grandmother's voice encouraged her to share her fears, however, just as it always had. Here in this kitchen, she had revealed a hundred secrets during her adolescence.

And this—whatever was going on—wasn't even a secret. If she could share the particulars of her daughter's nightmares with some dismissive stranger in Montgomery, surely she could confide in her family. Almost the only family she had left.

"Delores, would you get us some of that pound cake you made yesterday?" Her grandmother took Blythe's arm to guide her away from the window, apparently taking her silence for consent.

"Yes'm. You all want some preserves to go with that?"

Delores Simmons, the ancient black woman who had looked after the household since Blythe could remember, was almost as old as her mistress. Although the two elderly women were closer than sisters, the traditional formalities that had existed between them for more than half a century were still maintained, even in private.

"Preserves?" Blythe's grandmother asked, pulling

out a chair at one side of the kitchen table and gesturing toward the opposite one. "Or apple butter, maybe. I made both, so I guarantee they're good."

Blythe slipped into the place, shaking her head in response to the question. "Not for me."

"Just the cake, Delores. And make sure you don't cut none of that sad streak either."

"Now you know Miz Blythe always likes a bit of sadness with her sweet."

Despite the fact that the women were talking about a common flaw that left a swath of butter-rich denseness through center of the cake, the words seemed symbolic. A little too apt.

"You said she calls you. That that's how it starts."

Surprised by the change in subject, Blythe looked up from her coffee. Her grandmother's faded blue eyes were focused patiently on her face. "She calls Mama."

Blythe wasn't sure when the thought had crept into her head, but since it had, she couldn't dislodge it. Because she was no longer sure Maddie was calling *her.* Just as she was no longer sure—

She shook her head, refusing to take the next step. If she did, it might take her down a road she didn't want to consider.

"And you go to her, of course," her grandmother prodded, "and then what?"

"That isn't all she says."

"Something besides Mama?"

"I don't know whether or not she says more the longer the dreams go on or whether I understand more each time. Most of it is just...sounds. Screams. No words. But at the very beginning... Before she gets so hysterical... There are words."

"What does she say?"

"Help me. Mama, help me. Daddy. No. Daddy."

"If she's calling for her daddy, then maybe— I mean didn't that psychologist tell you this was connected to John's death?"

"Not exactly. She said the stress of his death combined with the stress of the move. But...a four-year-old? How she can be stressed?" Blythe asked. "Does she *seem* stressed to you?"

"She's just having a nightmare, baby. Everybody has them."

"But what does she see that terrifies her so much she can't get her breath?"

"And she's crying when she says all that?"

As she asked the question, Delores set a glass dessert plate down in front of Blythe. A thick slice of pound cake, the promised sad streak bisecting its perfection, rested in the center on a paper doily. Despite the presentation, Blythe felt a wave of nausea at the thought of trying to eat it.

"Is she crying? A little. At first. Then she starts begging for somebody to help her. Then... 'Please, Jesus, help me,'" Blythe whispered, her eyes holding on the black ones of her grandmother's housekeeper.

"That pure don't sound like it's got nothing to do with Mr. John, whatever that doctor told you. That baby's afraid of something."

Blythe nodded, relieved to have her own conclusion put into words. To find someone who understood the fear she felt as the episodes escalated. "She's terrified. After a while the words become screams. Shrieks. As if someone is—"

"Hurting her," Delores finished softly when she couldn't go on.

"Nobody's ever hurt that child in her life," her grandmother said dismissively. "Why in the world would she have a dream about somebody doing it?"

"Dreams ain't always because of something that's happened to us. Dreams are sometimes more than what we know in our heads."

"Don't you start that nonsense, Delores. Not in this house. We're Christians here."

"I'm just as good a Christian as you, Miz Ruth. That doesn't mean I don't know things they don't talk about in Sunday school. Mine *or* yours."

Maybe if she hadn't already crossed this line in her own imagination, Blythe might have ignored the housekeeper's theory. Some indefinable something about the words and phrases the little girl uttered—something Blythe couldn't explain to anyone who hadn't heard them night after night—had already led her to the conclusion that whatever was happening in her dreams might not be happening to her daughter.

"What kind of things?" she asked.

The two old women, squared off for a religious battle they had probably fought a dozen times through the long years of their acquaintance, turned to look at her. Their faces indicated surprise, either over the interruption or her question itself, so she repeated it.

"What kinds of things do you know about dreams, Delores?"

"She don't know nothing that the rest of us don't know," Ruth said. "Dreams are dreams. That's all they are. Everybody has 'em. Sometimes they scare us, but that don't mean we have cause to be scared."

"That angel's been dreaming the same thing since you all moved down here." Delores ignored her mistress's comments as if they were unworthy of a response. "Is that right?"

Blythe nodded and watched the old woman's lips tighten.

"And she didn't ever dream this before?" Delores went on. "Or anything like it?"

"I don't think Maddie has cried out in her sleep since she was a baby. Certainly nothing like this. And believe me, I'd remember. I swear," she said, turning to her grandmother in an attempt to convince her of how out of the norm this was, "it sounds as if someone's killing her."

Despite the opinion she'd just stated so adamantly, her grandmother's brow furrowed in quick sympathy. She reached across the table to lay her hand over Blythe's. "Oh, child."

"I don't know what to do," Blythe went on, speaking hurriedly, trying to get the words out before the force of the emotions she'd kept hidden for almost two months overwhelmed her. "I can't believe this is about losing her daddy. Why would that start now, almost a year later? Why not immediately after his death? And don't tell me she's upset about the move. She seems happier here than she has been since John died."

Her grandmother's eyes had filled with tears of love and sympathy as she'd talked. Her fingers closed tightly around Blythe's, adding their own silent comfort. "I don't have any answers for you, sweetheart. I don't even know where to tell you to go for answers. Maybe if you took Maddie back to that doctor in Montgomery—"

Blythe shook her head, not bothering to explain the dismissive attitude of the psychologist or her loss of faith in her advice. At first Blythe had attempted to obey her dictate not to try to wake Maddie, but the terrors had seemed to intensify as well as increase in frequency. And if something unnatural *was* going on at the house to cause them…

Once more the question hovered on the tip of her tongue. Ruth and Delores had lived in this town for more than eighty years. If that house had a history of violence or death, they would know about it.

Are you seriously considering asking them if the house you're living in could be haunted?

Blythe pressed her lips together instead, knowing how much a question like that would worry her grandmother. In Ruth Mitchell's world, when people died, they went to heaven or to hell. They didn't hang around knocking on windows or causing little girls to have nightmares.

Besides, if Blythe really wanted to know what had happened at the place she was renting, there were other ways to go about it. Ways that wouldn't alarm anyone or make them question her sanity. Something she was doing quite nicely, thank you, all on her own.

4

Ada Pringle had been the librarian in Crenshaw since Blythe was a child. Despite the more than fifteen years since Blythe had seen her, the woman had changed very little.

Her hair and penciled brows were still coal-black, which made Blythe realize that the former had probably been dyed even then. And Ada's eyes still peered disapprovingly at her over the top of a pair of tortoise-shell half glasses.

Although the library was deserted at this time of the afternoon, the effect of that look was the same as when Blythe had been twelve and asking for help to find information needed for school. As if she had no right to pester Miss Ada with a request for service.

"Good afternoon, Miss Pringle."

"Blythe Mitchell, as I live and breathe. Heard you was back."

Blythe waited, expecting the conventional welcome-home comments. None were forthcoming.

"For almost two months now," she said with a smile.

"Not living at your grandmother's, I hear."

"Well, there's moving home, and then there's moving home." It was quickly obvious her attempt at humor had fallen flat. There had been no change in the brown eyes. "We decided to get our own place."

"Heard you have a little girl."

"Maddie. She's four. I've been meaning to bring her by. She loves books as much as I did when I was that age."

"Children ain't allowed till they start school. Same as it's always been," Ada said. "Now what can I do for you?"

Blythe suddenly remembered why, voracious reader that she had always been, she hadn't enjoyed coming here. And if there were any other option for what she needed, she would be tempted to walk out now.

"As I remember, you have bound copies of the *Herald.*"

The *Crenshaw Herald* was a weekly, but it was the only game in town. Most of its pages were devoted to church and club activities and athletic events at the school. The editor had always thoughtfully included anything newsworthy that had happened between issues, although it was probable that everyone might already know all the details through the ever-efficient community grapevine.

"Since the beginning. Most libraries have gone to microfiche, but as long as the pages hold together, I'll keep the papers themselves," Ada said. "That's how I like to read 'em. I figure I'm not the only one."

"I'd like to see them, please."

"Of course." Ada's words were abrupt, but she lifted the hinged section of the counter she'd stood behind, moving briskly past Blythe and toward the tall shelves at the back of the room. By the time Blythe arrived, Ada was pointing to a row of huge, leather-bound books, each marked in gold on the spine with the words *Crenshaw Herald* and a year.

"Anything in particular you're looking for?"

Accustomed to the anonymity provided by a city like Boston, Blythe hadn't anticipated the question. Given the objective of her research, she didn't intend to share that information with a gossip like Ada.

"Just a little local color."

"Local color?"

"Stories about the people and the community. I have several years to catch up on."

"You still writin' those articles, are you?" Ada's tone sounded slightly disapproving.

Blythe had written three or four short travel essays for one of the regional magazines while she'd been in college. She hadn't thought about them in years, but she was sure Ruth had made certain everyone in Crenshaw was aware of them. She might even have donated copies of those issues to the library.

"It's always a possibility," Blythe said, seizing on the excuse Ada had offered. "*If* something interesting turns up."

All she wanted was to be left alone back here with the newspapers. Maybe this was a wild goose chase, but she believed that if there had been any sort of violence associated with the house she was renting, it would be detailed in the *Herald*.

When she'd dropped her daughter off this morning, she had asked her grandmother to keep Maddie this afternoon as well, pleading the need to investigate a couple of opportunities for employment. She would do that, too, before she picked the little girl up, but only in the most current issue of the *Herald*, which came out today.

"What kind of 'interesting'?" Ada prodded. "More touristy stuff?"

The deprecating tone rankled. Granted, Blythe didn't consider herself a writer, but she had been paid for that work. "Whatever will sell. As I said, something interesting."

Ada's eyes considered her over the top of her glasses. "If you're looking for something that'd make money…"

The librarian ran her finger along the row of books until she found the one she was looking for. "I know it happened this year. Same as the flood in Sanger. My aunt's house was damaged in that. And I know it was in the winter, so…" She pulled a volume off the shelf and laid it on one of the long empty tables and began flipping pages.

"I'm sorry?" Blythe had no idea what Ada was looking for.

"Sarah Comstock," the librarian said, glancing up at her quickly before she went back to thumbing through the newspapers.

Blythe hadn't thought about the Comstock murder in years. She'd been a little girl when it had happened, maybe five or six years old. Just slightly older than Maddie, she realized.

Although no one had talked openly about the murder in front of her, she had known. *All* the children in Crenshaw had known that Sarah had somehow been stolen from her room, taken from a bed where she'd slept beside her sister, and brutally murdered.

Blythe had come to the library looking for some incident of violent death. Yet for some reason, she had never thought about Sarah Comstock's.

The newsprint continued to turn under Ada's long, thin fingers. Suddenly the librarian's hand stilled. She smoothed the pages on either side of the open book so that they lay flat and exposed.

"December. Thought so, but I wasn't sure. I'll get the next one, too, 'cause I know those stories ran for months."

She turned back to the shelf, leaving the first volume on the table. The grainy picture in the center showed several men in uniform standing in the area the locals had always called Smoke Hollow. There was no body visible in the photograph, and Blythe was infinitely relieved not to have to view even a picture of a child-size corpse. With the sickness that thought created in the bottom of her stomach, she almost reached out and closed the book.

Before she could, Miss Ada laid another beside it. "First few months of this one, too. I don't think the paper carried the story in depth much longer than that. Not a lot to cover."

"Thank you." Blythe set her purse down on top of the picture in the opened volume, as if to claim ownership of it.

"Cold cases always grab the interest of the reading public," Ada said.

"Cold cases?"

"Unsolved crimes. Particularly murders. Why, you remember Mark Furman, don't you? Made a mint on that girl's murder in Connecticut. Don't re-shelve 'em when you're done. Just leave 'em out, and I'll do it. Most everybody gets it wrong."

"No, I won't. And thank you, Miss Pringle." Despite the passage of years and her own maturity, Blythe couldn't bring herself to call the woman Ada.

"Sorry for your loss." The librarian's words were slightly awkward. "Good you came on home, though. Your grandmamma needs you."

Blythe opened her mouth, trying to think of an appropriate answer. Before she could, Ada had turned and headed back to her counter.

Left alone, Blythe took a breath before she looked down again at the newsprint, sliding her purse to the side to reveal the picture. With her other hand, she found the back of one of the wooden chairs that had been shoved under the table. Without taking her eyes off the story that surrounded the photograph, she pulled the chair out far enough that she could slip into it. As she began to unbutton her coat, her mind was already occupied by the words that had been written a quarter of a century before.

* * *

"Time to close."

Blythe blinked as she looked up. Ada was hovering at her elbow, a black vinyl purse hooked over her arm.

As she'd moved, Blythe had become aware of a stiffness in her neck and shoulders. Not surprising, she acknowledged. If it was indeed closing time, she must have been reading in this same position for hours.

It wasn't only the gruesome details that had emerged from the yellowed pages of the *Herald* that held her rapt. She had been fascinated by the microcosm of the rural county's society the investigation into the little girl's murder had revealed. Since she had known most of its principals all her life, she had become completely caught up in the unfolding story.

Law enforcement, in the person of Sheriff Hoyt Lee, had admitted from the start that the lack of physical evidence was not only baffling, but virtually insurmountable. The child's mutilated body, stripped of its nightgown, had been washed clean by the swift, icy current of the stream that cut through the hollow. There was no trace evidence, at least none that the technology of the day had been able to discover. No footprints. And as there appeared to have been no sexual assault at the time of the murder, no DNA had been preserved.

"May I check these out?" Blythe asked.

She couldn't come back here every afternoon. She had already imposed on her grandmother enough. Lost in the articles on the murder, however, she hadn't even looked for anything relating to her house.

"The newspapers? Oh, those don't circulate."

"I'd be very careful with them, I promise." The schoolgirl feeling had come flooding back.

"Can't make exceptions. Then everybody expects them."

As Blythe debated whether anything might be gained by further argument, Ada reached over and closed the first book she'd taken down. "You should talk to Hoyt." She juggled her purse as she prepared to lift the heavy book back up onto the shelf. "He's bound to know stuff that never made the papers. Evidence, I mean." The three syllables of the word were individually and distinctly pronounced, the accent on the last.

Despite her annoyance at being treated like a child, Blythe had to admit the idea was intriguing, but not because of the Comstock case. The former sheriff would be the ideal person to ask about the house she was living in. Not only would he know if anything had happened there, he would never gossip about her inquiry.

Hoyt had shown her extraordinary kindness while she'd been growing up. Maybe because he'd been friends with her father. Maybe he'd felt sorry for her because of his untimely death. Whatever the reason, he had treated her like a fond uncle, even escorting her once to a father/daughter church banquet.

"That's a *very* good idea, Ada. Thanks for the suggestion," Blythe said, pushing back her chair and gathering up her coat and purse.

The librarian's eyes had widened at her use of her given name, a reaction that Blythe found surprisingly satisfying.

The Sheriff's Department had expanded to take in the adjoining buildings in the years she'd been away. Obviously there was a greater need for law-enforcement officers with the growth of the population and the county's changing demographics.

In the few weeks she'd been back, Blythe had become aware of the problem of meth labs, which seemed to spring up overnight in this mostly rural area. Even the redoubtable Sheriff Lee would no longer have been able to control things with only three or four deputies. Judging from the row of patrol cars parked in front of the building, there were far more than that now.

As she approached the door, her eye was caught by the neat gold letters, all caps, on its top half. DAVIS COUNTY SHERIFF'S DEPARTMENT. And below that, in both lower and upper case, Sheriff Cade Jackson. She had already reached out to grasp the doorknob when memory stopped her hand in midair.

Cade Jackson. She hadn't thought about the object of her first teenage crush in at least a decade, but the image evoked by his name was still colored by those long-ago fantasies.

The reality would probably be much different. She'd run into a couple of her former classmates, both of whom had succumbed to the dangers of a regional diet heavy on fried foods and starches. Their bellies had drooped over their belt buckles, and one had already begun combing his thinning locks across his pate in an unsuccessful attempt to hide the aging process.

It would verge on blasphemy if that had happened to Cade, she thought. Given that he was still living here in Crenshaw, however, it was probably inevitable.

And why would you care if he's fat and bald?

She would, she realized. Something about schoolgirl dreams and first loves. Even if Cade had never known about either.

She debated turning around and going back to her car. She had come here to see Hoyt, and it was obvious he was no longer employed by the county. Cade would probably know no more about the history of the house she was living in than she did.

Despite that logical conclusion, she turned the knob and pushed the heavy door inward. The kid at the desk looked to be about the same age as Cade the last time she'd seen him. A high-school senior, he'd soon left the county, heading to Tuscaloosa and a football scholarship at the University of Alabama.

Blythe, who had been twelve at the time, had grieved with all the emotion she'd been capable of. Which, as she remembered it, had been quite a lot.

That had been her first experience with loss. Although the memory of that pain had faded with the passing years and especially with the reality of true loss, within her chest stirred a shred of the apprehension she would have felt as a pre-adolescent had she known she was about to come face-to-face with Cade Jackson.

"Help you?" the young deputy asked.

"Sheriff Jackson, please?"

"May I ask what your inquiry is in reference to?"

At least the kid had been well trained. The question was both polite and efficient. Score one for Sheriff Jackson.

Tell him I'm trying to discover if my house might be haunted.

Since she couldn't divulge the truth, she said, "I'm trying to get in touch with Hoyt Lee."

The kid held her eyes a moment, his assessing. Then he reached for the phone on the desk in front of him, holding the receiver in the same hand he used to punch in a couple of numbers.

"Lady out here wants to talk to you about locating Sheriff Lee."

He listened, lips pursing slightly at whatever was said by the person on the other end of the line. His eyes met hers again as he nodded in response to what he'd been told.

He put down the phone and nodded toward another glass-topped door at the end of a short hall. "You can go on in. Sheriff's expecting you."

"Thanks."

She had taken only a couple of steps when the door she was headed toward opened. A man stepped through it and out into the hall. Although the overhead light cast a shadow on his face, his body in the light-colored uniform he wore was silhouetted against the darkness behind it.

If anything, Cade was leaner than when he'd played quarterback for the Davis County Warriors. The shoulders were still as broad. His height the same, of course.

As he walked toward the well-lit reception area, her mouth went dry. Her first thought was that he hadn't changed at all, but he had, of course.

The features that had been almost too fine at eighteen had strengthened. The straight nose had at some point been broken, so that a narrow ridge marred its perfection. The lips were thinner, more mature. More masculine, she conceded.

And far more sensual.

She was shocked by the thought. More shocked by the physical reaction that had produced it.

Cade Jackson had been a good-looking boy. He was a compellingly attractive man.

She couldn't remember the last time she had responded to a man in this way. Other than John, of course. And John had been dead for almost a year.

Maybe this was simply a natural progression in the long process of grieving. Maybe nature had decided it was time she began to notice members of the opposite sex again.

Sex.

Something else she hadn't thought about in a long time, she realized. And didn't want to think about right now.

Especially not as the man who had epitomized every adolescent daydream she'd ever had advanced toward her across the room, holding out his hand. If

Ada Pringle's rudeness could reduce her to an adolescent state, what effect would placing her hand into Cade's have?

"Cade Jackson."

It was obvious he didn't remember her. But then, she was very different from the twelve-year-old she'd been when he'd left Crenshaw. Maybe she should have been flattered that he didn't make the connection.

"Blythe Wyndham." She put her fingers in his, aware of their calloused hardness.

His handshake was firm and brief, without any of the cheesy lingering hold men sometimes used to prolong contact with an attractive woman.

Because he doesn't find you attractive?

"Wyndham?" A tiny furrow appeared between the dark brows.

His eyes hadn't changed either, she realized. Surrounded by thick, dark lashes, they were an unusual blue-green, almost aquamarine. Their paleness contrasted to the darkness of his skin, still deeply tanned despite the season.

"Née Mitchell," she offered, and then wondered if he would even know what that meant.

"Blythe Mitchell. Of *course.* I heard you were back."

She waited for the obligatory expression of sympathy, but he didn't offer one. Maybe the town gossip hadn't provided him with the information about her husband's death. Or maybe he'd forgotten it.

She became aware that he, too, was waiting. After all, she had asked to talk to him.

"I have what may seem a strange request."

The lips she'd just thought of as being sensual quirked slightly at the corners and were quickly controlled. "I doubt it's any stranger than most of the ones we get in here."

He glanced at the kid at the desk, who, Blythe realized, had been hanging on their every word. Despite the convenient excuse Ada Pringle had suggested, Blythe didn't want it spread around that she was investigating the town's most notorious murder. That would only provoke more gossip about her situation, something she'd had enough of.

"Do you think we could talk in your office?"

She knew by the momentary hesitation before he answered that she'd taken Cade by surprise. It took only a second or two for him to recover. He turned, using his hand to direct her toward the hallway and the still-open door.

She stepped past him, once again aware of him physically. Of his size. Of the faint aroma of soap or aftershave that seemed to cling to his body along with the scent of laundered cotton.

She wondered who did his laundry. Maybe he had a wife, someone who had taken the time to lovingly put that knife-edge crease into the khaki pants.

Then, concentrating on what she'd come here for, she determinedly banished any thought of Cade Jackson, the man. He was simply the current sheriff of Davis County.

That was the only role she was now interested in

having him play in her life. She had long ago outgrown the other.

His office was small, but neat. There were only two chairs, a battered leather swivel on the far side of the desk—obviously Cade's—and a straight-back wooden one, very like the chairs in the library, on the other. Blythe waited until he entered behind her, leaving the door open. She watched as he crossed the room to stand behind his desk. He gestured, indicating that she should sit down.

"Jerrod said you want to get in touch with Hoyt Lee." He had waited until she was seated before he settled into his own chair. "That doesn't seem such a strange request to me, although I would think Miz Ruth would have been able to help with that."

"Actually, I didn't realize he wasn't sheriff anymore. I came here thinking I could talk to him."

"Would you like for me to call him? Set up an appointment?"

"No. You're right. My grandmother will have Hoyt's number. Actually..." She was repeating herself, she realized. Of course, she'd never been very good at prevaricating. "I do freelance articles for magazines," she began again. "At least I did."

"And you want to write an article about Hoyt?"

Cade's elbows were on the arms of the chair, long brown fingers tented so that their joined tips touched the slight depression in the middle of his chin. It wasn't deep enough to be classified as a cleft, but it had always fascinated her. It was a little disconcerting to realize that it still did.

She wondered if she should just tell Cade the truth. Wouldn't he be bound by his office to keep anything she told him confidential? If she'd been willing to confide in Hoyt, why not in the current sheriff of Davis County?

"My grandmother suggested that doing so again might provide...a source of income."

His brows lifted slightly. "And..."

"I've spent the afternoon researching the town's history. Reading back through the old issues of the *Herald*, trying to find something that might be interesting to the outside world."

"Did you?"

"Ada reminded me of the Comstock murder. And that it's still unsolved."

"That's right."

Judging by the shortness of his answer, she wondered if Cade disapproved of what she said she'd come here to do. Again she fought the urge to tell him the truth. He might believe she was an idiot, but at least he wouldn't think her a ghoul.

"Was that a case where the police knew the killer, but couldn't prove it?"

"Not in my opinion."

"Then you've read the file?"

"I read through all the unsolved cases when I took office."

The sheriff of Davis County was an elected official. Blythe wondered what credentials Cade had brought to the job other than some long ago prowess on the football field. Of course, in this state that might have been recommendation enough.

"May I look at it?"

"Why?"

"I told you—"

"I know what you told me." He lowered his hands, resting them on the edge of his desk. "Now I'd *really* like to know why you're so interested in a murder that happened twenty-five years ago."

"Cold cases catch the public's attention," she said, repeating Ada's words. "And maybe editors'."

"So you're thinking of a book deal?"

"I really haven't gotten that far. Besides, there may be nothing there—"

"There's plenty there. For the curious. There's just no evidence. Certainly not enough to lead to an indictment. And no way you're going to be able to come up with the murderer."

"I'm sorry?"

"What kind of story would you have without a conclusion?"

She relaxed a little, believing that she understood his objection. "I'm not trying to solve the case, Sheriff Jackson. I don't have the skills to do that. I assure you I'm interested in doing exactly what I said. Writing an article. Preferably one I can sell," she added.

There was another of those thoughtful silences. "I'm sorry for your loss."

When Cade began the sentence, she had believed

he was about to apologize for giving her a hard time. By the time he finished it, she realized that he had connected John's death with the article. He obviously believed she needed the money. Which was the truth, she acknowledged.

"Thank you."

"I'll have Jerrod get you the file. There's an office across the hall you can use. I can't let you take anything out of course, but there's a copier in the reception area."

Cade stood, indicating that their conversation was over. Except she hadn't asked him anything she'd come here to find out. She had been morbidly fascinated by the Comstock murder, and it had provided an excuse for her research, but what she really needed to know…

"Are there any other…" She hesitated, unsure how to phrase what she wanted to ask.

"Murders as gruesome as Sarah's?"

Again she sensed his disapproval. "Acts of violence," she said, finishing her interrupted question. "Other incidents of violent death."

"A few brawls and farm accidents. Are those the kinds of things you're looking for?"

"Not really. Someone mentioned that something violent had happened in the house I'm renting. It's the two-story frame house at the end of Wheeler Road."

"Not that I've ever heard of. However, your grandmother or Hoyt would be a better source for that kind of information than I am. Both have lived here all their lives."

"You're right," she said, finally getting to her feet. "I'll check with them. Thank you for your time."

She turned and walked through the door of his office, aware that he was following her. The kid watched as they came into the reception area. She smiled at him as she passed the desk.

"Jerrod, would you get Ms. Wyndham the file on Sarah Comstock, please?"

Realizing that she had been about to walk out without looking at the material she had professed to want to see, Blythe turned, making a point of glancing down at her watch. "Actually..." *Again.* "Would it be all right if I come back another day and read through the material? I'm late picking up my daughter. They'll be wondering what's happened to me."

"Of course. Whenever Ms. Wyndham is ready, Jerrod."

"Yes, sir," the deputy said. "Anytime, ma'am."

"Thank you. Thank you both." She started to the door.

"Good to see you again," Cade said. "And since I didn't say it before, welcome home."

She smiled her thanks. A smile he didn't return. Cutting her losses, she opened the door and escaped those considering blue eyes by stepping out into the cold twilight.

5

Her first thought was it was too soon. It had been only four nights ago that Maddie's screams had awakened her, and now—

Not screams. Whatever she was hearing didn't follow the normal pattern of the nightmare. And then, in a blood-chilling flash of recognition, she knew the sound for what it was.

Smoke alarm.

There was only one, located at the top of the stairwell. She'd meant to buy another for the kitchen, but with everything involved in the move and with what had been going on since—

She threw off the covers and leapt out of bed, adrenaline flooding her system. She was halfway to the door of the second bedroom before she encountered smoke. As she ran, her mind analyzed the possibilities. None of them were comforting.

It was thicker in the hall, but she didn't slow. As long as whatever was burning didn't keep her from getting to Maddie, she wasn't concerned with it right now. Once she had her daughter, she'd think about the terrifying reality that in the middle of the night her rented house was filled with smoke.

As she neared the door to the main bedroom, where Maddie had been sleeping since Blythe had heard the tapping on the window, she fought her panic, reassuring herself that despite the density of the smoke there was enough breathable air....

The little girl was sitting up in bed, her eyes wide as the alarm continued to sound its warning. "Mama?"

Blythe threw back the quilts and scooped her up off the bed. Maddie clung to her neck, her legs automatically wrapping around her waist.

She carried Maddie into the hall, heading toward the stairs. In the darkness, framed by spindles at their top, she could see the glow of flames, already licking up the stairwell.

The most immediate danger was the smoke, which was already thick in the upstairs hall. Toxins would be released by the burning furniture, and the smoke itself would rapidly eat up the life-sustaining oxygen.

How long did that give her? Blythe wondered, reversing course. How long would there be air for them to breathe? How long did she have to try to find a way out?

Running now, she carried Maddie toward the window at the end of the short hall. One look at the two-story drop below it made her rethink that solution. She turned away, glancing over her shoulder at the glow from the stairwell.

Mentally she reviewed the windows on this floor.

The one where she'd heard the tapping overlooked the roof of the screened-in porch. And apparently the fire had started on the other side of the structure….

She hurried into what had been Maddie's bedroom. She leaned over the secretary, putting her forehead against the cold glass. Below stretched the gently peaked roof of the addition.

She bent, setting Maddie on the floor. "Lie down and stay down," she ordered, in her I-mean-it voice.

She jerked the desk away from the wall as if it weighed nothing. Even if she decided the drop to the roof below was too great, once she opened the window, they would at least have fresh air.

She turned the metal latch at the top of the sill and then tried to push up the sash. No matter how much pressure she applied, the window refused to budge, not even when she bent, using the muscles of her thighs and buttocks. Either moisture had caused the wood to swell or it had been painted shut.

She looked back toward the hall, which was now thick with smoke. There had to be another way. Another window. Some other access to the roof.

Even as she mentally sought other possibilities, she knew there were none. The other windows on this floor offered a straight drop to the ground two stories below. And there was no guarantee that any of them would be easier to open than this.

Her eyes fastened on the small desk chair that had been shoved into the keyhole of the desk. When she'd moved the secretary, it had carried the chair with it.

Coughing, she jerked the chair free, holding onto the back of it with both hands. It seemed incredibly light, far too fragile to accomplish what she needed it to do.

"Keep your head down," she ordered Maddie.

She moved back to the window, swinging the chair at the bottom half, the part without the wooden mullions. The first time the legs and seat hit the broad pane of glass, they bounced off.

The second time she swung the chair with all the strength she possessed. The glass cracked, and when she struck it the third time, it shattered.

She took a deep breath of the cold night air rushing in through the opening. Behind her, the fire crackled and hissed with the renewed flow of oxygen. The sound destroyed her sense of euphoria, replacing it with another burst of panic.

Using the chair and her hands, she broke out the shards that clung to the frame. Then she turned, picked Maddie up off the floor and started back to the window.

"Mama? What are you doing?"

"It's okay," Blythe said. "We're going out the window. Just do what I tell you, okay?"

Against her body she felt the little girl's nod.

Dear God, don't let me lose her, too.

The broken window loomed before her. For a moment she couldn't decide if she should drop onto the roof and then have Maddie jump down so she would be there to break her fall.

It took only a second to realize too many things

could go wrong with that plan. She could be knocked unconscious by the fall. Maddie could refuse to jump. The fire could reach her before—

She destroyed the thought as she set Maddie on her feet. Then, putting her arms around the little girl's torso, Blythe locked her hands around her back. She lifted her daughter and lowered her body through the open window.

The roof below looked much farther away than before. She would have to drop the little girl on the right side of the peak so that when she fell, she would roll down into the valley formed by the wall of the original house and the roof of the addition. If she dropped her on the other side, Maddie might roll off and onto the ground below.

Blythe edged nearer the right side of the window, ignoring Maddie's sobs. One chance to save her daughter's life. If she blew it…

She bent as far out as she could, so that her belly was pressed against the bottom of the frame. She could feel a piece of the broken glass that had clung to it slice her skin, but she ignored the pain, carefully positioning Maddie for the drop.

Blythe's shoulders screamed for relief from the weight they held, but she ignored them, too. Instead, her left arm still around Maddie's back, she managed to slide her right hand up until it was fastened around Maddie's wrist. She closed her eyes, anticipating the strain on her shoulder as she held on to the small, dangling body with one hand while with the other she completed the same maneuver to grasp Maddie's other wrist.

She thought she could feel the heat of the fire behind her. She could definitely hear it. Despite the length of the drop and the chance of injury, she had to release her daughter and let her fall.

Only chance...

"I'm coming, Maddie," she said, pitching her voice to carry over the noise of the inferno behind her. "I'm coming. Just stay there, and I'll jump down beside you."

Opening her hands to let Maddie go was the hardest thing she'd ever done in her life. Heart in her throat, she watched as the small body, clad in its white flannel gown, fell. The little girl rolled over twice, coming to rest in the protection of the valley, just as Blythe had planned.

She waited just long enough to see Maddie raise her head to look up at the window. The intensity of the heat behind her allowed no further hesitation.

She put one leg over the frame, turning so that she could hold onto the inside edge of its sill with her fingers. That would allow her body to extend to its full length before she let go and dropped to the roof. Through the pall of smoke in the bedroom, she could see the glow of the conflagration that was now consuming the upper hall.

Only chance...

She let go, falling hard onto the side of the peaked roofline. As she slid down into the valley between the two rooflines, she tried to slow her progress by grabbing at the shingles, scraping her hands as well as her hip.

"Mama."

She turned to find Maddie looking up at her, her eyes wide. In the moonlight, which seemed bright as day, there were no visible injuries. Even if there were…

"We're okay," Blythe reassured.

She pushed onto her feet, putting one hand on the wall of the house to keep her balance as she moved toward her daughter. She tried to keep her right foot in the center of the flashing, which, compared to the roof itself, was relatively flat.

She held out her free hand. "Come on," she ordered as she pulled the little girl to her feet.

Afraid of what she'd see, she refused to look up at the window through which they'd exited. As she moved toward the front of the addition, she listened instead for the wail of fire trucks. There was nothing but the sound of the fire, devouring the rich heart pine from which the little house had been constructed.

Please, God, let me get her down. Don't take her away from me. I'll do whatever you want, if you just won't let anything happen to Maddie.

When she reached the edge of the roof, holding tightly to Maddie's hand, she stooped to look out over it. The concrete patio that had probably been constructed at the same time as the screened porch was directly below them. There was no sign of the fire here at the very back of the house. If she could get them down, they should be safe.

But there was no drainpipe. No conveniently placed tree. Nothing.

She couldn't remember how close the trees on the other side of the addition were. She knew there *were* a couple, however. And shrubbery. But they would have to go over the peak of the roof to reach them.

She shifted her grip on Maddie, so that she held her wrist rather than her hand. It would be too easy for those small fingers to slip away from her.

"Where are we going?"

"To the other side."

Maddie shook her head, tears welling. "I'm scared, Mama."

Me, too, baby. Me, too.

"I've got you. I won't let go. It's going to be all right, Maddie. I promise." As she made the pledge, she started up the incline.

Although she had to bend in order to maintain her hold on Maddie's wrist, she managed to reach the peak with relative ease, using her free hand on the shingles for balance. Only when she reached the top did she realize that the real danger would be going down. How could she ensure that she wouldn't slip on that slanting surface, carrying Maddie with her?

She eased down so that she was sitting on the peak of the roofline. She drew Maddie to her, relishing her small, solid warmth. The little girl was trembling like someone in a chill, but the act of comforting her gave Blythe hope. And it renewed her determination. After all, they had made it this far.

She looked again at the downward slope. Although it wasn't steep, for someone barefoot and guiding a terrified four-year-old, it would be treacherous.

"You remember when Daddy used to ride you piggyback?" Blythe leaned back, sweeping Maddie's bangs from her eyes, as she looked into her face.

The little girl nodded.

"Think you can do that again?"

"Up here?"

"Hold on around my neck and put your legs around my back. I'm going to scoot down on my bottom."

In the silence that followed, Blythe could hear the fire again. She had no idea how long it had been since the alarm had awakened her. It felt like an eternity, yet there were no fire engines. For the first time she realized they might not come until it was too late.

With that incentive, she brought her other leg over the peak and, still holding onto Maddie, scooted down perhaps a foot. Her nightgown rucked up under her, but there was nothing she could do about it. The shingles would abrade her buttocks and thighs, just as they had her hands.

"Piggyback," she said, trying to position the little girl behind her without losing the grip she had on her arm. "Put your legs around my waist and hold on."

"I don't want to."

"You have to, Maddie. You have to." Again she made her voice hard. Demanding.

She knew the child was at a breaking point, but she couldn't deal with hysterics. Not up here. She had to get her off the roof now, even if it meant dropping her over the side as she had dropped her out of the window.

"Get on my back," she said, pulling sharply on Maddie's arm. "Do it now, Maddie. Do you hear me?"

Trembling arms fastened around her neck, almost choking her. She reached down and lifted her daughter's legs to wrap them around her body. She had to push the constriction of the little girl's gown out of the way, but finally the child was in position, clinging to her back, her cheek resting against Blythe's neck.

She could hear Maddie sobbing, but she ignored it. She ignored everything except what she had to do.

Using her palms and her feet, she inched down the sloping roof. Given the size of the addition, it was a matter of less than a minute before her toes were at the edge. Then she realized that she wasn't sure how to proceed from there.

Try to position herself, with Maddie still on her back, to dangle from the roof as she had from the window? But there was nothing here to hang onto. Even if there had been, she wasn't sure that her arms could support their combined weight—not even long enough to extend her body over the edge.

Drop Maddie, as she had done before? The grass below would be softer than the roof, and she'd suffered no serious injuries from the previous fall. Of course, working on the slanting surface would be much harder than standing on the floor of the bedroom and lowering her out the window had been.

Her eyes searched the area below. Stripped by the

winter of their leaves, the foundation plantings looked like stakes, pointing upward, ready to impale them.

The ground then, she decided. Even the dead brown grass would offer some cushion. And what choice did she have?

She glanced up and back. Tongues of flames shot out of the window she'd broken. They had only a couple of minutes at most before the fire would involve the rest of the house, including the place where they were sitting.

"I'm going to swing you off the edge, just like we did before." She reached up, trying to pry Maddie's hands from around her neck.

"No. No, Mama. I don't want to." The child's denial was mindless. Panicked.

Blythe didn't have time to reason with her. Ruthlessly, she pulled at the child's right wrist, breaking its hold. In response, Maddie's legs tightened around her waist as she clung like a limpet to what she perceived to be safety.

"Maddie, let go. We have to get down."

A wail answered her. The wrist she'd captured was ripped from her hold as Maddie again locked both arms around her neck, threatening to cut off her supply of air.

"*Look* at it. Look up. Do you see the fire? We have to get off the roof, damn it. We *have* to."

Uncertain whether her words would have any impact against the child's fear, she reached again and pulled the clenched hands apart. This time she didn't let down her guard and allow Maddie to free her wrist. This was life and death. And it was up to her to make sure the choice was not the latter.

Ever mindful of how near the edge they were, she tried to drag the child around in front of her. Realizing she wasn't going to be able to do that one-handed, Blythe lifted her other hand off the roof, using it, too, to try to manhandle the little girl off her back.

Now beyond any threat that might coerce her to obedience, Maddie struggled desperately to maintain her position. Eventually Blythe's superior size and strength won out. She wrestled the child forward, breaking the hold of those trembling legs.

As soon as she realized what was happening, Maddie lunged upward toward the peak of the roof, trying to escape. Blythe was forced to turn to keep hold of her daughter. As she did, her foot slipped on the shingles, sending her sliding toward the edge of the roof. Although the distance she traveled was small, her left foot dropped over, almost unbalancing her.

She let go of Maddie, throwing herself prone in an attempt to stop the downward slide. Moving carefully, she pulled the dangling foot back onto the roof and, then using her feet and hands, painstakingly inched her body up the incline.

Although the exertion required had not been great, she was panting, breath sawing in and out of her lungs. When she finally felt secure enough to move again, she turned her head, searching for her daughter.

Maddie was sitting halfway up the slanting roof. Her arms were wrapped around her knees, which had been drawn up to her chin, her nightgown draped over them. Her eyes were the only dark spot in a face literally without color.

In the sudden stillness between them, Blythe was aware of heat beneath her body. The fire had apparently reached the porch. Once it broke through…

"We have to do this now, Maddie. You can't fight me or we'll both fall off."

Or worse. She couldn't say that, of course. The child had clearly moved beyond the reach of reason. Reminding her of the fire would only drive her further into hysteria.

Blythe pushed up, still moving carefully after the near disaster. She reached one hand out imploringly to her daughter.

For a long moment nothing happened. She had begun to despair when the little girl finally moved. With the same crab-like motion Blythe had used to make the descent, she edged down the incline.

Blythe took the child's left wrist in her right hand. "I'm going to swing you off and drop you down on the grass. Bend your knees when you hit. You'll be fine. I swear, Maddie, you'll be fine."

She expected resistance. Arguments. Something. The little girl nodded instead.

There was no time now to do anything other than swing her over the side and then let her go. One chance. One chance.

She took Maddie's other wrist, pulling her around in front. Then, fighting to keep from falling off the roof, too, she swung the little girl over the edge, her shoulders screaming again with the strain.

She bent forward, her breasts touching her knees, in an attempt to hold Maddie away from the house. She took a final glance at the ground to verify that her daughter would fall onto the thick zoysia below. Then she closed her eyes for a final wordless prayer, before she allowed her fingers to release, dropping the child to the ground.

Blythe's eyes followed her descent. For a long heartbeat, Maddie lay where she had fallen. Then slowly, more slowly than Blythe believed she could bear, she began to sit up.

"Maddie? You okay?"

Another eternity before the small blond head moved up and down. Blythe stifled the sob, knowing there was no time for tears, not even of relief.

"You have to run," she said.

Despite the moonlight, the woods that stretched behind the house seemed dark and frightening. But if she sent Maddie toward the front, she wouldn't be able to see her. She couldn't be sure that the child wouldn't go back inside the house to find a toy or because it had once been a place of safety.

"The woods," she said. "Can you run to the woods and wait for Mama?"

"I want to wait here. You said you were coming."

"I am. I'm right behind you. But you need to get

away from the house. Away from the fire. Go on, Maddie. Just to the edge of the woods."

She watched as her daughter reluctantly climbed to her feet. As soon as Maddie moved out of the way, she would jump down. Even if she broke an ankle, she'd still be able to get away from the fire. *Even if I have to crawl...*

"Go on, Maddie. To the edge of the woods and wait for me."

As Blythe said the words, she raised her eyes to the thick pine forest that marked the property line. Something in the trees caught her eye. A shape, darker than the trunks themselves, was moving along the edge of the woods.

She blinked, trying to make sense of what she was seeing. When she looked again, whatever she'd seen seemed to have melted into the shadows. Still...

A movement below drew her gaze from the forest. Looking like a small, white ghost in her pale nightgown, Maddie was running across the back lawn toward those woods. Just as Blythe had told her to.

And she was running directly toward whatever—or whoever—had been moving there.

6

Eyes straining against the darkness, Blythe searched the property line again. There was nothing there now but the trunks of the trees, standing stark against the moonlight.

She knew in her heart that she hadn't been mistaken. Something had been moving among them. Something upright. Too tall to be an animal.

That thought was almost as unnerving as the other. *Whatever* was out there, she had to stop Maddie and then get the hell off this roof. In that order.

"Maddie? *Maddie,*" she screamed.

The little girl didn't slow. Maybe she couldn't hear above the noise of the fire, which seemed to have grown louder in the last few seconds.

Blythe looked down at the place where she'd dropped her daughter. The quickest way off the roof—and the quickest way to get to Maddie—would be to jump.

Behind her a whoosh erupted. A flare of heat, strong enough to be painful, assailed her back.

Without looking around, Blythe scrambled to her

feet. Her body poised on the edge of the roof, she tried to remember everything she'd ever read or heard about how to fall.

Bend your knees when you hit. Roll. There was nothing else. That was the sole store of her knowledge. Too little. And way too late.

She bent her knees, mentally as well as physically preparing herself, and then leaped out over the edge. The ground rushed up, giving her no time to be afraid.

For a second after she landed, she was aware of nothing. Not of pain. Not even of the impact itself. All she knew was that she was lying on her side on the cold, wet grass.

Then everything seemed to flood her consciousness at once. The burning house, flames and sparks shooting upward into the night sky. And the more frightening realization that Maddie was running toward whoever had been standing in the woods.

Blythe rolled over onto her hands and knees. When she put her weight on her right foot to push off the ground, she realized that she hadn't escaped the jump unscathed. Even if her ankle was broken, it wouldn't be enough to keep her from getting to Maddie.

As she got to her feet, her eyes found the small, ghostly figure. Maddie was almost at the edge of the forest, the white nightgown outlined against its darkness.

Blythe began to run, too, her speed hampered by

her injury. She didn't waste breath on shouting, knowing now that she couldn't be heard above the fire.

Far enough, Maddie. Stop and look back. Look at me.

Even as Blythe willed her daughter to stop, the little girl drew closer and closer to the line of trees. Blythe's gaze searched them, trying locate again whatever she'd seen before.

When she did, terror squeezed her chest. Although the shadowy form she'd spotted from the rooftop had been moving *away* from the property, that was no longer the case. The child in the pale gown and the dark shape moving among the trees now appeared to be on a collision course.

"Maddie. Stop, Maddie."

The words had no effect. As Blythe's eyes shifted to the other figure, she realized that it at least had stopped. Watching her?

Ignoring the agony in her ankle, she tried to increase her speed. Surely Maddie wouldn't go into the woods. Surely she had understood…

"Maddie!"

Despite the awkwardness of her hobbling run, Blythe was gaining on the little girl. Encouraged by that realization, her eyes again lifted to search for the figure in the woods.

The shape was no longer in the place where she'd last seen it. Her gaze trailed along the edge of the forest, trying to find that dark anomaly.

Eyes on the trees instead of the ground in front of her, she stumbled, pitching forward despite her frantic efforts to regain her balance. Even as she broke her fall with her outstretched hands, she looked up to locate her daughter.

Perhaps emboldened by her fall, the shadowy figure at the edge of the woods seemed to once more be moving toward the little girl. The light of the fire clearly illuminated what was happening.

Blythe scrambled to her feet, again screaming her daughter's name. Finally—unbelievably—the little girl turned, looking back across the yard. Looking directly toward her. Slowing. Stopping just short of the woods.

Still Blythe ran, adrenaline pumping so fiercely through her veins that she was conscious of nothing but getting to Maddie before he could. She caught the little girl in her arms, holding the small body against her own as she turned to run back toward the fire.

Its known horror was less now than the unknown that lurked at the edge of the forest. She threw a glance over her shoulder, but the shape seemed to have again melted into the shadows.

Then Blythe, too, heard the sound that had undoubtedly driven him back into the darkness from which he'd materialized. Faintly from the distance came a wail of sirens.

Finally. Finally.

By the time she'd reached the gravel driveway beside the house, which was now totally consumed by the conflagration, the first of the fire trucks had arrived, their sirens drowning out the noise of the blaze.

* * *

When the sheriff's cruiser pulled into the drive, probably twenty minutes after the first of the firefighters, Blythe was sitting on the open back of the paramedic's van. Someone had wrapped a blanket around her shoulders, but she couldn't remember who or when that had happened.

Perhaps it had been while they'd checked out Maddie, which she had insisted they do first. Or maybe it had been before the paramedic, who seemed hardly more than a kid himself, examined her ankle. He'd told her that he didn't think it was broken, but she'd need to have it X-rayed to be sure.

Now her daughter was huddled in her lap, her legs again wrapped around Blythe's waist. Despite the activity that swirled around them as the men fought a losing battle against the fire, the little girl hadn't lifted her head from her mother's shoulder.

Although Blythe had pulled the blanket around them both, Maddie's body was occasionally racked by tremors. Not the result of the cold, but of the incredible stresses of this night. As soon as they got to Ruth's, Blythe told herself, Maddie would be okay.

Okay. Incredibly, they both were. Considering that the house where they'd been sleeping was now engulfed in flames, that was a miracle.

Thank you, Father.

She glanced up at the sound of a car door slamming. As she watched, Cade Jackson walked up her drive. Although she couldn't see his face beneath the uniform Stetson he wore, she realized she would have recognized that distinctively athletic walk anywhere. Anytime.

She hadn't expected Cade to show up out here, but she should have. This was his county. His responsibility.

He stopped to speak to one of the firemen. The man pointed toward the van where she and Maddie were sitting. It had been pulled toward the back of the yard, well away from the house.

To express his thanks for the information, Cade touched the brim of his hat. As ridiculous as it might have seemed to outsiders, there was something about the gesture that was touching. Crenshaw had been caught in a time warp as far as the traditional courtesies were concerned, and she liked that.

Cade was moving more quickly now that he had a location. He would be here before she'd had time to prepare for the questions he would ask. Right now, she didn't want to have to think about what had happened tonight. Or why.

Despite the fear the memory still evoked, she also didn't want to talk about the figure in the woods. Either Cade wouldn't believe her, making her feel like a hysterical fool. Or even worse, he would.

That would make it real. More frightening, somehow, than the fire.

"Ms. Wyndham."

As he said her name, Cade again touched the brim of his hat.

Tears started at the back of Blythe's eyes. She blinked to control them.

"Are you okay?"

The deeply masculine voice, its accent comforting, was full of concern. And that, too, touched her emotions, which were battered and too near the surface.

"We're alive."

Bottom line. And all that mattered.

"Thank God for that. Any idea what happened?"

She shook her head. "The smoke alarm woke me. I ran to Maddie's room to get her, and by the time I had, the staircase was on fire."

She hesitated, trying to think if there was anything else about what had occurred while they were inside the house he should know. At the time, she hadn't been thinking about anything but finding a way out.

"That's where the alarm was," she added. "I had meant to put one up in the kitchen, but..." She let the sentence trail, again feeling as if she'd done something wrong. As if she hadn't made a great enough effort to protect her daughter.

"So the fire was already at the staircase when the alarm went off?"

"I... I don't know," she said, shaking her head again as she tried. "There was smoke in the upstairs hall. Actually, the alarm is up there. At the *top* of the stairwell. By the time I got Maddie and was back out in the hall, I could see the flames coming up the stairs." The words ran down, as she was overwhelmed by having to relive those moments of sheer terror.

"What did you do then?"

"I broke a window in the other bedroom and dropped Maddie out onto the roof of the screened porch."

Cade's eyes widened slightly. Not questioning, but apparently surprised.

But then, she was telling this in fits and starts. It probably made no sense to someone who wasn't there.

"There's no other way out from the upstairs," she explained. "I didn't believe we could get down the stairs. I didn't want to try. Not with Maddie."

"Good thinking. And then after you dropped her out the window, you climbed through and...?"

"We crossed over the top of the roof of the porch, and I dropped her onto the grass on the driveway side. I couldn't think of another way to get her down."

"And then you followed."

She nodded.

"Any idea how it started? You leave a coffeepot on or something? Light some candles before you went to bed?"

"No candles. No open flame. The furnace is gas, but..." She shook her head. "We haven't had any trouble with it. Or with anything else here."

"We'll get the fire chief to check it out. I just thought you might have some idea. A place to start. I'll tell him what you've said."

His right hand started upward in the gesture she'd already seen him make twice. Halfway to their target, the long dark fingers changed direction. He leaned forward, bending to put his hand on the top of Maddie's head. It rested there a moment, but the little girl didn't respond.

"She okay?" The aquamarine eyes lifted to Blythe's, the question in them as well.

"Physically."

There was a moment's hesitation. "Kids bounce back from things like this quicker than adults. You'll be surprised."

She didn't answer, but her eyes held his. Of course, he couldn't be aware of everything that had gone on in the little girl's life. Losing her father. The move. The nightmares. And now this.

After a moment, he nodded, clearly a dismissal. He had already begun to turn away, no doubt intending to talk to the fire chief as he'd indicated. Before he'd taken two steps, the words she wasn't sure she had wanted to say had been launched into the air between them.

"There was someone here. Standing at the edge of the woods." She turned her head, glancing toward the dark trees.

When she looked back, she realized that Cade's gaze had followed hers. He regarded the woods for several seconds before his eyes returned to hers. Again they were questioning.

"Some*one?*"

"A shape. That's all I saw." Now that she'd decided to tell him, the words spilled out. "It was too tall and upright to be an animal. I think... I'm sure it was a person. He was standing at the edge of the woods looking toward the house."

"He?"

Examining her memory, she realized she couldn't have determined that based on what she'd seen. "I shouldn't have said that. I assumed it was a man, but… There was nothing that defining about what I saw. It was a shape," she reiterated, trying to stick to the facts. "It was different from those around it. And it moved. That's why I noticed it."

"How do you know that whoever was out there was looking at the house?"

She wasn't sure why she'd said that either. She certainly hadn't been able to see features of whomever she'd seen.

"I don't. It just seemed to me that he was. Or that he had been."

"I would think anyone who saw a house on fire around here would come to help."

As a general comment about the community, that was probably accurate. Still, she knew what she'd seen. That kind of logic wasn't going to change her mind about it.

"Whoever was out there didn't come to help. I'd sent Maddie toward the woods after I dropped her off the roof. I wanted her away from the fire. I looked at the trees to see how distant they were, I guess. To judge whether that was a safe place for her. And…there he was."

"Watching Maddie?"

She examined her memory, trying to see if that fit.

"I don't think so. I think he must have begun moving when she started that way."

"As if he didn't want her to see him?"

"I don't know." Unconsciously, she shook her head again, the movement slight. "I don't know what he was doing out there. Or what he was thinking. I only know that I saw someone standing in those woods watching my house burn."

The hysteria she'd managed to deny up to this point had crept into her voice, and she hated it. For as long as she could remember, she had considered any loss of control a failure of will. It seemed especially important now that she be strong for Maddie.

"Then there should be footprints out there," Cade said, "as much rain as we've had."

There should be, she realized, which would be proof of what she'd seen. To give Cade credit, however, she had detected no trace of doubt in his voice. No skepticism, despite her emotional outburst.

"That'll have to wait for morning," he went on. "I don't want to go blundering around out there with a flashlight and obliterate whatever signs are there."

"Thank you."

She wasn't sure he would understand her expression of gratitude. After all, he was only doing his job. The fact that he was doing it on her word alone meant more than she could say.

"I'll need to make sure the area is taped off. After that, I can take you to the hospital. Unless you'd prefer to ride in the ambulance."

"I'd prefer not to go at all. The paramedic doesn't believe anything's broken. I don't either. I ran on my ankle to get to Maddie." A hobbling effort, but still a run. "Surely if something were seriously wrong—"

"Adrenaline can mask injuries, even severe ones."

He said that with the surety of someone who knew firsthand. Of course, an injury was why his football career had ended prematurely. Or so she'd heard.

"The safest thing to do is have it checked out," Cade finished.

"I'll get it checked out first thing tomorrow, I promise. Right now… Right now I just want to go to my grandmother's. I need to get Maddie back to bed."

Cade hesitated before he turned to look over his shoulder, probably searching for someone to drive them over to Ruth's. His job was here, especially considering what she'd told him.

He turned back, looking down on Maddie. "I'll take you."

"Are you sure?"

"Doug can hold down the fort. We aren't going to be able to do much out here until daylight, anyway. In any case, I need to go back to the office and call the state fire marshal."

"The fire marshal?"

"Since someone was lurking at the back of your property, at approximately the same time a fire broke out in your home, we're going to need to check for arson. That's the state's job."

Despite the figure in the woods, the thought that

someone might have deliberately set the fire that had destroyed the rental house had never crossed her mind. Things like that didn't happen. Not in Crenshaw.

"Do you really think—"

"It's a possibility we can't afford to overlook."

"Warm enough?" Cade glanced over his shoulder into the backseat of the cruiser.

"We're fine," Blythe lied.

Maybe he'd been right about the effects of adrenaline. Although the sheriff had insisted she keep the paramedic's blanket, she had begun shivering shortly after they'd gotten into his car, and she hadn't been able to stop.

Even Maddie's solid warmth, still pressed against her body, hadn't helped. Since there was no child restraint seat in the police cruiser, Blythe had fastened the seat belt around both of them. Hardly an ideal situation, but in light of everything else that had happened tonight, it seemed a small enough risk.

She hated to wake her grandmother. She glanced to her left, trying to gauge time by the sky. A thin tinge of yellow hovered just above the horizon, not yet strong enough to lighten it, but surely a precursor of dawn. By the time they'd driven the remaining five miles or so to the house, Delores would probably have breakfast started.

"You want me to call?" Cade asked, glancing back again.

"I'm sorry?"

"You want me to call your grandmother and tell her we're coming?"

The offer was tempting. Even if Cade explained, Blythe knew she would still have to answer the questions of the two old women. It would be better not to worry them until she had to.

She shook her head before she realized he wouldn't be able to see her. "She may not be up. Let's let her sleep as long as possible."

She wasn't sure how her grandmother would react to the news of the fire. Right now, she wasn't sure about anything.

She and Maddie had nothing left, not even a change of clothes. The little that had remained of John's insurance had almost been expended in the move. Like it or not—and she didn't—she would be dependent on her grandmother's hospitality for a while.

There was no doubt in her mind that Ruth would welcome them without reservation. Her grandmother's feelings had been hurt that Blythe had wanted her own place. And truthfully, that had been a decision Blythe herself had not been completely sure of.

Now that decision had been taken out of her hands. She had no choice but to move back into the family home. No choice but to allow herself and Maddie to sink back into the comfortable existence she'd known as a child. Her grandmother would pet and pamper them both. Delores would feed them, look after their clothes, and pick up after them if Blythe let her.

That was the thing she had feared most when she'd

decided to come home. That the cocoon of family would again create the deadly inertia she'd had to struggle against after John's death.

She had been determined to make her own way, even here. Although the idea of writing again had been only a cover story provided by Ada's misconception, it had generated an undeniable sense of excitement. The thought of being able to make a living for the two of them by doing that...

"Is that where you got the idea to write about Sarah Comstock?"

Cade's question seemed to fit so well into her internal dialogue it took her a few seconds to realize that, unless he was psychic, he couldn't have known what she'd been thinking. Which made her wonder what he was talking about.

"I'm sorry?"

"The house. Living there."

There could be only one meaning for the combination of those two phrases. Despite having reached it, she still didn't understand. "Why would you think that?"

"Then it wasn't? Somehow, when you came to the office the other day I thought it might be."

"You're talking about the house that burned. Why in the world—" Some premonition of what Cade must have been about to say stopped her breath.

It would explain so much if there was, as he'd intimated, a connection between the house they'd been living in and the murdered child. It wouldn't explain everything, of course. Not unless you were willing to believe that the dead maintain some bond with the things of this earth, but still...

"From what you said that day, I thought maybe you knew. Audra Wright grew up in that house. Lived there until she married Abel Comstock. Old Miz Wright lived there until her death, maybe sixteen, seventeen years ago."

"Audra Comstock," Blythe repeated softly, beginning to realize the implications.

"Sarah's mother."

And the Miz Wright Cade had mentioned would be Sarah's grandmother, Blythe realized, thinking of the strength of that tie. In her experience, an unbreakable bond. Especially in this locale, where family was the cornerstone of one's existence.

All this time she and Maddie had been living in the home of Sarah Comstock's maternal grandmother, and she hadn't even known it. Not until the same night that house had been reduced to ashes.

7

Blythe had been wrong about the impending dawn. Delores's old Chevrolet wasn't yet parked in the driveway of her grandmother's house. Nor could she see any lights on inside.

"Doesn't look like Miz Ruth's up." Cade's comment reinforced her own assessment.

"What time is it?" She leaned forward to look through the windshield as he pulled the cruiser parallel to the front steps.

"A little before five."

"Delores should be here soon."

Neither of them said anything for several seconds. Finally it dawned on her that Cade undoubtedly had other things to do.

Like put a call in to the fire marshal.

"We'll get out and wait on the porch. My grandmother will be awake in a few minutes. She always gets up to unlock the door for Delores."

Blythe could remember her mother arguing that the housekeeper should have a key to the house "just in case." Neither her grandmother nor Delores had wanted that. She suspected that what they primarily objected to was any proposed change in the way they'd done things for so long.

"Actually, I'd rather you all wait inside the car, if you don't mind."

"Why?" Blythe's fingers were already wrapped around the door handle in preparation of getting out.

There was a slight hesitation before Cade answered her. "Because right now I don't know what went on out at your place tonight. Until I do...I prefer both of you to be where someone can keep an eye on you."

The idea that they might be in danger hadn't crossed Blythe's mind, despite the shadowy figure on the edge of the woods and Cade's mention of arson. Was he suggesting that whoever had been out there might have followed them here?

To do what? Take a potshot at them as they sat in the porch swing? The notion was ludicrous.

More ludicrous than someone setting fire to your home and watching it burn?

"You think he might have followed us here? Is that what you're saying?"

"*Nobody* followed us. I can promise you that. As I said, it's just that until I know what's going on, I'd rather be safe than sorry."

So had she, of course. Especially where Maddie was concerned.

She removed her hand from the handle, putting her arm back around the little girl. She wondered if Maddie was asleep. She'd hardly moved since they'd gotten into the car.

She glanced down at the child she held. Nothing was visible from this angle but the top of her head.

For an instant the image of Cade's long, dark fingers resting over the blond hair was in her mind. Then a flash of light hit the window beside her, drawing her attention outside.

The twin beams of a set of headlights cut through the darkness. Blythe recognized the sound of the battered Nova's engine long before she could see the car itself.

Delores guided it carefully around the police cruiser and into her usual parking place at the side of the house. Almost before the motor died, the housekeeper was out of the car and hurrying back to Cade's.

He had quickly opened his door and gotten out to meet her. Although the interior light was briefly blinding, after a few seconds Blythe could see Delores's wrinkled face peering into the car, her dark eyes wide with concern.

"Lord, child, what y'all doing in a *police* car?" The housekeeper leaned forward to pitch the question in through the open door.

"We're all right," Blythe reassured her. "We just need to stay with Grandmamma for a while."

Delores looked at Cade, as if she expected him to provide some explanation for that necessity.

"House fire," he obliged.

"Fire at you all's house?" Delores's gaze snapped back to Blythe.

"Everything's gone, Delores." It was the first time Blythe had put that reality into words. The concern in the old woman's eyes drew the admission from her. "There's nothing left."

"Sure there is, baby. We're left. Me and your grandmamma. And we're gonna take care of you. Both of you. You get 'em out of the car, Mr. Cade, and I'll go wake up Miz Ruth. Something told me to get over here early this morning. I knew something was wrong before daylight. I knew it in my bones."

The last two sentences, muttered rather than spoken, floated back to them as the old woman hurried toward the front steps. Cade turned to watch her before he, too, bent to look inside the car.

"I think we've been given instructions. You want me to carry her?" He lifted his chin to indicate Maddie.

"It's probably better if I do. I think she's asleep."

"I'll come around and open the door for you. Hang on."

He closed the door on the driver's side. Blythe's eyes followed him as he walked around the front of the cruiser and then to the back door on the passenger side. He opened it, holding out his hand to help her out.

She slid across the back seat, trying not to wake Maddie. Once there, she hesitated, for some reason reluctant to accept Cade's hand. Just as she had been that first day.

Knowing that getting out with the child in her arms would be awkward, she finally put the fingers of her right hand into Cade's, allowing him to practically pull them from the car. In the process, the blanket fell off her shoulders.

As she stepped away from the car, favoring her ankle, which had stiffened during the short ride, Cade reached back inside to retrieve it. He was in the act of draping it around her when the porch light came on above them.

They looked up as Ruth Mitchell opened the massive front door. She had already stepped back to allow Delores room to enter when she spotted the three of them standing together at the foot of the steps.

"Lord have mercy. What in the *world?*" Her grandmother came out through the open door, almost pushing the housekeeper out of her way.

"We're all right," Blythe said again.

"What's happened?"

"A fire," Cade offered.

The rehearsal with Delores's questions seemed to have cemented their roles. Too tired to break the pattern, Blythe said exactly what she had before.

"Everything's gone, Grandmamma. There's nothing left."

"Oh, my dear. You come on inside. Bring that baby in here," her grandmother directed, letting Delores brush by her to enter the house. "You all are the only things that can't be replaced. The rest of it… The rest of it's just 'worldly goods,' like the Bible says. You put those things right out of your head, Blythe Mitchell, and come inside this house."

She had already started limping up the steps when Cade's hand fastened under her elbow, offering support.

Like touching his hat, it was the kind of thing that came naturally to him. Part of his upbringing. Still, the gesture touched her emotions exactly as the other had. Almost unconsciously, she turned her head to look at him.

Since he was trailing a step below her, they were eye to eye. His were once more filled with concern. Underlying it, was something that sent a shiver through her lower body.

The sensation his look created was enough to cause her to jerk her gaze away. She focused instead on the open door and her grandmother.

As soon as she was safely inside, she would have time to examine what had just happened. To sort through the combination of emotions that had caused the surge of what was clearly—again—a sexual response to Cade Jackson.

An echo of that schoolgirl crush? Or, more likely, she acknowledged, a growing realization that she was still alive. Still a woman. A young woman with all the normal needs.

"You come on in, too, Cade. Looks like you could use a cup of good, strong coffee. Delores has probably got the pot on the stove by now."

Blythe didn't turn to gauge whether or not he would obey. She didn't dare. Not once she had realized the interior of the house might not be the sanctuary she'd believed it would be.

"Thanks, Miz Ruth. I could use some of Delores's coffee right now, but I don't have time. I've got some things to do concerning the fire."

With Cade's words, Blythe breathed a mental sigh of relief. To hide her reaction, she lowered her head, taking the opportunity to shift Maddie's weight slightly so that her hold was more secure.

"I got foam cups," Ruth said. "You can take it with you. I won't take no for an answer now, you hear?"

Ruth Mitchell was not easily put off. Not when she had her mind made up.

"To go, then," Cade said, giving in far more gracefully to her grandmother's iron will than Blythe had ever managed.

By now they were at the front door. Cade stood back to allow her to enter first and then followed her into the dark hallway. Ruth closed the door behind them before she turned, holding her chenille bathrobe against her thin bosom with one hand.

"I'll take Maddie upstairs and put her down." Blythe needed time to compose herself, and that wouldn't be possible down here. Not with Cade here. "Which bedroom do you want us to use?"

"Why, any of them, child. They're all made up."

They always were. With sheets that smelled of lavender.

Blythe wondered if Delores changed all those every Monday as she had when Blythe was a child and someone had actually slept in those beds. She probably did, she realized, considering that things never changed around here. Right now, that was a comfort.

"Let me carry her for you."

Cade's offer stopped her at the foot of the stairs.

Narrow and steep, their tread was worn with the countless footsteps that had gone up and down them during the past century. Carrying Maddie up them would be hard enough in the best of circumstances. With a sprained ankle—

Before she'd had time to make it, Cade took the decision out of her hands. While she hesitated, he had moved to her side, reaching for the little girl.

She was conscious of his closeness, just as she'd been in his office. Tonight the acrid smell of smoke clung to his uniform instead of the scent of laundry starch.

And that particular memory reminded her of the question she still had no answer for. Despite her lack of knowledge about Cade's marital state, when he took Maddie from her arms, just the accidental brush of his hand against her stomach caused the same reaction she'd experienced earlier. As soon as the transfer had been made, Blythe stepped back, putting a more comfortable distance between them.

Maddie turned her head against Cade's shoulder, looking at her. *Not asleep*, Blythe realized.

And yet not protesting the fact that she was being carried by a stranger. Blythe wasn't sure that was a good sign. Maybe the little girl was just exhausted. Or traumatized.

And who wouldn't be?

"Mama?"

"I'm coming. I'm going to tuck you in, safe and sound."

Please God, no nightmares. There had been enough for one night. For Maddie *and* for her.

"Are we going to live here now?"

"For a while," Blythe said, following Cade up the stairs.

At least until I can figure out where the hell we go from here.

Cade stepped out on the wooden porch, closing the front door behind him. He held the promised cup of coffee in his hand, its heat welcome against the bite of dawn's cold.

Blythe Mitchell.

It wasn't until he'd seen her daughter that he'd fully made the connection to the little girl who had never quite fit in with her relatively rowdy schoolmates. Mostly what he remembered about her was the straight blond hair and downcast eyes. And the same delicate features reflected in her daughter.

He had noticed her watching him a couple of times when they'd been in school, but it had evoked nothing but a passing curiosity. She must have been… What? Five or six years younger than he was. Maybe more, since the county school at that time had served all grades. Young enough in any case that she hadn't made an impression on him.

Which was no longer the case. Her hair had darkened through the years, although there were still streaks of blond. He wasn't knowledgeable enough to know whether they were natural, but he didn't suppose it mattered. They were becoming. As was the style in which she wore it, little different than when they'd been in school. And the makeup she'd worn the afternoon she'd come by the office had been subtle, something else he liked. Of course, she had looked pretty damn good this morning wearing no makeup at all.

If Blythe Mitchell's appearance is all you got to think about right now, you ought to look for a different line of work.

Still, it was hard not to speculate. When Blythe had come home a couple of months ago, there had been plenty of talk. About her husband's death. Her daughter. The fact that she had refused to live in Ruth's house.

Now she'd be forced to. By circumstances that were, at the very least, tragic. And at the worst, dangerous.

As he came down the steps, Cade looked up at the sky. By the time he got back to the scene of the fire, it would be full daylight. If Doug had done what he'd been told, Cade would be able to examine the area where Blythe claimed to have seen someone watching her house.

He wasn't sure that was the case, but he *was* sure she believed it. That fear had been in her eyes, underlying both the exhaustion and her own need to deny its reality.

Her house had burned down to the ground. She'd had to take her daughter out over the roof. And she thought someone had been standing at the edge of the trees watching everything unfold. Enough to generate the look he'd seen in her eyes.

A look he had wanted to erase. An emotion that had far less to do with duty than it ought to.

He opened the door to the cruiser and climbed in, setting the coffee down in the center console's cup holder. Before he did anything else, he sat in the quietness of the car a moment, trying to put his impressions of tonight's events into context.

What he saw instead were earnest blue eyes lifted to his. *There was someone here. Standing at the edge of the woods.*

If there had been, there would be some sign. Some evidence to back up her story.

And if there wasn't…?

Then the stress of what she'd been through would be enough to explain away what she thought she'd seen. Still…

He believed her, he realized. As unlikely as it seemed, he believed that someone had been lurking on the edge of the property.

Watching the fire? Given the circumstances, that was the only thing that made sense.

Ignoring the coffee, he picked up the radio and punched the call button. When Logan Medders answered, Cade didn't have to think twice about the instructions he gave.

"Put in a call to the state fire marshal's office. Tell them we've got a house fire down here I'd like them to take a look at. Ask them how long it will be before they can get an investigator out here."

"You think the Wright place was arson?" Logan sounded surprised.

"I believe it's possible. Verifying whether I'm right or not is their job. And tell them we need someone out here sooner rather than later."

"They ain't gonna like that," Logan said with a laugh.

"Yeah? Well, I'm not *real* fond of somebody trying to burn down a house in this county with a family inside. I guess me and the investigator will both be in the same frame of mind when he gets here."

"You coming in?"

"I'm going back to the scene. I'll be there if you need me."

Without giving Logan time to respond, he flicked the switch and put the radio back into its stand. Then he touched the key that was still in the ignition.

Instead of starting the car, he again sat in the relative darkness of its interior, thinking about the woman he'd just brought home. He'd always been a sucker for a hard luck story. Based on town gossip, Blythe Wyndham would already have qualified. For something like this to have happened to her in Crenshaw...

Meant that she'd probably pack up and head back up North. Something that might be better for his peace of mind, he admitted.

With that acknowledgment, Cade wrapped his fingers around the key, turning it with more force than was necessary. The engine roared to life.

Before he put the car into Drive, he glanced back at the front door of the Mitchell house. In that upstairs bedroom he'd carried her little girl to, Blythe would be putting her daughter to bed. Singing to her, maybe. Reassuring her, just as Ruth had reassured Blythe, that everything was going to be all right.

And as long as she was living in Davis County, making sure neither of them was wrong was up to him.

8

Blythe stopped in the kitchen doorway before she entered the room. Delores and her grandmother were seated at the table, hands clasped and heads bowed. An open Bible lay between them.

She wasn't sure whether this was their normal morning devotion or if their prayer had been prompted by the events of last night. Probably the former, considering the role religion played in their lives.

She had promptly broken her own vow not to offer any more prayers to the Almighty while she'd been trying to get Maddie out of the burning house. The old saw about there being no atheists in foxholes was obviously true.

"Amen," her grandmother said, raising her head to meet Delores's eyes. She squeezed the frail black hands clasped within her own before she released them.

The housekeeper glanced up, finding Blythe in the doorway. "You get that angel to sleep, Miz Blythe?"

"Finally. And I could really use that cup of coffee you were offering earlier. If there's any left."

She was relieved to find Cade wasn't still here. Although she was sure he intended to follow through immediately on the things they'd talked about, she was also sure the coffee's warmth and anticipated kick would have been as tempting to him as it now was to her.

"Plenty," Delores said, pushing her chair back. "And plenty more where that came from."

"I'll get it," Blythe said quickly, stepping through the door and walking toward the stove.

"Not in my kitchen, you won't, missy. You sit down by your grandmamma. I remember just how you like it. White and sweet."

Although Blythe had given up milk and sugar years ago, the remembrance of her first sip of creamy, sweetened coffee, which had taken place here at this very table, was suddenly in her head. It was those kinds of memories that, like the people who lived here, made this house a sanctuary. One she needed more than she ever had before.

"Thank you." Changing course, she pulled out a chair from the side of the table and sat down. As she did, her grandmother's fingers wrapped around hers.

"It's gonna be all right, baby. Don't you worry about a thing. There's plenty of room here for as long as y'all need to stay."

Blythe leaned over and pressed a kiss against Ruth's cheek. Her grandmother's skin smelled faintly of the lavender that scented the sheets she'd tucked around Maddie. "Thank you."

"This is what families are for. Times like these.

If your mama was here, she'd tell you the same thing."

Blythe's mother had died three years ago from a rare and virulent pneumonia. She'd been gone almost before anyone had realized she was ill.

Blythe's father had been killed in a hunting accident when she was only a toddler. That was why she and her mother had moved in with Ruth. That and her mother's depression, brought on by her father's untimely death. It was an illness she had never completely shaken.

What families are for…

Were she and Maddie about to repeat that pattern? That had been one of the reasons Blythe had been so adamant about their having their own house. Now…

The plan she'd so carefully constructed before she'd moved back was unraveling. And it seemed there was nothing she could do to prevent that from happening.

Of course, maybe the fire at the rental house had been a blessing in disguise, given what had been going on out there. And with what she'd learned from Cade this morning…

"Did you know the house Maddie and I were living in had once belonged to Sarah Comstock's grandmother?"

"Miz Eula Wright," Delores said, setting a cup down in front of her.

Despite the generous portion of cream the old woman had added, the heady scent of the chicory-flavored coffee made Blythe's mouth water. Ignoring her grandmother's gaze, she lifted the cup, taking a sip.

"Her girl's the one that married that Comstock man," Delores added as she slipped into her place across from Ruth.

"Abel," her grandmother supplied. "Some folks say he's the one that done it. That he killed his own baby."

"His wife said he didn't leave the house that night," Blythe said, remembering the articles she'd read in the *Herald.* "Would you lie for a man who was capable of doing that to your daughter?"

"Maybe. If I was scared he'd do the same to me," Delores said.

"He beat her," Ruth verified. "I know that for a fact. Saw the bruises myself."

She was talking about Sarah's mother, Blythe realized. "You knew her?"

It was a stupid question. In Crenshaw, everyone knew everyone else. Still, given the difference in their ages…

"Little old washed-out mouse of a woman," her grandmother went on. "Wouldn't say boo to a snake. Sure wouldn't have said it to Abel."

"I can't believe any mother would be capable of that." Blythe took another draw of her coffee, feeling the caffeine begin to work its magic. "Of lying to protect a man who could do that to her child."

"I expect that's 'cause you ain't never *been* beaten."

Delores was right. It was easy to make that kind of judgment when you didn't know the situation. Or the pain.

"Is she still alive?"

"Miz Comstock? Lord, she died… What, Miz

Ruth? Half a dozen years ago, I reckon. Flu or somethin'. Worked her to death more likely. Ain't that right, Miz Ruth?"

"I don't keep up with the likes of the Comstocks, Delores."

In spite of her innate kindness, an occasional touch of the arrogance bred long ago among the plantation houses of St. Francisville came out of her grandmother's mouth. Of course, Ruth Mitchell *didn't* associate with people like the Comstocks. Either old woman would have felt justified in using the phrase *poor, white trash* to describe them. It was probably apt.

"*He* is, though," Delores went on, ignoring her mistress's correction. "Last time I heard."

"Sarah's father?"

"Still out in that same little old shacklety house."

The Comstock place was separated from "downtown" Crenshaw by a deep woods and the stream that bisected Smoke Hollow. One of the theories Blythe had read was that Sarah's killer had passed by the house on his way back to town. Perhaps he'd looked into the uncurtained windows, it had been speculated, and had seen the two little girls sleeping together. No one had been able to figure out how he'd gotten in and grabbed Sarah, however, without waking her sister.

"Did you know Sarah's grandmother?"

"Eula Wright." It was Ruth who answered this question. "A fine Christian woman. Younger than me, but I knew her."

"Was she close to Sarah?"

Ruth shook her head. "Doubt it. Knowing her daddy. Eula didn't want her daughter to marry him, of course, but she'd got in a family way. Didn't have no choice. Not back then. Abel kept Audra away from her family as much as he could. I don't know about the children. I expect they would have needed a grandmother's love. Poor as church mice. The whole bunch of the Comstocks. Always was."

"But there must be *some* connection to that house."

As soon as the words were out of her mouth, she knew she'd given too much away. No matter their age, these two were too sharp not to pick up on the implications of that.

"Why would you say that, Miz Blythe?"

Because something—or someone—tapped on its windows late at night, demanding admittance. And because while we lived there, my daughter dreamed about things that made her scream in terror.

"I guess because I was so drawn to that little girl."

"Any woman would be. Any mother, leastways," Ruth said.

"I think it's more than that."

"You got you a little girl, Miz Blythe. You gotta feel for that other baby. And for her mama."

"Is that why you're planning to write a book about her murder?" her grandmother asked.

"*What?*"

"Ada said you were planning to write about Sarah's murder."

"*Ada* told you that? When?"

A more important question, Blythe realized belatedly, was *where.* If Ada had been telling that story all over town—

"Women's Aid Society, I think. 'Course, my memory ain't as good as it used to be."

"I believe it was," Delores said. "I'd cooked a roast for the night you came home and told me. That was on Tuesday."

"And she said that in front of all those people?"

"Emma Spencer said you was going through all the official files on the murder. Said Cade had given you permission."

Blythe didn't believe Cade had shared that information, but he hadn't been the only person in the office that day. "Is Emma Spencer's son named Jerrod, by any chance?"

"That's him. He works at the sheriff's department. I don't think he's a deputy, but he's in training or something."

There had to be some link between these seemingly unrelated events. Between Sarah's murder and their living in her grandmother's house. Between the unexplained noises they'd heard there and Maddie's night terrors. *Between Ada's gossip...*

And the fire? My God, was it possible that—

"There was somebody out there tonight," Blythe said softly.

She needed to talk to someone about what she was thinking. Whatever she said would sound insane. Of all the people in the world, these two would be the least likely to believe she was.

"Some*body?*" her grandmother repeated sharply.

"Standing out at the edge of the woods. When I dropped Maddie off the roof, I sent her there to get her away from the fire. When I looked out there, I saw him."

She had done it again. Called the figure she'd seen a "him." Despite what she'd told Cade, there must be some subconscious justification for that. Size. Shape. Something.

"At the back of the property?" Delores asked.

Blythe nodded, turning to look at her.

"You got any idea who it was?"

"It was just…a figure. A shape. But…if Ada's been telling people I'm going to write a book about the Comstock murder or suggesting that I'm trying to investigate it—"

She should have remembered how things worked here. Anything out of the ordinary in this sleepy little community occasioned excitement. And gossip.

"Isn't that what you told her?" her grandmother asked.

"*No.* Of *course* not. I mentioned the previous articles I'd written. And that I'd like to do others."

Ada was the one who had brought up Sarah's murder. She was the one who had said how interested in cold cases people were and how much money Blythe could make. From there it had probably taken only a small leap of the imagination for Ada to decide that Blythe *was* going to write about it. And then she'd simply added fuel to the fire by her visit to the sheriff.

"You *had* to have mentioned that murder, Blythe Mitchell. I've known Ada Pringle all her life. She has characteristics I can't admire, bless her heart, but she's not a liar."

"*She* mentioned it. *She* took those volumes of the *Herald* off the shelf and found the articles about Sarah. I admit I read them, but..." Blythe shook her head at how out of control this had gotten. "How that ever came to *this*..."

"Are you suggesting that what Ada's been saying has a connection to what happened tonight? To the *fire?* That's... Lord, I don't know *what* it is. Pure craziness, honey. This isn't New York or Boston or Atlanta. Things like that don't happen here."

"Sarah Comstock's *murder* happened here. And her murderer has never been caught. If he were told I intend to write a book about the case—"

"He must have thought you were gonna solve it and send him to jail? Is that it?" Her grandmother seldom resorted to sarcasm, but that comment had been heavy with it.

Given the constraints placed on her generation, the idea of a woman pursuing a murderer probably *was* ridiculous. In all honesty, it had never crossed Blythe's mind. The murderer—thanks to town gossip—would have had no way of knowing that.

"If he thought my writing about it would attract attention to the case, he might. Cade Jackson strikes me as someone who would be interested in any unsolved case in his jurisdiction."

That was fact, not supposition. Cade himself had told her he'd read the files of all the unsolved cases.

"And just how were *you* gonna find any new information on that little girl's murder? Thumbing through some old issues of the *Herald*? Or reading stuff in a twenty-five-year-old file the best sheriff this county ever had couldn't use to catch Sarah's killer?"

Blythe took a breath, acknowledging how far afield from the reality of what she'd set out to do this had come. "I wasn't trying to discover new information. I was simply following Ada's suggestion and reading about a crime I barely remembered." There was no point in mentioning her fascination with what she had read that day.

"Then why in the world would you think Ada running her mouth would incite somebody to burn down your house?"

"'Cause Miz Ada let on there was more to it than that, didn't she?" Delores's quiet question made Ruth's head swing toward her. "It ain't important what Miz Blythe *meant* to do. What's important is what somebody *thought* she was doing."

There was a moment of silence, and then Ruth said again, "That's pure craziness."

"So is somebody standing in the woods watching my house burn. Even Cade said that didn't make sense. Not around here."

"Cade Jackson's opinion notwithstanding," her

grandmother said, "we got plenty of folks around here with that much meanness in 'em."

"Miz Ruth, do you mean to say that you think there's somebody in this town wicked enough to set a house on fire with a woman and a baby inside and then stand there an' watch it burn?" Delores demanded.

With the time of night at which the fire occurred and the distance of the house from the volunteer fire department's nearest station, there could have been only one intent for such an action.

"We already know that there's someone in this town wicked enough to brutalize and kill a child," Blythe reminded them softly. "And as far as anyone knows, that person is still living right here among us."

9

Blythe had been surprised to learn from her grandmother that Dr. Etheridge was still practicing. He'd seemed old to her when she was a child. Of course, almost everyone had back then.

At least he hadn't moved his office, she thought as she pulled into the tree-shaded drive. Dwight Etheridge had always seen patients in the same office where his father and his grandfather had seen theirs—inside the family home.

She got out of the car and slammed the door, the sound echoing along the quiet residential street. An elderly couple, bundled up against the cold, sat in the porch swing of the house across the street. Although she couldn't come up with the name that went with their almost-recognizable faces, she lifted her hand to wave at them. Both waved back.

"Glad you're home," the woman called.

"Thank you." Blythe almost added, as she had so many times in the last two months, that she was glad to be back. After last night, she was no longer sure that was the case.

Keeping her hand on the car for support, she limped up the drive. Her ankle seemed to have stiffened again, but that was hardly unusual for any injury, even a minor one.

Just don't let it be broken. Please don't let it be broken.

For some reason, the dread of wearing a cast while dealing with salvaging things from the house, talking to her landlord's insurance agent, and with the responsibility of replacing the items of daily living she and Maddie would have to have seemed overwhelming. Rationally, she knew her anxiety was not so much about the injury, but the result of an accumulation of stresses from the last few days.

Still, she felt that if Doc told her the ankle was broken, it would be the last straw. She would find a hole to crawl into and pull it in over her head.

She rang the bell next to the door on what had always been the "professional" side of the huge Victorian and waited. After more than a minute, she rang it again.

"You got to go to the other door, dear."

Blythe turned to find the female half of the couple across the street at the end of the Etheridge driveway. "I'm sorry?"

"Dwight don't keep office hours. You have to call ahead. Or ring the other bell. The one on the house side."

"My grandmother told me he was still practicing."

Blythe limped to the edge of the porch to lessen the need to shout.

"He is. He'll see you. Just ring the other bell."

"Thank you."

"You're welcome, dear. Give Ruth my best now, you hear."

Blythe nodded and waved again. The woman turned, hurrying across the street to rejoin her husband. When she had, both of them resumed watching Blythe's every move.

So much for HIPAA, she thought as she turned and limped over to the other door. She rang its bell, listening to the melodic chime echo inside. She hadn't had time to turn to politely contemplate the street before the door was opened. She stepped back to allow the screen to be pushed outward by the man who had tended every bump and bruise and fever she'd experienced throughout her childhood and adolescence.

"Blythe? Blythe Mitchell? As I live and breathe. Heard you were home, but I never expected you to come visiting."

"Hello, Dr. Etheridge. I'm home."

"Well, don't stand out there in the cold, girl. We'll both catch our deaths."

As he stepped aside to let her pass, he, too, waved to the couple across the street. Once Blythe was inside, he closed the door, shutting off what little light there'd been in the foyer.

"Can't say the cold hurts them none," the old man said, turning to walk toward the formal room on the left of the hallway. "Those old bats are determined to live forever just so's they don't miss nobody coming or going on the street."

"They told me you still see patients."

He turned at that, looking her up and down. "They were right, but you don't look sick to me. You look just fine, if you'll pardon an old man's admiration."

"I sprained my ankle. At least I think it's a sprain. I don't believe anything's broken."

"You got a broken bone, Blythe, you need to go to County."

There was only one hospital in the area, which served all of Davis County and much of the populace of the surrounding counties. There had been quite a controversy when it had been built in the nearby community of Dawsonville, rather than here in the county seat.

"It's not broken," Blythe said. "I know it isn't. But I promised the paramedic I'd have it checked out."

"Paramedic?"

"It was an accident."

"You didn't have a wreck, did you?"

"Not that kind of accident"

The shrewd brown eyes held on hers for several seconds. When she didn't elaborate, the old man nodded. "Let's go see what we got."

He headed toward the other side of the house, an area Blythe had visited dozens of times during her childhood. When he opened the door to the examination room, everything was exactly the same as it had been then. Even the prints on the wall were unchanged.

"You know the drill. Get up on the table so I can look at it." The old man walked over to the sink to scrub his hands.

Blythe pulled out the metal step, settling on the end of the paper-covered examination table. Her eyes drifted around the room, taking in the objects she'd always used to distract herself from whatever unpleasant procedure she was here for.

"Let's see what we got," Doc said again. He bent, picking up her foot to remove her shoe and sock.

The ankle he revealed was swollen and slightly discolored on one side, but Blythe still couldn't believe it was broken. Surely she would be unable to walk on it if it were.

"What kind of accident?"

The doctor didn't look at her this time. His hands, their fingers gnarled by arthritis, gently manipulated her foot, taking the joint through its full range of motion. When he turned it to the right, she sucked in a breath at the jolt of pain.

His eyes lifted, examining her face. "You fall?"

"Actually… I jumped off the roof."

"Bored?" Although he was again working the joint, the teasing note was clear.

She laughed. "Not at the time. My house was on fire."

His eyes came up again, quickly this time. "You don't say? Leave the stove on?"

"No."

"Your girl?"

"She's four. She's precocious, but she doesn't cook."

"She okay?"

"She's fine," Blythe said, and then wondered if that were the truth. "She's with my grandmother."

"How bad?"

"I'm sorry?"

"The fire. How bad?"

"I haven't been out there this morning. I was on my way, but I'd promised the paramedic to have this checked." She kept saying that. As if it had been some kind of sacred vow. "I'm going over as soon as I'm done here."

"Fire trucks get out there pretty fast though?"

"Not fast enough," she admitted softly.

"I figured you wouldn't be jumping if they had."

"I think everything's gone." The words were easier to say than they had been last night.

"Need X-rays to be sure about this. I can call and tell 'em over at County that you're coming."

"How much is that going to cost?"

There was a small silence, as the dark eyes once more focused on her face. "E.R. charges. X-rays. Probably a couple hundred. Could be more, depending on what they have to do."

"Like putting it in a cast?"

"Calling in a specialist. Lots of variables."

None of them good. Or cheap.

"I don't have insurance, Doc. And frankly…"

"I expect your grandmother would be good for it," Etheridge said with a smile.

"We're going to have to move in with her. At least

until I decide what to do next. Maddie and I will need to replace some necessities that burned. If there's anything *you* could do..."

She let the sentence trail, wondering belatedly what she thought he could do. He didn't have the equipment to take the X-rays he'd said she needed. He probably thought she was asking for a loan or something. Or to get the hospital to discount the bill, neither of which had been her intent.

"I mean if it's possible that it's *not* broken—" she started to clarify.

"I know what you mean. You think after all the times you come in here I don't know you well enough to read between the lines? You got no insurance and money's tight. And you don't want to burden your grandmother any more than you have to. You willing to trust an old country doctor's gut?"

"About my ankle?"

"What else we talking about, girl?"

My lack of resources. And my pride.

"You know I trust you," she said aloud. "I always have."

"Yeah, well, I thought maybe you'd gone big city on me."

"No."

"Then my gut says this ain't broken. Could be some kind of hairline fracture, but even if it is, it'll heal. I can wrap it for you. Give it some support. You come back next week and let me look at it. How does that sound?"

"Sounds like a plan to me." She wasn't sure where those corny words had come from. Maybe from her sudden relief-generated euphoria. Despite everything else that had happened, Doc's agreement not to send her to the hospital felt like a victory of sorts. There hadn't been many of those lately.

"It'll be better to stay off it, even taped, but I expect you ain't gonna do that."

"I don't think I can. Not with everything I need to take care of."

"You staying?"

"I'm sorry?" She felt like an idiot. Almost every question he'd asked, she had stammered and stuttered around it.

"*Here*. In Crenshaw."

He meant for good, she realized. A question she hadn't yet answered for herself.

It would take time to see to things. And money to replace what they'd lost. She couldn't replace everything, but both she and Maddie would need more clothing than the outfits and jackets she had bought for each of them this morning. Shoes. Toiletries. The stuff of daily life.

"For a while. I expect there'll be a lot of things I'll have to tend to about the fire. Forms. Insurance. Sheriff Jackson said he was going to call the state fire marshal to check it out."

"*Fire* marshal. Cade think this was arson?"

"I'm not sure. Maybe he just wants to be safe."

"I expect he does. *You* think it was arson?"

"I can't imagine why anyone would do something like that," she said carefully.

"Not here," Doc said. "Not in Crenshaw. 'Course, I guess like everywhere else we got our share of dunces. Still, it would take someone downright evil to endanger a child, don't you think? Though our history proves we got some of those here, too, doesn't it? Heard you were interested in that."

"You've been talking to Ada Pringle."

"You want something spread around, you tell Ada. Is that what you did?"

"Hardly. I went to look up information on my house."

"On your *house*? You have a reason for that?"

"Just…some things that didn't feel right about it."

His palm again around her heel, the old man lowered her foot. "Don't sound like you're talking about bad plumbing?"

"Bad dreams. Nightmares actually. Not me," she added quickly, seeing the question in his eyes. "My daughter. Maddie. She started having night terrors. And *I* heard things. Things I couldn't explain. I just thought that there might be some explanation for them."

"An explanation in the history of the house?"

"Maybe it was a stupid idea—"

"I didn't say that. If there's one thing I've learned in this business, it's that not everything can be explained by science. And I consider myself a man of science. I've also learned never to discount a mother's instinct. Not where her child's concerned."

"You've lived here a long time," she began, wondering if Doc would be someone she could confide in to an even greater extent than she already had. He seemed open to hearing her out.

Besides, like her grandmother, the old man knew everyone in this town. And most of their secrets.

"All my life."

"Did you know Eula Wright?"

"Most of *her* life. And I don't know anything about her that would explain your daughter's bad dreams or any noises you heard out there. What kind of noises, by the way?"

She hesitated, but in the end she told him because she desperately needed to tell someone. "Tapping sounds. On one of the windows, but… There wasn't anything there to cause it."

The brown eyes again considered her face. After a moment, Doc's mouth pursed, but he didn't ask any more questions. "Eula Wright died peacefully at Snow's Nursing Home. I was there at the time. Her husband passed away years before of a heart attack. They'd taken him to UAB for some kind of treatment they'd hoped would make a difference. There was nothing violent or unfinished about either of those deaths. And neither occurred in that house."

"I didn't mean to imply—"

"So neither of them should be haunting you. Or it. *If* that's what you're suggesting."

"I honestly don't know what I'm suggesting. Just

put this entire conversation down to stress," she said, smiling at him.

"Of course, you already know that not everyone Eula loved died so peacefully."

The unspoken name lay between them for a few seconds like a closed door. One she wasn't sure she wanted to open.

"Sarah Comstock," she said finally.

"Prettiest, sweetest little girl I ever saw. Kind of shy, but she just blossomed if you showed her any kind of attention. I suspect she didn't get much. Nobody out there had time to see to her or any of them young'uns."

"You treated her?"

"What treatment any of 'em ever got. Her mama brought her in a few times. Once with a broken arm, I remember. I made sure their inoculations were up to date. Did what I could, but… I guess nobody did do enough."

"The broken arm. Could it have been…?"

"Abuse? I wondered, of course, but then kids fall and break bones. It wasn't the kind of injury I could have said definitively was caused by anything other than that. She still had that same shy little smile. Trying so hard not to let on she was hurting. So damned anxious to please."

The old man's voice had softened. Blythe knew the memories were powerful, and that this wasn't the first time he'd remembered that day.

"I was county coroner when she died. Did you know that?"

She hadn't. She wasn't sure she would have

broached this subject if she had. Doc knew more about Sarah's murder than Blythe wanted to hear. Maybe more than she could bear.

"That office was elected. Just like it is now," Etheridge went on. "That was the only qualification. Some counties use morticians. In some it's preachers or the occasional furniture salesman. I ran for that office because my daddy had done it before me and not 'cause I wanted to. We figured it was better for a medical doctor to serve in the position. That was the only murder I had during the ten years or so I served."

"Doc—"

"There are things nobody should have to see and know. Not even a doctor. Not even a 'man of science.' You know what everybody around here believed about the murder, don't you?"

"That her father had done it."

The old man laughed, the sound hard. Unamused. "Yeah, some thought that. I never subscribed to the theory myself. I don't believe a man could do those things to his own flesh and blood. That ain't what I'm talking about."

"Then… I *don't* know. I don't remember any other suspects mentioned in the *Herald*—"

"This wasn't the kind of thing anybody's gonna put in the newspaper. Still, there was plenty of talk. I heard it. I know Hoyt heard it, too."

Despite the fact that she had started this, Blythe didn't want to know what he was talking about. She already knew more than would let her sleep at night.

"'Course everybody was thinking that kind of thing back then. It was all over the TV. In the papers. They put folks in jail on account of rumors like the ones that were running rampant around here. Whole day cares supposedly filled with Satan worshippers. They'd bring in psychologists to talk to the kids. Ask 'em questions that would implant memories so that they'd really come to believe those awful things had been done to them."

None of this had been in the materials she'd read. It, too, was the kind of thing that might have been whispered about out of the hearing of children. Even if it had been, however, surely Doc Etheridge couldn't believe there was anything to it.

"The only difference was, in this case those things *had* been done to that baby."

The paper had mentioned mutilations, but they hadn't been more specific than that. She wasn't sure if the old man was suggesting Sarah had been the victim of some kind of satanic ritual or that the murder had been done in such a way as to suggest that.

"Are you saying that you think there was some kind of...devil worship involved?"

"I'm saying some in this town thought so. And none of that made-up garbage I read about in those other cases was worse than what that little girl had suffered. That's another reason I don't believe Abel had anything to do it."

"The paper quoted Hoyt as saying that the violence of her injuries seemed to indicate it was personal."

The sheriff's statement appeared to contradict what Etheridge was suggesting. But then both came to this from their own very different areas of expertise. "He said that random victims of violence are usually killed for gain—money or goods. And that the killing is as fast and as efficient as the killer can manage."

"I'll go along with Hoyt on part of that. 'Cause I sure as hell don't believe Sarah was chosen at random. I don't think someone passing by the Comstock place just looked in and saw two little girls sleeping in the moonlight and decided to drag one of them out and butcher her. And I damn *well* know that whoever killed Sarah had no interest in being fast. But as far as I could tell—and since I'm the one who did that autopsy, I don't think I'm wrong—Sarah Comstock's murderer *was* certainly efficient. Too *goddamned* efficient, if you ask me."

10

"Doesn't tell us much, does it?"

His deputy was right, Cade thought, his eyes examining the ground under the trees at the back of the property where the Wyndhams had been living. He had hoped for tracks. At least one clear impression of a footprint. Something that could be measured and analyzed. Some kind of proof that the story Blythe had told him wasn't a figment of an overactive imagination.

"You sure none of the firemen were out here?"

"Not unless it was before we arrived," Doug Stuart said. "And I can't imagine why any of them would have ventured back this far. Maybe to take a leak or something, but..." The deputy shrugged. "There's just not much to go on."

A layer of pine straw and rotting leaves covered the ground under the trees. In a few places the debris looked as if it had been disturbed, but it would be hard to argue that those constituted proof someone had been walking around out here last night. Even at the edge of the woods there was exposed loam, which would have taken prints.

One hand on the ground for balance, Cade swiveled, looking back toward what he'd grown up calling the Wright house. Wisps of smoke rising from the pile of rubble it had been reduced to blended with the morning mist.

He had expected Blythe to be back out here as soon as it was light. It was almost impossible for people who were victims of a fire *not* to come and survey the damage or try to find any of their personal mementos that hadn't been destroyed.

Given the speed with which the wooden structure had been consumed, he doubted there would be much left. And no news that he could give her concerning the figure she claimed to have seen out here in the woods. That would be another blow added to those she'd already suffered.

"Why don't you take some casts?"

"Of *what?*"

Doug's surprise was understandable. Under any other circumstances Cade would probably have let this go. If this *was* a crime scene, it wasn't going to be a fruitful one.

"How about the areas that appear to be disturbed."

"You think somebody was covering up their tracks?"

"Maybe."

"Out here in the dark." Doug's tone was skeptical.

"It's possible," Cade said evenly. "By the time I arrived, the fire was lighting things up pretty good."

"You see anybody out here?"

"No, but that doesn't mean there *wasn't* someone. Ms. Wyndham is convinced she saw a man standing among these trees."

"A man who didn't leave footprints."

"The leaves and pine straw would prevent that. The areas that aren't entirely covered are the ones that appear to have been disturbed. Doesn't that make you wonder?"

"Birds digging for worms. Squirrels rooting for acorns. Or the neighbor's cat using it for a litter box. Just 'cause there's some dirt turned over, that don't mean somebody's been out here hiding their trail."

"Just do the casts. See what we get."

Cade got to his feet, deliberately not looking at his deputy. He knew Doug thought he was being asked to do a job that wasn't going to be productive. He might be right.

Since there was nothing else going on in Crenshaw this early in the morning, Cade felt he could afford to waste a deputy, who was already on the clock, and a little plaster of Paris to verify—or disprove—Blythe's story. What he didn't understand was why he cared so much that it was the former.

"You're the boss." Still Doug didn't move, maybe hoping that Cade would rescind the order. "Can't say that I blame you either. She's a looker."

"What?"

"The Wyndham woman. Got that kind of city polish about her. You can spot it a mile away."

She did, but that was something Cade hadn't

wanted to think about. Jean had had that same unmistakable air of sophistication.

"She grew up here." Cade glanced over at the younger man.

The deputy was pretending to look at the smoldering ruin. "Yeah, well, she must have spent a few years somewhere else. You can always tell."

Apparently Cade wasn't the only one aware of the aura that surrounded Blythe. Maybe it was the way she dressed. Or the way she carried herself. Not as if she were better than anyone else, but slightly aloof. Untouchable.

The word echoed in his head before he dismissed it as a thought that was inappropriate in their situation.

"Check under the windows, too," Cade added, his eyes following the deputy's back to the house. "Around the doors. Just stay out of the house itself."

"The firemen will have left prints all over those areas."

"Cast whatever you find. We can sort them out later."

"Could take a while."

"You got until whoever they send out from the fire marshal's office shows up."

"They're gonna get somebody out here *today?*"

That was what Cade had been promised. Of course, knowing how things worked in Montgomery, he wasn't going to hold his breath waiting for that to happen.

"That's what they say."

"We got company," Doug warned.

Cade's gaze tracked to the end of the driveway. He

watched as Ruth Mitchell's big old Oldsmobile turned in, pulling up even with what would have been the house's front porch.

Blythe climbed out of the car, her eyes locked on the remains of the structure. She didn't seem to be aware they were back here, despite the two cruisers parked beside the detached garage where her car had been sheltered from the fire.

Cade realized that Doug was looking at him. He turned, raising his brows at his deputy, who shook his head.

"Nothing. I'll go get the plaster and get started. You better tell her not to walk around."

"Can you get out?"

"Plenty of room to make a U-turn back here. Unless you want me to cast for tire marks, too."

Despite the sarcasm, the comment triggered something he should have thought of earlier. Cade turned, looking back through the trees.

"Not here," he said. "Look for tread marks on the other side of these woods. All along Salter Road."

"You think whoever was out here came through the woods?" There was a note of interest in the deputy's voice.

"I think it's possible. Actually, why don't you do that first. Stop there on your way back from the department."

It was probably their best shot. Even if Doug found a place where someone had pulled off the road, it wouldn't necessarily mean that the driver of that car had been the person Blythe claimed to have seen.

That would have been the easiest access to the house, other than the road that led directly to it. And the fact that the guy had been waiting back here while he'd been watching the house burn argued that might have been his planned escape route.

Doug nodded, apparently following the logic that had led Cade to that conclusion. At least he wasn't arguing about what he'd been asked to do.

"And don't hurry over it," Cade added.

If someone had parked on the road that paralleled the back of these woods, then there were probably a dozen places where he could pull off and hide his car from passing traffic. Finding that location would be more important than doing casts of what would almost certainly turn out to be the prints of the volunteer fire department.

"Want me to disappear for a while, huh?" Doug's smirk made it clear what he was thinking.

For some reason the implication that Cade wanted to be alone with Blythe sent a flood of anger through his body, so strong it was almost a physical reaction.

"What I *want* is for you to do the job the citizens of this county are paying you for. You got that?"

The grin was quickly wiped off the deputy's face. It wasn't often that Doug felt the brunt of Cade's displeasure. It wasn't often he deserved it. At the look in the kid's eyes, Cade knew he'd gotten his point across.

"Okay if I get Phillip to help me? That's a long stretch of woods."

"As long as he's got nothing else going on."

"Thanks, Cade. If it's back there, we'll find it."

"I know you will." By now he was ashamed of his overreaction. And calm enough to want to analyze why Doug's suggestion that he was interested in Blythe would set him off.

Because there's more truth in it than you want to admit?

"I think she's spotted us. I'll go on and get started. You can give her the bad news."

It took a fraction of a second too long for Cade to realize that his deputy meant the information about the lack of footprints. *That* would be bad news, he knew. Blythe had been convinced someone was standing here watching her house burn.

And waiting while her daughter ran toward him.

"Let me know if you find anything," he called after the departing deputy, who was making his way toward his patrol car.

"You'll be the *first* to know."

Deliberately ignoring Blythe's approach, Cade watched as Doug folded his lanky frame into the driver's seat. Maybe it was the deputy's suggestion that he was attracted to her. More likely it was the reality of that—something he had just been forced to acknowledge. For whatever reason, Cade found he wasn't prepared to deal with the reality of *her* right now.

"Sheriff Jackson?"

There weren't many people in Crenshaw who called Cade by his title. Or by his last name, for that matter. When you'd grown up in a town this size, no matter what you achieved in life or how far you traveled before you came home, you were always going to be known by your first name.

"Ms. Wyndham," he said, touching the brim of his hat.

She continued to walk toward him, but her eyes had followed the gesture before they came back to his. Her cheeks were reddened by the cold, giving her skin a flush of color it hadn't had last night. He would bet that, as fair as she was, any change in temperature or the slightest exertion would cause that same heightened color.

"Did you find his prints back there?" Her gaze swept the line of trees behind him. When he didn't answer, it focused again on his face. "You didn't, did you?"

Underlying her obvious disappointment was something Cade couldn't quite read. Anticipation that he hadn't believed her?

"The ground's covered with dead leaves and pine straw. We're going to take casts of a few areas, just to see what turns up, but as of right now—"

"You haven't found anything."

"Nothing conclusive. You hear anybody outside last night?"

"Before the fire?" She shook her head, her eyes again examining the trees. "We were both asleep. Probably more soundly than I would have been otherwise."

"Ma'am?"

She looked at him, her blue eyes seeming to evaluate whether or not she could trust him. Apparently he passed whatever standard she'd applied.

"Maddie hasn't slept well since we've been here. At first I thought it was just the move. The unfamiliarity of the house. But the longer we lived here, the worse they got."

"They?"

There was a moment's hesitation before she answered. "Night terrors. Those are very severe nightmares, by the way," she explained when he didn't respond. "And they look exactly like what the name implies."

An instinct developed by the ten years he'd spent in this job kicked in. There was something else going on here, something she wasn't telling him. He could feel it in his gut.

Her little girl looked too young and innocent to have set this fire, but troubled kids could be amazingly precocious. And damn devious. Devious enough that not even their parents suspected what was going on. Not until it was too late.

"She's had a pretty tough year," he said aloud.

Blythe nodded. "I told myself that. The psychologist I took her to said the same thing. And maybe if those were all—"

She stopped, looking like a suspect who'd realized she'd said too much. When that happened, nobody could take back the words that had let the cat out of the bag. Neither could she.

"There's something else? Something besides the nightmares?"

She shook her head. Her lips had tightened, as if she were determined not to let herself say anything more.

That was one of those involuntary physiological reactions that were almost impossible to control, which meant there was definitely something else. And if it had anything to do with what had happened here last night, letting her get away with guarding a secret was a luxury he couldn't afford.

"Ms. Wyndham, it's going to be impossible for me to get to the bottom of this if you keep things from me."

The color he'd noticed along her cheekbones deepened. Her mouth flattened even more before she opened it again. "I've heard noises."

Whatever he'd expected, it wasn't this. And he wasn't sure what to do with it. "What kind of noises? Somebody prowling around outside? Trying to break in?"

"*If* they're trying to break in—" she began, and then once more stopped herself.

"Ma'am?"

"Please stop calling me that. My name is Blythe."

He couldn't tell whether she was annoyed because she no longer considered herself to be part of the regional tradition that demanded he use that form of address. Or annoyed because she thought he ought to remember her and believed he didn't. Whichever it was, how he referred to her wasn't the issue on the table right now, so he ignored her objection.

"If they're trying to get in?" he repeated.

She shook her head, her eyes focusing again on the woods behind him. When she turned to look at him, her chin went up fractionally, as if she were daring him not to believe her.

"There's a tapping. On an upstairs window in Maddie's room."

Again, not what he'd been expecting. "A window on the second floor?"

"Actually the window we climbed out of last night. The one above the addition. The screened porch. What *was* the screened porch," she corrected. "And before you say anything, I checked for branches. A loose shutter. For anything that could be in a position to hit the glass. Believe me, there was literally *nothing* up there that was close enough to touch it."

"Then...what do you think it was?"

"I don't know. The first few times I heard it, I assumed it was one of the things I just mentioned. The last time, it was storming. I was carrying a flashlight because I was afraid the power might go out. I heard the tapping from downstairs and then again after I got to Maddie's bedroom. It had grown louder, but when I looked out the window—"

This time he waited through the pause, recognizing that whatever she was about to tell him now was at the heart of her reluctance. Was *that* when she'd seen the figure in the woods, rather than last night? Or maybe there had never been anyone in the woods. Maybe she had gotten so spooked living out here by herself—

"When I looked out, there was nothing there," she finished softly, interrupting his speculation. "I could hear the sound. It was right in front of me. I could even see the glass tremble, so I should have been able to see whatever was striking it, but..." She shook her head, her eyes not focused on anything in the present. "Even when I shined the light on that particular pane, there was nothing out there."

"Are you saying...?" He stopped, unsure *what* she was saying.

"I'm saying that on more than one occasion I heard a tapping on one of the windows in my daughter's bedroom when there was nothing there to cause it."

"Nothing you *saw,*" he corrected gently.

"I'm not crazy. And I don't believe in ghosts. At least..." She hesitated, seeming to gather her composure. "Look, I know how this sounds. Believe me, I've told myself everything you're thinking right now. But there was *nothing* out there. No trees. No shutters. No animal."

"And you're sure the noise wasn't coming from the attic—"

"Squirrels in the attic," she said with a laugh. "Or bats. No, Sheriff Jackson, whatever I heard *wasn't* in the attic. It was right outside—"

"Cade."

"I'm sorry?" She seemed genuinely confused by the interruption.

Why shouldn't she be? He was. What the hell did he think he was doing?

"You asked me to call you Blythe. I thought I'd return the request."

Her mouth opened, but nothing came out. She shook her head again, apparently in disbelief this time. "I'm sorry?"

He was making a fool of himself. Whatever had happened out here, she clearly believed something strange had been going on. And it was his job to get to the bottom of whatever it was, even if that turned out to be nothing more than an overactive imagination.

"What do you think it was?" he asked, trying to get the conversation back on track.

"I don't know. Maybe whatever sets off Maddie's terrors. Something… Something I can't explain."

"And that's what you were trying to do when you came to the office. To find out why there might be something…strange about this house."

"If you'd seen my daughter as I have, paralyzed with fear, screaming hysterically night after night, you'd pursue any avenue to try to get to the bottom of what was going on. Even one as ridiculous as that."

"As ridiculous as thinking the house might be haunted?"

"I did. At least I was beginning to. Enough to try to investigate the possibility anyway."

"And?" Maybe the past tense she'd switched to was related to the fire, but maybe there was something else that changed her mind.

"Doc Etheridge says there's no reason to believe the Wrights aren't resting easy in their graves. Neither of them suffered a violent death. And according to him, neither passed away inside the house." She turned, looking toward the ruin. "I suppose *whatever* was going on out here is academic now."

If she'd imagined a tapping on her daughter's window, maybe she'd also imagined the figure in the woods. As of yet, there was no physical evidence to prove its existence. And with what she'd just told him—

"By the way," she said, "I had hoped there might be a little more professionalism in your department."

"What does that mean?"

"The kid at the front desk that day… Would his last name be Spencer?"

"Jerrod? What about him?"

"His mother informed the Women's Aid Society that you'd given me permission to review the files of Sarah Comstock's murder. According to her and Ada Pringle, I'm planning to write an exposé about the case. Of course, in order to do that, I'll have to solve it first. I can't help wondering if that possibility might be making someone nervous."

"The possibility of you solving the Comstock murder?"

Cade hadn't meant that to sound mocking. He just wasn't sure where this was going. All he knew for certain was that he'd have Jerrod's hide as soon as he got back to the office.

"Yeah, that took me by surprise, too," she said, laughing again. "But still…I can't help but wonder if it might have something to do with this." She turned to look at the burned-out shell of the house.

For a long moment neither of them said anything. Cade was trying to process what she'd just suggested. To examine the idea from a law-enforcement standpoint. Motive? Or more small-town gossip?

"You *will* let me know what the fire marshal says."

Her eyes had returned to his face, he realized. No longer focused on what had once been her home.

"As soon as we know something, I'll call you."

"I'll be at my grandmother's." She remembered as soon as she said it that he would know that since he was the one who'd taken her there. Her cheeks colored again. "For the time being."

"You're thinking about looking for another place?"

There wasn't much rental property in town. Or near it. None Cade believed she would be willing to live in. Still, he could put out the word that she was in the market.

"Actually, I'm thinking about going back to Boston."

He wasn't surprised. Although she'd grown up here, she had obviously forgotten what small-town life was like. Or wanted to forget.

"Is that where you lived before?"

She nodded. "This hasn't quite worked out like I anticipated."

"Your grandmother will be happy to have you as long as you need to stay. You know that."

"I know. Until I can figure out what to do, you know where to reach me." She looked again the still-smoking pile of rubble before she turned and started back toward Miz Ruth's big car, her hands in the pockets of her jacket and her eyes on the ground in front of her.

Whatever pleasant memories Blythe Wyndham had once had of Crenshaw, they'd been replaced by strange sounds in the night, shadowy figures and a fire that might or might not have been arson. It wasn't as if anyone could blame her if she wanted to cut her losses and run away, but Cade found himself hoping like hell that she wouldn't.

11

"Not much doubt about it. Signs of accelerant use are clear, particularly in this area."

The investigator from the fire marshal's office pivoted on the balls of his feet to look up at Cade. The guy had been squatting over an area of the burned-out shell that Cade believed, based on his knowledge of other homes from this era in the area, had been either the living or dining room.

"Probably broke a window and then tossed the stuff on whatever was in here," the investigator went on. "Doesn't look like there was much furniture in the room."

"I doubt this family had much."

"Well, they got less now. Once he got the fire started, wooden structure like this, it would have gone up in a matter of minutes. You say everybody got out?"

"A mother and her four-year-old daughter. They crawled out a second-story window and onto the roof of the addition."

"Maybe the door was closed down here. That might

have contained the fire long enough for them to hear the alarm and get out. Dodged a bullet, if you ask me."

"So if whoever set this knew there were people inside..."

"If he knew, he wasn't worried about whether or not they got out."

Or didn't intend for them to. Given the scenario the inspector had laid out, the fact that Blythe and her daughter had escaped seemed almost a miracle. And gave credibility to her claim that she'd seen someone watching the house burn.

"What's the chance he'd hang around to see what happened?"

"Excellent to one hundred percent," the inspector said, pushing to his feet. "What's the fun of setting something off if you don't get to see it go up?"

"The woman who lives here claims someone was standing at the edge of the woods in the back."

"Should be a great view of the house from there. She's probably right."

Cade felt like a bastard for having doubted her. And it made him wonder how much of the other things Blythe had said he should take seriously.

"You think he might have been hanging around before? Watching the family, maybe from those same woods? Doing little things to frighten them?"

"An arsonist doesn't get off watching people. Or frightening them. He gets his jollies watching stuff burn. If this guy's getting them from something else, that's your area of expertise more than mine. Wouldn't take a genius to do what he did here. All it would take is a general lack of concern about being caught and a *total* lack of concern about whoever was inside the house going up with it."

"What if that's what he wanted? What if seeing the house burn was secondary?"

"Then, like I said, what you've got on your hands, Sheriff Jackson, isn't arson. It's attempted murder."

"Could have been somebody from the high school out parking. I'm not saying that what we got is conclusive, but as much as me and Phillip could follow them, those tracks led into the woods and in the direction of the Wright place."

"You cast 'em?"

"Tire tracks and prints. Like I said, though—"

"I heard what you said. Go on back over to the Wright house and see what you can find there."

"You got it."

Doug's distaste for the job he'd been given had apparently been erased by the possibility that the tracks they'd found on the road behind the woods might be important. He was more than willing now to try to find matching prints at the house.

"And keep everybody away from there until you get through."

"I'll let you know if we find anything."

The comment reminded Cade that he had promised to let Blythe know what the investigator had discovered. That was something he wasn't looking forward to, despite the fact it vindicated her impression of last night.

There had been a note in her voice when she'd talked about leaving Crenshaw that had let him know she was on the edge of despair. Even though the information he needed to give her would validate what she thought she'd seen, it couldn't possibly be construed as good news.

He flipped open the case of his cell and realized he didn't have Miz Ruth's number. He could call information or he could backtrack a couple of miles and go by the Mitchell house. Considering the nature of the information he had to convey, it would undoubtedly be better delivered in person.

Maybe there were other things that had happened before the fire that Blythe hadn't thought to tell him. Something besides the noises and the nightmares.

He hadn't asked if she'd seen anybody hanging around the place or noticed anyone in town acting strangely. Women were usually intuitive. She might have some idea who felt strongly enough about her—

To burn her house down over her head? To risk her life and the life of her daughter?

Any way he cut it, this was an act that went beyond arson. That was simply a place to start.

Delores answered the door, ushering him in as if he were an expected guest. "Miz Blythe's in the kitchen with her grandmother. You come on back, Mr. Cade, and I'll cut you a piece of cake. Make some fresh coffee to go with it, unless you'd favor some sweet milk."

"Nothing thanks, Delores. Do you think you could ask Ms. Wyndham to come out here?"

"Something you don't want Miz Ruth to hear?"

"It might be easier."

"Lord, I swear I don't know how much more that child can bear." Delores's words floated back to him as she made her way down the dark hall toward the back of the house.

The guilt Cade had felt since the investigator had given his verdict increased. Although he'd tried to keep his doubts about Blythe's story hidden, he was sure she'd known what he was thinking. And if she hadn't, he still regretted thinking it.

He hung his hat on the hall tree, shrugging out of his jacket to loop it over the hook under it. He blew out a breath, dreading the coming confrontation.

So far Blythe had managed to keep herself together. He had a quick mental image of her chin lifting defiantly as she'd told him about the tapping on the window.

Her footsteps sounded on the hardwood floor of the hall. Cade raised his eyes to watch her walk toward him. She was wearing the same jeans she'd had on earlier. He hadn't seen the dark red sweater because she'd been bundled up in a jacket, which had added bulk to her figure.

Despite the fact that it had been only a few days, she appeared to have lost weight since she'd come by his office looking for Hoyt. Stress from the noises she'd told him about? Or her daughter's nightmares. Or arson.

Enough to kill anybody's appetite.

"Sheriff Jackson? Delores said you wanted to see me."

"Think your grandmother would mind if we used her parlor?"

"I think she'd be embarrassed I haven't already invited you there."

She led the way, indicating one of two wingback chairs that had been set before the fireplace. While he was wondering if he was likely to leave soot or dirt on the pale brocade, Blythe took a match from a box on the mantel to light the gas logs.

"I'll get that." As he spoke, he began to move in front of her, holding out his hand for the match.

Somehow they ended up trying to occupy the same space. She laid the match on his palm and then stepped back out of his way.

In the brief contact between them, he'd been aware of her with every sense he possessed. Her height. The brush of her shoulder against his. The fragrance of her skin, clean and light and far more tempting than the darker, stronger perfume his ex-wife had worn.

He turned on the gas and lit the logs. When he turned back around, she was watching him.

"Since you're here, I take it the investigator confirmed there were no candles involved in what happened last night."

"He found clear evidence of an accelerant."

"What does that mean?"

"That the fire was definitely set. He believes someone broke out a window in the downstairs room on the far left of the house, threw whatever he was using in through the window and then set it alight. Although there didn't appear to be a lot of furniture in the room, the blaze caught."

"There were a lot of boxes in there. Things I hadn't gotten a chance to unpack. I guess that's one thing I can mark off my to-do list." What had clearly been intended as some sort of gallows humor fell flat.

Cade ignored the comment even as he gave her marks for trying. "You usually keep the door to that room closed?"

"Since I wasn't using it. Except for storage, I mean. It made the rest of the downstairs warmer."

And it would be cheaper. He knew that she was working for Ray Lucky, but only part-time. Finances were probably tight.

"The inspector thinks that's why you were able to get Maddie out before the whole thing went up."

"Because I'd closed that door?" she asked with a disbelieving laugh. "Probably the first thing I've gotten right since I came home."

There was nothing to say to that, either. Cade's impression that she was ready to cut her losses and leave was even stronger than it had been this morning.

"Thank you for telling me," she said when the silence stretched. "And for coming by to do it personally."

"A couple of the deputies found tracks on the other side of those woods that back the Wright place. I don't know that they're connected to what happened last night, I sent them back to your place to see if there's anything we missed this morning."

"What kind of tracks? Footprints? You think he came through the woods?"

"It's possible. They're relatively narrow. There were tire tracks as well. An indication that someone had pulled off the road and parked almost directly behind your house."

"And walked through the woods carrying…what? A can of gasoline?"

"Or kerosene. The report from the fire marshal's office should give us more details."

"And then he just stood in the trees and watched us try to escape the fire he'd set."

Even if that had been a question, Cade couldn't see any point in answering it. "I was hoping you might have thought of something else. Something you didn't mention this morning. Had you seen anyone hanging around the house in the last few days? Or noticed a car parked nearby?"

"Neither. Actually, nothing unusual has happened *outside* the house at all."

"You think he could have gotten inside? Sometime before last night?"

"I don't think what was going on inside that house had anything to do with someone coming in from the outside."

They were back to the haunting. Despite the fact that she had apparently been right about the figure in the woods, he was no more inclined to buy the supernatural business than he had been this morning. Since he wasn't, there seemed little point in continuing this discussion.

"If you think of anything, would you call me?"

"Of course. And I'll hear back from you regarding the fire marshal's final report as well as any progress on those tracks?"

"You'll be the first to know." He stood, nodding to her. "Thanks for your time."

"I'm not ungrateful. No matter how that might have sounded. It's just that I've been trying to make sense of this for weeks and haven't been able to. Now I'm trying to explain it to someone who clearly doesn't want to hear it."

The accusation was well deserved. Still, even if the Wrights were playing restless spirits in their old home, they hadn't left tire tracks on Salter Road or thrown kerosene around the dining room.

"Anything else happened since you've been back that made you… I don't know. Uncomfortable somehow?"

"I don't understand."

"Anybody in town look at you strangely? Seem overly interested in you or in Maddie? Anything that set off your personal weirdness alarm?"

"When you're a thirty-one-year-old widow who's come home again to raise her daughter, almost everyone's reaction seems forced. People never know what to say. Or how to say it. Especially to Maddie. 'I'm so sorry your father died. Or do you even remember him, dear?' So…to answer your question, yeah, I found about half the people in this town to be strange."

"Frightening strange?"

She shook her head. "The only things I've been afraid of since I've come back all took place *inside* the house where we were living. I can't offer you a suspect, Sheriff Jackson. Or a motive, other than the fact that Ada Pringle, with the help of your receptionist, has been telling people I'm going to solve the Comstock case."

"And you think that has something to do with the arson?"

They were still standing, facing one another. For the first time Blythe broke eye contact, looking down at her clasped hands. She still wore her wedding ring on the left, he noticed with a stab of something that felt ridiculously like jealousy.

She raised her eyes finally, meeting his. "I don't know. I've thought about it a lot since last night. Sarah's murderer has never been caught. Maybe he took Ada's nonsense seriously."

"And tried to make sure you didn't catch him by burning the house down around you?" He hadn't been able to prevent that trace of sarcasm, but she didn't seem to resent it.

"There have been plenty of motives for murder that made no more sense than that. Besides—"

"Besides what?" he prodded.

"Sarah's grandmother lived in that house. Maybe there is some connection."

"Between the house and Sarah's murder?"

"Between what's happening now and what happened then."

"It's been a long time. Twenty-five years. We don't even know if the murderer is still alive."

"*Or* if he's dead."

"Or if he's dead," he conceded. "If no one has identified him after all those years, do you think he'd be that concerned at the idea of a freelance writer trying to figure out a murder that has baffled law enforcement for a quarter of a century?"

"Haven't you heard? According to Ada, I'm the next Mark Furman." Her voice lost that mockery. "Maybe that isn't what has him frightened. Maybe he's figured out that law enforcement isn't the only entity who wants him brought to justice. After all, what was going on in the Wright house is what made me start researching."

Cade had been willing to cut her some slack after all she'd been through. And admittedly a lot of intelligent people believed in the spirits. He drew the line at the idea of her ghostly visitor trying to encourage her to seek out the killer.

"You think that tapping you heard is some kind of Morse code from the great beyond?"

"I think Sarah Comstock's grandmother and grandfather lived in that house," Blythe said, her voice patient. "It's not beyond my belief system to think they might want the monster who brutalized and then murdered her to be caught."

"I've never known a better law-enforcement officer

than Hoyt Lee. Sarah's murder was his case, and he did everything in his power to solve it. Seems to me if Eula and Buck wanted to give somebody hints as to the murderer, they would have started with him rather than you."

Her eyes had widened at his bluntness. "I guess it's all moot now anyway. If the Wrights *were* haunting that house, they've been displaced as surely as we have. So...thank you again for coming by, Sheriff Jackson."

Clearly a dismissal. And he was more than ready to let this go. "I'll call you about the tracks."

"You do that. And if I hear any more tapping, I'll see if I can figure out the message for you. In the meantime, I need to check on my daughter. I'm sure you know your way out."

12

As he closed the door of the Mitchell house behind him, Cade reviewed their conversation. He'd come over here with bad news, expecting Blythe to have a meltdown when he told her the fire had been set. Instead she'd seemed more concerned about the noises she'd heard while she'd lived there than about the fact someone had apparently tried to kill her and her daughter.

He stopped at the foot of the steps, his mind reiterating the thought. He believed that, he realized.

He might not buy the hocus-pocus about things that went bump in the night, but he didn't believe what had happened last night was a simple case of arson. Someone had tried to murder Blythe Mitchell. As difficult as it might be to fathom, right now the only motive he had for that attempt was the story Ada Pringle had spread around town.

Had a killer who'd gone undetected for twenty-five years panicked because he'd heard some writer was doing a story on the case? It didn't make sense. Not unless the murderer knew something he didn't.

Obviously, Cade acknowledged bitterly. Like who the hell he was and why he'd killed an innocent little girl. Nobody, not even the redoubtable Hoyt Lee, had been able to figure that out.

But the ex-sheriff *would* remember everything there was to know about the crime. Before he sought the old man out for his take on all this, Cade had his own investigation to carry out.

There was a file on the Comstock murder a couple of inches thick. He had read it before, back when he'd first been elected, more out of curiosity than anything else. This time he'd be reading with an eye to any connection between those events of a quarter century ago and what was going on right now.

Blythe's anger carried her almost to the kitchen before she began to feel ridiculous. It was one thing to wonder if the tapping at the window and Maddie's nightmares could have a supernatural causes. It was something very different to tell the county sheriff that you suspected a murdered child's grandparents were trying to steer you to her killer.

Even she didn't believe that. She had allowed her exhaustion and her anger with Cade's dismissal of her concerns to goad her into going too far. In the process, she'd lost all credibility with him.

It didn't matter, she decided, trying to regain her composure before she had to face her family. Why should she give a rat's ass what some country-bumpkin sheriff thought anyway?

Because he's Cade Jackson. And because you still see him through the eyes of an impressionable adolescent.

"What did Cade have to say, dear? Seems that young man is quite taken with you."

Despite how far from the truth that statement was, especially right now, Blythe managed a smile for Maddie, who was standing on tiptoe beside Ruth as the old woman mixed what appeared to be piecrust. Blythe could remember when she'd been a little girl watching those skillful fingers with the same fascination her daughter was displaying.

"What don't you run upstairs and get our jackets, Maddie? I think we have time enough before dinner to go out back and swing. What do you think, Grandmamma?"

"I think you should probably have daylight out there until just about the time I take the corn bread out of the oven."

"And you'll push me?" The eagerness in the little girl's eyes made Blythe realize how little time she'd spent with her daughter since they'd been here.

"As high as you want. Would you like that?"

"Yes."

"Yes, ma'am," Ruth corrected. "You remember what I told you about ladies and their manners."

"Yes, ma'am," Maddie echoed.

"Then run on upstairs and get our jackets." Coats had been an immediate necessity, one she'd taken care of on the way to see Doc this morning.

Blythe waited until the child was out of earshot before she turned back to her grandmother, who was adding ice water to the dough, a careful tablespoonful at a time and then blending it in with an economy of motion.

"Cade Jackson certainly isn't interested in me. And saying things like that in front of a four-year-old is just asking to have them repeated at the wrong time and to the wrong people."

"What in the world would it matter if she repeated it?" Ruth asked without looking up. "You're both single. Folks around here have been expecting Cade to set his sights on *somebody* since his wife walked out on him five years ago. Thought she was too fine to be married to a rural county sheriff. If ever a man deserved some happiness—"

"Maybe so, but he isn't looking for it with me. This was an official visit. He came about the fire."

"Well, what did he say?" The gnarled fingers paused, as Ruth looked up.

"That whoever they sent out from the state found signs of an accelerant."

"A what?"

"Gasoline. Kerosene. Something to start the blaze."

"Lord have mercy. Even with all the wickedness these days, you don't expect something like that. Not in Crenshaw."

Crenshaw. Where long before the current day's wickedness a child only a few years older than Maddie had been murdered.

"So what's he gonna do about it?"

"Who?" Her thoughts on Sarah's murder, as they increasingly had been lately, Blythe hadn't made the connection.

"Why, *Cade*. What does Cade aim to do about what happened?"

"They're looking for prints. Tire tracks. He thinks they might have found some on the other side of the woods that run behind the house. I'm not sure Cade wants that to become common knowledge, though," Blythe warned. "Just keep that to yourself until I check with him."

"I can tell Delores, can't I?"

Blythe suspected it would do little good to say no. "Just tell her not to spread it around."

"We ain't gossips in this house, young lady," her grandmother said, throwing a little flour on the dough that she'd now taken out of the bowl and shaped into a ball. "No need for all your warnings."

"I'm ready."

The announcement made them both turn. Maddie had donned her own jacket, and she held Blythe's out to her.

"I know you're not," Blythe said softly, reaching out to touch Ruth's hand. "I didn't mean that."

"Go on then. I'll call you when supper's ready."

Knowing from experience that her grandmother's pique would be short-lived, Blythe walked over to take her coat from her daughter. She slipped it on, and then put her hand on the back of Maddie's head, guiding her toward the back door.

It felt even colder outside than it had this morning, a dank and dreary winter afternoon. Maddie seemed oblivious to the temperature, running happily toward the swing.

Blythe followed more slowly, unable to put the events of the day out of her mind, despite her determination to make the most of these moments with her daughter. By the time she reached the oak, Maddie had already crawled up into the tire, small, chapped fingers wrapped around the rope it hung from.

Blythe moved into position behind her, pushing the surprisingly heavy swing forward. She stepped back a foot or so, and then gave it a harder shove when it swung back to her.

Maddie leaned back, scuffed tennis shoes pointing toward the lowering sky. Somewhere, sometime since they'd moved down here, she'd learned how to propel the swing with just the movement of her body. Another milestone she'd missed, Blythe realized. Another thing someone else had taught her daughter.

Through the months of John's sickness and death, poor Maddie had gotten the short end of the stick. She'd been clothed and fed and loved, of course, but the little things, the store of memories that mattered most to a child—

Maybe the psychologist had been wrong, Blythe thought as she pushed the swing again. Maybe those night terrors were Maddie's way of demanding attention. An attention the little girl was more than entitled to.

"Did you have fun today with Miz Ruth and Delores?"

"She let me stir the corn bread."

"She used to let me do that when I was growing up. One day when you're older, and if you promise to be very careful, she'll let you dip the batter into the tins."

"I could do that now."

"Then we'll tell Miz Ruth. What else did you do?"

"Me and Delores looked at the photo album of you when you were little."

"You did?" Although Blythe knew those pictures existed, she would never have thought of showing them to her daughter.

"Delores says you looked just like me."

"I guess I did at that." Several people in Crenshaw had commented on the resemblance.

"I saw your mama and your daddy when he was a little boy."

"He was Miz Ruth's little boy. Did Delores tell you that? She loved him very much."

"And then he went to heaven to live with the angels. God rest his soul." The little girl intoned the words as if she had been saying them all her life.

There was something amusing and endearing at the same time to hear that near anachronism come out of her mouth. Almost as if she were channeling the two old women inside the big house.

As long as they lived here, Maddie would be exposed to the same influences Blythe had been as a child. Manners and religion. Family and tradition.

Which doesn't seem to have hurt you any.

Except she wasn't sure Maddie didn't need something more than those shields against a world that was increasingly more dangerous than it had been when her grandmother was growing up. Different even from when Blythe was a child.

"I didn't see her though."

"Her?"

"That little girl."

"My mother? That's because she didn't live here when she was a child. She lived in Atlanta. Her grandmother probably had all those pictures in a photo album at her house."

"Can we go see it?"

Blythe's maternal grandmother had been dead for years. She realized that she had no idea what would have happened to her things. Although her mother had had a brother, they hadn't been close. He hadn't even come to her funeral.

"I expect it's long gone."

"Gone where?"

"I don't know. I think you'll have to make do with Miz Ruth's pictures."

She pushed the swing, sending it once more in an upward arc. There was no noise in the big backyard other than the creak of the rope. The birds were huddled against the chill of twilight, and it was too late in the year for the hum of insects that was constant during the summer.

In that peaceful stillness, Blythe's tension had

begun to ease, helped by the mindless, repetitive motion of pushing Maddie and even by the familiar noise the swing made. As the tensed muscles in her neck and shoulders began to relax, she drew a breath, releasing it as a long sigh.

"What's wrong?" Maddie asked.

"Absolutely nothing."

It was true. At this moment, there was nothing more important in her world that what she was doing. This was what life was about. Or it should be.

"Who's that?"

Maddie's left hand unclasped the rope, causing the tire to cant slightly as it swung back toward Blythe. As her gaze followed the child's pointing finger, she failed to send the swing forward again.

A man stood at the back corner of the house, watching them. Shadowed by the trees that grew just beyond the fence, she couldn't see his features. Before her stunned mind could command her body to move in order to get a better look, he turned, disappearing along the side of the house.

"Mama?"

"I don't know." But she wanted to, damn it.

Blythe hurried toward the fence to see if she could identify whoever had been watching them. By the time she reached it, there was no sign of the figure. She leaned as far over the top of the pickets as she could, but the house and the overgrown foundation plantings blocked her view. And the gate, she realized belatedly, was on the other side.

"Stay here," she ordered, throwing the words back at the child in the swing as she sprinted across the yard.

She pushed up the latch on the gate and slipped through, automatically taking time to close it behind her. Then she ran toward the front of the house, eyes searching in all directions.

No car other than Ruth's was parked in the circular drive. With most of their dinner already prepared and warming on the back of the stove, Delores had gone home for the day.

The sun had sunk below the horizon, lengthening and distorting the shadows in the yard. In the fading light Blythe searched first the front yard and then the side where she'd seen the intruder. It was as if he had vanished into thin air.

Or, she realized, he'd gone inside. That would explain everything. Even his survey of the back garden.

Whoever she and Maddie had seen at the side of the house had been a legitimate visitor. Someone who'd come to see her grandmother. Hearing voices at the back of the house, he'd come there looking for Ruth. Given the events of the last few weeks, it was no wonder she'd let her imagination run away with her.

She hurried up the wooden stairs, her footsteps echoing as she crossed the broad cypress planks of the porch. The front door was unlocked, just as it always was during the day. The lights in the hallway had not been turned on, however, making her question the explanation she'd just formulated.

"Grandmamma?" she called.

After a moment, Ruth appeared at the end of the long hall, a dish towel in her hands. "What's wrong?"

"Was someone just here?"

"Now?"

"A visitor."

"'Course not. Who'd come calling this time of day? It's suppertime."

"There was someone out back—" Only with those words did the enormity of the mistake she'd made explode inside Blythe's head.

Without another word, she turned and ran out the front door, slamming it behind her. She headed around the side of the house where she'd first seen the man. Eyes darting from side to side, she realized that in the few minutes her search had consumed, what light there had been in the evening sky was now gone.

From the windows at the back of the house, a soft glow poured out into the growing darkness. It was enough to light her path, and enough to see, when she reached the corner, that the tire swing, still moving gently back and forth, was empty.

13

"Maddie?"

Like bits of glass in a kaleidoscope, the images she'd formed of Sarah Comstock's death swirled through her head, even the distorted ones created by the whispers she'd overheard as a child. She destroyed each unspeakable picture as it took shape, but its place was taken by another and then another. As her panic grew, it became impossible to keep them at bay.

"Maddie? Answer me, Maddie!" As she screamed, she leaned over the fence, peering into the backyard. Her eyes frantically searched every dark corner, every shrub, every visible inch of ground.

"What in the world is going on?"

Blythe turned at the question. Her grandmother was standing behind her. In the gloom, Blythe could see the white of the dish towel she carried in her hand and her hair, its silver made gold by the light shining from the kitchen window.

She would never find them, Blythe realized in despair. He might be holding Maddie, keeping her quiet with his hand over her mouth. And in this light, she would never see them.

"Maddie. He's taken Maddie."

"Who's taken Maddie? Land's sakes, child, calm down."

"Whoever was *here*. He was standing right here watching us, and when I went inside— He must have taken her."

"I didn't hear anything. Maddie would have screamed if someone tried to carry her off."

Of course she would, Blythe realized with a sense of relief. Maddie knew the drill. She knew what to do if someone tried to abduct her. They'd gone over it time and time again.

They even had a code, so that she would know if her mother ever sent someone to pick her up at day care. Maddie would have screamed if anyone had laid a hand on her.

If he'd knocked her unconscious? Or drugged her? Or, as she'd thought before, simply held his hand over her mouth?

"Maddie?"

Her cry echoed through the nighttime stillness. The same stillness she had thought so peaceful only minutes before.

"Maybe she went inside."

The logic of her grandmother's suggestion broke through Blythe's terror. She'd left Maddie in the swing to disappear just as night fell. Why wouldn't the little girl go inside, where the kitchen windows beckoned with light and warmth?

"Come on," Blythe said, turning to grasp Ruth's arm.

"You go on. I'll stay out here and keep callin' her. If she's in there, stick your head out the door and let me know."

"I can't leave you out here alone."

"In my own *yard?*"

"I left Maddie, and now she's gone. You're coming with me. We'll check inside."

"She's probably in the kitchen," her grandmother said, giving in to her urgency. "Maybe if she is, she'll think to take the pie out of the oven. I expect it's gonna burn to a crisp with all this running around."

Despite her anxiety, Blythe had slowed her pace to match her grandmother's. Because of the uneven ground and the darkness, she kept a firm grip on the old woman's elbow as they made their way back to the front.

Even if Maddie hadn't gone into the house, Blythe would still have had to go back inside to turn on the outside lights. And to call the sheriff.

The thought was unwanted. Once she placed that call, this nightmare would become real.

Dear God, let her be inside. Let her be sitting at the kitchen table eating one of the corn muffins she helped to mix.

Remembering the excitement in the little girl's voice as she'd talked about those brought tears to Blythe's eyes. Such a short time ago they'd been together. Despite the fire, they'd been talking about all the things they should have been talking about. And for the first time in what felt like years.

"You go on," Ruth said, putting her hand on the banister that ran beside the front steps. "I got the rail here. I'll be fine. You go find your baby."

Blythe didn't argue. She released her grandmother's arm and ran for the front door. As it slammed shut behind her, she began to call again, her words echoing along the long, dark hallway. "Maddie? Maddie, are you in here?"

There was no answer. And the brightly lit kitchen, when she reached it, was empty.

She could smell the pie. And the corn bread. Even the greens simmering on the back of the stove.

"Maddie." Not a cry, but a whisper of fear and despair.

This had been her last hope. If her daughter wasn't here, she was out there somewhere. In the darkness. A darkness where he was.

Fighting the images that once more crowded her brain, Blythe ran over to the back door, flicking up the switch that controlled the backyard lights. She hurried down the steps, not bothering with the railing, her gaze again sweeping from one side of the enclosed garden to the other.

The shapes that had been nearly indistinguishable from outside the fence resolved themselves into familiar objects. The potting shed. The well, long covered. Trees and shrubs she had known from her own childhood.

"Maddie? Maddie, where are you?"

When there was no answer, she ran toward the back of the lot. With the floodlights on, there were only a couple of places inside the fence that weren't illuminated.

The top of the well was still covered, but she took time to try and lift the boards that had been nailed across its top. Then she made for the shed.

There was a lock stuck through the hasp that held the door closed, but it hadn't been closed. The creak when she opened the door reminded her so strongly of the swing that she even glanced back to make sure that Maddie wasn't there. That she hadn't somehow missed seeing her in the depths of her terror.

The movement of the tire that she'd noticed before had stopped. Empty, it now hung motionless from the oak.

She stepped inside the dimness of the shed, the smell of fertilizer and compost strong, but not unpleasant. Gradually, as her eyes adjusted, the items inside it became identifiable. A rotary lawn mower hung by its handle on one wall. A wheelbarrow was propped against another. Every inch of shelf space was covered with pots and sacks and tools.

She bent to look under the counter where her grandmother repotted her flowers, certain that despite the lack of light she would be able to spot Maddie's pale jacket. There was nothing there but a couple of market baskets, a clutter of tomato cages and some tin pails stacked one inside the other.

"Oh, Maddie." An expression of regret for having left her daughter unguarded for those few crucial minutes. A mistake in judgment she could never take back.

A rustling at the back of the small structure caused Blythe to whirl, eyes widened with hope. "Maddie? Is that you?"

The sound came again, even as Blythe pushed aside a sack of fertilizer in an effort to reach the back wall. She stooped, literally feeling along its length. Trying to find the warm, still breathing body of her daughter.

"Maddie!"

"I'm here."

Her heart leaped into her throat. "Where, Maddie. I can't see you."

"Back here."

Behind the shed, Blythe realized. Not inside, but behind.

She ran out through the door, throwing it back so hard it hit the outside wall of the shed. Before the sound had faded, she was at the back of the building.

There was a narrow space, perhaps a foot wide, maybe less, between the back wall and the fence. Maddie huddled there, the small, pale oval of her face raised to look up at her.

"Why didn't you answer me?"

In spite of her joy, she couldn't prevent the question. If Maddie had only called out, she wouldn't have gone through these terrifyingly endless minutes. All she would have had to do—

"Is he gone?"

For a fraction of a second, Blythe didn't understand the question. Then that, too, came flooding back. She meant the watcher. Whoever had been standing at the edge of the house.

"Did he come back here?"

In the darkness, Maddie's featureless face moved from side to side, denying. "She told me to hide."

Blythe examined the words, trying to fit them into the context of what had happened. Or of what she believed had happened. "*Who* told you to hide?"

"The little girl. She said he's the one."

"The one?"

"Who taps on the window. She told me to hide from him."

A chill began on the back of Blythe's neck, the hair there lifting. "Who told you to hide, Maddie?" She bent so she was eye level with the child who still crouched in the shadows.

"That girl. The one he hurt."

"Do you know her name?" Blythe asked, her voice very soft. "The girl who told you to hide. Do you know who she is?"

The oval moved from side to side again.

"Was she out here? Here in this yard?"

As far as she knew, Ruth's house had no connection to the murder. Or to the Comstocks. Maybe she could accept the things that had happened at the Wright house, but this…

There was no explanation for this. Not any she could bring herself to consider.

"I don't remember."

"Of course, you remember," Blythe said, her voice too harsh. "It was only a few minutes ago that we saw him."

"I don't want to swing anymore." Maddie sounded on the verge of tears, tired and petulant. "It's too cold to stay out here. I want to go inside where it's warm."

Inside. Where Ruth was waiting to hear. And by this time, she might already have called 911.

"Come on," Blythe said, holding out here hand. "Miz Ruth has supper ready. You can eat the muffins you helped make. Would you like that?"

Whatever was going on, she wasn't helping her daughter by her anger and impatience. Maybe Maddie *didn't* remember. Or maybe she had imagined the girl and the warning. Or maybe…

Maybe we're all going insane. That was what this felt like.

"Did you find her?"

Blinking back tears, Blythe turned to look at the back door where her grandmother stood, silhouetted against the light.

"She's here," she called. "She was behind the shed."

"Well, praise the Lord. Y'all come in now and get warm."

"Maddie?" Blythe turned back, holding out her hand again.

"Is he gone?"

For now. Blythe wasn't sure where the thought had come from, but it represented a truth she had accepted. He was watching them. As he had been last night. And more than likely that meant he was the one who'd set the fire.

"I'm sure he is. With all the lights on out here."

Maddie turned her head, trying to look toward the house as if she had just become aware of the floodlights.

"Miz Ruth's waiting supper for us. Are you hungry?"

"Yes, ma'am."

"Me, too." Blythe stepped closer, turning sideways to enter the shadowed area behind the shed. "Come on. Let's go inside now."

A small, cold hand reached up to grasp hers. She pulled, lifting the little girl to her feet.

Together they began to walk toward the back steps, where her grandmother kept vigil. Halfway there, Blythe slipped her hand out of her daughter's to put her arm around her shoulders. As she held Maddie against her side, they crossed the last few steps to the warmth and light and safety of the big house.

"Right there," Blythe said.

She had chosen to direct him from inside the fence where she'd been standing when she'd seen whatever she'd seen. Cade stopped, shining the flashlight he'd brought from the cruiser down on the spot she'd indicated.

"Are there prints?"

He hated to destroy the note of hope he heard in her voice. The truth was he could tell nothing from the packed earth. "The ground's pretty hard here."

"So there's nothing there."

"Not that I can see tonight. We'll come back out in the morning and take another look."

"Just like after the fire."

"When the light's better—"

"Maybe he doesn't leave prints."

"I'm sorry?"

The edge of hysteria that had been in her voice when she'd talked to him on the phone was back. She was trying to control it, masking her fear in sarcasm, but he'd talked to enough victims to understand that attempt at bravado.

And that was what she was. Whatever was going on, Blythe was first and foremost a victim of a crime—maybe two—that had been committed in his jurisdiction.

"Maddie said he's the one who taps."

Despite their earlier conversation about the Wright house, there had been nothing in her call tonight that had made him think she was going to start that again.

"On her window." Although he'd been trying to sound nonjudgmental, the words had been flat. She was smart enough to pick up on that.

"She also said that the little girl he hurt told her to hide. So she did."

"Blythe—"

"I know. I just thought you should have all the pertinent information while you're conducting your investigation."

The sarcasm was back, this time seemingly directed

at him. Hell, he was here, wasn't he? Without supper. Without catching up on the sleep he'd lost chasing her phantoms last night.

"Do *you* think your daughter's communicating with Sarah Comstock's ghost?"

The floodlight attached to the corner of the house where he was standing illuminated her face. Something changed in it with his question. Maybe he should have put it into words before now. Maybe once she heard how this sounded—

"I don't know. I don't know what to believe anymore. I wish I did. I *do* know what I saw. And what I heard. And I know what Maddie said."

"Could I talk to her?"

"To *Maddie?*"

"Yes."

"She's four years old."

"She talks, doesn't she? At least I understood from what you just said that she does."

"Of course she talks."

"Then I'd like to hear what she has to say."

"I told you what she said."

"It's my job to interview witnesses. I can't take information from them secondhand."

"She's *four,*" she said again. "Have you ever *talked* to a four-year-old, Sheriff Jackson?"

Not that he could remember, but he wasn't going to admit that to her. "I'm not going to frighten her. I'm not going to badger her. I'd just like to hear what happened from her perspective."

"After I found her... She said that she didn't remember whether the little girl had been here or not."

"The little girl who told her to hide?"

"Look, it's obvious from your attitude—"

"Somebody set fire to your house last night. Apparently the same somebody was out here in the dark at your grandmother's tonight. I'm trying to do everything in my power to discover who's involved. If you'll let me."

"And you think *Maddie* can help you with that?"

"Since she seems to be involved in whatever's going on?" he said patiently.

"What do *you* think is going on?"

"I think you've seen someone watching you and your daughter on two separate occasions. If this is the same person who set that fire, then I think..." He hesitated, trying to think of another way to phrase this. There wasn't any. "I think you're in danger. Or she is."

That was something Blythe knew in her heart or she never would have called him. Now that she had, she didn't get to dictate the direction in which this proceeded. That was his job.

"Is she asleep?" he asked, pressing his advantage.

She shook her head. She was standing with her arms crossed over her chest, as if she were cold despite the jacket she wore.

"Then why don't we go inside and let me ask my questions while this is still fresh in her mind."

"I'm not sure it is."

"What does that mean?"

"She never remembers the nightmares. She said she didn't remember if the little girl was here or not."

"Maybe she sensed that talking about her upsets you."

He could tell she was thinking about the possibility. Unable to deny that she had been upset.

"What can it hurt to try?" he prodded. "I promise I won't scare her. You tell me to stop, and I will."

It was a promise he shouldn't have made, and he regretted it as soon as he had. Still, if this was the only way he was going to be allowed to talk to the child…

She nodded, the single motion quick. Then she began walking toward the back of the house. "I'll let you in the front. I told Ruth to lock the door after us."

As he moved along the side of the house, Cade shone his light over the ground. Just as there had been no sign of anyone in the woods this morning, there was none here. Maybe the kid wasn't the only one seeing ghosts.

What was that disease where the mother made the kid sick so she could get attention? Maybe this was something like that—the mother pretends the daughter sees ghosts so she will be given attention. Except there was nothing in Blythe's manner that would lead him to make that conclusion.

If anything, she seemed reluctant to talk about what was going on with her daughter. As far as he knew, she *hadn't* talked about it. Not until someone had set fire to her house with her and the little girl inside.

Besides, every instinct he'd developed over the

course of the ten years he'd spent in this job told him that whoever had thrown gasoline or kerosene in the window of the Wright place had been flesh and blood. And that their reasons for doing that had had nothing to do with a haunting.

14

"Maddie, this is Sheriff Jackson. He wants to talk to you about what happened tonight."

As introductions went, this one hadn't been designed to instill comfort, Cade thought. Although Blythe had agreed to this interview, it was obvious she was doing so under duress. Her reservations would undoubtedly be communicated to her daughter, if not by word then by attitude.

Still, he didn't have much choice but to pursue this. The little girl had been involved in everything that had happened. Apparently no one, however, including her mother, had questioned her at any length. Of course, the difficulty of doing that with a four-year-old rapidly became evident to him.

Maddie hadn't looked up when her mother had spoken. She was holding a small teddy bear, which looked to be brand-new.

Which made sense, considering that whatever toys the child had would have been destroyed in the fire. He fought the surge of guilt that realization produced, stooping down in front of the couch on which the little girl was sitting.

She looked poised to run. If she'd made eye contact, he would have tried to reassure her with a smile. Instead, eyes downcast, with small, slightly grubby fingers, she worried at the ribbon that had been tied around the bear's neck.

"Hey, Maddie. I hope you won't mind answering some questions for me."

There was no response other than the momentary stilling of her fingers.

"You mama says that you're the one who saw the man at the corner of the house. Is that right?"

Her head moved up and down, but she didn't meet his eyes.

"Can you tell me what he looked like?"

The motion this time was side to side.

"Was he tall?"

Another nod.

"Tall as me?" Cade asked, standing so that she would have something to measure by. "Or maybe more like your mama?"

He was nearly six-two. He judged Blythe to be closer to five-eight or -nine. It was a range that should give him a general idea of the size of the person they were dealing with.

The little girl's eyes followed him as he got to his feet. He'd forgotten how blue they were. Darker than her mother's, they were widened now as if she were trying to figure out what he wanted her to say.

"I don't know," she said finally.

"*All* adults seem tall to her."

He glanced at Blythe. Despite her comment, her face was devoid of censure. Her eyes were focused on her daughter, and she appeared oblivious to anything else.

He gave in to her superior knowledge of how a kid this age thought. "Then how about if you just tell me what you saw."

The child ducked her head, fiddling again with the ribbon.

"Maddie, tell the sheriff what happened. We were swinging…"

"We were swinging," the little girl repeated dutifully.

"And then you saw…" her mother supplied.

The room was so still as they waited that Cade could hear the crackling of the fire in the grate. A real one, he'd noticed, unlike the gas logs in the parlor.

"Maddie."

"*You* know what I saw. *You* tell him."

The child's tone was so adult it took Cade by surprise, particularly after her previous monosyllabic replies.

"I *have* told him. Now he wants *you* to tell him. You may have seen something I didn't."

The blue eyes lifted again, studying Cade rather than her mother. Apparently, whatever the little girl saw reassured her.

"He was standing by the corner of the house watching us."

"Could you see his face?"

She shook her head.

"Could you tell *anything* about him, Maddie?"

"It was dark all around him."

Again there was something strange about that phrasing, but Cade decided to ignore it in the interest of keeping her talking. "And when your mama went running toward him, he left."

Another nod.

"What did you do when she followed him out of the yard?"

"I hid."

"Behind the shed."

An affirmative movement of her head.

"Why would you do that?"

"Because it was dark and I was afraid to be by myself."

He allowed the silence to build again as he tried to think what to ask next. Blythe took the decision out of his hands.

"You said someone told you to hide."

No response.

"Maddie? Tell the sheriff what you told me."

Nothing.

"You told me that the little girl told you to hide. Is that what happened?" This time Blythe waited the child out, forcing her to respond.

"I don't remember."

"But you *do* remember telling me that, don't you?"

A nod.

"So why did she tell you to hide?"

"I don't know."

"You *do* know, Maddie. You *know* what you told me?" Blythe's composure was clearly beginning to slip.

"Did you make that part up, Maddie?" Cade asked softly. "Did you make it up because you were afraid your mama would be mad you hadn't answered her?"

Blythe turned to look at him, mouth open, but he ignored her. He had known she'd be upset by his suggestion, but considering the child's reluctance to repeat whatever story she'd told outside, that explanation made sense.

More than a ghost child's warning from the great beyond.

"I was afraid he'd find me if I answered."

"But he was already gone, wasn't he?"

The small shoulders lifted in a shrug.

"Did you make up the little girl, Maddie?"

What Cade believed was at the root of this lay in Blythe's question. Still the child remained silent until her mother spoke again, her voice low and serious.

"Did you lie to me, Maddie?"

"No, ma'am."

"Then if it was the truth, you need to tell the sheriff what you told me."

"She said he's the one who taps on the glass."

"Do you know her name, Maddie?" Cade asked, squatting in front of her again. "Did the little girl you talked to tell you her name?"

She met his eyes briefly before she dropped hers to the bear. There was something in their depths he couldn't read. Something that again struck him as too adult. Too knowing.

"Maddie?"

The sharpness of Blythe's question made him wonder if she had seen whatever he'd noticed. If Maddie's expression bothered him, with his lack of a connection to this child, how would her mother react to it?

"I don't know her name. She doesn't tell me."

"But you've seen her more than once," Cade asked.

"Yes."

"In the backyard tonight and…when else?"

"I don't remember."

"At the other house?" Blythe suggested. "Did you talk to her there?"

"I *told* you I don't remember." The words were petulant. "Can I go sit in the kitchen with Miz Ruth? She said she'd tell me a story. You said she could."

Blythe turned to him, brows lifted. Since it was obvious this was getting them nowhere, he decided to cut his losses.

Maybe if he didn't alienate the little girl, he might have another chance to talk to her. If he kept on with this—which even to him was beginning to feel more and more like badgering—she'd never trust him again.

He nodded to Blythe, giving permission to put an end to the interview. Her head tilted as if she were surprised at his agreement.

"Tell Miz Ruth I said… Tell her to tell you Cinderella. That was always one of my favorites."

The little girl unperched herself. Without giving either of them a backward glance, she crossed the room at a run and disappeared through the door.

"I only repeated what she told me," Blythe said when Maddie was out of earshot.

"You believe she was telling you the truth."

"She was terrified. I think she was too frightened to lie."

"A lot of kids have imaginary playmates. Maybe this is something that makes her feel not quite so alone. She probably doesn't know many other children yet—"

"So my daughter has created an imaginary playmate who tells her that some man will hurt her? Where do you think she'd get an idea like that?"

"Maybe on TV. Or maybe she overheard someone talking. All I know is I find it easier to believe that she's got an imaginary friend than that she's communing with the dead."

"You find it more *acceptable* to believe."

"I would think you would, too."

"I heard things I can't explain in that house. Just as I can't explain what happens to her during those nightmares. I sincerely wish I *could* believe that either had been caused by an imaginary playmate."

"If you think there's a connection to Sarah Comstock, let's put that to the test."

Her eyes widened, reminding him of her daughter's. "How?"

Putting the idea he'd just had into words seemed

another cruelty. Like badgering a four-year-old? Refusing to believe what a distraught mother was telling him about her child?

"Whatever is going on started when you moved into the Wright house?"

"That's right."

"No night terrors, no strange noises until then?"

"Not even immediately after John died."

"You believe both of those have something to do with Sarah Comstock's connection to that house."

"Her grandmother lived there. Sarah must have spent time there. Given what I now know about the family, I thought the house might have been…a haven for those children."

"Somewhere they felt safe."

"Yes."

But Sarah hadn't been sleeping at her grandmother's the night she'd died. She'd been taken from her own bed in that shack Abel Comstock still called home.

"What do you think would happen if you exposed Maddie to somewhere Sarah *didn't* feel safe?"

"I don't understand."

He could tell by her eyes that she did. She just didn't want to entertain the idea. He could hardly blame her for that.

"Smoke Hollow."

"You want to take Maddie to the place where Sarah was murdered?"

"Believe me, there's no evidence of what took place

there. It's been twenty-five years. The spot's as beautiful as it was when you were a child."

She shivered, crossing her arms over her body again. Her right hand made a back-and-forth journey from her shoulder to her elbow. "Still…"

"Has she ever been out there?"

She shook her head.

"You tell her anything about it? Anything at all?"

Another negative motion.

"Has she even heard the name?"

"I doubt it. I can ask Ruth and Delores, but… I can't imagine why they would have said anything about that place."

"Then we take her there and see what happens."

"No."

"Why not?"

She laughed, the sound without amusement. "If you don't know, then I can't explain it to you."

"You think there'll be some kind of what? Psychic energy out there? Residual pain or terror?"

"A little girl *died* there. I don't think it's so far-fetched that there might be something…"

"Something that would traumatize your daughter? That would prove your point, wouldn't it?"

"My *point?*"

"That whatever is happening with Maddie—and whoever is stalking the two of you—is connected to Sarah's death."

"Why go through this charade? You've made it abundantly clear you don't believe that."

"Prove me wrong."

"By exposing my daughter to a place where another child was butchered?"

"If I'm right, there's no risk, because Maddie won't know what happened there. If *you're* right..." He hesitated, searching for a reality that wouldn't frighten her. "If you're right, then we'll have somewhere to start."

"To start what?"

"Putting an end to this."

"So now you're going ghost hunting?" Anger dripped from her question.

"If we can prove this is connected to Sarah's death—the fire, the man who was watching you tonight—then I won't be hunting for her ghost. I'll be hunting for her murderer."

15

Ray had asked her to stay late today to catch up on some correspondence. Although Blythe was grateful for the extra money, she now worried whenever she was away from Maddie, despite her grandmother's solemn promise to keep the doors locked during the day.

She had resisted the thought of Smoke Hollow ever since Cade had suggested taking Maddie there. Still, the location had been in the back of her mind during the last two days, especially when she drove past the path everyone had always used to get to the creek. This afternoon the pull was too strong to ignore.

Despite Cade's words about the beauty of the spot, she needed to see for herself what the place was like now. Her childhood memories didn't include anything that could be classified as beautiful. Of course, she couldn't remember ever setting foot there after the murder. Whatever the reality had been, her impressions would have been clouded by the snatches of conversation she'd overheard about Sarah Comstock's death.

She got out of the car and closed the door, for some reason taking care not to slam it. Maybe because of the absolute silence emanating from the forest.

She held her breath, listening for the creek that had, during her childhood visits, tumbled noisily along its rock-strewn bed. Long before swimming pools and community centers, that stream had lured the town's children out here to wade during the heat of south Alabama summers.

She could hear the water now, but more faintly than she'd remembered. Perhaps with the growth in population in Davis County—although nothing compared to other areas of the state—much of its flow had been diverted somewhere upstream.

Before leaving the car, she glanced up and down the highway. The blacktop was empty as far as the eye could see, increasing the sense of loneliness the silence had fostered. Still, even within the hollow, she would be only a few hundred yards from one of the county's main thoroughfares. And despite the lowering clouds, it was still mid-afternoon.

Maybe Cade was right. Maybe she'd become obsessed with the decades-old murder. Seeing, hearing and fearing things that didn't exist. All she wanted was a quick look at the crime scene. If for nothing else, to prove to herself that Cade had been telling the truth when he'd said there was nothing there now that would evoke the tragedy that had occurred here.

Denying her uneasiness, she moved forward, walking around in front of her car. Hand on the right fender for balance, she stepped across the narrow ditch that edged the two-lane. Without giving herself time for second thoughts, she moved purposefully across the right of way, heading toward the path she had followed dozens of times as a child.

As soon as she entered the line of trees, it grew dim. What little sun escaped the clouds seeped weakly through the branches of the pines, dappling the ground before her, but not really illuminating it to any degree.

The farther she went into the woods, the louder the noise of the stream grew. Only when she reached the source of that sound did she understand what Cade had meant about beauty. In spite of the season, water ran over algae-covered rocks and between the reaching fronds of a dozen different varieties of fern.

She stood a moment, looking down on the water. Despite the green of the vegetation surrounding it, she knew it would be ice cold. She took a step nearer the creek bed before she bent, reaching out to lower her fingers into the swift-moving current. The water's temperature was first shocking and then numbing.

She looked around, trying to orient herself. Although she had felt a sense of familiarity when she'd studied the black-and-white news photos, she wasn't certain now that she was in the right spot. The banks had seemed higher in those pictures. Maybe if she walked farther along the stream…

She pushed to her feet, wiping her fingers on her pants. She put her hands into her pockets, huddling inside the jacket that had been warm enough for running from the house to the car and then into the office. The chill out here seemed to cut through the wool as if she were wearing nothing.

Cade had been right about one thing, she decided as she followed the stream deeper and deeper into the woods. There was nothing frightening here. Nothing anyone should react to—not unless they knew the story. And Maddie couldn't, of course.

The terrain had gradually risen as she'd walked. The creek bed now lay well below the level of the ground, creating banks that were perhaps three feet high, matching those in the photographs. She stopped, her gaze scanning the area where she was standing, as she tried to correlate her memory of those pictures with her surroundings.

For the first time since she'd entered the woods, she was again conscious of the stillness. It was as if time had been suspended. As if the outside world had disappeared, leaving only the patterns of broken light and shadow and the sound of the stream. She shivered in reaction.

She wasn't sure she had reached the spot where Sarah Comstock's body had been found, but she'd seen enough. Whether a desire for the truth or morbid curiosity had brought her here, it was time to leave.

Her initial instinct had been right. This was not a place where she wanted to bring Maddie. If the little girl was somehow attuned to Sarah, the eeriness here would affect her. Just as it was affecting Blythe.

That or your overactive imagination.

Which was exactly what Cade had suggested Maddie had. Was it possible that Blythe had communicated to her daughter her own childhood fears about Sarah's murder?

Except she hadn't thought about Sarah in a dozen or more years. Not even when she'd moved back. And she hadn't read about the murder until after the tapping and the nightmares had begun. In any case—

She turned, intending to head back to the car and then to the warmth of her grandmother's house. A man stood in the path between her and that intended destination.

He wore overalls over a flannel shirt, but no jacket, and his work boots were caked with mud. Combed back from his face, his dark hair was liberally streaked with gray. His skin was stained with patches of red that ran along his cheekbones. She couldn't decide if his high color was the result of the temperature or some emotion.

His eyes, when she met them, were the color of mud. And as cold as the water that had numbed her fingers a few minutes before. For what seemed endless seconds they stared at one another before he broke the silence.

"This here's my property."

That had not been the case during her childhood, when everyone had come here for picnics and to wade in a vain attempt to escape the heat. This land, and the pine trees on it, had belonged to one of the large paper companies.

Of course, after all these years that could have changed. Even if it hadn't, she wasn't inclined to argue with someone who seemed so…menacing.

He did, she realized. As if he were taking pleasure in threatening her.

"I'm sorry. I didn't realize this had changed ownership. I used to come here as a child. We all did."

"Well, you're trespassing now. And you ain't welcome. None of you."

"I didn't know," Blythe said again. She took a step toward the man, but he didn't move.

His eyes had narrowed, and he appeared to be studying her face. "I know you. You're Ruth Mitchell's granddaughter. The one that just come back from up North."

The fact that he knew her grandmother should have been reassuring, but it wasn't. With the stories circulating in town about her intent to solve Sarah's murder, she wasn't sure that being recognized out here was a good thing.

"You come to see where she died?"

That was exactly why she'd come, but the urge to deny it was strong. Even if she did, she knew he wouldn't believe her.

"Well, this ain't it," he went on without waiting for an answer. "It's on up the hollow. I can show you."

"I really need to be getting home. My grandmother's expecting me. Probably wondering what happened to me."

She wanted him to be aware that someone was

waiting for her. Someone who'd be concerned if she didn't show up soon.

"Won't take but a couple 'a minutes. It's what you come for. Since you're here, you might as well get what you want."

The last thing she wanted was to go deeper into these woods with some strange man. And in this case, the adjective didn't just denote a lack of familiarity.

"I appreciate the offer, but—"

"It's thataway." His chin jerked, indicating the area behind her.

As if compelled by the gesture, Blythe turned, looking in that direction. The woods seemed darker there than where she was standing. More threatening.

"I really have to go," she said, turning again to face him. "They're waiting for me at home."

Head down so that she wouldn't have to meet his eyes as she told the lie, she began walking toward him. There was enough room to skirt beside the path he was blocking. She just needed to get the hell out of here.

As she came nearer to where he stood, she could smell him. A combination of stale sweat and dirty clothes, with an undernote of something alcoholic. Bourbon or whiskey. Or maybe, since this was still a dry county, it was moonshine.

She stepped off the path, preparing to edge by him. Like a snake striking, he reached out, hard fingers grasping her forearm. When she tried to pull away, his grip tightened.

"They say you're aiming to find out who killed her. That right?"

Blythe's eyes had automatically focused on the flat, spatulate fingers wrapped around her sleeve. Their reddened knuckles were so chapped they had cracked. Her senses acutely on edge now, she could see the pores in the weathered skin on the back of his hand.

"No," she said, raising her eyes to his. There was an intensity in them that had not been there before.

"They said you're gonna write a book about it."

"No," she said again, shaking her head.

"*Somebody* needs to. Somebody needs to find that bastard, so she can finally rest in peace."

The words paralleled her own thinking. If Sarah Comstock *was* reaching out to Maddie, it had to be because of the manner of her dying. And because her murderer had never been brought to justice.

Blythe, however, wasn't the one to do that. She was only a mother trying to protect her own child.

"I can't do that. Believe me, I wish I could."

"You told Ada you was."

She shook her head again, not sure she would be able to push words past the tightness in her throat.

"You need to see where she died. Everybody needs to see it. They all done forgot. All of 'em except me."

Was that why he'd bought this land? Because he had some connection to the girl who'd been murdered here?

"Why haven't *you* forgotten?"

"'Cause she was mine."

"You're Sarah's father."

The man many believed had slaughtered his own child.

The coldness in his eyes had been replaced by a fervor understandable in a grieving father. Blythe could see why people suspected he'd played a role in Sarah's death. There was something unsettling about them. As if the mind that functioned behind them was out of tune with reality.

"I know what they told you," he said. "That *I* kilt her. Could you kill your young'un? Could anybody you know kill their own child?"

But people did. All the time. The newspapers and the courtrooms were full of those cases.

"No," Blythe said, compelled to answer by the tinge of madness she saw in his eyes.

"That lie had as much to do with killing her mama as losing Sarah did. That everybody believed I'd done it. That they all thought she'd married a monster who could cut up his own baby just like slaughtering a hog."

Bile rose in the back of Blythe's throat. She swallowed against the urge to be sick. To physically spew out the horror his words created.

"Even if you'd 'a kilt her by accident, could *you* have cut up your baby that way, Miz Mitchell?"

Even if you'd 'a kilt her by accident…

Was that what had happened? Had this man beaten his daughter to death for some imagined infraction? Or had he hit her too hard in a fit of drunken rage? If not, then why would he introduce that idea into this conversation?

"I asked you a question. Could *you* 'a done that to your girl?"

"No," she whispered again. "No."

"I told 'em that. Told anybody who'd listen. But they never did. Nobody but Hoyt."

"Sheriff Lee believed you?"

"Only reason I wasn't took to court. He knew I couldn't 'a kilt my own baby."

It was said that the reason Hoyt Lee was such a good lawman was that he understood human nature. Could he tell a lie from the truth by looking into a murderer's eyes?

"Then who did?" Blythe asked.

Maybe he was drunk enough to tell her something. It wouldn't change what had happened to his child, but it might protect hers.

"Don't you think if I knew, I'd 'a done somethin' about it? Don't you think I'd 'a made them pay for what they done?"

"You have no idea?"

"Somebody she trusted. That much I know."

"How do you know?"

"'Cause he didn't break in my house and take my girl. I'm the one who got up that morning and found her gone. I'm the one who searched that room and then the house and then the woods. The latch on hers and Rachel's window was turned. Unlocked from the inside. Whoever did that to her, she let 'em in."

"Maybe she just forgot to lock it before she went to bed. Sometimes—"

"*I* locked it. She asked me to. Had to run 'em to bed, the two of them. They was huddled up by the fire, but the next day was school. Told 'em to skeedaddle to bed, or I'd whup 'em both. Rachel went on, but Sarah… Sarah hung back, pulling on my sleeve. 'Daddy, come and check our windows.' I didn't let my young'uns tell me what to do, you understand, but there was somethin' about the way she was beggin'…" He stopped, closing his mouth to swallow, the whiskers on his trembling chin moving with the effort at control. "That's the last thing she ever said to me. Last thing she ever asked me to do. Praise the Lord He give me sense enough to do it. It's been hard all these years. Knowing what folks thought. If I hadn't 'a gone in and checked that lock…"

Blythe couldn't know what Abel Comstock had told the sheriff all those years ago, but if it had been conveyed with this same emotion, she understood why Hoyt believed him. No matter what the people of Crenshaw whispered behind their hands all these years.

"Her or Rachel unlocked that window. And Rachel swore to me till the day she died she didn't do it."

"She knew him." Blythe breathed the acknowledgment.

"She knew him," Abel repeated. "And trusted him. Least ways enough to open that window."

"But you still don't have any idea—" She stopped because that had been asked *and* answered. And because she believed what he'd told her.

There was no doubt in her mind she was capable

of killing anyone who would ever hurt Maddie. If Abel Comstock had had even a suspicion that one of his neighbors was guilty of the murder of his daughter, Davis County wouldn't have needed a trial to ensure justice for her killer. It would have been meted out without one.

"I'll take you to where he kilt her. It ain't far."

Blythe realized that her mouth was still parted on that broken sentence. She closed it, thinking of the warmth and safety of her grandmother's house. Of Maddie—

Of Maddie. Who had had someone tapping on *her* window. And who screamed in terror as she slept.

"All right."

"You mean you're coming?"

Why wouldn't her agreement surprise him? Most of the town believed he'd murdered his daughter.

Blythe was no closer to an answer to what was going on with Maddie than she had been before, but she now knew, with as much certainty as she was capable of bringing to her search, that whoever had killed Sarah Comstock, it hadn't been her father.

16

When Blythe made it downstairs the following morning, Ruth was teaching Maddie to cross-stitch. They were sitting at the kitchen table, a profusion of brightly colored embroidery thread spread over its surface.

Maddie didn't even look up when Blythe entered the room. The little girl's tongue, caught between her teeth, protruded from her mouth as she guided an outsized needle up and across one of the blue markings.

"Very good," Ruth said, arthritic fingers sorting through the piles of thread. She was separating various shades of green on one side and the blues on the other.

Without speaking, Blythe crossed the room to look over her daughter's shoulder. A stamped pattern of leaves and flowers trailed along the edge of a white pillowcase.

"When you finish that, I'll teach you how to crochet some lace to go on the edge. You can put 'em in your hope chest."

"What's a hope chest?" Maddie asked, lifting her eyes from her project.

"It's where you keep all the things you'll need when you get married," Ruth said.

"Or when you get your first apartment," Blythe broke in.

"Look what I'm doing, Mama."

"I see. And a very good job you're making of it, too."

"It's gonna be cases for some pillows."

"They'll be very beautiful ones, I know."

Blythe bent to press a kiss against the razor-straight part in her daughter's hair. That, too, would have been Ruth's work, of course. That and the hot-pink plastic clasps that held what had been Maddie's bangs back on each side.

"They're for her hope chest." Her grandmother's tone said, *And I don't want to hear any more on the subject.*

"Or maybe she'll want to sleep on them now." Perversely, despite all that she owed her grandmother for taking them in and caring so diligently for Maddie, Blythe couldn't seem to help challenging Ruth's growing influence over her daughter.

"Can I, Miz Ruth?" the little girl begged. "Could they be mine to sleep on now?"

Her grandmother glanced up, meeting Blythe's eyes. "I don't see why not. If you don't want to save them."

"I'd be careful with them," Maddie promised.

"Of course you would," Blythe said. "Miz Ruth knows that."

"There's coffee."

Ruth's change of subject indicated that as far as she was concerned, the discussion was finished. Having made her point, Blythe was more than willing to let it drop.

"Can I pour you another cup?"

"My goodness, no. I've been drinking it since sunup. Any more and I'll be turning cartwheels."

"I can turn a cartwheel," Maddie offered, her eyes on the pillowcase as her fingers guided the needle through the cloth.

"But you can't drink coffee," Ruth teased, reaching over to push a strand of hair behind the little girl's ear. "Only grown-ups like your mama and me can do that. Ask your mama if she remembers how to make a French knot."

"What's that?"

"Something you'll need to know so's you can make the centers of your flowers."

"Do you, Mama?"

"I expect I can still make a French knot." Blythe smiled down at her daughter. "I'll show you just as soon as I've had a couple of cups of Miz Ruth's coffee."

She walked over to the stove and took a mug off the metal tree beside the pot. She poured the steaming black brew into it, breathing in the aroma, which was always better than the taste. Holding the cup in both hands, she brought it to her lips as she turned back toward the table, savoring the first long sip. She was even getting used to the hint of chicory.

"You slept mighty late. Must have been catching up."

She had been, Blythe realized. And for once she'd slept the night through without any disturbance.

"It's nice not to have to get up and dress for work. It's nice to be here with the two of you."

She could see that Ruth was pleased by the comment. There was evidently still some lingering hurt that Blythe hadn't agreed to move in here when she'd first returned.

If you had, maybe none of this would be going on now.

"So...do you have plans for the day?" her grandmother asked.

"Only to spend it with y'all."

As if to put a lie to that, the bell at the front door rang, its deep chime reverberating through the house.

"Lord have mercy," Ruth said, pushing back her chair. "Reckon who that could be this time of the morning?"

"I'll go," Blythe offered quickly, turning to set her cup down on the counter.

As she walked down the front hall, still relatively dark despite the morning sunshine, she, too, wondered who could be calling this early. Maybe someone from Ruth's church, she thought as she opened the door. Or maybe—

Though he'd been looking out on the winter-browned front lawn, Blythe had no trouble recognizing their visitor. Even without the uniform, Cade's height and the width of his shoulders were a dead giveaway.

He had turned at the sound of the door. For a few seconds, neither of them said anything. The connection she'd felt from the first day in his office was still there, apparently stronger than it had been before their argument.

"Sheriff?" The word was intended to reveal her curiosity about why he was here.

"Ms. Wyndham." A couple of long brown fingers touched the brim of his Stetson.

If anyone but Cade did that, she would have laughed. Instead her eyes followed his hand and then held on his face.

"Although I appreciate good manners as much as the next person, the kid at the car wash calls me Blythe. I think by now we can safely dispense with the formality."

"Especially since I acted like a royal bastard the last time we talked."

Both the word and the confession surprised her, but not unpleasantly. "I'm not sure what a *royal* bastard is, but..."

"You'll concede the other."

"Yes."

He nodded. "Then you'll understand why I've come."

"Actually, I don't, but I'm willing to be informed."

"I wanted to apologize. I had no right to suggest what I did."

"That I should take Maddie to Smoke Hollow."

"I don't blame you for being angry. The only excuse I can offer is my frustration with the investigation."

"Of Sarah's murder?"

"I was talking about the fire."

"And you don't see any connection between the two."

"I didn't say that."

"You didn't have to."

"Look..." Cade began and then stopped. He closed his mouth and took a breath. A muscle jumped in his jaw, sending an unexpected jolt of heat through her stomach.

What the hell was it with Cade Jackson and her libido? Did she have to react sexually to every move the man made?

"I didn't come here to argue with you," he said.

"Just to apologize."

"Believe it or not."

"I don't have any reason *not* to believe it. In all honesty, I don't want to argue either. And...after you left, I wondered if there wasn't something to what you'd said."

"About taking Maddie to the Hollow?"

"I thought maybe you were right. That it might prove something one way or the other."

"So...are you now saying you *want* to take her?"

"I'm saying I thought about it. So seriously that *I* went."

The furrow formed between his brows. "To Smoke Hollow?"

"I thought if there was anything to what I've been thinking, then there should be some kind of... I don't know. Residual energy or something." She lowered her eyes, recognizing how ridiculous that sounded. "God, I can't believe I just said that. Until we came here... Believe me, something like that wasn't part of my vocabulary. So…I know what you're thinking. I can even sympathize with it."

"You don't have any idea what I'm thinking."

She glanced up, puzzled by what was in his voice. He was looking down at her intently, with no trace of ridicule or amusement in those aquamarine eyes.

And he was right. She didn't have a clue what that look or his tone meant. She wasn't sure she wanted to.

"You said it was beautiful," she said instead of pursuing the opening he'd provided.

"You didn't find it to be?"

"Okay, I confess I don't know about 'residual energy,' but there was something about the place that made me uneasy. And it was the middle of the afternoon."

"You shouldn't have gone there alone."

"That's something else I figured out after it was too late."

"If you want to go back—"

"That I *wasn't* alone."

It took him a second or two to get it. "There was somebody out there?"

"Someone who claimed to be the owner of the property."

"The county owns that land. They have since Longleaf closed their mill in Draper."

"Then he was lying about that. But…I don't think he was lying about the rest."

"The rest?"

"About Sarah. Her death."

"He told you something about the murder?"

"Several things, actually."

"Blythe? Who is it, dear?" Her grandmother's voice came from the other end of the dim hallway.

Blythe should have known that Ruth's curiosity would demand she come out to see who their visitor was. She shook her head, trying to indicate to Cade that he shouldn't say anything about what she'd just told him. Then she turned, finding her grandmother standing in the doorway, silhouetted against the light from the den.

"It's Sheriff Jackson, Grandmamma. He came to talk to me about the fire."

"Well, for goodness sakes, child, don't leave him standing in the cold. You want some coffee, Cade? Got a pot on the back of the stove."

"I'm fine, Miz Ruth. Thanks."

"Well, come on in and close that door. You're lettin' out all my heat. You two can talk in the parlor. I'll make sure Maddie won't trouble you."

"Thank you." Blythe met Cade's eyes again, trying to convey her apologies with the look.

She knew now that she hadn't been mistaken when she wondered if Ruth had picked Cade out for a little matchmaking. She could only hope he hadn't figured out the plan as well.

"After you," he said.

The front room was better, she acknowledged, its warmth seeming to provide some distance from what had happened in the Hollow. She bent to turn up the fire in the logs. When she straightened, Cade had removed his hat and was shrugging out of his jacket. To him the parlor probably seemed stuffy and overheated.

"Sorry," she said. "We could have gone outside to talk."

"Do we need to?" He stopped, one arm still enclosed in the sleeve of the jacket.

"I didn't mean that. I just meant... It doesn't matter."

"Did he tell you his name?" Cade finished removing the jacket, laying it over the back of one of the wingbacks in front of the hearth.

"He didn't have to. He told me he was Sarah's father instead."

"Abel Comstock? He was out there?"

"I wasn't even at the location of the murder. Once I got there, nothing looked like I expected it to from the newspaper photos. I figured I must not have gone deep enough into the woods, but by that time, I didn't want to go any farther. I turned around to head back to my car, and there he was."

"He scare you?"

"At first, I didn't know who he was. He made me uneasy. I think anyone would have, given the situation. It was pretty clear he'd been drinking. And then, when I knew who he was—"

"You know he was everybody's prime suspect at the time of the murder."

"Except Hoyt's, apparently."

"As much as I respect Sheriff Lee, I'm not sure he was right in this case."

"Abel asked me if I knew anybody who could do

that to their own child. I don't. I can't even imagine it. And then I remembered all the children who are abused every day, and I confess I wondered…"

"If he might be capable of that."

"I think he could have killed her," she admitted. "Everybody says he was mean. Abusive. To his wife and his kids. That he was an alcoholic. I think maybe, given the right set of circumstances, he could have hit one of his children too hard. Shoved them away from him and caused them to fall. Or struck them in a drunken rage. Slammed them into a wall or a cabinet or something. A terrible accident…" She ran down, having produced all the scenarios she'd thought about on the way home from the Hollow yesterday.

"But?"

"How did you know there is one?"

"It was in your voice. You think he might have hit her, maybe even hard enough to kill her, *but*…"

"I don't think he could mutilate her. He said she was cut up 'like slaughtering a hog.'"

"Judging from the autopsy photographs, that isn't far from an accurate description."

"Who could do that to a child?"

"Someone who was very, very angry with her. Out of their mind with rage. Make no mistake. What happened beside that creek was a personal act of violence, committed by someone who had strong feelings for the victim. It was not a random murder. Not the killing of some unknown child who'd been snatched from her bedroom by someone who saw her as he was passing by."

"That's exactly what he said."

"Abel?"

"That she knew him. That she had opened her window to him. That Sarah had to have been the one who turned the latch and let her murderer in."

"Unless he was *already* in. There's something else the autopsy showed. Something that wasn't made public back then."

"What?"

"Long-term sexual abuse. Whoever murdered Sarah that night had probably been periodically raping her for a long time. And the most likely candidate for that..."

"Was her father," Blythe finished softly.

17

That made two people he needed to talk to, Cade thought as he descended the front steps of the Mitchell house. He just couldn't decide which one he was going to call on first.

Logic argued it should be Hoyt Lee, but something about the thought of Abel Comstock proclaiming his innocence at the scene of his daughter's murder made him want to think with his gut instead of his brain.

And if it had been someone other than Blythe he'd pulled that stunt on? Would you still be itching to slam your fist into his lying mouth?

Lee might be right that Comstock hadn't killed his daughter, but the drunken bastard was never going to win an award for being father of the year. He'd sent his wife and a couple of children to Doc Etheridge's office long before Sarah's death. For him to now pretend to be some kind of victim…

Cade took a breath, trying to control the surge of anger that thought provoked. Although Sarah had been dead for a quarter of a century, just thinking about what she'd suffered during her short life was enough to make his blood boil. He couldn't imagine how people who had to work on cases like that kept from committing physical violence against a suspect.

The same way good law-enforcement officers always gain control. They distance themselves from the victim.

That was the first thing Hoyt had taught him. If your gut was tied in knots and your hands shaking with rage, you couldn't be an effective force in bringing the perpetrator to justice.

Cade took another long, slow breath, remembering the man who'd taught him everything he knew about the job he held. Maybe it was time for a refresher course.

"I didn't arrest him because I didn't think he'd done it."

"I know you well enough to know you had to have a reason for thinking that," Cade said.

"I didn't teach you about gut instinct?" Hoyt questioned with a laugh.

Cade's mentor didn't seem to have changed much in the year since Cade had been out here. He hadn't realized it had been that long, but he knew better than to argue with Hoyt about it. If it had come down to it, his former boss could probably have provided him with the exact day and time of his last visit.

The former sheriff's hair was completely white now. And for the first time there was an almost imperceptible stoop in his near-military posture. Nothing had changed about the keen intelligence in those faded blue eyes, however, which were looking at Cade now as if their owner were simply waiting for the other shoe to fall.

"I just never heard you admit to using it to solve a case," Cade said.

"I didn't. Wish I had. Solved the thing, I mean. That's the one that still gives me nightmares, even after all these years."

"Because of the way she died."

"And the way she lived. The fact that somebody could do something like that to a helpless little girl and then melt back into this community like he'd done nothing out of the ordinary."

"He never killed again."

"Far as I know. Until I left office, I used to try to keep up with child murders in the surrounding states. I always had it in the back of my mind that one day..." The sentence trailed.

The old man lifted the beer bottle from the scarred table beside him and took a long draw of its contents. Cade knew him well enough to know that was to cover an emotion he wouldn't want anyone to see. Apparently this was one victim even the legendary Hoyt Lee hadn't been able to get distance from.

"So why not Abel?"

"I don't know. Hell, he was mean enough to kill—her or anybody else that crossed him. And he was probably drunk enough to have done it the night it happened. I've often wondered if she called for him, and he didn't hear her because he was sleeping off a binge."

"But you didn't arrest him."

"I saw him that morning. When they found her body. Didn't look hardly big enough to be a nine-year-old girl. 'Course the way it'd been left..." Hoyt shook his head. "There wasn't a man out there that wasn't affected. Even those like me who considered themselves real Alabama hard-asses. I wept that morning for Sarah Comstock. I don't mind admitting to that."

"And her father did, too? Maybe a sign of remorse."

"He didn't cry. Maybe if he had..." Hoyt paused reflectively before he lifted the bottle to his lips again. When he brought it down, he wiped his mouth with the back of his hand. "He looked like the heart had been cut out of him. She was his baby, you know. The youngest of that scraggly brood. That's why her and her sister was sleeping in that little ol' bitty lean-to he'd added on to the house. It'd make sense to anybody but the Comstocks to move the babies into the warmest part, now wouldn't it? Abel just built the two newest additions a room and stuck 'em out in it, rain, wind or shine. Never did have the gumption God give a goose. And sorry as bat hoobie to boot. But...if you'd 'a seen his eyes that morning, you wouldn't be asking me why I didn't arrest him."

There wasn't much Cade could say to Hoyt's comment that wouldn't sound disrespectful. He took a draw on his own beer as he tried to figure out what to ask next. The old man took the problem out of his hands.

"Why *are* you asking, boy? You ain't been to see me in more'n a year, and now you come all the way out here to ask about a girl that's been dead for twenty-five."

"It's a long story. And I don't know how much of it I believe myself."

"Well, I ain't got no pressin' appointments this afternoon. Actually, I'm pretty much free for the rest of the month, if it's all that long. Why don't you try me out and let's see how much *I* believe."

"Are you sure I wouldn't be imposing?" That was one thing he'd tried not to do when Sheriff Lee had retired. He'd figured the man had earned all the uninterrupted fishing and hunting he could manage before he passed on.

"I been setting out here by my lonesome all winter watching some World War II documentaries I've seen a couple 'a dozen times. What makes you think telling me a story, believable or not, ain't gonna be preferable to that?"

"You believe her?"

It was the only question Hoyt had asked during the fifteen or twenty minutes it had taken Cade to lay the whole thing out for him. And after all, it was the only one that mattered.

"I don't know. If *you* were telling *me* this same stuff, I would have told you no without any hesitation. But listening to her... All I can tell you is that she believes it."

"Lord protect us from ghoulies and ghosties and

things that go bump in the night. My grandmamma used to say that."

"Did you believe her?"

"I was a kid. Hell, when I was a kid, I believed anything."

"And now?"

"Now I'm an old man. And I ain't half so sure of all the things I thought I knew when I was a young one."

"You think Sarah Comstock's ghost is trying to use Blythe Wyndham's daughter to reveal who murdered her?"

Cade could hear the sarcasm in his question. There seemed to be only one interpretation for what Hoyt had just said, which made the comment about being sure of things when he was young feel like a slap at Cade's disbelief.

"I think if ever a spirit had reason to be restless," Hoyt said, "it's that little girl's. Maybe she thinks I let her down, although, as God is my witness, I swear I tried."

"Then why isn't she haunting you?"

"Same reason she ain't haunting you. Neither one of us would 'a listened if she tried. Maybe a four-year-old would. Especially one who's sensitive right now to loss and grief. One that's also living in your grandmamma's house. Maybe Sarah finally found a receptive audience."

"You're telling me you believe there's something to what Blythe Wyndham claims is happening."

"I'm telling you that I'd like to go with you when you take that little girl out to Smoke Hollow. I'd be real interested in hearing whatever she has to tell you."

* * *

Cade couldn't remember the last time he'd driven by the Comstock place. Must have been three, maybe even four years.

Whenever it was, nothing had changed. If the house had ever had a coat of paint, it had long ago weathered off. A couple of rusting automobile carcasses, one set on cement blocks, graced the grassless front yard.

Broken windows had been stuffed with newspaper and rags, except for those in the lean-to addition Hoyt Lee had described. There they had been ignored, leaving that room open to the elements.

Cade would bet those hadn't been treated like the rest because Abel Comstock never set foot in that part of the house. Guilt? Or simple grief?

Despite the former sheriff's conviction that Abel Comstock hadn't murdered his youngest daughter, Cade would have banked on it being the former. After all, who the hell would still live like this in these days of so much state and government support for the indigent?

Maybe an alcoholic father who feels responsible for not protecting his daughter…

He climbed out of the cruiser, deliberately slamming its door as a warning of his arrival. Despite the noise, nothing stirred on the property other than a plastic grocery sack that, carried by the afternoon's cold wind, scurried along the ground.

"Abel?" He waited through the answering stillness.

He surveyed the entire compound, looking for any sign of life. Maybe Comstock was inside, insulating himself against the cold with some of Pete Carraway's finest. Or maybe he was down in the hollow waiting to confront the next trespasser.

"Abel Comstock?"

Still no answer. Although it was only a little after four, the light was beginning to go. The temperature had probably dropped six or seven degrees since he'd left the office.

His conversation with Hoyt had sent him back there to reread all the material in the file on the Comstock murder. He'd come away with a sickness in the gut and more questions than answers.

It didn't seem likely he was going to get any of those this afternoon. As long as he was out here, however...

He walked up to the front door. He knocked forcefully a couple of times, and then out of politeness turned, once more contemplating the desolate front yard. After a minute or two he knocked again. Still no response.

Of course, it was always possible that Abel had seen the patrol car and decided not to answer. Maybe he thought Cade had come about his encounter with Blythe yesterday.

And he wouldn't be wrong about that.

The thought of the bastard hiding from him made him almost as angry as Abel's claim about owning the hollow. That was something else he'd checked out in his trip back to town. The property was still in the town's name. As if Abel could have managed to put together enough to even make an offer on it, he mocked his own gullibility in checking the title.

Cade had already turned to go back to the car when on impulse he reached back and grasped the doorknob. When it moved under his fingers, he pushed the door inward, revealing a front room that was dark and almost as cold as the outside.

Although there was a stack of wood by the hearth, the ashes in the grate were gray and dead. For the first time a tendril of uneasiness curled through his stomach. As cold as it had been last night, if Abel had passed out and let the fire go out…

"Abel? It's Sheriff Jackson. I need to talk to you. You in here?"

Nothing. He pushed the door open a little wider, primarily to let more light into the room, and then stepped inside.

A miasma of odors assailed him. He could identify the scent of wood smoke from the fireplace, a trace of bacon grease, body odor, and despite the season, a strong smell of mildew.

A single armchair sat before the hearth. On a small table beside it an unlabeled bottle half-full of cloudy liquid sat on top of what appeared to be, judging by its size, a family Bible.

Leaving the door open, Cade crossed the front room to explore down the narrow hallway. There was a bath and a couple of bedrooms. The bed in the one at the end of the hall was unmade, with clothes lying in an untidy array over its brass foot rail. None of the rooms were occupied.

He retraced his steps, looking into the kitchen. It,

too, was empty, dishes stacked in the sink and the counters cluttered with empty cans and boxes.

"Abel?" he said again, pitching his voice loudly enough to carry through the small house. No response, and there was now only one place he hadn't looked.

He walked across the front room and, without giving himself time to think of a reason not to, he opened the door to the addition.

He'd been wrong. The interior of the house wasn't as cold as the outside, but with its broken windows, this was.

A double bed sat against the wall of the house. It was made, a thin quilt pieced from a variety of scraps serving as a spread. A small chest, the only other piece of furniture, stood against the wall to his right. Directly in front of him were the two windows, which had been ineptly set into the outer wall.

For a moment he wondered why they'd even been added. And then he realized that there was no ceiling fixture. No bedside lamp. Those windows would provide the only light in the room.

As well as a means of entry from the outside…

If Abel and his wife's bedroom had always been the one at the end of the hall, then it was possible that whatever had happened in here, they couldn't have heard anything. Certainly not a tap on the window.

This was where Sarah Comstock had spent the few short years of her life. Was it any wonder that if she had chosen to come back, it wouldn't be to this place?

If she chose to come back. And he was still a long way from buying any of that.

He turned and reentered the front room, pulling the door to the lean-to closed behind him. It was clear that Abel wasn't here. Judging by the ashes in the grate, he probably hadn't been all day.

Was it possible that he spent his days in the hollow? Waiting for the next trespasser to show up, so he could convince them that he wasn't guilty of his daughter's death.

Given the unpleasantness of his surroundings, Cade didn't plan to wait for Abel to come home. And although it was probably less than half a mile by foot to the scene of the crime, he wasn't going to walk it. Not this late in the day. He'd take the road and follow the trail in as Blythe said she'd done yesterday.

If Abel was hanging around there, he'd warn him off. Cite him for harassment or something. If he wasn't...

Then it was probably for the better. Given the mood Cade was in, he was the last person Comstock would want to run into.

If Abel *was* out here, the son of a bitch was even crazier than Cade had thought. Although the description of the place where the murder had taken place was fresh in Cade's mind from his reading of the files, he'd already come farther from the road than he'd expected to.

On top of that, it was almost dark. In the murky twilight under the canopy of pines, he was having a hard time seeing the ground in front of him. The sound of the creek to his left would take him into the heart of the hollow. If he didn't trip over an exposed root and break his leg first.

The deeper he went into the woods, the more conscious he was of the isolation. His military background told him this would be the perfect place for an ambush. With the waning light—

He stopped, head cocked to identify whatever he'd just heard. It had definitely come from in front and slightly to the left. Even over the noise of the water, the sound had been sharp and distinct.

Although he hadn't hunted since he'd come home, he had spent enough time in the woods as a kid to know that hadn't been the kind of noise game made. Besides, he was upwind of the area it had come from, which meant any animal who'd been here before he'd entered the hollow was by now long gone.

Still frozen in place, he reached down and undid the snap on his holster. Although his intent hadn't been to take out his weapon, his fingers seemed to wrap around the butt as if they had a mind of their own. As soon as he felt the comfortable heft of the Glock settle into his palm, some of the anxiety he hadn't even been aware he was feeling seeped out of his body.

He eased a breath and then expelled it in a cloud of white. The temperature had continued to drop, and the humidity along the creek bed made it feel even colder.

Or maybe this is the chill ghosts are supposed to cause.

Despite his uneasiness of a moment ago, the thought amused him. Whatever he'd heard, whatever he was feeling, he was pretty sure it wasn't the spirit of Sarah Comstock. More likely the drunken stumbling of her sorry-assed daddy.

Weapon in hand, Cade began to move again. The toe of his boot caught on a rock or a root, sending him stumbling forward a couple of steps before he could regain his balance. At least the misstep reminded him of the flashlight on his utility belt.

With his left hand, he freed it. The cone of light it provided illuminated only a few feet in front of him, but that was enough to allow him to stride more freely.

He thought more than once about turning back, heading to the patrol car and then to the Town Square Diner for supper. Even if Abel was out here, Cade would play hell making any kind of charge against him stick. That had been thinking with his gut again.

He probably would have followed that instinct to give this up as a bad idea except for the realization that he'd reached the area where the murder had taken place. He stopped, directing the flashlight over the location in a wide circle.

The light reflected off the trunks of the trees, creating wavering shadows between them. After a moment, he switched off the distorting beam, allowing his eyes to adjust to the murky dimness. Once they had, it became clear that the spot indeed matched the crime-scene photographs he'd looked at this morning.

He expelled another breath, watching the white mist that formed when it hit the air drift in front of him. Apparently Abel didn't have the place staked out to warn off trespassers. Or if he did, he was still sober enough to recognize that he would be pushing his luck trying to get rid of Cade.

"Abel? You out here?"

There was no sound except the noise of the creek.

Even if Comstock was here, he wasn't going to answer. This whole thing had been a waste of time from the start. He'd do better to go back to town and then return to the Comstock place tomorrow. He could take some photographs of the tire tread on Abel's truck. Do something that suggested investigation rather than personal vendetta.

Or a ghost hunt.

"If you're out here, Abel, be aware I know what happened here yesterday. What lies you told Ms. Wyndham. You sure as hell aren't the owner of this property. The county is. And that means *you're* the one who's trespassing."

By the end of that speech, delivered at volume, Cade was beginning to feel more than a little foolish. First of all, he didn't know whether or not Comstock was here. Secondly, he seemed to be threatening Abel with trespassing, a relatively toothless charge, even for Crenshaw.

He just needed to get the hell out of these woods. Find someplace warm. Grab some food.

And some perspective.

He turned, at the same time shoving the semiautomatic back into his holster. He hadn't completed that action when the bark on the tree beside him exploded outward, fragments striking the unprotected side of his face. Then, at almost the same instant, the sound of the gunshot that had struck the trunk echoed through the clearing.

18

Cade's reaction was pure reflex. He threw his right hand up to shield his eyes, bringing the semiautomatic with it. As he did, he dropped into a crouch, pivoting on the balls of his feet so he was facing the direction from which the shot had come.

When he'd completed that turn, the Glock was already out in front of his body, left hand cupped under the right to steady it. He pumped two quick rounds at the place where he believed the gunfire had originated before he sidestepped, positioning himself behind the tree the bullet had struck.

Then, holding his breath, he listened for any noise that might reveal the shooter's position. He could hear nothing over the ever-present gurgle of the creek.

Eventually he eased a breath, trying to think of the best way to get out of here without getting his head blown off in the process. He had no doubt that had been the intent of his assailant's shot. If he hadn't begun to turn at the exact second he had…

Rather than worrying about what might have been,

he concentrated on formulating a plan. He wasn't going to sit out here in the woods all night. Although it wasn't cold enough to be dangerous, it would be damned uncomfortable.

He also didn't intend to do anything that would allow Abel to take another shot at him. Judging by the accuracy of the last one, the bastard hadn't drunk enough today to spoil his aim. Of course, he reminded himself, Comstock had supplied meat for his family for years from these woods. And judging by his long-standing habits, most of those times he'd gone out hunting, he would have been intoxicated. Abel could probably shoot as straight drunk as Cade could sober.

Son of a *bitch*. The expletive didn't help. And the fact that he couldn't express it aloud added to his frustration.

He could edge around the trunk and then work his way through the trees until he was behind his assailant. Despite the recent rain, however, there would be no way he could do that without making enough noise to alert Abel to his approach.

Or maybe he should let him hear. Maybe if Abel knew Cade was coming for him, he'd leave. Melt back into the shadows and head for home. After all, as things stood now, there was no way to prove who had fired that shot. Comstock had probably already thought of that. Maybe that was why he hadn't fired again.

Hell, maybe Cade had even been wrong about his intent. Maybe the drunken bastard *was* good enough to graze the tree beside him without hitting him.

Cade shifted his weight, leaning to his left to peer

around the other side of the trunk. Even in the few minutes since he'd taken shelter here, it had grown darker. Enough so that he could barely distinguish the trees from the spaces between them.

His eyes strained to spot any anomaly, any area of more solid blackness among the shadows and the vertical lines of the pines. There was none.

With the semiautomatic leading the way, he moved in a low crouch to the left of the tree and began to circle back toward the location from which the gunfire had come from. He moved slowly, taking as much care as possible. Still, the occasional crack of a twig or rustle of leaves seemed to echo through the stillness.

During the times he halted to listen for any answering movement from his opponent, he could hear nothing but the stream to his back. It would mask his progress as well, he told himself as he drew nearer his destination.

As his distance from the creek increased, its noise faded. When he moved into the area from which he believed the shot had originated, there would be an even greater need for stealth.

He took another careful step forward. As he lowered his boot, it encountered an obstacle that caused him to hesitate, balancing on one foot. The surface he'd just touched lacked the solidity of wood. Nor had it moved, like the foliage on the fallen branches he'd stepped on before.

There had been something different enough about the feel of this to make him take a backward step and then stoop to investigate. The Glock still grasped in his right hand, with his left he reached out, fumbling in the darkness. What his fingers discovered caused the rhythm of his heart to skip before it resumed its steady beat, but much more rapidly than before.

He traced along the fabric-covered surface his intellect had already identified as the torso of a body. There was no discernable warmth beneath the flannel shirt. When his fingers reached its open collar, he slid them into position on the side of the man's neck, feeling for the life-sustaining pulse of the carotid artery.

Because of the stubble of whiskers beneath his fingertips, there was no question about the gender of the victim. And after a few seconds, no possible doubt that he was dead. And judging by the coolness of the skin, that he had been for a while.

Despite the shock of his discovery, Cade hadn't lowered his guard. Logic argued that, unless there were two murderers wandering these woods at the same time, the person who'd taken the shot at him had also killed the man at his feet. And if that person was Abel Comstock—

Something—maybe the lawman's instinct Hoyt always talked about—replaced that thought with another. Cade moved his hand upward to braille the features of the dead man. Although he'd had no experience at that particular skill, the fleshy nose and the deep-sunk eyes beneath bushy, untamed brows assured him that his gut had been right.

Abel Comstock wasn't the one who'd fired at him because his was the body Cade had stumbled over.

Which meant whoever *had* taken that potshot was still out there in the darkness.

Waiting for him to make this discovery? Or leading him to it?

The question caused him to shift position slightly, his hand trailing first along the right arm of the corpse and then groping around on the ground nearby. Near the outstretched hand was the object he was searching for. Abel's rifle lay as if he'd dropped it when he'd fallen.

Cade paused again to listen to the stillness surrounding him, taking another visual survey as he did. After a few seconds he leaned over the body, locating the end of the rifle's barrel. Any prints on the weapon should be on the stock or trigger rather than down there.

He raised the muzzle to his nose and inhaled. As he'd suspected, the gun had been recently fired. Recently enough that he didn't believe Abel's hand had pulled the trigger.

Not unless you believe in ghosts...

He didn't. Not ghosts that fired rifles. Or even ones that tapped on windows.

He placed the barrel back on the ground and got to his feet, both hands again closing around the grip of the semiautomatic. If he was right in what he was thinking, his attacker was already gone.

The attempt on Cade's life had been a spur-of-the-moment action. The murderer couldn't have known he was coming. Cade hadn't been certain of that when he'd left the Comstock place.

Apparently when the killer had seen him following the creek to the site of that long-ago murder, he'd decided to try for some misdirection to cover up what he'd done. If Cade were killed with Abel's rifle, Comstock would surely be blamed for his death. And as cold as it was, Cade doubted the coroner would be able to pinpoint the times of the two deaths accurately enough to dispute that scenario. Not with a medical certainty.

He didn't know how the killer intended for law enforcement to explain Abel's death, but Cade would be very interested in finding out its cause. If Comstock had been shot, would it be with the same caliber weapon Cade carried? Or had he been killed with his own gun? An apparent suicide?

He had no doubt, now that he'd worked through all the possible permutations, that the killer's plan had been formulated as the events had played out rather than in advance. Unfortunately for the murderer, it hadn't worked. Which meant there would be a thorough forensic investigation of Abel's death. Cade would see to that, since it was something the killer obviously had hoped to avoid.

But there was a larger and more important question as far as Cade was concerned. What connection did what had happened in Smoke Hollow tonight have to the other murder that had taken place here? Given all he didn't know about those two crimes, there was one thing he was absolutely certain of. When he solved one, he would also know the solution to the other.

* * *

Since the incident in the back garden, there had been a blessed lull in the night terrors. Although Blythe would have expected the fear Maddie had experienced that night to have increased their frequency, the opposite seemed to be true.

She had no explanation, but she'd been relieved enough not to question the reason behind that turn of events too closely. Something to the effect of not looking too closely at a gift horse. Especially one that brought a much-needed respite from lost sleep and endless worry.

What she hadn't realized was that, despite the quietness of the last few nights, she was still awakening several times to listen for the now-familiar screams. And those weren't what she heard tonight.

It took her a few seconds to identify the soft sobbing that came from her daughter's room. Another few to decide that, although not nearly as frightening as the nightmares, this, too, required comforting.

She slipped out of bed, glancing at the bedside clock as she did. It was only a little after eleven. No wonder she'd awakened so easily. She'd not been asleep more than an hour.

She grabbed her robe from the foot of the bed, shrugging into it as she hurried down the hall. She couldn't remember the last time Maddie had cried. Even during the fire, her stoicism had been remarkable.

She had just finished belting her robe as she entered the little girl's bedroom, noticing that it seemed several degrees colder in here than it had in her own. Her eyes were automatically drawn to the windows where the drapes had been pushed back, revealing the expanse of dark glass.

Satisfied with that explanation for the chill, she ignored them, moving straight to the bed. In the glow from the nightlight, she could see that Maddie was lying prone, her face buried in the pillow as sobs racked her body.

Blythe sat down on the edge of the bed. "Hush, baby," she whispered, conscious of the open doorway and of Ruth sleeping next door. "Shh… Everything's all right."

As with the nightmares, her words seemed to have no effect on the sobbing child. The same suffocating fear that always filled Blythe's chest when she heard the familiar words of the nightmare stirred, but she denied it. This was something different. Something far more normal.

"Maddie. Wake up. I'm here, baby. It's all right." This time she took the child by her left shoulder, lifting it so that Maddie rolled onto her side.

The little girl's eyes were open. As Blythe watched, tears welled from their blue depths and rolled down her cheeks, but the eyes themselves were as blank as they always were when she was in the throes of a terror.

"Maddie!" She shook her gently, trying to wake her. Instead her head lolled lifelessly, making Blythe afraid to shake her more forcefully. "Wake up, Maddie!"

Uncaring now if she disturbed her grandmother,

Blythe raised her voice to try to break through the seemingly impenetrable barrier separating her from her child. After a moment, like a miracle, the blue eyes cleared. They focused on her face and then widened as if in surprise.

"Did you know?"

"Know *what?*" Blythe asked. As baffling as this was, at least it wasn't a repetition of the terrifying scene they'd already lived through too many times.

"My daddy." Maddie's voice broke on the word.

Then her eyes filled again, a tear streaking down the curve of her cheek as Blythe watched. "Were you dreaming about Daddy, Maddie?"

Maybe the psychologist had been right. Maybe John's death had been the root of everything. An unresolved grief that for some reason manifested itself only in her sleep.

Maddie nodded, swallowing as if to suppress a sob.

"It's okay," Blythe said, lifting her against her chest. "I dream about him, too. And I miss him. Just like you do."

The small body lay motionless against hers. After a moment, Blythe leaned back so she could see her daughter's face. She brushed a strand of tear-dampened hair away from her cheek to smile down into her eyes.

"Do you want to tell me what you dreamed? Sometimes it helps to talk about nightmares. Or we can talk about Daddy if you want. We can remember all the good times the three of us had together. Would you like to do that?"

The small head moved from side to side.

"Okay. Then..." At a loss, Blythe hesitated, trying to remember the advice the psychologist had given her.

"It was dark," Maddie said, her voice low enough that Blythe had to strain to catch the words. "And cold. So cold."

The uneasiness that had gradually dissipated as she held her daughter began to stir again. Blythe wasn't comfortable with any aspect of John's death being associated in her daughter's mind with cold and darkness. Those were not the images she'd tried to instill. Influenced by her upbringing, Blythe had talked about Daddy being in heaven. About him looking down on both of them and protecting them. This...

This was anathema to everything she had been taught as a child. And to everything she'd taught her daughter.

"It's all right," she said again, trying to draw the little girl back into her arms.

"*He* was so cold. And I couldn't wake him."

"Maddie, don't."

"I tried to find him at first, but it was too dark. Just like—" The words cut off as the blue eyes widened again.

Despite Blythe's discomfort with what was happening, there was something about the broken sentence that compelled her to ask, "Like what, Maddie. It was like what?"

The little girl's eyes focused again on hers. As Blythe watched, something began to happen within them. A change—almost a transformation—until they were once again...present. She didn't understand the use of that word in this context, but it was the one that her mind supplied.

"Like what, Maddie?"

"I don't know. I don't remember."

"Another nightmare?"

Her grandmother's question caused them both to turn. Ruth stood in the open doorway, her robe lighter than the backdrop of shadows in the hall.

"Something—" Blythe began and then stopped. Had it been? Certainly it had not been like the others, but something had happened here. "Something a little different this time."

"Maybe some warm milk to help her sleep?"

Blythe shook her head, unsure her grandmother's remedy for anything involving lost sleep would work in this case. As she turned back to her daughter, she realized the little girl's eyelids were already drooping. She knew from past experience that if she released her, Maddie would snuggle down under the covers and be sound asleep in a matter of seconds.

Without answering Ruth, she laid the child down on her pillow, pulling the quilts up over her. Unable to prevent the gesture, she again swept the disordered hair away from her temple to drop a kiss there. If not for its dampness, she might have believed she was the one who'd been dreaming.

She watched, still sitting on the edge of the double bed, as Maddie's breathing steadied into a slow, regular rhythm that didn't change even when Blythe stood up. She hesitated a moment more, but it was obvious the little girl was fast asleep.

Only when she turned did she realize that Ruth was still standing in the doorway. As Blythe made her way across the room, she stepped aside, allowing her to move out into the hall.

"What was that all about?" her grandmother asked.

"I'm not sure."

"Didn't sound like what you've described."

"It wasn't. It was nothing like the other."

"She was talking about her daddy? That's good, isn't it? Isn't that what that woman told you?"

It was obvious that Ruth, too, had been awakened by the sobbing. She must have heard more of their conversation than Blythe had been aware of.

"She... There was something about the things she said..."

"The psychologist?"

"Maddie. She said it was cold and dark. That *he* was cold."

"Lord have mercy. Now where would she get an idea like that? You don't suppose somebody's been talking to her about death?"

"I don't know who that would be. She doesn't see anyone but you and me. And Delores. You don't think *Delores*—"

"'Course not. She wouldn't fill the child's head full of that kind of nonsense. You know better than that."

She did. Delores cared for Maddie as if she were her

own grandchild. That was evident in everything she did. Still…

"Maybe she was talking about something else, and Maddie got confused."

"Hush, now. Whatever that baby's confused about, you ain't gonna lay it at Delores's door. Next thing you'll be accusing me of filling her head with nonsense about her daddy."

"Not that kind, at least." Blythe's smile was tenuous, but the old woman answered it by reaching out to take her hand.

"This was just what it seemed. A nightmare. Don't you go making anything else out of it."

"She said she tried to wake him. She wasn't there when John died. I don't know where that could have come from."

"From her imagination, of course. She's a little girl who lost her daddy, and she wants him back. Seems pretty straightforward to me. Maybe she heard that in one of the hymns at church. Asleep in the bosom of the Lord. One of those. A child that age… Well, you can't tell how twisted up things get in their little minds."

It made sense. Maybe because Blythe needed it to. She needed some kind of rational explanation for what had just happened, and Ruth's was as good as any. She could even remember some of the misconceptions about religion she'd harbored as a child. Things that she'd been too embarrassed to confess to when she'd finally grasped the correct theology.

"You need to start sleeping in my room so you can hear her if she cries. We'll swap in the morning."

"I can't take your room, Grandmamma."

"Why not? It's you she needs, and not me. Besides, at my age, I need my beauty sleep. Can't be jumping up and down all night. Now how about some warm milk for you and me? I expect we both could use some."

"Include a shot of Granddaddy's bourbon in mine..." Blythe put her arm around Ruth's shoulder and pulled her close. She recognized the thoughtfulness that had prompted the offer of a room swap, no matter how it was couched. "And we've got a deal."

At least tonight hadn't been a replay of the other nightmares. And Ruth had provided a logical explanation for what had occurred. All Blythe had to do now—

Was convince herself the anxiety she was feeling wasn't valid. And that whatever had happened tonight wasn't really more terrifying than the nightmares.

19

It was Delores who brought the news of Abel Comstock's murder the following morning. Although much of what the old woman said Blythe believed to be speculation based on gossip, the essential part of the story, which Delores related with obvious enjoyment, was that Abel had been found dead in Smoke Hollow, right at the spot where his daughter had been murdered so long ago. According to Delores, he'd been killed with his own gun. The authorities hadn't yet determined whether the gunshot wound had been self-inflicted.

"Guilt finally caught up to that man," the housekeeper pronounced as she set Blythe's coffee down in front of her. "'Bout time, too, after what he did to that baby."

"Hoyt Lee never believed Mr. Comstock killed Sarah." Nor did she, Blythe realized. Not based on what had been in his eyes and his voice when he'd talked about his daughter.

"Hoyt's been wrong a time or two in his life," her

grandmother said, sipping her own coffee. "Not to hear *him* tell it, of course."

"Why else would he have done it there, right at the very spot where he killed her?" Delores demanded.

"You said there was some question about whether or not it was a suicide."

"Not to me, there ain't," the housekeeper said with an audible sniff. "Not a question in this world."

"More than likely Abel had been drinking," Ruth put in. "Same as he did every day of his life."

"He went out there, and that place got to him. The memory of what he'd done."

Delores's words brought back the eerie feeling Blythe had experienced there. Still, that wasn't how she'd read Abel. Grief, yes. A degree of guilt perhaps, the kind any parent who had lost a child under those circumstances would feel. But not the deep remorse a father would feel if he'd brutalized his own daughter in that way.

"I expect we'll hear soon enough whether he took his own life," Ruth said. "'Course you know this is just going to keep stirring everything up."

"What does that mean?" Blythe asked.

"Why, about Sarah's murder. When Ada started telling everybody you were gonna write a book about it, that generated a whole lot of excitement in this town. Now with Abel's death, I expect there'll be a whole lot more."

Since the excitement Ruth referred to had apparently precipitated the arson, Blythe wondered what the news of Abel's death would bring. Of course, if

Sarah's father had been behind the two incidents—the fire and the scare in the back garden, she should be feeling relief. If he hadn't been, it was imperative she know how his death was connected to those events. And there was only one person who could give her the answer to that.

"I need to check on Maddie," Blythe said, pushing back from the table. "It isn't like her to sleep this late."

"Let her be," Ruth urged. "She's just catching up on what she missed last night."

"She have another nightmare?" Delores asked.

"Not the same kind," Ruth said. "This one was normal. Crying over her daddy. That'll be healing, I would think."

If the nightmare had been normal, her grandmother might be right. To Blythe, it hadn't been. Whatever the dream had been about, it had been full of images she'd been careful in talking with her daughter *not* to associate with John's death.

"I'll be back," Blythe announced unnecessarily.

She wasn't sure why she was hiding from the two of them that she intended to call Cade. Maybe because she hadn't told them about her own visit to Smoke Hollow. Without revealing that, it would be difficult to say why she resisted the idea that Abel Comstock had killed himself. And if he hadn't—

If he hadn't, someone had murdered him. In a place where there hadn't been a murder in the last twenty-five years—when Abel's daughter had been slaughtered in the same location where his body had been found.

Given that connection, and the mistaken one the town had made between her and Sarah's murder, that meant Abel's death, too, was linked to her. And, more frighteningly, linked to Maddie.

Blythe climbed the stairs, deciding to use the phone in Ruth's bedroom rather than the one in the front parlor. There was less chance of being overheard up here. And she could also do what she'd said she intended and check on Maddie.

She did that first, looking into her daughter's room on the way to her grandmother's. The little girl still seemed to be sleeping soundly. From the doorway, Blythe watched the regular rise and fall of the quilt spread over her daughter's shoulders.

After a moment, reassured, she reached inside the room and pulled the door almost closed. Then she walked to Ruth's bedroom next door.

Her grandmother's bed had been made, probably as soon as she'd crawled out of it. Not an item was out of place anywhere in the room. Even the pictures in their silver frames, which covered the dressing table, were all carefully aligned.

Feeling like an intruder, Blythe crossed the hardwood floor and sat down on the edge of the bed. She had already picked up the phone before she realized she didn't have the number of the sheriff's office. Since this wasn't an emergency, she didn't want to dial 911.

She opened the drawer of the bedside table, looking for the telephone directory. On top of her grandmother's Bible lay a gun—a very lethal-looking semiautomatic pistol.

Shocked, Blythe immediately pushed the drawer back in as if to hide what she'd seen. Then, remembering that a four-year-old was now living in this house, she pulled it open again.

The gun had belonged to her grandfather, his Army Colt. This was still a society that took the phrase "a right to bear arms" literally. That had been even more true in his day.

Ruth had lived here alone for many years. Although her grandmother would have said that the community was perfectly safe, it wasn't so surprising, given the culture she'd grown up in, that she would keep the gun beside her bed. What *was* surprising was that she hadn't put it away when Maddie had moved in next door.

Gingerly, Blythe picked up the weapon. Its solid weight was unexpected, so that as she held it, the barrel drooped slightly, revealing that the magazine was in place. And if this had been intended for protection, that made perfect sense. Just as putting it where a four-year-old couldn't reach did now.

She stood, taking a quick survey of the room. There was a narrow drawer at the very top of the chest of drawers. That would do for the time being. The next time Cade was here—

Cade. She'd almost forgotten why she'd come up here. She walked across the room and slipped the gun into the hiding place she'd chosen. She would have to tell her grandmother what she'd done, of course, and insist that Ruth not put the weapon back into the bedside table.

She'd already turned to go back to the phone, intending to call information, when she heard a sound from next door. She stopped, listening for a repetition of whatever it had been.

Maddie was talking, she realized. Her voice was very low. Almost as if she were whispering.

Maybe Delores had come upstairs to get started on the bedrooms. Or perhaps Ruth had followed Blythe up here. It would be just like her grandmother to check up on both of them.

As she neared the open doorway of Ruth's bedroom, she could hear her daughter's voice more clearly. She could even distinguish the occasional word. She thought she heard "daddy." Remembering Maddie's agitation last night, she stepped out into the hall and hurried toward the little girl's room.

She was surprised to find that the door she'd pulled to had not been opened. If Delores or her grandmother—

As she pushed the door inward, she realized that she could no longer hear her daughter's voice. And then she saw that Maddie was in the same position she'd been in when Blythe had checked on her a few minutes ago. The quilt still covered her shoulders, which rose and fell with each steady breath.

Puzzled, Blythe looked around the room, but there was no one here. And there was no radio or anything else to explain the conversation she'd heard.

She took a step inside and then another. From that vantage point she could see Maddie's face. The little girl was sleeping on her side, her hand tucked under her chin. Her lashes lay unmoving against her cheek.

Unwilling to discount what her senses had told her when she'd been in the bedroom next door, Blythe again scanned the room. Pale winter sunlight, slipping in through the slats of the blinds, painted a pattern on the gleaming wood floor. The pink sprigged spread that she had folded back across the foot of the bed was undisturbed. As was Maddie's robe, which lay over the arm of the only chair.

Nothing was out of place. No one else was here. And her daughter was still asleep.

So who had she just heard?

"Maddie?" Despite what her eyes were telling her, she wanted to know that the little girl was all right.

And what do you think could happen to her here in your grandmother's house?

"Maddie, it's time to wake up now."

The blue eyes opened, looking at her for a moment without any sign of recognition. And then her daughter smiled, breaking through the cold, mindless terror that during the last few seconds had gripped Blythe's heart.

"You're already dressed." Maddie's voice rose on the last, making it almost an accusation.

"I've been up a while. Come on, Miss Sleepyhead. The day's a-wasting."

That was something Ruth had always said to her when she was a little girl. Time in her grandmother's day was never wasted. It still wasn't.

"What are we going to do?"

Not, apparently, call Cade, Blythe thought with a twinge of regret. Or maybe she could do that while Maddie ate her breakfast. If not, the questions she had to ask him could wait. After all, he would undoubtedly be very busy this morning.

"I'm not sure. We can talk about it over breakfast. You can come down in your jammies if you want." She watched Maddie push back the cover with her feet and then crawl out of bed. "You need to go to the bathroom?"

"Yes, ma'am."

"Want your robe?" Blythe walked over to pick it up from the chair, but when she turned, Maddie was shaking her head.

"I don't want it. I want to put on my clothes."

"You go on to the bathroom, and I'll lay them out."

Obediently, the little girl started toward the door to the hall. Before she reached it, Blythe asked the question she had decided not to give voice to.

"Were you dreaming, Maddie?"

Her daughter turned, the blue eyes filled with a reassuring innocence. "Just now?"

"Right before I woke you."

"I don't think so. I don't remember it if I was."

"I heard someone talking. I was next door in Miz Ruth's room, and I thought it was coming from in here."

"I didn't hear anything."

"And then when I came in, you were asleep. So…I wondered if maybe you were dreaming. Talking to someone in your sleep."

"I don't think so."

This was getting her nowhere, but Blythe couldn't seem to let it go. She needed to understand what was going on. She needed to know what was happening to her little girl.

"You dreamed last night. Do you remember *that?*"

The blond head moved back and forth, sun-touched strands of hair brushing against her shoulders. The nearly colorless brows drew together as if in concentration.

If this was the breakthrough the psychologist had talked about—an acknowledgment of the depth of Maddie's loss—then it was something they desperately needed to talk about. Even if it was painful to them both.

"You dreamed about Daddy. And you were crying. Miz Ruth and I both heard you."

"I don't remember."

Frustration made Blythe's voice sharper than she intended. "You said it was cold and dark. You said *he* was cold."

Maddie shook her head, looking bewildered.

"And just now… Just now you were talking. Were you talking to someone, Maddie? Was there someone in here with you?"

As she threw the questions at the little girl, the big

blue eyes widened. Slowly they filled with moisture, which welled into tears that spilled down her cheeks.

"Stop crying, Maddie. I need to know what's going on. Something's happening here—" Blythe stopped, appalled by the harshness on her tone, something the child couldn't possibly understand.

"I didn't *do* anything."

"I know," Blythe said, taking a calming breath. "I know you didn't. I'm just… I'm just out of sorts. You've got a cranky old mommy."

"Because of the fire?"

On top of everything else.

"That's part of it."

"I don't remember dreaming about Daddy."

"I know. I know you don't. You go on to the bathroom, and I'll get your clothes. Then we'll find something fun for us to do today. Okay?"

"Okay. You're not mad anymore."

"Not at you. You and I— You and I are a team. Just like we have been since Daddy died. We'll be all right as long as we stick together."

"Okay."

The little girl turned, disappearing into the hallway. Blythe closed her eyes. When she opened them, she blew out a breath, loud enough to be audible.

What the hell are you doing? Browbeating a baby because she doesn't remember dreaming about her dead father? Or talking to a ghost?

It was the first time she could remember actually

admitting the possibility. She'd beat around the bush in her conversations with Cade, but…

Did she really believe her daughter was conversing with Sarah Comstock, a child who had been dead for a quarter of a century? Or did the fact that she was even considering that as an explanation for what had gone on since they'd moved to Crenshaw make her crazy?

She walked over to the chest of drawers where she'd put the three outfits she'd bought for Maddie after the fire. Refusing to think about anything but making it up to the little girl for these few unpleasant moments, she methodically ripped off tags, tossing each garment onto the unmade bed as she did.

"I really *don't* remember."

Blythe looked up to find Maddie standing in the doorway watching her. Her hands hesitated as she tried to think how to heal the breach she'd caused. "I know you don't."

"I'd tell you if I did."

Maddie *had* told her about the little girl the night they'd seen the figure lurking outside the backyard. Maybe she didn't remember the dreams. Maybe she was telling the literal truth.

"I know you would. It's… It doesn't matter. I'm sorry I got upset. How about the playground in the park?"

There was only one, centrally located just off the town square. In the summer, the slides and swings were shaded by hundred-year-old oaks. Blythe couldn't ever remember going there in the winter. However, she also couldn't think of any other treat to offer. Except…

"And a hamburger and fries and a milkshake for lunch," she added. "Does that sound good?"

"Yes, ma'am."

"Then you get your clothes on, and I'll go down and get our jackets from the front closet."

In the room next door, the phone rang. Together they listened, neither of them moving until someone downstairs picked up. Still they waited in silence, as if expecting bad news.

Finally, from the foot of the stairs Ruth's voice floated up. "Phone for you, dear. It's Cade."

Blythe stepped to the door, putting her hand on Maddie's shoulder as she called down to her grandmother. "I'll get it in your room. Thanks. Go on," she said, giving her daughter a gentle push toward the bed. "I'll meet you downstairs. You can tell Miz Ruth and Delores what we're planning. And ask them to give you a banana to eat on the way."

Without waiting to see if Maddie obeyed, Blythe stepped by her, heading for her grandmother's bedroom. When she reached the doorway, she looked back, but the little girl had disappeared inside her own room.

After only a moment's reflection, Blythe eased the door closed and then crossed to sit on the edge of Ruth's bed again. She took a breath before she picked up the receiver.

"I've got it, Grandmother."

She waited until she heard the click signifying that the other phone had been placed back on its cradle.

"Blythe?"

She reacted to the sound of his voice. An unexpected warmth that penetrated the chill at her core that she hadn't been able to shake since she'd heard about Abel's death.

This was nothing like the sexual response she'd experienced before. It was more like the feeling of relief when you'd been lost, driving down unfamiliar streets, and you suddenly spotted some landmark you knew. A sense of safety. Of homecoming.

"I'm here."

"You heard about Abel?"

"Delores told us. She said that they thought it might be suicide."

"If they did, they'd be wrong."

The silence stretched as she considered the implications. "Someone killed him. At the same place where Sarah was killed."

"Close enough."

"Do you know—"

"We need to talk."

Clearly not a request. "You mean not by phone."

"I'd rather not. Actually… Why don't you come down to the office? There's been enough misinformation put out about this."

"What does that mean?"

"That whatever Delores or your grandmother overhear will be repeated at circle meeting and prayer meeting. I'd rather not supply them with any more gossip. Not even the factual kind."

"I promised to take Maddie to the park."

Another pause, this one slightly longer. "How about if I meet you there? Say…twenty minutes."

She wanted to meet him, she realized. Just as she had reacted to Cade's voice on the phone, she wanted to see him face-to-face. Just to be able to talk to someone to whom she'd already revealed the worst of her fears.

"Twenty minutes," she agreed softly.

The sibilance of the last syllable hadn't faded when she heard the click that signaled he'd hung up. And although they were no longer connected, she was still strangely reluctant to put down the phone.

20

As he pulled the cruiser up along the curb, Cade turned, looking out the driver's side window at the only two people in the park. The day was cold enough to have kept everyone else indoors, so that Blythe and her daughter had the place to themselves. Which suited his purposes.

The serenity of the scene he was watching, however, made him want to delay the inevitable. Blythe was pushing her daughter in one of the swings, the little girl leaning back as far as she could at the top of each arc. Her long blond hair, glinting in the winter sunlight, almost touched the ground. They looked like any other mother and child, out to enjoy some time together.

Within the next few minutes, Cade knew he was going to shatter their tranquility. Maybe forever.

Pulling his gaze away, he picked up the radio from its stand on the dash. When he reached the dispatcher, he made his message as vague as possible, considering the investigation most of the department was involved with right now.

"I'll be out of touch for a few minutes. I'll check back as soon as I can. Anything short of another body can wait."

He replaced the radio and then opened his door. Once on the sidewalk, he deliberately slammed it. The noise had the desired effect, attracting Blythe's attention.

Even at this distance, their eyes held for a few seconds. He could almost feel her mentally preparing for whatever he was going to say.

So now you're psychic, too? Must be going around.

As he started toward them across the dead grass, Blythe stopped the swing. She leaned forward to whisper something into her daughter's ear. The little girl looked up at her before she turned her head to locate Cade.

For a heartbeat there was something watchful, almost wary, in her eyes. Then, in response to what she'd been told, Maddie slipped off the plastic seat and ran toward the nearest slide.

Blythe's gaze followed her daughter before it came back to him. The same wariness he'd seen in Maddie's eyes was reflected in hers. And there was nothing he could do to alleviate the sense of dread all of them seemed to feel about this meeting.

"You said someone killed him," Blythe said as he approached.

He glanced toward the little girl. She was far enough away that she wouldn't hear their conversation. Not unless it got more heated than he anticipated.

"Maybe Abel made his claim of ownership of the Hollow to the wrong person."

"Someone who had a different reason for holding a vigil out there." Blythe's comment was etched with a bitterness she made no attempt to hide.

"Or someone who decided that for Sarah, justice hadn't been served, so they decided to do something about that."

"Some…good citizen, you mean. Just doing what law enforcement hadn't done."

"It's possible."

"You don't believe that." Her tone was very sure.

"No."

"Then what *do* you think happened?"

"I think Abel was doing the same thing yesterday he was doing the day you ran into him."

"Visiting the scene of his daughter's murder?"

"And he stumbled onto someone else doing the same thing."

She waited, holding his eyes. "And?" she prompted finally.

"I don't know. Maybe something was said that made Abel suspicious. Maybe he made an accusation that whoever was out there was afraid he'd repeat, even when he was sober."

"So…you're saying whoever killed Sarah, someone who has evaded suspicion for twenty-five years, just killed again because of something the town drunk said to him."

No more far-fetched than believing the murderer was

so worried about the book she was supposed to write that he'd tried to kill her. If you could swallow one, why not the other?

"I don't *know* why he killed Abel. We may never know. But for what it's worth, I don't think it was premeditated. I think he was caught off guard and simply reacted."

Blythe glanced over to where her daughter was playing. When she turned back, she asked, "So where does that leave us?"

"Something's changed. At least he believes it has, and he's reacting to it."

"What does that mean?"

"All these years he's been content to let things lie. To let people suspect Abel. Or Satanists. To blame whoever they wanted to blame. Now..." Cade hesitated, wondering if there was any way to couch this warning that wouldn't scare her to death.

"Now?" she repeated.

"Now, for some reason he's afraid."

He could see her thinking about that. After a moment she came up with the only logical scenario for Abel's murder.

"He's afraid someone is going to figure out that he's the one. Is *that* what's changed?"

"I think so."

She laughed. "He thinks I'm going to do some research and figure out who killed Sarah? That I'm going to do what Hoyt couldn't, not with all the resources of the county and state at his fingertips?"

Cade said nothing, knowing that she'd eventually get there on her own. Maybe that was better.

"You really think he's afraid of *me?*" she demanded.

"Maybe," Cade said. "Or maybe... Maybe he's afraid you've got help."

"*Sarah?*" She laughed again. "Look, I know I said some things about the Wrights wanting him brought to justice, but you have to know—"

"Maybe living with his guilt all these years has made him more susceptible to the idea that a hand from the grave is going to reach out and finger him."

"Pun intended, I assume."

"Look, I've never denied that I don't buy the idea that your daughter is somehow in contact with Sarah's ghost. That doesn't mean that whoever killed her doesn't buy it."

"Then why kill Abel? Wouldn't it make a lot more sense to go after Maddie?"

Her eyes had been hard and cold when she bit off that suggestion. When he didn't respond, something began to change within them.

Her lips parted as if she intended to say something else before she closed them again. Finally she shook her head. "You think *that's* what the fire was about. Not about *me*, but about Maddie."

"I think it's possible."

"But...how would he know?"

"In *Crenshaw?* How many people did you tell about the tapping?"

"The tapping? On the window?"

He could tell that had caught her off guard. Obviously she'd thought he was talking about something else.

"That would be significant to only one person," Cade said softly. "Only to whoever used to tap on Sarah's window at night to get her to come outside so he could rape her again."

Her mouth opened, this time in shock, as her eyes held his. "Is that what it meant?"

"I don't know. There's too damn much we don't know. What I *do* know is that Abel Comstock is dead. And that someone tried to burn your house down with the two of you inside. So...like I said, after twenty-five years something's obviously changed."

She glanced again toward her daughter, who had migrated to the set of swings on the other side of the playground while they'd been talking. "Maddie? That's too far. You need to come back over here."

"I'm all right." The childish voice, carried away by the wind, seemed faint. Distant.

"Mind me, Maddie," Blythe called, her tone clearly saying that she wasn't brooking any argument. "Come back here right now or we're going home."

Together they watched as the child trudged reluctantly over to the slide where she'd been playing before. This time she didn't climb the steps, but leaned against them, head down.

Blythe turned back to him, anxiety written on every feature. "What do we do?"

We. He wasn't sure whether or not he should welcome her linking of them in this effort.

Still, it was a fair question. Whatever else he was, he was the sheriff of Davis County. If Maddie Wyndham needed protection—and that she didn't wasn't something he was willing to take a chance on—then it was up to him to provide it.

"First, we assume he'll try again."

"Another fire?"

"Anything's possible, I guess, but…"

"You don't think that's the way he'll go."

"I think this time he might want to try something more…"

"Certain?" she finished for him, the bitterness back.

"Thanks to you, he didn't have much success with arson."

"Maybe he'll just shoot her like he did Abel." Unconsciously, she had crossed her arms over her body. "God, why is this happening? Why Maddie?"

As she said the name, her gaze again left his face to seek out her daughter. The little girl was sitting on the bottom of the slide, scuffing the toes of her sneakers in the soft dirt beneath it.

"We're leaving," Blythe said, turning back to him.

"Leaving?"

"Crenshaw. We should never have come back."

"So you're going to run."

"Don't. Don't even try that. I don't owe you or Crenshaw anything. Especially not my child's life."

She had already turned and started toward the slide where her daughter was sitting, when he grabbed her arm. She looked back at him, eyes wide with shock.

"What do you owe *her?*"

"I'm her mother. I owe her everything. Protection. My life for hers, if that's what it takes."

"I didn't mean your daughter."

It stopped her efforts to pull her arm out of his grasp. In response, he released her.

"*Sarah?* I thought you didn't believe—"

"I don't. *You* do."

"I don't owe her anything. I didn't ask for this."

"Maybe Maddie did. Or maybe she was just more open to whatever's happening than anyone who's lived in that house since Sarah was there."

That was what Hoyt had told him, and on some level it made sense. Even to him.

"That house is *gone.* Whatever connection—" She stopped in the middle of that assertion, closing her mouth and swallowing.

"Nothing's happened since you've been living with Miz Ruth?" The answer, one she obviously didn't intend to articulate, was in her eyes, so he pressed his point. "Do you really think she'll leave her alone?"

"Don't," she said again, but more faintly this time.

"You didn't initiate this. *She* did. And I don't think she's ready for it to be over."

"I don't care *what* she's ready for. Don't you dare try to feed me that crap. You haven't believed a word I've said since the beginning of this. Don't try to come on now like you do."

It was a legitimate argument. Except that sometime during the last few days—maybe when he'd stood in that cold, windowless lean-to out at the Comstock place—his conviction that either Blythe Wyndham or her daughter was crazy had lessened.

"I'm not trying to convince you of anything, Blythe. I'm just throwing out things you should consider. After all, only you know how close the connection between them is."

Her eyes changed again. Although they didn't lose contact with his, he knew she wasn't seeing him anymore. She was seeing something else. Something—

"Was it dark?"

"What?" Her non sequitur had thrown him.

"When Abel was killed. Was it dark?"

"I don't know. We haven't gotten the coroner's report back on the time of death. It was dark when I found him."

"Dark and cold," she said softly.

"That's right. Dark and cold," he repeated, unsure what she was asking verification of.

She turned her head toward the little girl sitting at the foot of the slide. Maddie was no longer kicking the dirt. She seemed to be looking out on the park. Her mouth was moving, as if she were singing.

After a moment, Blythe turned back to him, her eyes again hard. "What is it you want us to do?"

It was after eight before he got away from the office. After the loss of sleep last night, and with no opportunity to catch up on any today, he needed to grab a few hours in order to be able to think clearly. There was no room for error here.

And he couldn't remember the last time he'd eaten. Since he'd slept, of course, but when he tried to pin it down, all he could come up with was yesterday's lunch.

Something else that needed to be rectified, he acknowledged. It would be smarter to do that before he grabbed the hot shower and the few hours of sleep he hoped to manage. The quickest way to accomplish that in Crenshaw, other than the fast food places out on the highway, was the Town Square Diner.

He pulled up in front of the place, glancing up through the windshield and the wide plate-glass windows to assess the crowd. Since most of the county ate supper before six, there were as few people inside as he'd been hoping for.

He crawled out of the car, feeling in every aching muscle both the cold night he'd spent combing the crime scene in the Hollow and the endless day that had followed. He straightened, arching his back to stretch out the tightness.

He thought about checking in with the dispatcher, but decided Davis County had had enough of his time today. He had his cell phone. If they needed him bad enough, they'd find him. They always did.

He opened the door of the restaurant to a welcome rush of warm air and the smell of hot corn bread. Marilyn Becker was dumping corn sticks from a cast-iron pan into one of the warming pans on the service line. She looked up when the bell above the door sounded.

"Well, look what the cat drug in."

He couldn't argue with that. It was exactly how he felt.

"Coffee?" she asked, her tone suddenly compassionate.

"Black and hot." He put his hat on one of the hooks by the door before he shrugged out of his jacket, hanging it on the bottom prong of the same hook.

Marilyn was headed toward the table nearest the serving line, a mug and carafe in hand. She poured a steaming cupful as he slid into the chair.

"Whadda you want, Cade? I'll bring it."

"I don't know yet. Let me drink this, and then I'll get my plate."

"Good enough, honey. You just yell if you want me to bring you something, though. Be glad to. Y'all been at it all day?"

"And most of the night."

"Know who did it?"

"Not yet. But we will."

The hostess smiled and nodded before she went back to the register. Cade lowered his head, sucking in half the coffee in one gulp. It burned a trail all the way down to his stomach.

The reassurance he'd so glibly given made him feel like an idiot. Unless the autopsy or the state lab—

"You won't sleep after drinking all that caffeine."

He looked up to see Doc Etheridge smiling down on him. Cade knew the old man had served as county coroner years ago, which meant he would probably want to talk about Abel's murder.

"You could inject it straight into my veins and I'd sleep tonight. Besides, this is just to ensure that I make it to the bed before I pass out."

"Heard y'all been at it hot and heavy in the Hollow and over at Abel's place."

"Don't want anything important to slip through the cracks."

"I expect you learned that from Hoyt. No stone unturned."

"That's right."

"Any luck? Or is the state of the investigation not for public consumption?"

"We're waiting on the autopsy. Coroner fixed the time of death, and we have the bullets, but something else may show up in the postmortem. And we sent some samples we took from the scene to the state lab."

"Sounds like you're closing in." There was a note in the doctor's voice that seemed to say that he wasn't fooled by Cade's show of confidence.

Of course, when you'd practiced medicine in a place like Crenshaw for almost forty years, you developed a certain cynicism about the quality of the services available. After all, the town's only other murder in recent memory had never been solved.

"One thing leads to another." Cade kept his tone noncommittal.

"Well, good luck. Hope you do better than we did."

"We?"

"Hoyt and me. I was coroner back then. Thought you knew."

"I knew you had been at some point, but... I guess I didn't realize it was during the Comstock investigation."

"The *first* Comstock investigation," Etheridge corrected with that same edge to his voice.

"Any advice?"

That was the last thing he wanted or needed, but he'd always liked Doc. And right now the old man was just like everyone else in town—curious about how things were going.

"I've been thinking..." Etheridge began.

"Yeah?"

Cade lifted his cup to drain the remaining coffee, nodding to Marilyn as he set it back down. With its warmth and the jolt from the caffeine, he was beginning to relax. To feel less strung out. Mentally, he settled in to listen to whatever Doc had to say. Then he'd dip a plate of whatever they were serving and try to wolf it down before anyone else could corner him.

"Got to be a connection," Etheridge finished.

That was exactly what Cade had suggested to Blythe a few hours ago, but he was surprised to hear someone else thinking that way. And if Doc was, then Hoyt would be, too.

"A connection?"

"Between Sarah's murder and this one."

Marilyn's arrival with the coffee kept Cade from having to meet those shrewd brown eyes. He nodded his thanks to the hostess before he did. "What makes you think that?"

"You don't believe in coincidence any more than I

do, Cade Jackson. Don't try to make me swallow one of that proportion. Two murders in thirty years and both victims from the same family? You trying to tell me there *isn't* a connection?"

"Maybe one of the folks convinced Abel killed her decided to finally bring some justice to the situation." It was the same solution he'd offered to Blythe.

One she hadn't bought, he reminded himself.

Doc, at least, seemed to be thinking about it. "That your theory of the crime?"

"Right now I don't have a theory. Maybe when we get all the evidence we collected back. Talk to me then."

"You got somebody out at Ruth's?"

Cade wasn't sure whether Doc was asking or saying. It was possible the old man had seen the cruiser that Cade had sent out there after his conversation with Blythe, but the Mitchell house was a little too far off the beaten path to make that likely.

"Why? You think I should?"

"I've known Blythe most of her life. I just grinned when I heard all that talk about her writing a book about Sarah. Maybe somebody else took it more seriously."

"I don't see what that has to do with Abel."

"Maybe he was one of the ones taking it seriously. Always claimed he didn't have anything to do with the murder."

"So...he was thinking Blythe was going to clear his name?"

"Maybe. Maybe he started telling folks around town something to that effect."

It was possible. After all, Abel's encounter with Blythe had been the day before his death. Maybe he had gotten the idea that she was going to help him. He had apparently convinced her of his innocence.

"You know that for a fact?"

"Nope. Just speculating. You might want to try to figure out who Abel talked to in the days leading up to his murder."

That was something he would have pursued anyway. Of course, it wouldn't hurt to let the old man believe that he'd made a valuable suggestion.

"I'll do that. Thanks, Doc."

"Glad to help. That little girl's death always haunted me. I know it did Hoyt, too. He won't admit that, but… I'll never forget how tiny she looked on that table."

Cade nodded, thinking instead about another little girl. One whose mother he had just convinced to stay here—under his protection—until he could get to the bottom of whatever was going on.

"Well, I'll let you eat your supper in peace. I know you deserve it."

"Thanks, Doc."

"You got any questions, you let me know. I still got all those files. 'Course I expect Hoyt didn't throw any of that stuff away, either."

"Sarah Comstock's file was never closed."

"Well, maybe this time it will be."

21

Blythe couldn't explain the compulsion that had brought her to Abel Comstock's funeral. As she slipped into the small, whitewashed church on the fringes of the community, she was surprised to find so many people occupying the narrow wooden pews. Unlike the mainstream churches, most of which were within the town limits, this one had always been outside, beyond both the boundaries that were prescribed the town and those deemed "acceptable" to the majority of its inhabitants.

Almost everyone in Davis County took their religion seriously and their Bible literally. The congregants of the Holiness Brotherhood Synagogue, however, took both to the extreme. As long as Blythe could remember, there had been stories of snake handling and miracle healings associated with this congregation. There had even been talk of an exorcism, but like the whispers about Sarah Comstock's murder, that had been discussed outside her hearing.

As she sat down in the back of the small sanctuary,

she unconsciously surveyed the crowd. Sunburned men dressed in shirtsleeves, despite the cold, with their thinning hair neatly slicked down with pomade. Their wives, pale faces devoid of makeup, were, in contrast, dressed in their Sunday best, their uncut hair pinned in rolls atop their heads.

In a pew a few rows in front of the one Blythe had chosen sat Hoyt Lee. Despite the years since she'd seen him, she had no trouble recognizing the former sheriff.

She wondered if his motives in coming today were the same as hers. Abel had been vilified in life as the murderer of his daughter. Based on her conversation with him, Blythe didn't believe he had been. Neither did Hoyt.

There were few others she recognized. Even Ruth had declined her invitation to accompany her, and neither her grandmother nor any of her friends would voluntarily miss a funeral. This one, of course, had been placed beyond the pale, not only by its location, but by the reputation of the deceased.

As the man Blythe assumed must be the minister, simply because he was wearing a suit, walked to the front of the church, Cade Jackson passed her along the aisle, slipping into the pew directly in front of hers. She resisted the urge to reach out and touch his shoulder, concentrating instead on the man now standing before the small crowd.

His graying hair had been swept straight back from his round, florid face and was long enough to curl against the collar of his blue-gray polyester jacket. Under that he wore a dark blue shirt and paisley tie, a combination that had come straight from the eighties.

He began the service by reading from the Bible he held open in front of him him. His hands gave an appearance of strength at odds with his age.

Blythe didn't recognize the passage, which seemed inappropriate for the situation. As did his delivery, more suited to a fire-and-brimstone sermon than a funeral. After a moment, despite her good intentions, her eyes focused again on the man sitting in the row in front of her.

It was the first time she'd seen Cade in dress clothes. The navy wool blazer he wore emphasized the breadth of his shoulders. His hair, so dark in contrast to the collar of the white oxford-cloth dress shirt, displayed a tendency to curl she'd never noticed before.

Slightly disconcerted by her slavish attention to every detail of his appearance, she forced her thoughts back to the service. The minister was in the act of closing the Bible, which he then laid on the front pew. When he straightened, he launched into what should have been, given the situation, a eulogy.

"You all knew Brother Abel. You know what he suffered in this life. How he was condemned by many in this community for the death of his daughter. How he was as much a victim of those that took her precious life as little Sarah was. And now, praise God, he'll finally get to see her again. He'll be able to press her to his bosom and feel her loving arms close around his neck."

Considering the accusations of long-standing sexual abuse that had been levied against Comstock, the words seemed even less appropriate than the scripture choice had been. They were greeted, however, by a murmur of amens from the congregation.

"And those who caused their suffering," the minister went on, warming to his theme, "those whose perversions demanded the sacrifice of that sweet innocent, may they, like the rich man whose crumbs sustained Lazarus, look across that vast void between heaven and the earthly hell they created for themselves to watch Abel and Sarah rejoice in their reunion."

A stronger chorus of amens answered the rise in volume of the preacher's voice. Suspecting those would only encourage him to continue in that vein, Blythe glanced at the former sheriff of Davis County to see how he was responding to this assessment of the crime he'd been unable to solve.

Hoyt was sitting with his face tilted upward, as if studying the yellowed acoustic tiles that formed the ceiling of the building rather than the minister. Of course, he'd heard all this before. The devil worship and the sacrifice theory would be nothing new to him. Or to Cade, she realized, her eyes refocusing on the back of that dark, well-shaped head.

Had the two of them come here to pay their respects to Abel or to observe those who were attending his funeral? Did they expect the person who'd shot Comstock and butchered Sarah to show up here today? A tradition like the murderer revisiting the scene of the crime? Was that what had happened the afternoon Abel had been killed?

Unable to answer those questions, Blythe again tried to concentrate on the words of the minister. He was expounding on his theme, intent on exonerating his former parishioner by laying the blame on those he was convinced deserved it.

"They took that baby's innocence, and then they took her life. All in the service of their dark master. And to those in this town, those charged with bringing justice to little Sarah, those who couldn't admit to the possibility of Satan's minions living among us, I say to you that here is your proof."

He turned, laying his right hand on the pine casket that contained Abel's remains. "In the same place where they stole Sarah's life, they have claimed another sacrifice. Do you deny still the evil that lives among us? Will you tell me now, as you did then, that what took place in that forsaken place Lucifer has long claimed for his own *wasn't* a sacrifice?"

He paused, looking at Hoyt as if expecting him to answer. The former sheriff continued his concentration on the ceiling, ignoring the break in the rhetoric.

"I told you what had happened," the minister said, his voice lowered dramatically, "and you turned your face from the truth. I tell you now that they are still among us. They live among us, disguised as God-fearing Christians, when in fact they are anathema to Him and to all those who worship Him. Outcasts from hell, they carry on with their obscene rituals while you deliberately close your eyes to the truth." The volume increased as he warmed to his text.

"Abel Comstock's blood is on your hands, just as his daughter's was. And I tell you that for your disbelief, one day you, too, will be standing on the other side of that void, begging Brother Abel for one drop of water to quench the fire of your eternal damnation. And he will ignore your suffering as you ignored his."

Another smattering of amens greeted the last promise, which was almost shouted. In contrast, the following's "Let us pray" was spoken in a normal tone, as if, done with the theatrics, the minister was ready to get back to the business at hand.

Despite the almost universal bowing of heads among the congregation, Hoyt Lee's face remained tilted toward the ceiling. Smiling at that show of defiance, Blythe bowed her own head, observing that Cade had done the same.

The prayer was, thankfully, more conventional than the eulogy. The minister exhorted the Lord to welcome Abel with a "Well done, my good and faithful servant," and committed his soul into the Almighty's keeping. The congregation's amens, echoing the one that closed the prayer, seemed anticlimactic.

Blythe kept her seat as the men and women of the Holiness Brotherhood donned coats and jackets. Two by two, they filed down the narrow aisle, following the casket that the pallbearers would carry to the small cemetery adjacent to the church.

As the minister passed, he nodded to Cade. Then

he paused, his eyes focused briefly on her face. Unable to imagine what he intended, Blythe continued to look up at him.

"If you need my services, Ms. Wyndham, any of them, they're available to you. You don't have to be one of this flock to call upon the name of the Lord."

Unsure what that was supposed to mean, Blythe murmured a thank you. The minister held her eyes a few seconds longer and then moved on.

As soon as the last of the small procession reached the back of the church, Cade stood, turning to look at her. Belatedly she, too, got to her feet.

"Where's Maddie?" he asked.

"At home with Ruth and Delores. Your deputy's there."

Just as one of them had been since she'd agreed to remain in Crenshaw. That was a decision she had questioned during the last three days, but the fact that Maddie hadn't had a nightmare since she'd made it had gone a long way toward quieting her doubts. Even the fleeting ones she'd had about leaving Maddie at home today.

"I didn't expect you to bring her," Cade said. "Actually, I didn't expect you to be here."

"It just seemed the right thing to do. What do you think he meant by that?" Blythe glanced back at the door through which the minister had disappeared.

She couldn't help but remember that long-ago gossip about exorcisms. If Abel's minister was implying she should allow him to do something like that for

Maddie, he was sicker than that bizarre eulogy had suggested.

She turned back, but before Cade could comment on her question, Hoyt came up behind him and put his hand on his shoulder.

"So what'd you think?"

"I think I know why I stopped going to church," Cade said.

"Gotta say something at a funeral, I guess. And there wasn't much good to say about old Abel, now was there?"

"I don't believe the minister thinks much of your investigation into Sarah's death, Hoyt," Blythe said.

She had meant to commiserate with the old man over those highly prejudicial remarks, but her statement hadn't quite come out that way. Before she could think of something to mitigate what must have sounded like criticism, Lee smiled at her.

"You ain't changed a bit, girl. Still as pretty as your mama. And that's a real compliment."

"I take it as such," Blythe said, leaning forward to kiss his cheek. "It's good to see you, Hoyt. Even in these circumstances."

"Yeah, old Clarence ain't liked me much since I refused to push for an indictment of the bogeyman. I'd probably have had as much luck getting one for him as I would 'a had getting one for Abel. God rest his soul."

Blythe couldn't tell if the last was sarcasm. After the ambiguity of her initial comment, she decided to leave it alone, allowing an awkward silence to build between the three of them.

"Any progress in the investigation?" Lee finally asked.

For a second, Blythe thought he was asking about Sarah's murder. Then she remembered Crenshaw now had a second homicide investigation underway.

"Not yet," Cade said. "The slug the coroner removed from the body was a .45. Most people who have handguns in this state use that caliber. All I know for certain is that the tire impressions we took on Salter Road don't match the tires on Abel's truck. Since I'm not even sure those are connected to the arson at the Wright house, I don't know what that tells us."

"That, just like with Sarah, we ain't got much to go on. How's your girl?"

Hoyt meant Maddie, Blythe realized when she saw the blue eyes focused on her face. "She's fine. She's with her grandmother today."

"And how *is* Ruth? Been a coon's age since I seen her."

"Then you haven't darkened the doors of First Baptist in a while," Blythe said with a smile.

"You got that right. And the more Clarence ranted and raved, the more I knew why. Hell, I don't have to get up early on Sunday to be told I'm going to hell. Folks been telling me that since I was a kid."

"At least you've proved them wrong."

"So far," the old man said, eyes twinkling. "So far."

"I take it neither of you take the good reverend's theory seriously," she asked.

"Somethin' that was going around back then," Hoyt said. "Just not in Crenshaw."

"He sounded pretty convinced," Blythe said.

"Always was. Don't mean there was ever anything to it."

"Was he ever more specific?" Cade asked.

"Had a whole list of folks he suspected of being involved in devil worship. Most of 'em were people who didn't show up here every time the doors were open, mostly cause they were visiting Otis's on a right regular basis."

Otis Wolfe was the legendary local moonshiner. If he was still alive, like Lee, he'd be well into his sixties by now.

"Mostly it was Clarence's way to deflect attention from a suspect who was part of his flock. Abel's methods of discipline were right down these folks' alley. Spare the rod and spoil the child. I don't doubt they encouraged him in that. Preached beating the devil out of your kids from the pulpit."

"You said Doc treated some of the Comstock kids for suspicious injuries." Cade's comment was serious as compared to Lee's mockery.

"A couple. Both boys. They seemed to bear the brunt of Abel's anger when he was drinking."

"Either still around?" Blythe asked, wondering if those two could shed any light on what was going on now.

"Not since they were old enough to hightail it on out of here. 'Course when their sister was killed, I talked to all of them. Including Rachel, by the way. The one that was sleeping in the bed with Sarah that night. None of them gave me any information that helped."

"Maybe they would now that Abel's gone," Cade suggested.

"If anybody knew how to get in touch with them. Rachel's dead, and the boys… Hell, I doubt even their daddy knew where they are."

"I thought they might show up for the funeral."

Which probably explained why Cade had come, Blythe realized. No matter what he'd said, apparently he wasn't totally convinced of Abel's innocence.

"Didn't see them. You all going out to the cemetery?" the old man asked.

"Might as well," Cade said. "As long as we're here."

"I went to Sarah's funeral," Lee said. "Same reasons you're here today. Didn't do much good since the whole town showed up for that one."

"You think whoever shot Abel is going to come to his funeral?" Blythe asked.

"It's a possibility you can't discount."

"Or count on," Hoyt said. "But when you ain't got nothing else…"

"I better get out there," Cade said.

"I'll walk with y'all. Don't think I'll join you for the burying, though. I've paid Abel all the respect that's called for in his case, I reckon. I'm heading home to get out of this cold."

"I think I'll do the same." Blythe looked at Cade,

almost hoping he'd ask her to stay. Of course, he had more important things to attend to.

Like finding the person who threatened Maddie.

"I'll come by and check on things later on," he said.

"Thanks. And good luck."

"That's mostly what it's about in this business," Hoyt Lee said. "Luck and instincts. This one..." He put his hand on Cade's shoulder. "This one's got a good case of both."

And, Blythe thought as she allowed the former sheriff to take her arm, he was going to need them.

22

Blythe didn't recognize the car parked behind Delores's when she got home. Nor did she recognize the voice she could hear coming from the kitchen as she walked down the front hall.

She hesitated as she approached, trying to identify the person talking. Although she had intended to make up for the coffee she'd missed this morning by attending the funeral, she was reluctant to interrupt if the housekeeper was entertaining a friend. Only when she heard Maddie's distinctive treble did she step forward, pausing again when she reached the doorway.

None of the three people seated at Ruth's kitchen table seemed aware of Blythe's presence. An attractive black woman, her hair in neat cornrows, sat directly across from Maddie. They were holding hands across the scarred wood, the little girl's pale fingers a contrast to the long, dark ones closed around them. Although Delores was seated so that she was facing the door where Blythe stood, her attention was so tightly focused on the woman talking to Maddie, she seemed unaware of anything else.

"And she tells you things?" the stranger asked.

"Sometimes. But..." Maddie hesitated, the colorless brows pulling together as they did when she was perplexed.

"Sometimes what?" the younger black woman prompted, smiling encouragingly.

"Sometimes I just know what she wants to tell me."

"Without words."

Maddie nodded. "I just know."

"Are you ever afraid when she talks to you?"

Maddie shook her head. "At first... At first I didn't understand why she was there, but...I think she's lonely. I think she just wants a friend."

As Blythe listened, a slow chill started up her spine. Her instinct was to step forward and put a stop to whatever was going on. It was countered by an equally strong inclination, fueled by her long frustration over not knowing what was happening, to listen. To understand at last the forces that opposed the return to normality she so desperately wanted. Torn by those conflicting considerations, she must have made some sound or movement.

The housekeeper's eyes came up to find her hovering in the doorway. "Miz Blythe, this ain't what you're thinking."

"Then what is it?"

"Mama." Maddie freed her hands and jumped

down from the kitchen chair to throw herself against Blythe's legs.

She put her hand around the back of the little girl's head, pressing her to her body. After a moment the child stepped back to look up into her face.

Blythe could find no trace of fear or anxiety in the child's eyes. Clearly Maddie had been glad to see her, but she didn't seem to have been seeking a rescue.

When Blythe lifted her gaze from her daughter's face, both of the women who'd been seated at the table were standing. Delores's hands were twisting together nervously, but the young woman to her left appeared perfectly calm.

"What's going on here?" Blythe asked again.

"Miz Simmons thought that perhaps I could help your daughter. When she asked me, I told her I'd be glad to try, but there would be no guarantee, of course." Although her accent was local, the words were clearly, almost carefully enunciated.

"And who are you?"

"My name's Tewanda Hardy, Ms. Wyndham."

"And exactly how did Delores think you could help my daughter?"

The dark eyes left hers to focus briefly on those of the housekeeper. Despite Delores's obvious agitation, when they returned to Blythe's face, their tranquility was undisturbed.

"She said there had been some trouble. Nightmares. Even some incidents when..." For the first time the young woman's assurance seemed to falter. After a second, she looked down at Maddie, who appeared to be listening to every word. "Incidents when Maddie had contact, even when she was awake."

Had contact.

Blythe swallowed against the bile that rushed into her throat. "Contact with whom?"

"I think you know, Ms. Wyndham," Tewanda Hardy said softly. "I think we all know who's trying to work through Maddie."

Blythe had known for days, although she had never openly acknowledged it. Sarah had chosen Maddie, either because of her age or the child's proximity within her grandmother's home.

"What do you believe you can do for my daughter?"

Again the dark eyes touched on Delores's before they returned to hers. "Facilitate that communication."

"Communication with…a *dead* child."

"*If* that's what's happening here."

"Do you think it is?"

Blythe wasn't sure why she should care about this woman's opinion. Something about her air of confidence, though, made her want it.

"I think it's possible. The truth is, Ms. Wyndham, this isn't the first time I've been involved in something like this."

"Involved as what? Are you…a psychic? A medium? What?"

"I'm someone who, like your daughter, has been aware since childhood that there's more in this world than most people see and know. I only came today because I hoped to make this easier for Maddie."

"Easier?"

"By letting her know she isn't alone. That she isn't the only one who has this...ability."

Blythe almost asked what ability, but she'd played this out long enough. She had known all she'd needed to know since Tewanda Hardy had said "facilitated that communication."

"What did Maddie tell you?"

"We haven't had much time to talk. I was running late this morning. I had to take my baby by my mother-in-law's before I could get over here. And he was fussy. Maybe a touch of colic. Most likely because he knew I needed to be somewhere," she said with a smile. "I think they can sense when you're in a hurry."

It sounded so normal that for a moment Blythe's uneasiness about what had been going on when she'd arrived was soothed. This woman was a mother. Surely she wouldn't do anything that would hurt another child.

"Would you like me to finish?" Tewanda asked, her voice carefully neutral.

If Blythe refused, she had no doubt this self-possessed young woman, who had left a crying baby to come here today, would turn and leave. And no doubt she could shame Delores into agreeing not to pull anything like this ever again.

That was what a normal person should do. What

any caring mother would do. Protect her daughter against whatever mumbo jumbo had been going on around her grandmother's kitchen table.

"Where's Ruth?" For the first time she realized that her grandmother, who was supposed to be in charge of keeping Maddie safe, wasn't even here.

"They rushed Miz Delray's son to the emergency room this morning," Delores said. "The one that lives in Montgomery. They think he may have had a heart attack. Miz Ruth went over there to stay with Miz Delray until they hear."

The Delrays had lived in the next house up the road as long as the Mitchells had lived in this one. Lettie Delray, née Russell, and Ruth had played together as children.

Her grandmother had probably decided that as long as Delores and the deputy were looking after Maddie, Blythe could have no objections to her consoling a friend in her time of need. And Blythe was well aware that her grandmother's presence would have been no guarantee Tewanda Hardy wouldn't have been allowed to talk to Maddie.

"I can't stay much longer," Tewanda warned. "I'll need to get my little boy home for his nap. My husband's mama got rid of her crib a long time ago."

It was clearly an ultimatum. She had come as a favor to Delores. If her services were no longer wanted, then she had personal business to attend to.

"You got nothing to lose, Miz Blythe." Delores's voice was subdued because she recognized she'd stepped over the line. "You ought to go on and let her see what she can find out."

"By asking Maddie questions? Is that all there is to this?"

"If that's all you want me to do," Tewanda said. "Most of what happens, though, your girl doesn't have any memory of."

"Because *she* doesn't want to? Or because...because whoever she's talking to doesn't want her to remember?"

"I don't know. Sometimes... Most of the time, actually, children outgrow this pretty quickly. They lose the openness that allows communication. They...close in. Psychically, I mean. Like adults, they no longer see and hear what they did when they were babies. That may be why most of the contact comes to her through dreams. Maybe that's when Maddie's most relaxed. When she's most—" She stopped, her dark eyes suddenly filled with compassion.

"Vulnerable," Blythe finished bitterly.

"It's not what you're thinking, Ms. Wyndham. Really, it's not. She's too innocent to be open to something evil. It's adults that have to guard against that. With her—with someone her age—it's only the ones like Sarah. The lost ones. The unreleased."

"Because of how she died?" Aware suddenly that Maddie was listening to every word, Blythe put her hand again on the top of that fair, silken head, her fingers trailing down the soft strands of hair.

"Maybe. Or because she has...unfinished business." Tewanda's eyes acknowledged that it might be inappropriate to speculate in front of Maddie about what that business might be.

"How do you make her remember?"

"I try to get her to relax. I reassure her. Allow her to open her mind."

"How?"

Tewanda took a breath, releasing it slowly. "Some people call it a trance. Or hypnosis. I don't call it either. I'll just try to ease the natural restraints that tell her not to see what she sees or hear what she hears."

"And if she does that—" Blythe shook her head, unwilling to submit Maddie to something she didn't completely understand.

"I know you're afraid," Tewanda said. "And I understand why. But she's *already* seeing and hearing things she can't put into any kind of context. And from what Delores has told me about the dreams… Frankly, I don't know how this could get much worse. And…I believe I can make it better."

"But you can't promise."

"If there's one thing I've learned from living with this all my life, it's not to promise anything. My feeling is…" She paused, smiling again at Maddie. "I'd like to try."

With Blythe's permission, they'd cut off the overhead light and pulled the curtains over the windows, shutting out what little sunlight the overcast sky had allowed into the room. Although not totally dark, the kitchen was pleasantly dim.

After shuffling through paper diapers, a spit-up

cloth and a tiny blue sweater, Tewanda had taken a dark gray candle out of her voluminous purse, which apparently did double duty as a diaper bag. As soon as she'd touched a match to the wick of the squat, misshapen wax, its scent had begun to permeate the room. Not quite medicinal, it was like nothing Blythe had ever smelled before, but like the dimness, she found it neither unpleasant nor frightening.

Tewanda was once more holding Maddie's hands across the table. Delores and Blythe sat in the chairs on either side of them, completing the circle. It was clear, however, that they were only spectators. The young woman with the cornrowed hair was in charge, her assurance compelling. And reassuring.

Her voice had achieved an almost singsong quality as she talked to Maddie. Its low, yet vibrant timbre, as well as her words, was intended to soothe whatever fears the little girl—and her mother—might feel.

"There's nothing here that can hurt you. Nothing that should frighten you. Nothing but another baby, just asking for your help to find her way. Another little girl just like you. A little girl who played with dolls. Who had tea parties with her babies. A little girl who loved her mama and her daddy, just like you love yours."

There was a slight hesitation in that now-familiar rhythm, and then Tewanda began again, her voice as mesmerizing, although her narrative had taken a different tack.

"She saw you over at her grandmamma's house, and she wanted to play. She was *so* lonesome being there all that time with nobody to talk to. So she talked to you. Didn't she, Maddie? She talked to you."

Maddie nodded, her eyes half-closed, as if she were drifting off to sleep.

"What'd she tell you, Maddie? What'd that poor, lonely little girl tell you?"

For a dozen heartbeats there was no response. Blythe hadn't realized she was holding her breath until Maddie took one, deep enough to be visible, and began to speak.

"She used to sleep in my room. A long time ago."

"At her grandmamma's house."

"He couldn't find her when she was there." The cadence of Maddie's words mimicked those of the woman questioning her.

He. He couldn't find her…

Blythe remembered what Cade had said about the tapping on the window. That it had been a sign that Sarah should come out to him. Apparently, he didn't come for her when she was at her grandmother's.

"She *loved* to go to her grandmamma's," Maddie finished, her voice imbued with a longing Blythe recognized as a reflection of that other child's feelings rather than her own.

"And she came here, too, didn't she? She came to see you when you moved over here to live with *your* grandmamma."

"She was so lonely. She liked having somebody to talk to."

At the depth of the pain revealed in that simple and

childlike sentiment, tears burned Blythe's eyes. She blinked to control them, knowing they would distract from what was finally being revealed.

"Did she talk to you, Maddie? What did she talk about?"

"Her mama. And Rachel. Rachel was her sister. They slept in the same bed, but Rachel slept so hard she never heard him when he came."

"But Sarah did, didn't she? She heard him every time."

Maddie turned her head down and slightly to the side, as if she wanted to flinch away from those questions.

"She didn't want him to come, did she?" Tewanda prodded softly.

"No."

"Did she tell him not to?"

Maddie nodded. "But he told her—" The words ended with a gasp. This time the shrinking was unmistakable.

"You don't have to tell me if you don't want to," Tewanda reassured quickly. "Not if it scares you."

"He scares me."

"He scared *Sarah*, Maddie. He isn't here now."

"He *was*. He was in the backyard. She told me."

"What did she tell you?"

Blythe knew the answer to this one. Her stomach twisted remembering the terror of that night.

"She told me to hide."

Tewanda's eyes lifted to meet Blythe's. Despite the dimness in the kitchen, she could read the question in them. There was no decision to be made, however, other than the one she had made when they'd started this.

She nodded, giving permission to continue. If there was a way to put an end to this madness, she had to find it. And so far, Maddie seemed unharmed by this gentle questioning.

"Did she tell you who he is?"

The small blond head moved side to side, and the tightness that had built in Blythe's chest as she waited collapsed.

"Do you know what he looks like?"

"Big. He's so big."

There was something in Maddie's voice that hadn't been there before. Something Blythe didn't like.

"Tall?"

Maddie nodded.

"Fat or thin?"

"Just...big."

It was the same route Cade had taken, with the same results. Any man would seem big to a four-year-old. Maybe even to a thin little girl of nine. There had to be something else—

"What color eyes did he have?"

Maddie shuddered, a sudden revulsion reflected in her face. Her eyes had opened, but as they were in the clutch of the nightmares, they were unseeing.

"Maddie?" The same sense Blythe had that something was wrong was in Tewanda's question.

Blythe began to push up from her chair. The sharp negative motion of Tewanda's head stopped her. Palms flat on the table, Blythe hesitated, her gaze going back to Maddie's face.

"He's not here, Maddie," Tewanda said, her voice free of the panic Blythe felt. "There's nothing here to be afraid of."

There was no response in the child's eyes. It was evident something else was going on inside the mind that functioned behind that blank stare.

"Maddie," Blythe said, only to be warned off by the same quick motion of Tewanda's head.

"It's not real, Maddie. What you're seeing is something that happened a long time ago. Something that happened to Sarah and not to you. It's over and done a long time ago. Nothing—and nobody—can hurt you here."

Maddie's breathing was coming in gasps and broken inhalations, like an exhausted runner. Or like a baby who has cried so hard there are no more tears left. It was only when her head began to jerk back and forth with each snubbing breath that Blythe gave in to her instincts.

Ignoring Tewanda's attempt to restrain her, she rose from her chair and stepped to the side to kneel and put her arms around her daughter. Maddie's body, cold and stiff, was still racked by the occasional shudder.

"It's okay, baby. Mama's here. Mama's got you. It's only a dream. This isn't real. You're at Miz Ruth's. I'm here. And Delores is here. And nothing bad is happening. I won't ever let anything bad happen to you."

Slowly, so slowly that it seemed to take an eternity,

the rigidity began to seep out of the muscles of the child Blythe held against to her chest, trying to warm her frigid body. The jerking stopped, as did the ratcheting sounds of her breathing.

Blythe hadn't known she was crying, too, until she realized her nose was running. She sniffed, turning her head to wipe her face on her shoulder.

"It's all right, Mama," Maddie said. "Don't cry. Everything's all right."

"I know. I know it is."

She turned her head, looking across the table at the young woman who had come to help. "She can't do this."

"I don't think that decision is up to you, Ms. Wyndham. Or to her."

The reality of that was another blow. And there had already been too many of those.

"She isn't strong enough," she whispered in despair, pressing her lips against her daughter's hair.

For a long moment, Tewanda said nothing. Then she picked up the candle she'd placed in the middle of the table and brought the flame close to her lips. She blew it out with one long breath before her eyes lifted to meet Blythe's.

"You pray she will be. I will, too. I'll pray for both of you."

"What about—" Blythe realized that she didn't even know what to ask.

"She doesn't know who he is, but…she's seen him. It was through Sarah's eyes, you understand, so…"

She shook her head. "I don't know if she'd even be able to recognize him now. It's been so long."

Twenty-five years. A quarter of a century since he had haunted the nightmares of another little girl.

She was so lonely. She just liked having someone to talk to.

Poor Sarah.

And poor Maddie, who hadn't asked for this. And who didn't even understand what was happening. All she really understood was that her mother had just promised that nothing bad would ever happen to her.

Although that was a promise her mother was no longer sure she'd be able to keep....

23

"It's Cade, dear. He says he told you he'd come by to check on things after the funeral."

In all that had happened after she'd gotten home, Blythe had forgotten Cade's promise. Obviously, he hadn't. And right now, the thought of having someone she could talk to honestly, in spite of his professed disbelief, was appealing.

"Thanks, Grandmamma. Can you look after Maddie?"

She had been sitting with the little girl on the worn sofa in the den, an array of books Blythe had loved as a child spread out around them. Although she herself had not yet recovered from the session at the kitchen table, her daughter seemed to have forgotten it almost as soon as they'd left the room.

"I expect I still remember how to read. What do you want to hear next, baby girl?" Ruth settled into the place on the couch Blythe had just vacated.

"We haven't read any of those." Maddie pointed to the stack to her right.

"I used to read these to your mama when she was just about your size."

"Read this one first."

"*The Little Engine That Could.* I don't need the book for this one, Maddie-love. I can say these words by heart, I've read 'em so many times."

Her grandmother's voice faded behind her as Blythe hurried down the front hall. Cade was standing in the wide double doorway to the parlor. He wore a black overcoat over his navy blazer, which gave her an idea.

"Could we talk outside?"

"Get your coat," Cade agreed without discussion.

When she had retrieved her jacket from the hall closet, he took it from her, holding it out for her to slip her arms into. As she began to do up the buttons, she felt his hands fasten lightly over her upper arms. For a moment, she stiffened, and then, without any conscious decision to do so, she leaned back, resting against his solid strength.

He lowered his head, his lips finding her ear. "It's gonna be okay. Whatever's going on, we'll handle it."

The warmth of his breath against her neck produced a sweet heat deep within her body. The "together" at the end of that promise might have been unspoken, but she heard it in her heart.

She nodded, a strand of her hair catching in the late-afternoon stubble on his cheek. Although it took a conscious effort of will, she stepped forward, breaking the contact between them.

Once out on the porch, she drew a deep breath,

pulling the cold air into her lungs. Not only did it serve to mitigate the sexual pull of Cade's touch, after the heat and closeness of the house, it also helped clear her head.

"You upset about the funeral?" Cade had propped one hip against the banister, a position from which he could see her face.

"Something that happened after I got home."

"With Maddie?"

She could hear concern in his voice. He had promised to protect her daughter, and she had learned even in the short time she'd been back that Cade took his promises seriously. And he would that one. Even if he didn't buy into what he considered her harebrained theories about what was going on.

"Do you know a woman named Tewanda Hardy?"

She could tell by Cade's hesitation that he recognized the name. His answer, when it came, seemed carefully noncommittal.

"Let's say I know *of* her. Why?"

"She was here when I got home. Delores asked her to come over and see if she could help Maddie."

"Did she?"

"I don't know."

At the time, she'd believed the session had frightened the little girl, but she could no longer make that claim. Maddie had seemed perfectly normal the rest of the afternoon.

"Then…?"

"You were right about the tapping. That's how he

called Sarah to come out of her house. But he never came when she was at her grandmother's."

"The Wright place?"

She nodded. "Maddie said she loved being there."

"*Maddie?*" Her unthinking jump from one little girl to the other had obviously confused him.

"*Sarah,*" Blythe clarified. "Sarah loved being there because he didn't come for her at her grandmamma's. She was safe."

"But *you* heard the tapping there."

"I did, but…I'm not sure that wasn't some kind of message."

"A message? A message from who?"

"From Sarah. Maybe to let us know that's how he signaled to her that he was outside."

"So now you think the tapping you heard was Sarah."

She had known this wasn't going to be easy, despite what Cade had said in the park. His belief system was as deeply ingrained as Ruth's.

"Think about it. If someone *was* haunting the Wright house, it certainly wasn't him. It's now pretty obvious that whoever was abusing Sarah isn't dead."

Another hesitation. At least Cade was thinking about it rather than dismissing what she was saying out of hand.

"Maddie told you all this or the Hardy woman?"

"Maddie. Tewanda just…" Blythe shrugged. "She just asked questions."

"She charge you?"

Although she was shocked by the suggestion, she probably shouldn't have been. It was a perfectly reasonable question under the circumstances. After all, she, too, had been suspicious of Tewanda's motives.

"I would *never* pay for something like that. To be fair, she never asked. I almost told her to stop. To go home and leave us alone. But…despite my doubts, Maddie seemed to be remembering things she hadn't remembered before."

"What else did she tell you?"

"Maddie? That he was here that night. The night I thought she'd disappeared. That he's big. I know that isn't any help, considering the information is coming from a four-year-old's perspective."

Or a nine-year-old's.

She didn't bother to pass on Tewanda's belief that Maddie had only seen him through Sarah's eyes. Cade would probably dismiss that as he had the rest.

"Anything else?"

"She asked about his eyes. That's when Maddie seemed to…I don't know. She became really frightened. Almost paralyzed with fear. The same reaction she has during the nightmares."

"She has a nice little business on the side, you know."

"Tewanda?"

"Tells fortunes. Reads the cards. I don't know what all." Cade's voice expressed his opinion of those who would pay for those things as well as those who provided them. "It's a *job* to her, Blythe. A way to make money."

"That doesn't mean she doesn't have some ability. I wouldn't think she'd be able to stay in business very long if she didn't."

"In the first place, the people who go to her are gullible enough, and susceptible enough, to make whatever she says fit their situation. And she's figured out how to be vague enough that what she says will work most of the time."

"She didn't tell fortunes or read cards this afternoon," Blythe denied, holding on to her temper. Cade was trying to protect them. That was his job. "She also didn't ask for money. She tried to help Maddie remember. And I think she did. At least about Sarah."

"With enough information it wouldn't be hard for anyone to put that particular two and two together."

"I don't understand."

"You said Delores asked her to come. Don't you think she would have told Tewanda everything she knows? The nightmares. The noises. Your interest in Sarah's murder."

"I don't know what she told her. I can ask, but it wasn't anything like you're making it out to be. We weren't victimized. She didn't plant ideas in Maddie's head. She asked questions, and Maddie answered them. At least until she asked for a description of the man who tapped on her window. On Sarah's window," she amended quickly.

"A description might have been helpful, but I guess that was too much to ask."

Although Cade's tone had been mild, the comment

infuriated her. As if she didn't understand the importance of that.

"That's the *only* reason I didn't kick her out as soon as I got home. I thought *maybe* Maddie would say something that would put an end to this. Don't you think I know how much a description would mean? There's no one in this town who has a bigger stake in finding Sarah's killer than I do. Who the *hell* do you think—" She hadn't realized the tears had started until Cade took a step forward to put his hands on the outside of her upper arms again.

"Stop it." He shook her once, hard enough to put a stop to the words that had seemed to pour out without her volition.

She obeyed, closing her mouth. She sniffed, a reaction to the cold as much as to her runaway emotions. Releasing her shoulders, Cade took a handkerchief out of the side pocket of his overcoat, taking time to unfold it before he handed it to her. She wiped her nose with it, turning away from him to look out on the front yard as she did.

"You want to try it again with me there?"

She turned her head, meeting his eyes. "Try what?"

"Whatever the Hardy woman did."

She recognized this for the huge concession it was. She had said she was the one who had the biggest stake in finding Sarah and Abel's killer. Cade would undoubtedly be next in line. That was his responsibility. Just as was protecting Maddie until he'd identified the murderer.

"I don't know that it would help. If you could have seen her..." She shook her head, remembering Maddie's eyes.

"The forensics lab didn't give us much to go on."

"With Abel?" she clarified, trying to follow the shift in topic.

"We've got a couple of bullets, but no weapon to match them to. No footprints."

"Why would he kill Abel, Cade? I know what you said, but after all this time—"

"I told you. He believes something has changed. You. Maddie. Sarah. How much have you told your grandmother and Delores about what's going on?"

"They know about the nightmares. They have almost since the beginning. The fire, of course. And that you believe it was arson."

She shook her head, trying to remember what else she'd said to them. She had tried to protect her grandmother from the most troubling of her suspicions, but you had to get up very early to pull the wool over Ruth Mitchell's eyes. And whatever Ruth knew, Delores would be privy to.

"I honestly don't remember whether I told her what I believe about Sarah, but she may well have figured it out. My grandmother is nobody's fool."

"And she loves having a good story to tell."

"I can't deny that," Blythe said tiredly.

Everything she'd said to her grandmother and her housekeeper had undoubtedly been repeated to the ladies of the quilting circle and the women of the missionary aid society and wherever else she and Delores had met their friends. It would never have crossed Ruth's mind to do otherwise.

In this closed society, those women had shared every family trauma with one another since they were young. Births, deaths, divorces and maybe even the occasional straying husband had all called for prayer and shared comfort.

Why would a little girl's nightmares be any different? Or even the possibility of a haunting?

"I think it's better if I take tonight's shift."

Another change of subject. Another delay while she tried to process what Cade had just said in the context of their conversation. "Here?"

She lifted her eyes, finding the cruiser at the end of the drive. One of his deputies had been stationed there since she had agreed with Cade's assessment that running away wouldn't necessarily put an end to what was happening to Maddie.

"Inside. If that's okay with you and Miz Ruth. I'll leave the patrolman out here, but...I'll feel better if there was somebody *in* the house as well."

It wasn't that she objected to a police presence inside. And there was no one she would trust more than Cade. The fact that he felt the extra protection was necessary frightened her, however. A fear that ate at the sense of safety being in her grandmother's house had always provided.

"Ruth won't mind. Not when she understands the reasons." She was pleased her agreement sounded normal, despite how much Cade's concern had added to her anxiety.

"And you? Will you mind?"

"I told you. I'll do anything to protect my daughter. If you think someone needs to be on guard inside, then believe me, I have no objection."

When Blythe reentered the den, her grandmother was stacking the children's books that had been scattered over the couch and the coffee table. The little girl she'd been reading them to was nowhere to be seen.

"Where's Maddie?"

"I told her I thought there were some of your dolls where you found these." It was obvious the pronoun referred to the books she was still straightening, which had come from a shelf in the basement.

Despite the steepness of the stairs leading down to what had originally been the root cellar, there was no real reason for the rush of fear prompted by the realization that Maddie had gone down there alone. It was the same reaction she'd had to Cade's announcement that he intended to spend the night here. A response to the unexpected. To the possibilities it suggested.

"You let her go down there by *herself*?"

"You used to spend hours down there when you were little. I expect, cold as it is, she won't stay long. Where do you want these?" Her grandmother held out the books she'd stacked, her eyes innocent of the horrors Blythe was imagining.

"Anywhere," Blythe said. "It doesn't matter. I'm going to check on Maddie."

"Oh, dear. Did I do something wrong? You said we should keep her in the house, but the basement is part of the house, isn't it?"

Blythe was halfway to the kitchen by the time Ruth's plaintive question was completed. She didn't bother to answer. Instead, she hurried across the sunlit room with its ever-present fragrance of coffee. She avoided looking at the table where the medium had held hands with her daughter this morning.

"I'll pray for her," Tewanda Hardy had said.

Please God she is.

The door to the basement was inside the utility room. Blythe jerked it open and flipped the switch at the top of the stairs. Its light pooled at the bottom, leaving most of the basement in shadows, despite the half window on the opposite wall, a window that had been put in place of the original door to the cellar.

"Maddie?"

No answer.

"Maddie, are you down here?"

By that time she had descended the top three steps, far enough to see the shelf where she'd found the books. The little girl wasn't there. She turned, her eyes frantically searching the other side.

Her heart leaped in relief. Maddie squatted in the shadows, peering at the shelves that lined the other wall.

"Why didn't you answer me?"

The little girl turned, her eyes luminous in the dimness. "I was looking for something."

"It's too cold to be down here. Come on upstairs."

"Miz Ruth said there were dolls."

"Well, there aren't," Blythe snapped.

Her terror had been replaced by an unreasoning anger. Anger at Maddie for frightening her? Or at Ruth for not understanding the depth of her fears?

Why should she, when you've done your best to keep them from her?

"But Miz Ruth said—"

"If there were any more toys down here, they'd be over where the books were."

"But they aren't."

"Then they aren't down here. Come upstairs."

"We could look."

Blythe descended another few steps. The shelves where Maddie stood were filled with Mason jars, both full and empty. This was her grandmother's winter pantry, filled with the canned vegetables and fruits and jellies she'd put up last summer.

"Those are Miz Ruth's. I told you. Any toys would be on the other side. Come on. I'll show you."

She came down the rest of the stairs, holding out her hand. Reluctance clear, Maddie finally moved away from the pantry. She put her fingers, which were cold to the touch, inside Blythe's. With that contact—solid, familiar, flesh-and-blood—a wave of almost physical relief swept through Blythe's body.

She squeezed the small hand reassuringly. "Let's look together."

There was no reason not to satisfy the child's curiosity. Now that she knew Maddie was all right, Blythe was more than willing to do that. Maybe it would keep her from coming down here again.

There were no toys on the shelves where she'd found the books. Certainly no dolls. Whatever Ruth remembered had at some point been thrown out or given away.

"But she *said* they were down here," Maddie argued, despite the evidence of her own eyes. "She said they were the ones you used to play with when you were little."

"Well, they're not here now. But you know what? If I played with them all that long ago, they were probably not in very good shape when Miz Ruth put them here. I was pretty hard on my babies."

"Miz Ruth said you just loved them to death."

The regionalism jarred. Of course, right now any reference to death would have seemed inappropriate. Used in conjunction with babies…

"Would a new doll do?"

"Do you have a new one?"

"No, but I know where they sell them."

Something she should have done before now. Despite how tight money was. Despite her original plan to borrow as little from her grandmother as possible. A four-year-old needed more than the bare necessities to provide a sense of normality. She needed things to *be* normal. And for a little girl Maddie's age, that meant toys.

When Blythe had selected the few items of clothing she'd bought to tide them through until her next paycheck, she had also picked up a small stuffed bear to replace the one Maddie had slept with. She knew now that she should have added a few more things to her shopping cart that day.

"At the store?" Maddie asked, the hope in her voice heartbreaking.

"You want to go? We'll have to bundle up."

"A baby doll just like you had when you were little?"

"With a bottle and everything," Blythe promised.

The Wal-Mart out on the highway would surely have something that would fill the bill. The deputy on duty in the driveway could follow them. Or he could take them.

First she would have to call Cade and tell him what she planned. Maybe he could come pick them up and take them himself. Or at least meet them.

He wouldn't understand the necessity for this, but she thought he would acquiesce if she explained. And just the thought of having him there—

She deliberately pushed the pleasure generated by that to the back of her mind. There would be time enough to deal with her newly discovered feelings for Cade Jackson when this was over.

"But first I have to make a phone call," she hedged.

"Will it take long?"

"Five minutes. You go get your coat, and I'll be done by the time you get back. And then— Then we'll go get you a baby."

24

"I promised her a doll."

"You have to know this isn't worth the risk."

Cade had tried to be low-key this afternoon, but he'd thought she understood. Whoever killed Abel seemed determined to put an end to any threat of discovery. He couldn't take the chance the murderer didn't still see Blythe or Maddie as a danger as well.

"She's four years old. She has lost everything that ever mattered to her—"

"Except you," he broke in. "How do you think she'd deal with losing you?"

He heard her exhale, but he couldn't tell if that had been done in anger or frustration. When Blythe spoke again, however, her voice was less demanding.

"All I'm asking—"

"Is to take her out in a crowd. Wal-Mart will be working, alive with shoppers. You know how fast a kid can get away from you in that kind of situation."

"I *promised* her, Cade."

If he had believed the little girl was spoiled, he

might have continued to protest. But Blythe was right. Her daughter had lost everything. Wanting her to have a doll wasn't unreasonable. He just needed to make that happen without putting either of them in danger.

"What kind?" he asked.

"What?"

"What kind of doll did you promise her?"

There was a small silence. "A baby doll. With all the accessories," she added quickly.

"What accessories?" He pulled the notepad on his desk closer, writing *baby doll* at the top of the page.

"You know. Bottle. Blanket. Booties. A sleeper or gown. A passy."

He struggled to keep up, using his own form of shorthand. He had a vague idea about booties and a sleeper. "What was the last?"

"A pacifier. Doll-size. Usually all that stuff comes in the box with the baby. Are you going to look for one?"

"I can pick it up on my way out there. Boy or girl?"

She laughed, which he didn't understand. Didn't dolls come gender specific?

"Actually... Just look for one dressed in pink."

"Got it."

"Are you leaving now?"

He glanced at the clock. Despite the fact that it was twenty past six, he was still waiting on the state lab to fax the outcome of the tests they'd done on the items collected out at the Hollow. He didn't expect those to give much information, but he'd asked for priority processing due to a child being involved. They had promised to get the results to him tonight.

He had also intended to grab supper before he showed up out at the Mitchell place. He could stop for that at one of the fast-food places on the highway when he went to get the doll.

"Maybe a couple of hours. I'm waiting on a fax."

There was another brief silence on the other end of the line. "I promised her," Blythe said finally.

"I know. I'll take care of it. I'll get there as soon as I can. Just...don't get impatient and go yourself." The lack of an immediate response made him add, "Promise me you won't do that, Blythe."

"What if the deputy—"

"*Promise* me," he demanded. "You all stay right there. Where it's safe," he added, and then, turning the screws, "where *Maddie's* safe. Promise me, Blythe."

"Okay. We aren't going anywhere." The tone of resignation was more convincing than her words.

"I'll be there as soon as I can get out of here."

The only reply was a click on the other end of the line.

It was after nine before Cade climbed the steps and rang the bell at the Mitchell house. The discount store had been as crowded as he'd anticipated, and several people had stopped him to ask for the latest information on the Comstock shooting.

They were probably wondering what the hell he was doing in Wal-Mart while there was a murder investigation underway. He had wondered the same thing as he'd searched among the cellophane-covered cardboard boxes in the toy department.

There were dozens of baby dolls, all sizes and colors, each with a different array of accoutrements. He'd read a few of the descriptions on the packages before he'd given up, grabbing the one with the longest list. It had a pacifier stuck into a hole in its rosebud-shaped mouth and was wrapped in a blanket. Although he couldn't see enough of what it was wearing to put a name to the garment or to tell if it was shod, it was definitely dressed in clothing of some kind.

Close enough, he'd decided, as he threw a couple of miniature baby bottles into his cart, just to be safe. He had fished the list he'd made back in the office out of his inside jacket pocket, mentally checking off the items.

On his way down the aisle, his attention was caught by a tiny pink fold-up stroller shaped like an umbrella. Maybe Maddie would like to play mama and push her baby around, he decided, adding the stroller to the loot in his buggy. He wasn't sure the size was right, but to his admittedly uneducated eye, it looked as if the doll he'd selected would fit.

Despite the crowd, it had taken only a few minutes at the checkout. He'd spent a few more after he'd pulled into the Mitchell driveway, conversing with the deputy on duty. Leroy Smothers had been on watch since seven. According to him, everything had been as quiet as a tomb.

Cade hadn't been particularly taken with the comparison, but as he waited for someone to open the door, he found himself hoping it would stay that way. When no one responded to the bell after several minutes, he punched the button again.

He glanced at his watch and discovered he was almost an hour later than he'd told Blythe he'd be. Maybe she wasn't answering the door because he was so late.

When a couple more minutes had dragged on without a response, a frisson of anxiety began to build in his chest. As he reached out to stab the bell again, the door opened.

Although she was fully dressed, he could tell by Blythe's eyes that she'd been asleep. She crossed her arms over her chest, huddled against the cold coming in through the open door.

"Sorry," he said, examining her face in the glow of the porch light. The fragile skin under her eyes was dark, and her hair disarrayed.

"What time is it?" she asked.

"Almost nine-thirty. You okay?"

"I fell asleep. Maddie and I were waiting and then… I guess I drifted off, too. She didn't make it much past eight."

"I'm sorry," he said again. As if to make up for his tardiness, he held the plastic bag that contained the doll and the stroller out to her. "If it's not right—"

"It'll be fine. Come on in." As Cade stepped into the hall, she closed the door behind him, checking the lock. "I don't know that I can wake her. She's out like a light."

"You can give it to her in the morning. I'm really sorry it took me so long."

"I'll put it on the bed. That way when she wakes up, she'll see it."

Although he had as little experience with four-year-olds as with dolls, Cade nodded agreement. He unzipped his jacket and hung it, along with his hat, on the hall tree.

"Would you mind…?" Blythe hesitated.

"What's wrong?" The anxiety he'd felt outside was back.

"Nothing. I was wondering if you'd carry Maddie upstairs. None of us have slept very well around here lately. Actually, my grandmother's already gone to bed. Doc's promised to take her and Lettie Delray to Montgomery in the morning to see Lettie's son. You knew he had a heart attack?"

"I hadn't heard." Not surprising, perhaps, with the department so involved with the investigation.

"I just thought if I didn't have to wake Maddie—"

"I'll be glad to carry her."

"She's in the den."

She turned to lead the way down the hall. Even in the dim light filtering from the back of the house, Cade noticed how well her jeans fit, hugging slender curves and at the same time emphasizing the length of her legs. And providing exactly the kind of distraction he didn't need right now.

When they reached the den, only the lamp on the end table was on. Bathed in its pleasant glow, the little girl on the couch looked like one of the dolls he'd seen at the discount store. She was on her side, blond hair falling over her shoulder, a few strands touching her cheek.

"You want me to take her up now?" He was reluctant to disturb the picture she made. And with all that she'd been through, he couldn't help but wonder how the child would react if she woke up to find herself in the arms of some strange man.

"She should have been in bed more than an hour ago."

He had said he was sorry. He'd brought the doll, shopping for her when half the town thought he was slacking in his duty.

And what the hell do you care what they think?

He didn't, he acknowledged. And there was nothing he could do if Blythe was angry at him being late. He'd done the best he could under the circumstances.

He crossed to the couch and scooped up the sleeping child. She didn't wake, not even when he used his shoulder to push her head more firmly into the crook of his neck. Her hair smelled of shampoo and faintly of her mother's perfume.

Even the climb didn't awaken her. Blythe led the way to the same small bedroom where he'd carried her after the fire. He waited while she turned back the coverlet and sheets before he carefully laid the sleeping child in the center of the bed.

With an economy of motion that proclaimed long practice, Blythe slipped off her daughter's sneakers. She hesitated, maybe trying to decide if she needed to undress her.

Cade couldn't see any point. The knit sweatsuit would be as comfortable as pajamas. And leaving it on would reduce the risk of waking the child, something she had wanted to avoid.

Having apparently reached that same conclusion, Blythe pulled the sheet and one of the quilts up over her daughter. Then she retrieved the box that contained the doll from where she'd laid it against the leg of the bedside table. She held it a moment as if contemplating where to place it. Finally she leaned the package against the bedside lamp, where it would be clearly visible from the bed.

Then she bent, pressing a kiss against the little girl's forehead. There was no response.

Blythe straightened, looking at him across the narrow bed. The light from the hall was reflected in her eyes, which glistened with unshed tears.

"You sure you're okay?"

Her eyes tracked back to her daughter, but his whispered question had clearly not disturbed Maddie. When her gaze returned to him, she nodded. "Long day. *Several* long days."

He knew the feeling. "You'll sleep better tonight."

She smiled, the indulgent kind a parent gives a child who's just said something not particularly bright. "I hope."

Like the scene downstairs, there was something relaxing about the dimness of the room, with its faint scent of lavender. Restful. And if there was anything he would welcome after the last few days...

Not yet. Not tonight.

"Think Ruth will mind if I make coffee in her kitchen?"

"I know she won't," Blythe said, starting toward the door. "I'll make it for you."

He had expected her to disappear into one of the other bedrooms, so her offer surprised him. "You don't have to do that."

She turned in the doorway, looking back at him. "My grandmother doesn't believe in modern coffee-makers. Have you ever used a percolator?"

"I could figure it out."

"You probably could. Eventually. But if you want *drinkable* coffee anytime soon…"

Cade had watched closely as she'd gone through the process of filling the pot with water and then spooning the coffee into the mesh basket. The aroma released from the freshly ground beans wafted upward, making her mouth water.

Despite the temptation, she knew that caffeine this near bedtime was the last thing she needed. Cade intended stay up and keep watch. That meant—barring nightmares or visions or whatever it was Maddie had had several nights ago—she could afford to sleep more soundly. Someone else would be guarding her daughter tonight. Someone far more capable of ensuring that no harm would come to her than Blythe was.

"Then you put the top on and set it on the stove." She matched her actions to the instructions. "Turn it on high. When it's hot enough, the water will begin to percolate up into the bubble at the top." She put her hand on the glass ball to point it out. "I usually cut it off at that point, but Ruth and Delores just turn it to low."

"I think I'll try your version. At least that way I won't set the house on fire—" The sentence ended abruptly as Cade realized what he'd said. "Sorry. Bad memory, I know."

"One of many." She was too tired to hide the bitterness. Besides, good or bad, she'd been honest with Cade from the first. He had no illusions about her courage or her endurance.

"They can't *all* be bad."

"They aren't," she admitted. "But that's what I hate most about this. I came back because this was the place of *good* memories. Despite my father's death, I was happy here. In Crenshaw. In this house. I was cozened and pampered and spoiled rotten. That can be very appealing when life doesn't seem to be playing fair. And frankly, I didn't think it had been. John was too young to die. Maddie didn't deserve to be orphaned. I shouldn't have to cope with either of those things. So I ran back to the place where someone had always taken care of *me*. Classic coward's way of dealing."

"If that were true, you would have moved in with your grandmother like she wanted you to."

"And in the end, that would have been the smarter thing to have done. Even in that..." She shook her head over the irony.

Realizing they were still hovering over the percolator, she turned away from the stove to lean back against the counter. Unconsciously, she crossed her arms over her body again.

"No consolation, I know, but..." Cade hesitated.

She turned to look at him and realized that, although he hadn't moved from his position by the stove, he had been watching her. Something in his eyes was different. Although she couldn't have said exactly what it was, the realization that the difference was there caused that increasingly familiar sensation in her lower body.

A reaction that she'd already acknowledged as *sexual*. Only now, more than ever, this was not the time or the place for it.

What will be the time? When Maddie's grown? When you no longer have the total responsibility for her life and happiness?

Right now, the thought of sharing that responsibility, the same kind of sharing she and John had done, was almost as appealing as what she'd just glimpsed in Cade's eyes.

Again, the coward's way. Seeking the easy solution.

Still, she desperately wanted to know the ending to that broken sentence. Maybe Cade wasn't thinking what she thought he was. And it would be better to know that now before she allowed any more of those old schoolgirl fantasies a place in her head.

"But what?"

"I'm glad you did."

The reaction that quiet assertion produced was different, centered in her chest and crowding her breathing. "Why? I've brought you nothing but trouble. Including a murder."

"You don't know that. Besides..."

She waited through this hesitation, willing Cade to say any of the things she needed him to say. No matter what came of this—or didn't come of it—she wanted to at least hear them.

"No matter what, I'm glad you're back."

Not all she had hoped for, but more than she could have imagined he'd be willing to say only a few short days ago.

"Thank you. I don't know why you would, but—"

Before she could complete the sentence, he was beside her. As he had once before, he put his hands on her shoulders, using them to turn her to face him.

Although she was tall for a woman, he seemed to tower above her until he began to lower his head, his mouth descending to meet hers. At the last second, just before their lips made contact, he hesitated.

As frustrated by his hesitation as she had been when he'd stopped in mid-sentence, she didn't wait. She put her hands on his shoulders, stretching upward to bridge the gap between them.

His mouth closed over hers, his lips warm and firm. There was no awkwardness about the kiss. No hesitation on his part. Or on hers.

With the eagerness of her response, he gathered her closer, her breasts pressed against the wall of his chest. His tongue demanded admittance to her mouth.

She never thought about refusing, although for an instant the memory of John and all he'd meant to her was in her head. But John was dead, and she was still very much alive.

This was right. And she had no reason to feel guilty about responding to another man's embrace.

She stood on tiptoe, her arms locking around Cade's neck. As her body moved into a closer alignment with his, she became aware of his erection.

Excitement tinged with a touch of fear coursed through her veins. She had been ready for his kiss—had known she was ready long before she'd admitted it—but she wasn't ready for this. To pretend she was would be a lie. And unfair to him.

She pushed away, breaking the kiss. Cade refused to release her, but he raised his head, his eyes looking into hers.

"What's wrong?"

She shook her head, lips aching for the touch of his.

"Blythe? What is it? What's the matter?"

"I can't do this."

His mouth opened, but he closed it again without saying anything. His lips flattened, pressed together hard enough that the muscle she'd noticed before jumped in his jaw. After a moment, he stepped back. "I'm sorry."

"It isn't what you think."

She could only imagine what he was thinking. That

it was too soon after John's death. That she didn't want him to hold her. Or to kiss her.

"My grandmother's upstairs," she said, and then realized how that sounded.

"Are you warning me off? Or do you think we need a chaperone?"

She was relieved that there was amusement in his question. "Maybe both."

"Well, that's a relief."

She laughed. "I told you it wasn't what you're thinking."

"Then what is it?"

"This is just…a little scary."

His head tilted. "My kissing you? Or…"

"Yeah. The 'or' part. Do you have any idea how long it's been since I've done something like this? With someone other than—" She stopped, knowing how off-putting that must be. "It isn't John. He'd be the last person to want me to stop living, but… This is just new. Even thinking about…the possibilities."

"Then you *are* thinking about them?"

"Almost since I saw you again."

His eyes narrowed. "Again?"

"You honestly never knew?" She couldn't believe he hadn't been aware of her crush. Looking back on that time, she had believed it must have been painfully, blatantly obvious.

"I don't have any idea what you're talking about."

He did, though. Maybe he hadn't before, but his eyes had again given him away. After all, he'd been the heartthrob of Davis County High. Half the girls in the school had probably fanatisized about him. About this. He had to know that, too.

"I think you do."

"Are you talking about high school?"

"Junior high. For me, at least. I was twelve. I thought you had hung the moon."

"Along about then, I thought so, too. I figured out pretty quickly once I got out of Crenshaw that the rest of the world didn't have a clue about my importance to the universe."

"We spoiled you. All the adoring throng."

"Believe me, it wasn't permanent."

"I was a little surprised…" She hesitated, unsure how to express something she'd wondered about since she'd been home.

"Surprised?"

"That you weren't attached."

"I was married. It didn't work out. Once burned, I guess… In any case, there's nobody else."

"Not from any lack of opportunity, I'm sure."

"What does that mean?"

"You're still an attractive man."

He laughed. "Thanks. I think."

"You know what I mean. I thought at first the bright lights, big city had changed you, but…you're still here. Still in Crenshaw, so… I'm sorry. I know I'm prying."

"There's no secret about any of it. I spent some time in the military. Some of it in places that made me appreciate my upbringing. I came back because I wanted to."

"I see."

"You probably don't, but it doesn't matter. I wanted to be here. I just never found anyone here that I wanted to be with. Not until now."

Although that sounded promising, Blythe tried to rein in the surge of pleasure it gave her. Wanting to be with someone might mean something very different to Cade than it did to her.

"Thank you."

"You're welcome."

There was a small silence. For a second, looking up into his eyes, she thought he might kiss her again. She wouldn't have the strength of will to protest if he did.

Instead, he stepped back, increasing the distance between them. "Where do you want me to set up camp?"

"I'm sorry?"

"I think I'll move into the front parlor. The floor in the hallway is pretty revealing. I'll be able to hear anyone going up or down the stairs. And making trips back and forth for coffee will help keep me awake."

"Whatever you think is fine. I'm grateful you're here."

"Then take advantage of it. Try to get some sleep."

"I will. I should warn you. If you hear Maddie screaming, it may just be another night terror. And once she starts, there isn't much I can do until it runs its course."

"Maybe we'll get lucky."

His smile, slightly one-sided, made her heart turn over. An old-fashioned phrase for an old-fashioned feeling.

And as far as getting lucky was concerned, she thought that, despite everything, maybe—just maybe—she already had.

25

Cade had put his cell on vibrate after Blythe had gone up to bed, but he hadn't really expected anyone to call. Certainly not at...he looked down at his watch as he fumbled the phone out of his shirt pocket...2:24 in the morning.

He flipped the case open, dreading whatever this was. "Jackson."

"Something's going on out here." The voice belonged to Doug Stuart, who'd been scheduled to replace Smothers out front.

"Like what?"

"I don't know. Something was moving in the woods behind the house. Could have been a deer. Maybe a dog, but...I thought you ought to know."

"You still in the cruiser?"

"I got out to try and get a closer look. I'm alongside the front porch. To the left as you face the house."

"Stay there. I'm coming out the front door. I'll take the other side. There's a fence in the back. Watch out for it."

"Got it." The connection was broken.

Cade pushed up off the couch, adrenaline already beginning to make inroads on his exhaustion. He unholstered the Glock as he crossed the room.

He stepped out into the darkened hall while his mind replayed the call. When he glanced up, he saw a dark shape near the front door. Reacting instinctively, he brought his weapon up, both hands around the butt. Then, knees bent, he peered into the shadows, trying to bring whatever he'd seen there into focus.

Hall tree, he realized. His own jacket providing the bulk that had seemed man-shaped.

Blowing out a breath to release his tension, he straightened, lowering the gun. He closed his eyes to fight this second rush of adrenaline, one strong enough that, on top of all the caffeine he'd consumed tonight, he was almost light-headed from its effects.

Then he hurried forward, trying to make up for the two or three seconds delay his mistake had cost. As an afterthought, he grabbed his jacket off the hook as he went by. Switching the Glock from hand to hand, he shrugged into it.

His fingers had closed around the knob of the front door when he hesitated again, mentally preparing for whatever lay ahead. Doug's assessment was undoubtedly correct. Whatever was out there was probably animal rather than human. Especially with a couple of police cruisers parked in the front yard.

With the hand that held his weapon, he turned the dead bolt. Then he allowed his fingers to complete the movement they'd begun, opening the door wide enough to slip through before he pulled it closed behind him.

The cold was so sharp it took his breath. It also cleared the last of the brain fog caused by his tiredness.

Glock in his right hand, he reached behind him with his left and tried the knob. It turned, and the door moved inward. He reached inside and pressed the button, again pulling the door to. This time when he turned the knob, the door didn't open.

Although he would have to wake Blythe up to get back in, he wasn't about to leave the house unlocked while he checked out whatever his deputy had seen. He didn't believe this had anything to do with the murders, but that wasn't a chance he was willing to take.

He glanced to his left. In the moonlight, Doug crouched at the edge of the porch, watching him through the banisters. Cade raised his free hand, making a forward motion with its index finger. As soon as his deputy nodded his understanding, Cade began moving to his right.

He switched the Glock to his left hand and placed the other on top of the porch railing as he stepped over it. Before he dropped to the ground, he looked down the side of the house.

The leafless branches of the trees at the back of the property were stark against the sky. The picket fence gleamed in the moonlight, the potting shed a hulking shadow at its back. His eyes tracked left, taking in the other outbuildings.

Plenty of places to hide. Plenty of places for an ambush. And right now Doug was making his way back there alone.

Still holding on to the top of the banister, Cade jumped off the porch, hitting the ground with a small thud. He waited through a couple of heartbeats for any reaction to the sound before he began to move in a crouch toward the fence.

He stopped when he reached the back corner of the house. Leading with the Glock, he moved so he could see around it.

Doug was already at the opposite corner. He shook his head as Cade looked across at him.

Again Cade gestured him forward. Together they trailed along the fence on opposite sides.

The back garden, exposed by moonlight, was empty. The rear of the house seemed undisturbed as well, curtains drawn over the windows and the door closed. There was no sign of forced entry, at least none visible from here.

When he reached the shed Maddie had once taken refuge behind, he turned the corner of the fence, checking out the space between the pickets and the back of the small building. It was also empty.

That left the woods at the back of the lot, where Doug had seen something moving. More than a hundred feet of lawn lay between Cade's position and those trees.

Was the watcher Blythe had seen lurking at the Wright place the night of the fire out there now? Just as he'd been here the night Maddie had hidden behind the shed.

The crack of a broken twig on his right brought his body around, the Glock again outstretched. He had already identified the sound as well as the person who'd made it before his deputy threw up his hands.

"It's me, Sheriff. Sorry."

Cade straightened. "That's a *real* good way to get shot."

The kid nodded, his hands raised as if in surrender. "Sorry. Sorry."

With a mouth gone dry at the realization of how close a thing that had been, Cade asked, "Where'd you see movement?"

"Right over there." The area Doug pointed to was at the edge of the property, where the woods dipped off into a ravine.

If anyone *was* out there, it was unlikely he would have been headed in that direction. Not unless he had better night vision than most.

Something about this was beginning to set off alarms. Hoyt had said good police work consisted of luck and instinct. And right now his instincts were all telling him—

"Get your car and drive over there. Direct the headlights where you saw movement. If you see anything, call my cell."

He had already turned, starting back toward the house when Doug stopped him.

"What are *you* gonna do?"

"Make sure everything's all right inside."

"You think—"

"I think somebody ought to check," he said as he holstered his weapon. "Since I'm the one the family knows, I guess that ought to be me."

Unwilling to explain his sense of urgency, something he didn't completely understand himself, Cade started back the way he'd come. Before he got to the corner of the house, he had begun to run. At the same time, he reached inside his jacket and pulled his phone out of his shirt pocket.

He had added the number of the Mitchell house to his contacts list the last time he'd had occasion to need it. He slowed as he climbed the front steps, scrolling down until he found Mitchell and then punching the call button.

He could always ring the doorbell, but a phone call might be less frightening. No matter what he did, he was going to jerk Blythe and, more regretfully, probably Maddie and her grandmother out of sleep. This way at least they'd know immediately he was the one seeking admittance.

He listened through four rings, his anxiety growing as it had when he'd waited for her to answer the door. *Wake up, damn it. Wake up.*

"Hello?" Blythe's voice was filled with the same sleepiness as when she'd come to the door.

"It's Cade. Come down and let me in. I'm at the front."

"What are you doing outside?"

"The deputy on watch saw something. I came out to help him look around. I didn't want to leave the door unlocked while I did. Just come down and let me in."

"Okay."

"And check on Maddie."

He wasn't sure why he'd added the last. Now that he had, he had no inclination to take it back. He didn't know what his gut was trying to tell him, but through the years he'd learned to respect that niggling sense he got when something was wrong.

"What?"

"Look in on Maddie before you come down. Just make sure she's all right."

"What the hell is going on, Cade?"

As the cold night air had cleared the cobwebs from his brain, his suggestion that she should check on her daughter had brought Blythe to full alert.

"As far as I know, nothing. Just... Just look in on her."

She slammed down the phone. Cade stood for a moment with his cell pressed against his ear, breathing still ragged from his run.

Out in the driveway, Doug started the engine of the patrol car. Its headlights came up, bright enough that Cade raised his hand to shield his eyes. The deputy gunned the motor, sending the car roaring down the right side of the house.

Cade lowered his arm, finally remembering to look at his watch. The luminous hands revealed it was seventeen minutes until three.

He closed his phone and put his ear against the solid

wood of the door instead, listening for Blythe's footsteps. Which was stupid, he realized. She wouldn't put on her shoes. Not just to run downstairs to let him in.

Another couple of minutes went by, his tension increasing as he waited. It should have taken Blythe thirty seconds at the most to throw on a robe, look in Maddie's door, and then come down the stairs. What the hell was she—

The sound of the dead bolt turning interrupted that litany of impatience. A second later the door was flung open.

"She isn't there," Blythe said, eyes wide and dark in a face that was colorless.

"What do you mean she isn't there?" He pushed past her into the front hall.

"She isn't in her bed. She isn't in any of the other bedrooms. I've searched everywhere upstairs. If she's hiding..." Her voice faded behind him as he rushed down the hall.

Hiding. That's what she had done the night she had noticed the man watching them. Cade wasn't sure what she would be hiding from tonight, but since the house had been locked tight against intruders, that seemed the most logical explanation.

Taking Blythe's word that she'd searched upstairs, he headed toward the back of the house. As he passed the front parlor, he slowed for a cursory examination, but it was obvious the room was empty.

If Maddie had come downstairs in the middle of the night, either sick or frightened, she probably would have headed to where her mother had been when she'd fallen sleep.

As he entered the den, Cade flipped the switch of the overhead fixture. Behind him he could hear Blythe and her grandmother calling Maddie's name. He continued to hunt, even looking behind the massive TV cabinet and under the throw that lay in a tangle at one end of the couch.

As Blythe and Ruth continued to search the other rooms, periodically demanding that Maddie answer, Cade moved on to the kitchen, methodically opening the base cabinets and stooping to look inside each one before going to the next. When they had all been searched, he went into the utility room, a space that had obviously been partitioned off from the original kitchen.

He felt around for the light switch, finally locating it on the left-hand side of the door. As the overhead fluorescent flickered on, what it revealed caused his growing sense of disaster to escalate.

The door to what he had to assume to be the basement stood ajar. No light came up the stairs, but the first two or three were visible through the narrow opening. He could feel the cold air seeping through it and into the warmth of the house.

"I should have thought of that," Blythe said behind him.

He turned. "Thought of what?"

"My grandmother told her that some of my old dolls were down there. We looked this afternoon, but we couldn't find them. That's when I promised I'd get her one at the store."

She tried to move past him, but he caught her arm. "You think she's gone down there to look for those dolls again?"

"The one you brought had fallen off the bedside table. Maybe she didn't see it, so she came down here to look again for mine."

Given the whole have-to-have-a-doll business from earlier tonight, something about this was finally beginning to make sense. Using his elbow rather than his hand, Cade pushed the door open wide enough to squeeze through.

"There's a light," Blythe said.

Before he could stop her, she reached in behind him to flip the switch. The glow of the bare bulb that dangled from an old-fashioned, cloth-wrapped cord illuminated little more than the area at the base of the steps.

"Don't touch anything else," he warned.

He couldn't blame her for what she'd done. Her primary concern was to find her daughter. It was his, too. But he also had the responsibility of preserving evidence if this turned out to be a crime scene.

Crime scene. With that thought, the chill in his blood was back.

"Maddie?"

There was no answer.

"You call her," he ordered. If the child responded to anyone, it would be Blythe.

"Maddie? If you're down here, young lady, you better answer me."

"Tell her I'm coming down the steps," he said softly. "Tell her it's okay. That everything is okay."

"Maddie, Sheriff Jackson's coming down there. It's okay, baby. We just need to know where you are. Did you see the doll I got you? It's in your room. I put it against the bedside lamp, but it fell off. It's got bottles and everything you wanted. There's even a stroller so you can push her around."

Still no response.

Cade eased the Glock out of its holster again, sidestepping down the first few risers until he could see the entire basement. There was no sign of the child.

Although shelves lined two of the walls, there was no furniture. And no place for her to hide.

"Flashlight." He spoke the word without turning, continuing his slow scan of the basement as he listened to Blythe climb the stairs to obey. His eyes focused on the window on the opposite wall.

It was too high for Maddie to reach. If she'd come down here, she hadn't gone out that way.

Not unaided.

If anyone *had* come in or gone out that window tonight, there would be some evidence. Marks on the sill. Or in the dust beneath it. The one thing he didn't want to do—

"Here." Blythe touched his left shoulder with the flashlight.

He reached up and took it from her, pushing the

button as he descended four more steps. The beam revealed that there was no mud or leaves on any of them, not even those at the bottom.

He directed the light over the concrete floor. If there had been enough dust to leave footprints, he couldn't see them.

He came down the remaining steps, but even shining the beam directly on the floor from a distance of a couple of feet revealed no pattern. No dust. Nothing.

He stepped off to the side of the last riser and, skirting the center of the room, walked across it to the window. Slowly he played the light along its sill and then around the frame. No debris from the ground outside clung to either.

He slipped his weapon back into its holster, freeing his right hand. He ran the tips of his fingers along the part of the sill that extended beyond the frame and then held them out in front of him. There was no telltale smudge of dirt. Either the window had been wiped or…

"Delores clean down here?"

"Of course. It's my grandmother's pantry."

Wood that was frequently dusted would make it impossible to tell by this kind of examination if someone had come into the house this way. He directed the flashlight at the glass instead. Its blackness cast back their reflections, but he couldn't tell if there were any prints on it.

The window was the type that pushed out rather than up. With the same fingers he'd used to test for dust on the sill, Cade pushed against the bottom of the single pane. Its frame creaked and then moved outward. Despite the inherent dampness of its setting, it wasn't stuck. Nor had it been locked.

"What are you doing?"

Blythe's voice. Near enough that he knew she was no longer on the stairs.

"The window's unlocked." He turned and found her standing behind him in the middle of the room.

"I'm not sure it *can* be locked. It was put in to replace the original entrance to the root cellar. Since the door at the top of the stairs *does* have a lock, I don't think anyone cared whether the window did or not."

For a woman like Ruth, who had lived in Crenshaw her entire life, that made sense. In these circumstances, it hadn't.

"You think the door at the top of the stairs was locked."

"I checked it when we came back up this afternoon."

But as soon as she'd seen the open door, she'd thought Maddie might be down here. That must mean the child knew how to turn the button.

"But she could have unlocked it. Maddie knew how to do that, right?"

"I… I think so. She's seen all of us lock and unlock them dozens of times. But if she did…?"

Then where was she?

Without attempting an answer, Cade walked back to the stairs. Despite their steepness, he took them two at a time, bursting through the door at the top and practically running out of the utility room.

Before he reached the middle of the kitchen, he had an answer to the question that had driven him up here at a run. The button on the knob of the back door had also been turned, so that it, too, was unlocked.

"What is it?"

Blythe's question was in reaction to his race to the kitchen. She hadn't yet noticed the lock. When she did—

"Oh, my God. Maddie."

Again she attempted to move past him, but he grabbed her arm, holding on to prevent her from reaching the door. "There may be prints."

She turned to look at him, her eyes questioning. *"Prints?"* And then, when she realized what he was suggesting, she asked, "You think someone *else* unlocked the door?"

"Why would she go outside?"

"I don't know. Maybe she was scared. Maybe she had another night terror." She struggled to pull her arm from his grasp.

"So she goes out into the dark? And the cold?"

He'd been shocked at how cold it was out there. If the little girl was wearing only that sweatsuit—

"I don't know. I don't *know* what she did. I just want to find her. Please, Cade," Blythe begged, her other hand coming up to flatten against his chest as she struggled to make him release her. "Please, please, just, please God, help me find her."

26

"You aren't seriously thinking somebody got into the house through that basement window, are you?"

Hoyt's question was one of many Cade had been asking himself in the hours since Maddie's disappearance. And all the others were even more unpleasant than this one.

"What I'm thinking is a little girl is missing. You have another explanation for what may have happened to her?"

"You said the back door was unlocked."

"From the inside. And it *had* been locked. I checked them myself."

All except the basement door he hadn't been aware of. If someone had come in through the basement window and found the door at the top of the stairs unlocked, they wouldn't have gone out the way they'd come in. Why go to all that trouble when you could simply unlock the back door and walk out with the child in your arms?

Had that happened while Cade had been waiting

at the front door for Blythe to let him in? He believed now that whatever Doug had seen in the woods might have been a diversion intended to direct their attention *outside* the house.

Had the killer already been inside when Cade had taken the time to lock the front door behind him? If so, who or what had Doug seen?

"You're in the house," Hoyt went on. "You got a deputy outside. And you're trying to tell me somebody comes in, snatches the kid from her bed, and then just walks out with her. That, my friend, would take balls the size of Detroit."

Or a psychosis equally as large.

"What I'm *telling* you is that she's missing. That's all I know for a fact right now."

After he'd ordered the dispatcher to call everyone back on duty, he'd sent Doug on foot into the woods where he'd seen movement. By that time, more than twenty minutes had passed. As he'd expected, neither Doug nor the deputies who had quickly joined him out there had found anything.

He and Blythe had searched every inch of the backyard and the outbuildings. Then, on his belly, Cade had searched the crawl space under the house. Using the powerful utility flashlight from his patrol car, he'd directed a beam into every dark, cobwebbed corner while Blythe and Ruth had frantically looked through the house again.

Finally, with all his deputies already out combing the community, Cade had appealed to the law-enforcement units of the neighboring communities as well as to the members of the volunteer fire departments to join in the search. Word had spread like wildfire, as it always did when someone was in danger.

By daylight, with so many other people looking for Maddie, Cade had had to deny his own need to be physically involved. No matter how much he wanted to be out in the woods, he knew he would better serve her—and her mother—by organizing the volunteers into teams and assigning them to particular areas.

He'd dispatched half a dozen deputies to Smoke Hollow as soon as he'd determined Maddie wasn't on the Mitchell property. He'd sent two more out to the Comstock place. Another team, composed mainly of volunteers, was combing the woods behind the Mitchell house. Their instructions were not only to look for the child, but to check for any sign that someone had, in actuality, been out there last night. And volunteers were once again searching the outbuildings and the house as Cade continued to mobilize the available forces.

As of yet—almost four hours after they'd discovered she was missing—no one had found any trace of Maddie. As minutes turned into hours, Cade had had to deal with the reality that any chance they had of finding the little girl alive was rapidly fading.

If she *had* walked out that back door on her own—something he found hard to believe, given the conditions—she couldn't have gotten far. Not barefoot and without a coat. Dressed as she was, hypothermia was as much a danger to her as was whoever had killed

Sarah and Abel. Either way, the longer this went on, the less chance they had of finding Maddie Wyndham alive.

If she'd been abducted, there would be no reason for the killer to hold on to her. Cade believed he'd had one intent from the night he'd set fire to the Wright place. He had meant to kill Maddie because, for whatever reason, he thought she represented a threat. Why then would he delay in attaining his objective, once he had her in his possession?

"So what can I do?" The mockery had disappeared from Hoyt's tone, maybe because he'd discovered Cade wasn't wedded to any of the elements of the case the former sheriff found so hard to believe.

Cade's eyes rose from the map on which he'd been gridding search areas to meet those of his mentor. He started to suggest that Hoyt pray, but considering the old man's unconventional views, that would come across like sarcasm. There were already a multitude of prayers being sent up on Maddie's behalf by people on a more personal basis with the Almighty than Hoyt Lee.

Hoyt Lee's talents lay in other directions. Cade might as well take advantage of them.

"Tell me what else I should be doing."

Something sparked in the faded blue eyes, but the former sheriff nodded. "You ask the state to put out an alert?"

"A couple of hours ago, but we got nothing to give them except her description. They've listed her as a possible abductee."

"Description's a place to start." The old man leaned

over the desk, turning the map Cade had been working on to face him. "Put one of your teams out here."

He jabbed a finger down in the center of a triangle formed by the Hollow, Abel Comstock's house, and the western fringes of the community. Densely wooded and impenetrable except by foot, this was the area through which many believed Sarah's murderer had traveled the night she'd been taken from her bed.

Would the killer repeat that pattern in this abduction? Why wouldn't he? Cade thought. It had worked before. That was why he'd already sent so many men into the Hollow.

"Anything else?"

Hoyt looked up from the map. "Ask the state for their tracking dogs. May be too late by the time they get 'em here, but...if a body's all we're gonna find, they can help with that, too."

Despite the despair Cade had felt as time ticked away, hearing those words spoken so dispassionately made him sick. He wasn't ready to concede that Maddie was dead. Not until someone actually found the body Hoyt had made reference to.

"He used running water before to wash away the evidence," the ex-sheriff went on. "May not work as well today. Too much technology. But maybe he don't know that."

"You're thinking he's going to take her to a creek or a river?" Cade forced his mind away from the reality that that might be *after* he killed her.

"It's what he did before."

Hoyt was right. And that was something Cade should have thought of. He turned the map, looking at areas colored blue. There were a half-dozen tributaries of the Alabama River within the boundaries of the county alone. With a car…

With a car, the bastard could be anywhere by now.

Cade had always believed Sarah's murder had been an act of rage. Sheer impulse. Unplanned.

Maddie's abduction was different. The killer had had days to make his plans. Everything he'd done, no matter how risky or audacious, had seemingly worked.

And right now, Cade was no closer to knowing who he was than he had been the night of the fire when Blythe had seen that sinister shape at the back of her property.

"Maddie? Where are you, Maddie?"

As Blythe struggled through the tangled underbrush, one of the branches she had tried to push aside struck her face. Although she had flinched away in an attempt to protect her eyes, she was oblivious to the pain of the scratch, aware only of the relentless passage of time.

Ahead of her she could hear other searchers moving through the woods, but they were no longer calling her daughter's name. That change had occurred within the last half hour, and although no one had articulated aloud the thought that had driven it, she knew what they believed.

They were all aware of how cold it was. And they had undoubtedly heard the truism cited in dozens of abduction cases—that the first few hours were critical. Too many hours had passed since she'd discovered Maddie was missing.

"Where are you, baby? Answer me, Maddie. Answer Mama, please. Nobody's mad at you. There's a new doll waiting back at the house for you. Sheriff Jackson brought it last night after you were asleep. You just need to tell me where you are." She stopped again, straining to hear some response.

She knew, because Cade had told her before he'd left for the Sheriff's Department, that there were teams spread out all over the community. Just as there were in these woods.

Still, she had to do something. She was incapable of sitting inside her grandmother's house and waiting.

"*Maddie?*" As she paused again to listen, the noise made by someone approaching from behind her caused her to turn. Delores was picking her way through the rotten leaves and deadfall, holding the neck of her old, black wool coat together with a gloved hand. She wore a cloth cloche, held on by a plaid scarf she'd tied in a knot under her chin and tucked into her collar.

"Miz Blythe, you come on home now. That baby ain't out here. Mr. Cade told you that. They've already searched these woods. Even if she *was* here, she's not here now. There ain't no sense in you being out here."

"I have to do *something*."

"Then do something that makes sense. Something that might do some good."

"You tell me what that is, and I'll do it. Don't you understand—" Blythe's voice broke.

"'Course, I do. 'Course, I understand." The old woman pulled her into her arms, holding her tight. "That baby's like my own grandchild, but you ain't helping her out here. You *know* that."

Blythe nodded, the rough wool of Delores's coat brushing her cheek. She straightened, rubbing her nose with the back of her bare hand. Her face was cold to the touch. She was cold, freezing despite her jacket. And Maddie, poor Maddie, had been wearing only that thin little sweatsuit.

"I have to do something," she said again.

"I know. I know you do," Delores said, "but I'm thinking that there's something you can do better than this. Something I'll bet nobody else has thought of."

"I don't understand."

Delores held out her hand. Without a second's thought, Blythe put hers into it, feeling the housekeeper's fingers close around hers reassuringly. "You and me are gonna look for that baby another way. A way ain't nobody else looking for her."

Delores knocked again on the clear storm door of the neat brick house she'd driven them to. "Tewanda? You home?"

The delay as they waited for the Hardy woman to answer seemed interminable to Blythe. Just like every second that passed since Maddie had been gone.

Maybe Cade was right. Maybe what Tewanda did

was smoke and mirrors, but other than physically combing every square foot of Davis County herself—

"Miz Simmons? What y'all doing here?"

"You haven't heard," Delores said, her voice flat.

"Heard what? Y'all come on in." Juggling her little boy onto her hip, Tewanda opened the Plexiglas door. "What in the world's the matter?"

"She's gone," Blythe said, bringing Tewanda's eyes to her face. "Maddie's gone."

"*Gone?* Gone where, Ms. Wyndham?"

"That's what you got to tell us," Delores said. "You got to tell us where she is so they can get her before he does— You got to do it *now*, Tewanda. There's no time to waste."

The young black woman took a step backward, shaking her head. "Miz Simmons, I'm not sure I *can* do what y'all want. I told you it doesn't work that way."

"There isn't anything else," Blythe said, feeling the hope she should never have allowed to form beginning to slip away. When it had, there *would* be nothing left. "You have to try."

Dark eyes, full of concern, studied her face for a minute. Then, without saying a word, Tewanda held her baby out to Delores. Although he started to scream the minute she released him, she didn't look back.

"In here, Ms. Wyndham," she said, leading Blythe into the kitchen. "Sorry for the mess."

She cleared a stack of folded laundry, most of it baby clothes, off an otherwise spotless table. She laid the garments on the counter near the sink. Then from one of the upper cabinets she took the same candle she'd used that day in Ruth's kitchen and put it in the center of the table.

Picturing those small, pale hands clasped in the slim brown ones that were moving now with such efficiency brought tears to Blythe's eyes. She couldn't allow images like that into her head. There was only room there for the here and now. She couldn't think of anything else until every possible means of finding her daughter had been exhausted. And if this one didn't work—

"We need to sit down. You go on and sit over by the wall." As she gave those instructions, Tewanda moved around to all the windows, closing the mini-blinds.

Gradually the room took on the same twilight-like gloom Ruth's kitchen had had. Tewanda took a match out of a holder on the stove and used it to light the candle. Almost immediately the slight medicinal smell began to scent the air.

"Ms. Wyndham, you *do* understand—"

"Don't. Just tell me whatever you can. And if you can't tell me anything, then...then, please, tell me that, too."

Tewanda sat down in the ladderback chair on the other side of the table. Eyes earnest, she said, "It's not a matter of *trying*. No matter how much you might want to get something or reach somebody that doesn't mean you're going to make the connection. You have to understand..." She hesitated again, but perhaps she read the desperation in Blythe's eyes. "Maybe I can tell you something. She trusted me once..."

Blythe nodded because she was afraid the unsteadiness of her voice would betray her. As the fumes from the candle filled the space around them, the same doubts she'd had that first day came rushing back. What was she doing here when Maddie was somewhere out there, possibly in the hands of a madman?

She'd been a fool to listen to Delores. She was an educated woman, someone who had trouble believing in the more mystical aspects of the theology she'd been raised in. Why would she be sitting here with a self-proclaimed fortune-teller while everyone else in this town was out looking for her daughter?

Tewanda didn't reach across the table to take her hands as Blythe had expected. She lowered her head instead, closing her eyes and clasping her fingers together in front of her heart. They trembled like a leaves in a wind.

After a couple of deep inhalations, she shook her head. Blythe's heart seemed to hesitate, heavy with dread.

"It's *so* hard."

"What's hard?" Blythe had asked her to tell the truth. Now that it seemed she might, she didn't want to hear it.

"Getting everything else out of my head. Letting him in."

"Him?"

"Maddie probably doesn't know where she is."

Of course. If the killer had taken her somewhere, especially if he'd transported her part of the way by car, the four-year-old could have no idea of her location.

Blythe nodded again, but she wasn't sure the psychic had seen her agreement. Almost before she'd finished her explanation, Tewanda had again closed her eyes.

After what seemed an eternity, she said, "He's close. Closer than anybody knew. Except Maddie."

"How did she know?"

"The other one."

Her mind busy piecing together the message in that cryptic sentence, Blythe almost missed the following whisper.

"Somewhere safe. Gotta get somewhere safe. Both of 'em." Tewanda's speech had slipped back into the patois of the region.

Holding her breath, Blythe waited for the psychic to reveal the location of "somewhere safe." Instead, Tewanda raised her hands from their position in front of her breasts and lowered her forehead into them. After a moment she exhaled, blowing out the breath as if she were exhausted. Only then did she look up.

"She's gone. She won't talk to me any more. She's afraid he'll find out where she is if she tells anyone."

...she's afraid he'll find out where she is...

"Are you saying...she isn't *with* him?"

Tewanda shook her head. "She was running from him."

Hope moved again in Blythe's chest. "You mean... when she left Ruth's?"

"Yes, ma'am. He doesn't have her, Ms. Wyndham, but she knows he's looking for her. She'll stay hidden."

"Where?"

"She wouldn't tell me that. She was too afraid."

What had only seconds ago seemed a message of hope was worthless. *Somewhere safe.* And he's *closer than anyone knew.* Meaningless phrases in terms of actually *locating* Maddie, but exactly what any mother would want to hear about her missing child.

Tewanda Hardy had given her what she wanted. Just as Cade had said she would.

"She knows he's after her because *Sarah* told her he was?" Blythe could hear the growing emotion in her own voice.

Tewanda's eyes widened. "If you don't want to believe me, it's all right. A lot of people want to discount what I say, but…I swear I've told you everything I know. All she was willing to tell me. I'm gonna pray for your girl, Ms. Wyndham. I'm gonna pray that the Lord will take good care of her until you can find her."

"You're telling me that you just communicated with my daughter, but you can't say where she is."

"I told you. She wouldn't tell me because she's afraid that if she tells anybody—"

Blythe stood, pushing her chair into the wall behind her. "Sheriff Jackson was right."

"Sheriff Jackson?"

"This is just a source of income to you. A way to prey on the gullible. If I put some money on the table, would I get some more information? Of course, no matter how solid you'd have made that information seem, I doubt it would have told me any more than I know right now."

"That's *enough*, Miz Blythe. You've said enough."

She looked up to find her grandmother's housekeeper jostling the now-calm baby on her narrow hip, her little finger in his mouth. Delores's voice had held a warning, but Blythe was long past heeding it.

"You have any cash on you, Delores? Put some down on the table. Let's see how much better she can communicate with Maddie if I'm willing to pay."

"There's no call for that kind of talk," Delores scolded. She walked across the room and handed the little boy back to his mother. "I'm sorry. You try to forgive her, you hear. You think how you'd feel if it was yours that was missing."

Tewanda took the baby and cradled him against her chest, before she looked up at the housekeeper. "It doesn't matter, Miz Simmons. Sometimes when she can listen, you tell her I would have helped if I could. That's all I ever wanted to do."

Delores nodded. Then she walked over and took Blythe's arm, leading her like someone who was blind out of the room and then out of the house.

She never said another word to her, not even when the sobs that started before they'd left the driveway racked Blythe's body.

27

Cade had just gotten off the phone with the FBI office in Birmingham when Jerrod stuck his head inside his office.

"The kid's mother's outside. She's asking for you. You want to talk to her?"

Cade took a breath, thinking about what little information he had to tell Blythe. And none of it positive. That was something he wasn't looking forward to.

"Give me a minute."

"I'll tell her you're on the phone." The deputy disappeared.

Except Cade wasn't willing to lie to Blythe. Not even a small lie. Not in a situation like this. As Maddie's mother, she deserved the truth, no matter how unpalatable it might be.

"Jerrod," he called. After a second the kid stuck his head into the door again. "Go ahead and bring her back."

"Looks like she's been crying." Although the boy waited, as if he expected that to change Cade's mind, eventually he disappeared again.

Cade looked down at the map and the sheets filled with notes spread over his desk. He tried to think of anything he hadn't done, any avenue he hadn't investigated. If there was one, neither he nor Hoyt had been able to come up with it.

He raised his eyes from the clutter to find Blythe standing in the doorway. Jerrod was right. She'd been crying. The reality she had been trying to keep at bay earlier this morning had obviously set in.

"Any word?"

He shook his head, wishing he had something—anything—to tell her. "They've put out the alert. Maybe we'll get something useful from that."

"You think he'd take her out of the area?"

He didn't. And he could tell by her tone she didn't either. Still, the pattern they were all going by had been established twenty-five years ago and in circumstances that were totally different. What was to say the killer would do things the same way he had back then?

"I don't know. All I know is the more eyes we have looking for her, the better."

"It's so cold out there." Blythe had wrapped her arms across her body, despite the navy wool jacket she still wore.

There was nothing comforting Cade could say to that. What Maddie had been wearing was one of the first things they'd established, once they resigned themselves to the fact that she wasn't in the house.

The jacket Blythe had bought her after the fire had still been hanging in the closet. The only item of clothing missing was the pink sweatsuit they'd put her to bed in.

"We'll find her."

So much for telling her the truth.

He brushed the thought from his mind. There was a difference between lying and giving someone hope. And if Blythe couldn't find some reason to hope pretty soon…

He stepped out from behind his desk, drawn by the suffering in her eyes. He grasped her elbow, pulling her farther into the room. With his other hand, he closed the door, turning the lock. Almost in the same motion, he took her in his arms.

He expected resistance. Instead she leaned against him like a tired child, laying her head on his shoulder. With his hand, he soothed up and down her back.

After a moment she pulled away, looking up at him. "If we don't find her soon—"

"It doesn't do any good to think like that. We'll find her. There are too many people out there looking for her for us not to."

"Even if *he* didn't take her, Cade, it's too cold out there. So cold."

"Kids are more resilient than you think."

The same thing he'd told her the night of the fire, he realized. It had been evident she hadn't believed him then. Why should she now?

"Have you thought of anything else?" It was better to redirect her focus onto the search rather than its possible outcome. "Anything she said last night.

Anything—" He broke the question because she'd begun to shake her head.

"I've gone over everything. Other than going down to the basement to look for my dolls, nothing out of the ordinary happened yesterday afternoon. She wasn't agitated or upset. She seemed perfectly normal."

"If she left the house on her own—"

Another side-to-side motion of her head. "She's never done anything like that before. Going down into the basement maybe. I could see that because she'd been down there earlier in the day. But to unlock the door and go out into the dark? No." She shook her head again, more emphatically this time. "Maddie would have *known* that wasn't something she should do."

"Maybe she was going to the store."

"Without money? She understands you have to pay for things. She's a very bright little girl."

Blythe seemed more convinced than she had been last night that her daughter hadn't walked out that back door on her own. The only other option…

"Blythe, if he took her, then… You said the doors were locked. That there was no doubt in your mind. If he took her, then she had to unlock one of those two doors for him. You *do* understand that, don't you? She would have had to let him into the house. Why would she do something like that?"

If Maddie was as smart as her mother thought, why open the door to a stranger?

"Maybe…for the same reason Sarah did."

Abel had told Blythe that whoever killed Sarah had been someone she trusted. For Maddie, who'd been in town only a few weeks, Cade couldn't imagine who that could be.

"You think she *knows* him?"

For a long time Blythe said nothing, looking down at her hands. Finally she shook her head. "You asked me if there was anything else."

His gut tightened as he tried to imagine what she was about to tell him. Judging by her voice, it was nothing he wanted to hear.

"I went to see her, Cade. I thought maybe…if no one else could find her, she could."

"Who?"

"Tewanda Hardy. I thought maybe she could see where Maddie is."

"Blythe—"

"I know. I know now how stupid it was. You were right. She tells you whatever you want to hear."

"So…what did she tell you?"

He was careful to keep his question neutral. It was obvious that, whatever the psychic had said to her, she hadn't produced the results Blythe had been hoping for.

"She told me Maddie's safe, but that she was afraid to tell her where she is because if she did, he might find her." She laughed, the sound bitter.

"Then… I don't understand. What does that have to do with Maddie unlocking the door to someone?"

"It's not that. It's what the Hardy woman said before. At my grandmother's house. She said that Maddie had seen him, but only through Sarah's eyes. I thought… I thought maybe Sarah told her to open the door."

"To the man who *killed* her?" Despite his outward rejection of what Blythe was saying, even the thought made his blood run cold.

"Maybe for some reason she's repeating the pattern. Maybe *she's* in control. That's why I went there. I thought if Tewanda couldn't contact Maddie, maybe…"

"*Sarah?* You thought *Sarah* could tell us where she is?"

"If he took her, Maddie may not know where she is. Tewanda said that. And there's a kind of twisted logic to it. I thought maybe Sarah…" She shook her head again. "I know that's insane. But then, so is someone kidnapping a little girl because Ada Pringle said I was going to write a book. *Nothing* about this makes sense. It hasn't from the first." She stopped, closing her mouth and turning away from him.

"I'm going to get somebody to take you home."

"I don't *have* a home. I don't have anything anymore. Without Maddie—" Her voice caught on a sob.

"Is your grandmother still at home?"

"What?" The blue eyes came up, awash with tears.

"You said she was going with Doc to Montgomery today."

"Doc called and canceled the trip. He said he was going to join one of the teams."

Cade hadn't seen the old man, but that didn't mean anything. There were probably dozens of people out looking on their own. If he knew where Doc was, he would ask him to give Blythe something. It was time to start numbing the pain she was in. To deaden the emotions that were tearing her up inside.

"Everybody's out there. We'll find her."

Her eyes called him a liar, but she nodded. "I know." She said it because she couldn't say anything else. They both knew it.

"You go home now and get some rest. No more running around. I need to be able to get in touch with you as soon as we find her. You're going to be the one she needs most."

She nodded again, a glimmer of hope he'd had no right to offer in her eyes. She sniffed, using her fingers to wipe from her cheek the single tear that had escaped.

"Here." He took his handkerchief from the back pocket of his pants and handed it to her.

While she used it, he walked back to the desk and pressed the intercom. When Jerrod answered, he said, "I need someone to drive Ms. Wyndham home."

"Delores is here," Blythe said. "She's waiting outside. She drove me—" She hesitated, allowing him to fill in the blank.

Delores had been the one who'd taken her to see the Hardy woman, of course. She was the one who had brought the woman to the house the day of the funeral. He doubted Miz Ruth would have put up with anything that smacked of the occult.

"She'll take me home," Blythe finished.

"You *stay* there. Stay where I can find you. I'll call you as soon as I know something."

"You swear you'll call? No matter what?" Her eyes clung to his, demanding his oath.

"I swear. As soon as I know anything."

Her grandmother had insisted she lie down before she fell down. Plied with a strong whiskey and three aspirin, Blythe had finally given in. Eyes closed, she had listened as the two old women lowered the shades and then pulled the drapes across the windows in the bedroom Ruth had occupied since her marriage.

They wanted to tend to her, and it no longer mattered to Blythe where she waited. There was a phone on the bedside table. If Cade called—

She closed her mind to that possibility, trying to concentrate on something other than the two-edged sword hanging over her. No matter what happened, Cade had promised to let her know as soon as he knew anything.

No matter what...

She opened her eyes again, looking at the clock on the table beside the phone. Almost eleven. How many hours, she wondered, trying to add them up in her head, despite the slight buzz caused by the drink Delores had pressed on her.

More than eight. Eight endless hours.

How long had it taken him to do what he'd done to Sarah? No one knew, because no one had known when he'd abducted her. Just as no one knew how long Maddie had been gone when they'd discovered she was missing.

While she was kissing Cade in the kitchen? Had

someone come into the front of the house while they'd been back there? Maybe she hadn't relocked that door when she'd let Cade in. Maybe—

She forced her mind away from the fruitless merry-go-round of speculation. Cade had told her there was nothing to indicate anyone had entered the house last night. No evidence on the basement window. Or on the outside of the back door.

It was possible Maddie had done exactly what he'd suggested. Unlocked that door herself and walked out into the night.

Except Blythe didn't believe that. It made no sense. Why in the world would she leave the warmth and safety—

Somewhere safe. Gotta get somewhere safe. Both of 'em.

She turned her head on the pillow, closing her eyes to shut out the memory of Tewanda's words. There was a hot corner in hell for people who took advantage of those gullible enough to believe—

In ghosts? In restless spirits trying to communicate with the living?

Wasn't that what she'd begun to believe about the things that had happened since they'd moved back here? The night terrors. The tapping on the window—

She sat up straight in bed, her mouth opening and then closing as the memories swirled through her brain.

Rachel was her sister. They slept in the same bed, but Rachel slept so hard she never heard him when he came.

But Sarah did, didn't she? She heard him every time…

She used to sleep in my room. A long time ago.

He scares me.

He scared Sarah, Maddie. He isn't here now.

He was. He was in the backyard. She told me.

What did she tell you?

She told me to hide.

She loved to go to her grandmamma's. He couldn't find her when she was there.

Somewhere safe. Gotta get somewhere safe. Both of 'em.

She threw off the quilt her grandmother had spread over her legs, almost falling in her haste to get out of bed. Someone would have checked. She had told Cade yesterday what Maddie had said. He would have sent someone over to the Wright place. Surely he would have sent someone.

Even as she tried to reason with her excitement, she was pulling on her shoes, her hands trembling over the laces. There were literally hundreds of people out there searching. Surely someone—

Her hand closed around the receiver. She brought it up to her ear as her fingers hesitated over the numbers.

Finally she gave up trying to remember Cade's and punched in 911. It took half a dozen rings for the dispatcher to pick up, long enough that Blythe had had to fight the urge to slam the phone back down in its cradle.

"Davis County 911. What's your emergency, please?"

"I need to talk to Sheriff Jackson."

"Is this an emergency, ma'am?"

"This is Blythe Wyndham. My daughter is the little girl—"

"Yes, ma'am, I know about your daughter. Is she there?"

"What?"

"I thought maybe that's what you wanted to tell the sheriff. That you'd found her."

"No. Look, please, I just need to talk to him. Can you connect me? Or just give me the number?"

"To the Sheriff's Department?"

Dear God, Blythe thought, closing her eyes. "Yes, please. To Sheriff Jackson."

"I can connect you."

After a moment Blythe heard a phone ringing. She waited again, counting the rings.

"Davis County Sheriff's Department."

It was the kid who had taken her back to Cade's office. She recognized his voice.

"This is Blythe Wyndham. I need to speak to Sheriff Jackson."

There was the slightest hesitation. Maybe he was checking. Maybe—

"He's on another line, Ms. Wyndham. I think he's talking to the FBI. I can have him call you. You gonna be at this same number?"

"No."

Until she said the word, she hadn't made up her mind. She had intended to ask Cade if anyone had looked out there. Now, however…

"Could you just give him a message, please. As soon as he gets off the phone. It's very important."

"Yes, ma'am. Can you hold on one second…" There

were paper shuffling noises in the background. "Okay."

"Ask him— No. *Tell* him that I've gone out to the Wright house. Tell him that... Tell him that Sarah always felt safe there. Maybe... Maybe that's where she's gone."

"Sarah?"

"Maddie. My daughter. Tell him I think she may have gone to the Wright's house."

"Ms. Wyndham, don't you remember? The Wright's house burned to the ground."

His tone was one you'd use to a child. Or to someone whose mind was clouded with age. Condescending. Slightly pitying.

"I was *there,*" she said. "I'm not likely to have forgotten. Do you have the message?"

"Yes, ma'am."

"Then you see to it that Cade gets it as soon as he gets off the phone. Do you understand me?"

"Yes, ma'am. Whatever you say." Snotty, yet still polite.

"What I *say* is, if Cade doesn't get this message, I can assure you he isn't going to happy with the one who screwed up. In case *you've* forgotten, there's a homicide investigation as well as a kidnapping going on."

"No, ma'am. I haven't forgotten." Subdued. There was no longer any trace of youthful arrogance in the voice.

"Then whatever you do, don't forget this either."

Without waiting for a response, she carefully put the phone down on the cradle, struggling for control.

She took a deep breath, her promise to Cade echoing in her heart.

She had tried to get in touch with him. She'd tried to explain. After her reminder of what was at stake, she believed that the kid would tell him where she'd gone. And she had no doubt as soon as he knew what she was thinking, Cade would come.

The more she thought about this, the more certain she was that she was right. If she was, she owed Tewanda an apology. Tewanda *and* Delores.

Please, dear God, let me be right.

She was almost to the door when the thought struck her. If she hadn't been in this room, it probably wouldn't have crossed her mind, but since she was…

She turned, retracing her steps to the highboy. She opened the small middle drawer at the top. Her grandfather's Colt lay where she'd hidden it in an effort to protect Maddie.

Gingerly, her fingers curled around the coolness of its metal. She picked it up, again surprised by its weight.

Despite growing up in a culture that valued firearms, she had never been comfortable around them. Thanks to that upbringing, however, she knew how to fire a gun. As to why she wanted to take this one with her…

For the exact same reason she had put it away. In order to protect her daughter. And she would do that any way she could.

28

"Sheriff! Got a message here for you."

Jerrod's call stopped Cade before he could escape down the hall to his office. He had just spent twenty minutes in the street outside answering questions from the media outlets that had picked up on the alert.

When he'd stepped back inside, the reception area had been crowded with people. Volunteers who'd come to offer their help. Deputies from both Davis and the adjoining counties, who had just come in from the field. Townspeople who had stopped by for a progress report or to be a part of the excitement.

He turned to see the kid at the reception desk holding up a folded sheet of paper. At least Jerrod had sense enough not to blurt out whatever information it contained.

Cade walked over to him, nodding to a few people he hadn't yet spoken to this morning. He reached for the note.

"Oh, and the kid's mother called," Jerrod said as he placed the paper in his hand. "Said to tell you she was going out to the Wright place. Something about her daughter always feeling safe there."

"Are you sure it was Ms. Wyndham?" So much for convincing Blythe to stay put.

"Yeah, but... I think maybe she's losing it. I mean it's understandable and all, but she kept talking about Sarah. Like maybe she was thinking that her daughter... You know."

"How long ago was this?"

"Maybe...ten minutes. Could have been a little more than that. It's hard to keep track of when calls come in, with as many as we're getting. I know she called before I took that one." Jerrod nodded to the note. "That's from the police in Dothan. They think they may have a sighting."

Cade fingered the paper open and read the contact information for the Dothan Police Department. "Any details?"

"Just that. Said for you to call 'em."

Cade nodded. He turned, intending to do that from his office before he went out to the Wright place to check on Blythe. Hoyt was standing behind him, so close he'd almost run into the old man.

"They got something in Dothan?"

"Maybe. Doesn't sound too definitive."

"You'll get a lot of those. It's the price you pay with an alert. Every whiny, blond-headed kid who needs a nap and is being drug through the mall instead is gonna have folks spending a quarter to call the locals."

"You're probably right."

"You okay?"

"Just..." Cade shook his head. "Feeling pulled in a dozen directions and none of them leading anywhere."

"You're doing good. Just keep on doing what you're doing. There ain't any more you can do, Cade, believe me."

"I need to go check on Blythe."

"Want me to go over there?"

"She's gotten it in her head that Maddie might have gone back to the Wright place."

"She thinks he took her there?"

"I think she believes the kid went there on her own."

"That's probably... What? Four miles. She thinks a four-year-old is gonna walk that far. Even if she could find her way over there—"

"It's less than that if you don't stick to the roads."

"And that baby's gonna know those shortcuts? Sounds like the poor girl is clutching at straws. Even if the kid wanted to go back there—"

"It isn't that."

As Cade tried to think how to explain Blythe's obsession with Sarah's murder and that house, he became aware that other people were listening to their conversation. He took Hoyt's arm to draw him down the hall to the privacy of his office.

"So what *is* it?" Hoyt asked as Cade pulled the door to.

"Just..." Cade realized that nothing he could say would ever make the pragmatic ex-sheriff understand how a child who'd been dead for twenty-five years was playing a part in this. "I don't know. Maybe you're right. Maybe Blythe's gone off the deep end, but I still need to go see about her."

Hoyt said nothing for a moment. "Like that, is it? 'Bout damn time if you ask me."

"I didn't," Cade said shortly. "What I *am* asking you is to check with this guy." He held out the note from the Dothan police. "See how reliable their sighting is. If there's anything to this, get all the details you can."

Hoyt retrieved his glasses from his shirt pocket before he took the paper. He read the note through the bottom of the bifocals and then looked up at Cade. "When you get Blythe, you bring her here. By the time you get back, they might have apprehended whoever this is. Somebody'll have to go over there and identify the child."

Cade nodded, but his mind was still on the other message Jerrod had given him. It wasn't Maddie who'd felt safe at the Wright house. It was Sarah.

Because the killer had never come there to find her.

There was some logic to the idea that Maddie might go there. *If* she'd been running away from someone. And if, like that night in Miz Ruth's backyard, Sarah had told her to hide.

So now you've bought into Sarah guiding her? Sending her to the place where she *always felt safe?*

Which made him just as gullible as all those people the Hardy woman bilked out of their hard-earned money.

"You going?"

Cade looked up to find Hoyt watching him over the tops of his glasses. "Yeah. Yeah, I am. You can handle this?"

"Since before you was sucking on your mama's teats."

"Thanks, Hoyt."

"You bring her on back. Maybe we'll have some good news by the time you get here."

Blythe pulled her car into the drive, automatically maneuvering it to the space in front of the detached garage. Where she'd always parked when they'd lived here, she realized.

She hadn't been back since the morning after the fire. Not even to see if there was anything left to salvage.

The still-smoldering ruins had told her then all she needed to know. Looking at those same ruins through the car window now made her realize how ridiculous it was to think Maddie might have come all this way.

As long as she was here...

She took a breath and then opened the door. When she stood up, she could see the shell of the house over the top of the car. Behind it stretched the same swath of winter-dead grass she'd hobbled across that night in an attempt to stop Maddie from running straight into the arms of a madman.

The same reason that had sent her here today.

She closed the door, the sound seeming to echo in the surrounding stillness. She had been aware of the house's isolation during the time they'd lived here, but she'd never felt it more strongly than this morning.

This place seemed to exist on a different plane from the frenzy of downtown.

Everyone else was out looking for Maddie, and she was here. Once more listening to a cold wind sweep through the pines that lined the back of the property.

She walked to the front of the car and slipped the lock out of the hasp of the garage door. She pushed it open, hinges protesting as they always had. The thin winter sunlight filtered into its dim interior, exposing the few rusting tools hanging on the walls. Cans of paint whose colors she'd never had time to explore. Even the push mower her landlady had assured her she'd be welcome to use "come summer."

There was nothing else. No cabinets or toolboxes. No storage units. Nowhere to hide.

"Maddie?"

The word seemed tentative. Too soft. But the sound echoed in the empty space.

"Maddie, are you in here?" She had strengthened her voice, but there was still no response.

She hunched her shoulders against the cold and her growing sense of despair. As she turned to step outside, she started to put her hands into the pockets of her jacket for warmth. The right one encountered her grandfather's pistol, its metal colder than her hands.

Her eyes scanned the huge lot, skimming across the ruin, still surrounded by yellow crime-scene tape, and then tracking back to the trees. Her breath formed a white cloud of vapor before her as she began to walk toward the remains of the house.

Part of a wall on the far side was still standing. As she approached, she could again smell the acrid stench that had filled her nostrils during that terrifying flight across the roof. With it, the sense of panic she'd felt then returned.

They had almost died that night. Both of them.

That had been his plan. And except for a closed door, it would have succeeded.

She had reached the yellow tape, which was held up by stakes driven into the ground. She bent, slipping under it.

When she straightened, she could see over the pile of charred timbers that were all that was left of the walls on this side. The side where the fire had started.

"Maddie? Where are you?"

She had pitched her voice to carry across the shell. The wind, however, seemed to catch the words and throw them back at her, rendering them powerless.

She turned her face away from it, calling again. "Maddie? Answer me, Maddie? I've come to take you home."

I don't have a home. I don't have anything anymore. Without Maddie…

"Maddie, are you here?"

Something stirred in the rubble. A scurrying noise like rats in a wall.

Blythe's head snapped around as she tried to determine what she was hearing. Whatever had made the sound, it seemed to originate near the center of what had at one time been her home.

Holding on to the top of the pile of rubble in front

of her for balance, she stepped across blackened timbers and into the house. As soon as she put her weight down on her lead foot, whatever she'd been standing on shifted. She would have fallen had she not been holding on to something. As it was, her ankle, the one she'd injured the night of the fire, twisted.

She gasped with the pain, but then, determined to reach the place from where the sound came, she ignored it. Still holding on to the fallen timbers, she brought her other foot across.

Limping slightly, she picked her way across what was once the parlor, where most of their possessions had been stored. She didn't bother to look at the charred and waterlogged objects in her path, other than to avoid them.

Given the almost total destruction of the house, it didn't take long to become confused as to what room she was crossing. The blackened refrigerator, however, still stood against the wall the fire had not brought down. Using it as a point of reference, she began to move in that direction.

When she reached the area where she believed the sound had originated, she stopped. "Maddie? Maddie, where are you?"

Then she waited, listening for a repetition of what she'd heard. If it had been an animal, her nearness would cause it to freeze. If it had been something else—

A low creak sharpened her focus on the part of the ruin that had been the kitchen. As she watched, a small section of the floor seemed to undulate.

She blinked to clear the wind-induced moisture from her eyes, trying to figure out what she was seeing. The sheet linoleum had been burned away or melted by the fire, but the subfloor seemed intact. Despite the scorching they'd received, she could even distinguish the pattern of the boards.

The section that had shifted before moved again, literally lifting away from the surrounding planks, revealing a dark narrow line.

Trapdoor. Blythe's realization of what she was seeing was instantaneous. No longer conscious of the dangers of the uncertain footing, she ran toward it.

She grabbed the edge and tried to throw the door back, but its weight was too great. She stooped in front of the crack, putting her fingers around the raised edge, preparing to use the larger muscles in her hips and thighs to provide the leverage needed to lift it.

Before she did, she whispered the word she had shouted this morning until she was hoarse. "Maddie?"

"Mama?"

As if the trapdoor weighed nothing, Blythe lifted it and threw it back. It crashed into the burned floorboards, sending up a cloud of soot and debris.

Blythe was unaware of any of that. The world had shrunk to a pale, ash-smeared face and a pair of wide blue eyes looking up at her from what appeared to be a hole under the floor of the Wright's kitchen.

A well, she realized belatedly. An inside well, from the days before they'd had city water out this far. Covered over as it had been by the flooring, she'd had no idea it was here. How her four-year-old could have known…

She reached down, holding out her hand. After only the slightest hesitation, Maddie put hers into it. Blythe pulled, lifting her up and then squeezing her against her chest without allowing her feet to touch the floor.

"Maddie. Maddie."

She held the little girl away from her, unable to believe she'd really found her. Stifling the sobs that formed in her throat, she asked, "Are you hurt?"

The blond hair, as begrimed as her face and hands, swung against her shoulders as the child shook her head.

"What are you *doing* out here?"

As she waited for an answer, the blue eyes moved away from her face, seeming to focus on something behind her. The hair began to lift on the back of Blythe's neck. Almost afraid to turn and see what her daughter was looking at, she pivoted on her toes to face the road, keeping one arm around the little girl.

A police cruiser was pulling into the driveway. The rush of adrenaline eased, allowing her to take a breath. She hugged Maddie to her side. "It's okay," she comforted.

In response to that reassurance, the little girl melted against her. When the door opened and Cade stepped out of the patrol car, Blythe took another breath, her euphoria producing an inclination to laugh hysterically.

Why shouldn't she? She'd been afraid that she had lost Maddie forever, and yet here she was, apparently unscathed by her ordeal. And now Cade was here to ensure that whatever had happened to drive her daughter into the cold and the darkness last night wouldn't happen again.

"Blythe?"

"I found her," she shouted, the wind once more whipping the words away. "She was in the old well pit. She seems to be—"

She stopped because Cade's hand had jerked upward as if he were reaching for his hat. It flew off, spinning backward.

She had time to think that the wind had caught it before the sound of a rifle shot cut through the stillness, destroying any pleasant fantasy about what was happening.

Her arm tightened around her daughter to pull her closer. Unable to tear her eyes away, she watched Cade's body react again, the upward movement of his hand stopped in mid-motion to clutch at his chest. The second shot was an echo to the first, although everything seemed to be happening in slow motion.

"Cade!"

Her scream, too, was snatched away by the wind. Unable to believe what she was seeing, she watched as he began to fall backward. His body hit the ground hard enough that his head bounced.

And then he didn't move again.

29

Without thinking, Blythe straightened up and began to run toward Cade, again screaming his name. The third shot was so close the bullet brushed her hair, causing her to duck.

With the realization that the shooter was now targeting her, the shock she'd felt watching Cade fall was replaced by a fierce instinct to protect her child. She turned and grabbed Maddie, carrying her down with her, as she threw herself onto the charred boards of the kitchen floor. The pale pink sweatsuit would provide too clear a target against the blackened material around them.

She thought for a second or two about lowering Maddie back into the pit of the old well where she had been hiding and then crawling in with her. But what had been a place of safety then would now become a trap. All he would have to do would be open the trapdoor and fire down at them.

Like shooting fish in a barrel.

She pushed the image from her mind, trying to

think. Cade had fallen backward. And his hat had spun off in that direction. Which meant…

Keeping Maddie shielded under her body, she raised her head a couple of inches, her eyes searching the line of trees where she'd seen the dark figure the night of the fire. Had he again come through the woods from Salter Road?

If so, he would disappear back that way when he was finished, leaving no sign he'd even been here. No sign but their bodies.

Not Maddie, she vowed, remembering what he'd done to Sarah. She would never let him reach Maddie.

She could see nothing in the woods except the dark, straight trunks of the trees. She knew in her heart that he was out there, just as he had been the night of the fire. She could feel him. Waiting for her to make a mistake.

She turned her head, trying to see Cade. Of course, if he were still conscious, he would be doing exactly what she was—giving the killer as little target as possible.

"Cade?"

The killer knew where she was. There was no need for silence. If she could just know that Cade was there… That he was aware of what was going on…

"Cade?" Although this time she pitched her voice to carry against the wind, again there was no answer.

"Mama?"

"Shh," she soothed automatically, turning back to Maddie.

With her right hand she cupped the little girl's cheek, offering what comfort she could. She'd come too far to let him win now. She had Maddie in her arms once more, and she would never let anyone take her away from her. Not as long as there was breath in her body.

She looked back toward the woods, wondering what he was doing. Using the trees for cover, was he even now drawing closer to their position? The forest continued to the right of the property, forming a semicircle. And with the garage on the left…

She turned her head to survey that area. Although she could see nothing out of the ordinary, she wondered if he'd used the seconds she'd cowered here, head down, to flank them?

He had all the advantages. He could see her, but she had no idea where he was. If she tried to move, she'd expose both of them to that deadly rifle fire. There wasn't enough left of the house to provide cover for any maneuver she could think to make. And, forced to keep her head down as she was now, she might not even be aware of his approach.

"Mama?"

"Shh. Be quiet, baby. I need to listen."

The wind would mask most sounds. By the time the killer was close enough to make any she could hear, it would be too late.

With that realization, she eased her grandfather's Colt out of her jacket pocket. Despite acknowledging that it might be their only hope, she was strangely reluctant to have it so close to Maddie. Until today, she had seen her role as keeping guns *away* from her daughter.

Now... Now it was to defend her with one. As well as with her own life.

And there has to be a better place to do that than this.

Raising her head again, she examined as much of their surroundings as she could, given her limited field of vision. The refrigerator she'd noticed before made a ninety-degree angle with the one remaining wall.

If she could get Maddie into that corner, she would be protected on two sides. And the killer would have to come around in front of them. When he did—

When he did, then she would kill him, Blythe vowed with a cold determination. There was no doubt in her mind she was capable of that. She was capable of anything to protect Maddie.

A noise to her left brought her head around. Even before she identified its cause, she had swung the Colt around to point it in that direction and pulled back the slide. Instead of the figure she had expected, a piece of debris, disturbed by the wind, had tumbled off what remained of one of the interior walls.

When she'd controlled her panic enough to be able to think again, she knew they had to move. They were too exposed. Too vulnerable. They would be, until she found a location where she could see what was going on around her.

She turned her head, again looking at the refrigerator. It offered the only viable protection in what was an otherwise indefensible position. And to get them there…

"Maddie, can you do something for me? Something very important."

The small head moved affirmatively against her shoulder.

"You have to do *exactly* what I tell you. You understand?"

Another nod.

Blythe laid the pistol on the charred floorboards beside her. Then she took Maddie's chin in her hand and turned her face toward the kitchen.

"You see the refrigerator?"

Within the grasp of her fingers, the child's chin moved up and down.

"That's where I want you to go. I want you to go and hide in the corner between the refrigerator and the wall. The corner on the *right* side. You remember which is your right?"

Another nod.

"Show me."

The little girl held up her right hand. Blythe folded the tiny fingers down as she lowered it to keep him from seeing.

"Can you do it, baby? Can you go to the corner on the right side of the refrigerator?"

"Are you coming, too?"

"As soon as I can. I want you to go first, and then I'll come, but… It's like a game, Maddie. Like hide-

and-seek. You have to crawl. You have to crawl like a little baby. Without raising your head."

"Or he'll shoot me, too?"

What had she expected? That Maddie wouldn't know what had happened to Cade? As she'd told him, her daughter was a very bright little girl. From the beginning, she had understood far more about what was happening than the adults around her.

"He won't shoot at you if you crawl, because he won't be able to see you." Blythe had no choice but to take advantage of the child's quick perception of the danger they were in.

"And then you'll come too? As soon as I get there?"

"I promise. As soon as you're over there, I'm on my way."

"Could you just come with me now?"

"I have to stay here until you get there, sweetheart. Then I'll be right behind you."

"Are you going to shoot him?" Maddie's eyes fell to the gun.

If he gives me half a chance.

"You just stay down, okay? Just crawl like a little bitty baby. And I'll be right behind you. You ready?"

Maddie nodded, her eyes wide.

"Remember, to the right side of the refrigerator. Show me your right."

This was something Maddie had known for over a year. Her right hand from her left. Her right shoe from her left. Obediently, she again lifted her right hand, this time keeping it low.

"Good girl. Now just crawl to that side. And stay down. Understand?"

Another nod.

Blythe lifted her head again, scanning the line of trees. Then she rolled onto her side, freeing the child she'd been protecting with her own body.

"Go. Go now."

With one last pleading look, the little girl turned over and, as she'd been instructed, set out at a crawl across the few feet that separated her from the refrigerator.

As soon as she'd started crawling, Blythe had torn her eyes away, focusing again on the woods where the shots had originated. Propped on her elbows, she held the weapon out in front of her, her left hand attempting to steady the right.

Off to the side, she could hear the scrambling noises that indicated Maddie's progress. There was no response from whoever had shot Cade.

"Mama."

The plaintive whisper brought Blythe's head around. Maddie was sitting with her back in the corner formed by the wall and the refrigerator, exactly where she'd been told to go.

Good girl. My very good girl.

"You promised."

Blythe nodded, and then, throwing another look toward the tree line, she began her own journey. Keeping her head down, she used her elbows and knees to propel herself across the charred floorboards, the gun clutched awkwardly in her right fist. Although she presented a larger target than Maddie had, again nothing happened.

Unable to believe when she made it to the relative safety of the corner, she eased up into a sitting position with Maddie behind her. Then, her body again shielding her daughter's, and her grandfather's heavy pistol held out in front of her, she waited.

She knew he would come for them. He'd gone too far not to. It was only a matter of when and how he'd approach. And unless one of the teams of searchers came to this location…

As if in answer to that thought, she watched, unbelieving, as a Sheriff's Department cruiser rounded the curve in the two-lane and headed toward the burned house. She raised her left hand, waving to attract the attention of the driver.

Despite her position near the back of the house, by some miracle he must have seen her. The car pulled into the driveway behind Cade's.

Although Blythe couldn't tell who was driving, she knew she had to warn him. As soon as she heard the car door slam, she shouted, "He's in the woods. He has a rifle. He shot Cade."

By that time the driver of the cruiser had walked out far enough from behind Cade's car that she could see him. The distinctive shock of white hair left no doubt as to her rescuer's identity.

"Stay down, Hoyt," she yelled.

The former sheriff obeyed immediately, although he continued moving toward the house at a low crouch. Heart in her throat, Blythe watched as he stooped beside Cade.

With the piles of rubble between them, she couldn't see what Hoyt was doing, but she assumed he was feeling for a pulse. Maybe trying to staunch the bleeding.

After a few seconds, he straightened, bringing a walkie-talkie up to his mouth. Calling for an ambulance? Or reinforcements?

"Is he okay?"

"He's alive. Barely," Hoyt said. "What the hell happened out here? You got your girl?"

"She's here. She's okay. He was hiding out in the woods. He shot Cade. Please, be careful." If he shot Hoyt, too—

"Okay, I'm coming over. I'm gonna get y'all out of there."

"Did you call an ambulance?"

"Yeah, baby, that's all taken care of. Now let's see if we can draw this snake out of his hole."

Blythe watched in horror as the old man began a broken field run across the yard. Once more, however, there was no response from the shooter in the woods.

It made no sense. Whoever was out there had shot Cade, and yet he wasn't responding to Hoyt's open challenge.

As she watched the man she'd known since childhood run toward her and her daughter, the first inkling that something about this wasn't right was quickly followed by a dozen others.

Someone she trusted. Abel Comstock had said that about his daughter's murderer.

There would have been few people in poor Sarah's life those words would have applied to. Her father, of course. Her minister. Teachers. Her doctor.

A highly respected county sheriff?

As the links in the chain of thought that led her to that conclusion were being forged in her mind, Hoyt began to slow. And he was no longer crouching, Blythe realized. He was walking upright as he came directly toward the corner where she had taken refuge to protect Maddie from a vicious murderer.

A murderer Sarah Comstock had known and trusted?

A killer who had refused to arrest Sarah's father because he, of all people, had known that Abel wasn't guilty?

Those questions fought with her lifelong trust of a man who'd been like an uncle to her. Someone she had not only trusted, but loved.

Despite that, she began to bring her grandfather's Colt up, desperately trying to align its muzzle with the center of Hoyt's chest as he continued to walk toward them.

"Don't," she warned. "Don't come any closer, Hoyt."

"What the hell's the matter with you, girl? You know me. You've known me all your life."

Even as he chided her, he didn't slow. Measured and unafraid, he continued to come closer.

"So did Sarah. She knew you, and she would have trusted you."

"Put that thing down, Blythe. That's a bunch of foolishness, and you know it. Put that gun down 'fore somebody gets hurt."

"Not Maddie. Not *my* baby, Hoyt. You aren't going to do to her what you did to Sarah."

"That's plain crazy, Blythe. What in the world would your grandmamma say to what you're accusing me of?"

In spite of the fact the Colt was centered on his chest, Hoyt didn't seem concerned. For the first time Blythe wondered if what she was thinking *was* crazy. She *had* known Hoyt Lee all her life. He had been a friend of her father's.

A friend of Abel Comstock's as well.

And in all those years, Hoyt had never made an improper advance to her. Despite his protective, almost avuncular attitude, he had never once, by word or deed, stepped across that invisible line.

"Put it down, baby, 'fore you go and do something you'll regret the rest of your life. I know how much stress you've been under..." As he said the last word, Hoyt stepped across the rubble that had once been the front wall of the Wright homestead.

"I thought you said you'd called someone," Blythe accused, trying not to allow the heavy pistol to waver. "An ambulance for Cade. If he needs one, why aren't you over there seeing about him?"

"'Cause there ain't nothing I can do for him. And because the paramedics, who can, are already on their way."

She tried to think how much time had elapsed since he'd spoken into that walkie-talkie. Four minutes? Five?

Long enough that by now she should be able to hear their sirens in the distance. But all she could hear was the wind.

And then, as relentless and implacable as the tapping on the window had been, Hoyt Lee's footsteps as they moved across the scorched floorboards toward her.

30

"Don't, Hoyt. Don't come any closer."

Blythe raised the gun, trying to keep it aligned on his chest as he advanced. The reality that she might actually have to shoot him to make him stop had finally impacted on her brain.

She could feel Maddie cowering down behind her, trying to disappear. Any doubt she had about the killer's identity should have been destroyed by the child's reaction. The long years' memories of this man, of his relationship with her family, of his many kindnesses to her, warred with that conclusion.

"Baby, you need to put that down before you or your girl gets hurt. Ain't no telling how long it's been since that thing's been fired."

He was right, of course, but he was also trying to frighten her. To make her doubt his intent, which in the rational part of her mind she knew was to kill them. The emotional part, however, was still dealing with what would happen if she pulled the trigger.

"Don't make me do this, Hoyt," she begged. "Please."

He was close enough that she could see the blue of his eyes. So certain was he of her inability to fire, he still hadn't raised the gun he carried in his right hand.

"Give me that 'fore you hurt somebody." As he spoke, his tone one of exasperated amusement, Hoyt stepped around the opening of the old well where Maddie had hidden.

Hidden from *him*, Blythe remembered. Because Sarah had told her to. Sarah, who knew exactly who and what he was. Sarah—

He was almost on them, his hand held out as if he actually expected her to place her grandfather's pistol into it. If he got any closer, he would be able to reach out and take it from her. And if he did…

The time for warnings was long past. If she was wrong, she would have to live with the consequences. Because if she was right…

She began to squeeze the trigger, surprised by the amount of force it took to make it move. She applied more, as she watched Hoyt's eyes widen in realization. He lunged forward, attempting to knock the gun to the side.

The hammer fell, but nothing happened. The empty click of the misfire echoed inside her head as Hoyt's hand connected with hers, still joined around the butt of the Colt.

Despite the force of his blow, she didn't lose her grip. She tried to bring the gun around again, but Hoyt's second blow exploded against the side of her face.

Although it was powerful enough to turn her head,

she was unaware of the pain. All she was aware of was Maddie, her head buried against her back.

The Colt was wrenched from her hands. She grabbed at it, but Hoyt lifted it out of her reach. She scrambled to her feet, fingers curved into claws as she tried to get at his eyes.

Hoyt swatted her back with his forearm. As she fell, he dexterously reversed the pistol he'd taken from her, holding it by the muzzle as he raised the butt high above her head.

She dodged, lifting her arm to take the brunt of the threatened strike. The pistol came down on the bone of her upraised wrist, sending shock waves up her arm. The agony was so great that for a vital few seconds she was paralyzed by it.

In that moment, she became aware that Maddie was screaming, the same mindless shrieks she had listened to so many nights since they'd returned to Crenshaw. Was this the nightmare her daughter had seen in her dreams? This rather than Sarah's murder as she'd thought?

With the memory of what had been done to Sarah, Blythe struggled up again, only to be met once more with the butt of the gun Hoyt had taken from her. Because she'd been unable to get her arm up to deflect the blow, it struck her temple.

The air thinned and darkened around her head as she fell back. Although she never lost consciousness, she was unable to do anything other than watch as Hoyt tossed her grandfather's gun to the side.

Then, finally, he raised the weapon he had carried in his right hand. With the slow deliberation of a marksman, he held it out in front of him, targeting the forehead of the screaming child.

Fighting her way through the lethargy of near unconsciousness, Blythe tried to force her unresponsive body upright once more. Her own screams were added to Maddie's. "No. Don't. Please, Hoyt, don't."

He never looked at her, not even when she made it to her knees and began to lurch toward him. His total concentration on the target before him, Blythe watched in horror as his finger began to move against the trigger.

She heard the shot, the sound mingling with Maddie's terrified shrieks and her own drawn out "No." And then, as the echoes of both the shot and her scream faded, there was only Maddie's voice, her cries piercing in their mindlessness.

Maddie's voice...

Blythe lifted her eyes from their focus on the barrel of the gun in time to see Hoyt's body begin to tilt forward, his arms thrown out to his sides. The back of his head was covered with blood, too bright, too red, against the snow-white hair.

His forehead hit the edge of the refrigerator as his body struck the wood of the kitchen floor, throwing up a small cloud of soot. Maddie cowered in the corner Blythe had put her in, eyes tightly closed as she continued to shriek.

After a stunned moment, Blythe turned, looking toward the front of the house. Cade was kneeling on the dead grass of the yard, his own weapon held out in front of him, both hands wrapped around it. As she watched, the gun began to droop, as if it were too heavy to hold upright any longer. He put one hand flat on the ground, his head dipping as he tried to remain upright.

Somehow Blythe got to her feet. Her first move—instinctive—was to Maddie. She didn't look down as she stepped over Hoyt Lee's body.

She bent, picking Maddie up and settling her on her hip with the unthinking competence of long practice. Without attempting to comfort her daughter, she again stepped over the legs of the man who had brutalized another child so long ago. A man who would never terrorize anyone again.

When she reached the line of rubble that marked the front wall of the house, she stepped over it, too. Eventually, she set Maddie down in what had once been the center of their front yard. Then she knelt beside the man who had just saved both their lives.

Cade's head was still down, and he was still propped on that straightened right arm. She put her hand under his chin, gently lifting it.

He opened his eyes, long, dark lashes coming up to reveal pupils wildly dilated. Using the thumb of her other hand, she brushed back the trickle of blood seeping out of his hairline.

As she did, she began to try to evaluate how badly

he was hurt. His skin was ashen; his lips, colorless. And, she realized, as she bent to place her own over them, they were cold. So cold.

She had actually raised her eyes, again looking down the road for the paramedics Hoyt had called before she remembered that, whatever he had pretended to say into the walkie-talkie he'd carried, he hadn't placed a call for help.

"Cell," she said, leaning down to speak directly to Cade. She couldn't be sure how much of what she was saying he understood.

In response, however, he began to fish the phone out of the pocket of his leather jacket, eventually holding it out to her. As she accepted it, their fingers made contact. His trembled, either from the effort of remaining upright or from pain and loss of blood.

She flipped open the cell, dialing 911 with her thumb. As she waited through the rings, she turned to look at Maddie. Her cheeks were streaked with tears, but she was no longer screaming.

Although the child's eyes were fastened on Blythe's face, she hadn't moved from the spot where she'd been put down. Blythe motioned her forward, putting her arm around her and pulling her tightly against her side when she arrived.

"Davis County 911. What's your emergency, please?"

"This is Blythe Wyndham. I'm at the old Wright house on Wheeler Road. We need an ambulance."

"Can you tell me who's hurt, Ms. Wyndham?"

"Sheriff Jackson. He's been shot. I'm not sure… I'm not sure how bad it is, but…" She took a breath, forcing herself to go on, despite the fear crowding in her throat. "They need to hurry."

"Yes, ma'am, they're on their way. Are you all right?"

"I'm fine. My daughter's fine." Only as she said those words did she realize what a miracle they represented.

They were alive. Alive and unharmed. Both of them.

"I'm so glad, ma'am. I'll tell them. The unit's been dispatched. You stay right where you are. They'll be there before you know it. If you want to hold on, I'll stay with you."

"Thank you." Blythe laid the cell on the ground beside her.

With Maddie clinging to her right side, she sat down on the grass next to Cade. She pulled him to her, too, putting her arm around his back. After a slight resistance, he gave in, leaning his head against her shoulder.

"Thank you," she said.

The crisp dark hair was under her cheek. She turned her head to press a kiss against it.

"Thank God, she told me."

Blythe replayed Cade's words in her mind, trying to make sense of them. And when she couldn't…

"*Who* told you?"

"Maddie."

"But Maddie—" She stopped, thinking back through the sequence of events. Maybe Cade had heard the little girl's screams. Maybe those were what had awakened him to the danger they were in.

"You heard her," she attempted to clarify. "You heard her screaming."

He shook his head, his hair again moving under her cheek. "Whispered."

The word was faint, but unmistakable. Whispered? Maddie had done anything but.

"*Maddie* whispered?"

"She touched my face. Her hands were so cold. She touched my face, and then she told me… She told me I had to stop him. You don't remember?"

The prickle had begun at the back of her neck, the hair lifting as the chill his words created moved down her spine.

Not Maddie. Maddie had been with her. Whoever had touched Cade, warning him of their danger, it hadn't been her daughter.

Perhaps it had been another little girl who had, as Cade had once said, waited a very long time for justice.

And because of her connection to Maddie, finally, she had it.

Rest in peace, Sarah, Blythe prayed.

Then she turned her head, once more pressing a kiss against the midnight hair of the man she held. She asked no more questions, knowing that what had happened here today was as it was supposed to be.

She listened to the wind instead, holding the two people she loved most in this world, until finally in the distance she heard the sirens that had been promised.

* * *

When he opened his eyes, Cade wasn't sure for a few seconds where he was. The ceiling above his head was unfamiliar. Not home. Not anywhere else he recognized.

"Hey."

The softly spoken greeting, quintessentially Southern, drew his eyes to the woman sitting at his right. The metal railing that separated them helped to orient him.

Hospital.

With that realization, the memory of what had happened at the Wright place flooded back. "Maddie?"

"She's fine. And I think… I really think she will be. I think it's over, Cade. All of it."

All of it.

All except the grief. The pain of betrayal. For him, that would probably never be over.

"That's good." His voice sounded hoarse, and it had hurt his throat to push those two words out.

He closed his eyes, trying to come to grips with what had happened. And with what it might mean.

"I know he was your friend," Blythe began.

"He was a monster." He didn't open his eyes to watch the impact of that word on her face.

She had recognized the truth before he had. And if it hadn't been for her realization…

"You weren't the only one he fooled, Cade. Everybody in this town thought Hoyt was the soul of integrity."

The word lay between them, the reality of who and what Hoyt Lee had been mocking everything Cade had believed was true and real in his life. If Hoyt had been capable of doing what had been done to Sarah Comstock…

"Why?" The word echoed the bitterness of his earlier one.

"I think she finally refused him. Maybe he asked her to do something… I don't know. Something so horrible she couldn't imagine obeying him, no matter what he threatened her with. Or maybe she'd reached the limits of her endurance that night. Maybe she said she was going to tell. Whatever it was… Hoyt wasn't accustomed to people defying him."

Cade knew Hoyt had had the reputation in the old days of being mean. The gossip was that many a drunk had gone home from a stay in Sheriff Lee's jail covered with bruises. A couple with broken bones.

Of course, no one had ever filed suit because of those injuries. This wasn't the kind of place where you took legal action against the authorities. Not if you ever wanted to be accepted in the community again.

Cade himself could attest to Hoyt's hair-trigger temper. When he'd served as his deputy, he'd once pulled him off a man. That had been a domestic-abuse call. Hoyt had taken one look at the wife's battered face and decided to teach the husband what it felt like to be beaten.

Although he'd been new and green, Cade had stepped in to stop what was happening because he had literally feared for the man's life. Still…

"She was a little girl," he said softly, vomit climbing

into the back of his throat as he remembered that the man he'd considered both his mentor and his friend had abused and then murdered Sarah Comstock.

"Not to him, she wasn't," Blythe said quietly.

And that, too, was undoubtedly true. To Hoyt, Sarah had become something else. Someone else. Someone he believed he had the right to use as he wished. Until maybe, as Blythe had speculated, on that fatal night Sarah had refused him.

"I'm just glad I was the one who put an end to it."

Despite everything, he was. Glad he had stopped the lies that bastard had told for a quarter of a century. Glad he'd finally given Sarah the justice she deserved.

"Do you remember what you told me out there?"

He shook his head, too tired to try and figure out what she was talking about. Whatever he'd said—

"You said Maddie told you to stop him."

He searched his memory, but the order in which things had happened eluded him. The only clear remembrance he had was of trying to hold the Glock steady so he could pull the trigger. How he'd realized he had to do that had been lost in the haze of pain and shock.

He shook his head, setting off a pounding agony in his temples. "If I did..." He closed his eyes, trying to control the pain so he could finish the thought. "I don't remember."

"It doesn't matter. I just thought you might like to know... I think Sarah chose you. I think she knew all along you were the one who was—I don't know—

good enough, capable enough maybe, of doing what had to be done in order to end it."

"He could have changed all that in the woods that night. If he'd wanted to."

He had wondered then if Abel had deliberately fired high. Except it hadn't been Comstock who'd hit the trunk of the tree over his head. Either Hoyt had still viewed him like the son he'd always treated him as or, with his natural arrogance, the old man had dismissed the possibility that Cade posed a threat.

And he'd been right. The man Cade had loved would have been the last person on any list of suspects he'd composed.

"I don't understand," Blythe said.

He opened his eyes again to look at her. Despite the bruises on her face—another reason, if he needed one, that he was glad his had been the shot that had taken that murderous SOB out—she was the most beautiful thing he'd ever seen. If what she'd told him last night in her grandmother's kitchen was true…

"It doesn't matter. Just some things I don't want to think about."

"Then don't. Think about getting well."

"How long is that going to take?"

"I don't think anyone's said, but they did say you got lucky. The bullet didn't hit anything vital. You lost a lot of blood, and there's extensive soft-tissue damage, but other than that…" She let the sentence trail.

"You gonna be around?"

"What?"

"Crenshaw. You gonna be around long enough for me to get back on my feet?"

As he waited for an answer, he wondered if she had any clue how much what she said right now would matter. She'd been so eager that day in the park to get out of here—not that he could blame her for that, considering what had been going on.

"Do you want me to?"

"Don't play dumb. Nobody's gonna buy that."

Especially not me. Not after the way you figured out that Hoyt was lying.

"Is it dumb to want to hear you say it?"

"That I want you to be around?"

"Yes. For starters."

"Okay, I want you to be around when I get back on my feet."

"Why?"

"Why do you think?"

"I think I need you to say that, too."

"You're a damned demanding woman."

"You're the one making demands. I'm just asking to be told why."

She deserved that. If it hadn't been so hard to make that kind of commitment again, he would already have told her. As it was, he was lucky to get another chance.

"Because I want to finish what we started in your grandmother's kitchen."

Her lips parted, but she closed them again without saying anything. She shook her head slightly, causing a coldness in the pit of his stomach.

"You don't want that?"

"Yes."

"But?"

"I wish it didn't have to be here."

He nodded, remembering another woman who had chosen another place. Another man. One he couldn't be.

"This is my home. It's where I belong."

It's where you belong, too. You just haven't figured that out yet.

She shook her head again, the movement slow.

"You're not willing to give it some time?"

"It?"

"Crenshaw. Us. Coming home."

"So far...this hasn't been much of a homecoming."

"Let me change that. At least let me try."

Her eyes gleamed with tears she quickly controlled. Watching that effort, after all she'd been through today, made his burn in sympathy.

Damn whatever they'd doped him with. That was all he needed. To let her see how much this meant to him. She had a right to say no. A right to whatever life she wanted, wherever—

"When I was thirteen, just the thought of you saying something like that..." She stopped on a breath of laughter.

"Is that funny? My asking you to stay?"

"Not funny. Ironic, maybe. And strange how little seems to have changed after nearly twenty years."

He examined the words, wondering if they could possibly mean what they sounded as if they did. "So..."

"If there were a prom, I'd make you take me. Just so I could show you off."

There was only one way to interpret that. His heart rate accelerated and then steadied.

"I'll think of something," he promised.

He turned his head and closed his eyes before they could reveal too much. When she touched his hand, his fingers caught and then tightened around hers. He knew that next time he woke up, she'd be there.

For right now, that was really all that mattered.

* * * * *

Turn the page for an exciting preview
of multi-RITA®-Award winner
Gayle Wilson's new novel of romantic suspense
THE SUICIDE CLUB
coming in July 2007 from MIRA Books.

The stadium had already grown quiet as the crowd waited for the candlelight ceremony to begin. Lindsey felt isolated and alone out here in the ticket booth, second-guessing her decision not to go inside. Maybe she, too, needed the kind of closure saying goodbye publicly to Andrea would provide.

I'm so sorry, she thought, tears blurring the familiar scene through the ticket window. *I didn't know. I didn't understand. If only you'd told me.*

Suddenly the lights blinked out, eliciting a drawn-out ohhh from the crowd before a breathless silence again fell. As it did, Lindsey realized that not only had the switch for the field lights been thrown, someone had cut off the lights outside the stadium as well.

Across the parking lot, light from a street lamp glinted off the tops of the rows of chairs. Here, in the deep shadow cast by the overhanging bleachers, it was as dark as pitch. And then, in that sudden overwhelming darkness, she became aware of the smell of smoke.

She turned from the open window, looking toward

the door at the back of the booth. Although she couldn't see the smoke she had smelled, there was a flicker of reddish light visible along the crack at the bottom of the frame.

Fire?

She tried to picture the area behind the booth, but there was nothing back there but the steel Dumpster where the cleanup crew put all the trash that had been left in the bleachers after the games. There was no grass or weeds around the small, wooden building, only a mixture of dirt and sand.

Wooden, she realized, with a growing sense of horror. And by now there was no doubt it was on fire. She could not only hear the crackle of flames, but the smoke she'd smelled was getting thicker inside the booth.

She glanced back toward the window. Although the opening was probably large enough for her to crawl through, steel bars had at sometime in the past been installed three quarters of the way down. The space between them was sufficient for money and tickets to be passed through, but not nearly large enough to offer a means of exit.

Which meant the only way out was the back door. The same one that seemed to be on fire.

A minute of silence. That's what Dave had said. In sixty seconds, the lights would come up and someone would notice what was happening.

There was no need to panic. There were ten thousand people within shouting distance. Somebody would look around. Or somebody would smell the smoke and come out to investigate. Somebody—

With one last look through the narrow window, she ran to the door. She put her hands around the knob, feeling the heat of the fire conducted by its metal. If she opened the door, the flames would come inside. And there were a lot of combustible items stored in the building.

It might be better just to wait. Go back to the window, breathe the air that was still pouring in through that opening. Start screaming for someone to put out the fire and let her out.

Despite the logic of all that, she couldn't force her fingers to release the knob she gripped. She wanted out before the fire got any bigger. If it was just at the bottom of the door, she could jump over it. Even if she got burned a little it was better than taking a chance someone would discover what was going on before it was too late.

She turned the knob and pulled. The door moved slightly inward and then caught, refusing to budge farther even under her repeated and increasingly frantic efforts. Until finally she came to the only possible conclusion as to why.

Someone had slipped the padlock back through the hasp. Someone had intentionally locked her inside the burning booth....

* * * * *

GAYLE WILSON

32320 THE INQUISITOR ___$6.99 U.S. ___$8.50 CAN.

(limited quantities available)

TOTAL AMOUNT $________
POSTAGE & HANDLING $________
($1.00 FOR 1 BOOK, 50¢ for each additional)
APPLICABLE TAXES* $________
TOTAL PAYABLE $________

(check or money order—please do not send cash)

To order, complete this form and send it, along with a check or money order for the total above, payable to MIRA Books, to: **In the U.S.:** 3010 Walden Avenue, P.O. Box 9077, Buffalo, NY 14269-9077; **In Canada:** P.O. Box 636, Fort Erie, Ontario, L2A 5X3.

Name: ____
Address: ____________________ City: ____________________
State/Prov.: ____________________ Zip/Postal Code: ______________
Account Number (if applicable): ____________________

075 CSAS

*New York residents remit applicable sales taxes.
*Canadian residents remit applicable GST and provincial taxes.

MGW1206BL